NEVER GETTING Ahead

AMAZON BEST-SELLING AUTHOR
BETH GELMAN

Copyright © 2025 by Beth Gelman

All rights reserved under the International and Pan-American Copyright Conventions. By payment of the required fees, you have been granted the nonexclusive, nontransferable right to access and read the text of this eBook on screen. No part of this text may be reproduced, transmitted, downloaded, decompiled, reverse engineered or stored in or introduced into any information storage or retrieval system, in any form or by any means, whether electronic or mechanical, now known or hereafter invented, without the express permission of Insatiable Reader Publishing LLC

This book is a work of fiction. Names, characters, places, and incidents are the product of the author's imagination or are used fictitiously. Any resemblance to actual events, locales, or persons, living or dead, is coincidental.

ISBN: 979-8-9920340-2-8   *As listed in the Library of Congress*

Summary:

Woman plans, God laughs—Welcome to my life!

My dream college internship is set! I'm packed and ready to become a master gardener—until the program and my high hopes were canceled.

"Not to worry," my mentor says. "We have another great opportunity—on a farm." *Really?* I didn't spend the last three years killing myself to milk cows!

This disaster is causing my OCD to rage. If I have to pivot one more time, my head will explode. But milking cows is the least of my worries, it's the man I'll be working with that will be my demise.

We had history, but none of that mattered this year. I wouldn't let him screw up my chances of finishing this assignment. I had one focus and one focus only. Fix the soil, put in my time, and get the hell out unscathed. *Or broken-hearted.*

I may be a little stubborn and a little fixated on my plans, but nothing will keep me from graduating in the spring—not even Mr. Valize.

So why aren't my efforts ever getting me ahead?

Never Getting Ahead is Book #2 (of 3) in the *Dazed & Confused Steamy Romance Series*, highlighting neurodivergent brains in hilarious settings.

NEVER GETTING AHEAD

For information, address Beth Gelman directly at BethGelman.com or at BethGelmanWrites@gmail.com.

[1. Romance 2. Contemporary romance 3. Romantic comedy 4. Mental Health romance 5. Small Town romance 6. Multi-cultural romance]

Copy Editor: Dione Benson

Formatting Editor: Insatiable Reader Publishing LLC

Cover Design: 100Covers.com

First Edition

Contents

Dedication	VIII
Chapter 1	1
Chapter 2	7
Chapter 3	22
Chapter 4	30
Chapter 5	37
Chapter 6	47
Chapter 7	57
Chapter 8	72
Chapter 9	83
Chapter 10	91
Chapter 11	101
Chapter 12	110
Chapter 13	120
Chapter 14	131
Chapter 15	137

Chapter 16	145
Chapter 17	150
Chapter 18	159
Chapter 19	165
Chapter 20	172
Chapter 21	185
Chapter 22	198
Chapter 23	208
Chapter 24	218
Chapter 25	226
Chapter 26	233
Chapter 27	241
Chapter 28	255
Chapter 29	267
Chapter 30	280
Chapter 31	287
Chapter 32	298
Chapter 33	304
Chapter 34	318
Chapter 35	327
Chapter 36	335

Chapter 37	341
Chapter 38	351
Chapter 39	361
Chapter 40	371
Epilogue	383
Bonus Chapter	391
ABOUT THE AUTHOR	403
ACKNOWLEDGEMENTS	405
DISCOVER BETH'S CATALOG AND CONTACT INFORMATION	409
READ MORE: The Perfect Lessons	411

Dedication

To all the marginalized people and cultures that aren't being heard.

Chapter 1

SENECA

Senior year.

Finally.

Too bad I'm not twenty-one like most college grads. Apparently, I'm what they call a "late bloomer." Though, in actuality, I bloomed long before graduating from high school. If, for one minute, I thought my life would have unraveled the way it did, I would have started smoking pot early on. My ancestors did, except I don't think that's what Native Americans would have called it. I think it was called peyote. My dad may have mentioned it when my mom was dying of cancer. My brain shut down around then, and it's only been in recent years that it came back online. Thank goodness, because I had one purpose in life—getting my degree in horticulture.

I woke up this morning to a disturbing email that Dr. Abel, the Dean of the Horticulture College, and my mentor, sent late last night, based on the time stamp.

Dear Seneca,
We need to make some alterations to your internship this year. While normally we could discuss them in your weekly mentor

meeting on Wednesday, we can't wait. Please contact my office when you get this message and tell Olivia when you'll be coming by.

I'm sorry to start your day in a rush, though the sooner we meet, the better for all involved.

Sincerely,

Dr. Gregory Abel

What the hell did *alterations* mean? Do I need a special uniform to work at Longwood Gardens? *Probably.* I mean it's epic, and historical, and everything someone like me longed to be a part of. It's more than plants; it's a horticultural wonder. Pierre S. du Pont birthed the place, so it had to be magnificent. My internship there will be an integral part of history-in-the-making, making my resume stand out over everyone else in my field. This was my life-altering opportunity. If wearing an ugly jumpsuit made it happen, then so be it.

I dropped my phone on my nightstand and whipped off my beaten-up floral comforter. It was one of the few things my dad didn't throw away when he moved from Chicago to move in with his girlfriend, Belinda. She was nice enough but did everything in her power to clean up my dad's "tired" look, including dumping everything from his past, i.e., me. He allowed her to transform his life so long as he stayed in Cincinnati and did not visit me in Pennsylvania.

Up until this year, I endured several roommates, only to suffer annoyance by them or by me of them. I'd been humbled when my best friend, Abigail, offered to pay for my college tuition, room and board for four years. As much as I wanted an apartment of my own, I wouldn't be a slug soaking her for amenities that didn't matter. She paid me every summer to help her restore the gardens surrounding her home and barn. I helped her expand the community garden we installed four years ago after taking ownership of her ancestral mansion. I loved those gardens. If I didn't truly need the money, I'd have cultivated them for free. I took pride in finding all the perfect varietals to complement each other, giving Abigail a myriad of colors from spring to fall. I knew I had a talent for gardening, but a latent gift appeared one night in a dream. I had made an intricate Japanese meditation maze deep into Abigail's property. It was shielded by trees and inspired me to write it all down along with some preliminary sketches. I'd been waiting four long years to gather as much information as I could to make that dream come true. By next week, I'd be up to my ears in foliage and fertilizer, making a difference in the world at Longwood Gardens. If only I could force myself to move my body across the floor into the shower, I'd be on my way.

I held off calling Olivia, Dean Abel's department secretary, until I emerged from my shower with a clearer head. Some days were harder than others to motivate. Even days when I was excited to start the day could begin with my head feeling heavy or disoriented. Thinking about everything I needed to accomplish amped up my anxiety, forcing me to shut out the world until I had everything organized and settled. Today, I needed to reorganize my list with the addition of Dr. Abel's impromptu meeting, which made me late for everything else. This hiccup didn't happen all the time, but, when the pressure was on, that's when I began to slip up. I considered looking up all my idiosyncrasies once when I started school. A pattern was brewing, though I was too busy to address it. I shucked it off as college jitters. Except those feelings were still there halfway through my freshman year. After finally plugging my complaints into Google, it suggested I had obsessive-compulsive disorder. *Really?* I didn't have all the symptoms, not even two-thirds of them, but enough so that I succumbed to needing help. *Enter the school counseling center therapist.*

"Hi, Seneca. Sit wherever you like," Glenda Sheer offered sweetly, gesturing to three available seats. I took the single chair farthest from hers. *Why get too invested too soon?*

I smiled back, "Thank you, Dr. Sheer." I was the one who wanted to see someone, so I shouldn't be rude.

"Please. Call me Glenda. I'm not a doctor. I have my master's degree in social behavior and am a licensed therapist. I like to keep things informal anyway." She pressed her hands onto a pad of paper, sitting precariously with her crossed legs.

Her office was bright and spacious and gave me a fun vibe—if you can call therapy fun. There was a LEGO table in the corner with several other dolls and toys. In another corner by the window, she had fuzzy carpet on the floor with vinyl beanbags strewn about. The incredible collection of books that rose from floor to ceiling behind her was impressive, and I made a noise.

"Huh."

Glenda leaned in. "In reference to what?"

She was smart. I could tell by the way she knew I was referring to something I'd seen and not a reaction of concern.

My head swiveled, engrossed in the length and height of the wall. "Did you read all those books? It's impressive if you did." I sat back in awe.

She snorted. "Yeah, that *would* be impressive, but no. Maybe a quarter of them. I share an office with Dr. Delouise and two other therapists. We each have a few shelves for reference material. You're welcome to borrow one if you'd like." Glenda's eyebrows raised, inviting me to accept her offer. I was leery. *Who offers their stuff to strangers?*

I pursed my lips and tapped my thigh, considering her proposal carefully. If I borrow one, I have to care for it—not lose it. If I don't borrow one, then she'll think I'm disingenuous, and I don't want her to think I'm flakey. After two minutes of internal debate, I looked at her blankly.

"This is why I'm here. Simple decisions seem to lock me up. The internet says I am OCD. What do you think?" I could feel my eyebrows knitting tightly, and I forced myself to relax and sit back in my chair. *Why did I make everything so complicated?*

She stood up, walked across the room to the fuzzy, purple carpet, and plopped down in a beanbag chair. Looking at me intently, she said, "I don't know. Let's find out," and motioned for me to join her.

Fifty minutes later, I walked out of her office with my calendar filled with weekly appointments for the rest of the semester. She said we'd get to the bottom of it through several assessments, learn healthy coping mechanisms, and improve my self-talk. *Goodbye, imaginary friend.*

I reached the outer door to the hallway when she called out my name.

"Seneca?" Her head tilted slightly, her bangs falling across her eyes.

"Yeah?" I turned toward her hesitantly.

"It takes a lot of courage and self-respect to seek out help. I'm so glad you did. See you next week." Her face broke into a big, sincere smile. She waved goodbye as I pulled on the handle, feeling like a new door to a successful life opened as well.

Chapter 2
SENECA

Becoming a horticulturist was a natural transition from the Ojibwe heritage provided to me by my mother. My father's White male background didn't supersede that of my Native American mother. Growing up, she taught me to connect to the earth. After her tragic loss from pancreatic cancer when I was in middle school, I felt and saw her in my dreams. Her teachings allowed me to feel the earth, smell it, and hear it vibrating through and around me in a transcendent way. I wanted others to slow down and appreciate all the nuances and gifts Mother Earth could give us if we only would stop and listen. If Disney had one thing right about *Pocahontas, my mom* painted with the colors of the wind, only with flowers.

I arrived at Dr. Abel's office ten minutes earlier than planned. My heart raced as I climbed to the second floor of Landis Hall, the place I called home on campus. Most of my major classes at Delaware Valley University were held here. In four years, the only thing that had changed was a fresh coat of paint.

My favorite place on the executive floor was in this hallway of windows. The view from floor to ceiling consisted of an atrium filled with exotic orchids and Birds of Paradise to lichen that covered moist rocks. Anything that had to do with sophisticated horticulture started here. It was my nirvana. I focused on a beautiful burgundy Oncidium orchid —or "Dancing Ladies" as they are known. Each blossom cascaded down from the other with one petal exponentially larger than the others. It was a real stunner, and reminded me that life seemed very similar. Glenda would call it distortion, but I called it balanced with a burst of individuality. Either way, it made complete sense to me.

Remembering why I was here, I opened the reception door to Dr. Abel's office, and Olivia blanched when she saw me.

"Are you alright, Olivia?" I probed in earnest. She seemed fine until she recognized my face.

She shifted in her chair and pressed a curl behind her ear. "Terrific. I'm terrific. I'll let Dr. Abel know you're here."

Too nervous to sit down, I paced in front of the black leather couch. It didn't take long before I heard the booming voice of my mentor. "Seneca. Great, you're here. Please come in."

Dr. Abel was a masterful instructor and mentor, but his organizational skills were atrocious. It made me nervous whenever I came into his office, which was why I usually asked him to meet me anywhere else. Gulping back a knot of anxiety, I hoped we'd be done in less than ten minutes.

I took my usual seat in the deeply depressed leather chair across from his desk as he moved to his seat on the other side of it. His face looked odd. Different than his usual jovial self. His lips were pinched and his eyebrows knitted tightly, forming several deep crevices along his forehead. Something bad was about to happen. I knew it in my bones. The whole time I was getting ready, I recited my mantra to keep my shit together, but, now, there was no escaping whatever Dr. Abel was going to tell me.

He cleared his voice like staccato notes punctuated in a line of music. "It seems there has been a change of plans at the Longwood Gardens this fall." He paused, using his index finger and thumb to wipe the corners of his mouth. "They are losing some of their funding and rescinding their internship programs for the next few years until times are better. I'm so sorry to have to tell you this on such short notice, Seneca."

I gasped.

Wait. What did he just say?

"I'm sorry. Did you say that my required senior internship is canceled?" My mouth felt like the Sahara and my heart began to beat out of my chest. I jumped out of my seat, bending over at the waist, feeling sick.

I had planned my college experience perfectly.

*Honor Roll—Four years
*Dean's List—Four years
*Committee member for two horticulture groups—Two years
*Committee Chair for those same two groups—Two years
*ASHS Collegiate Scholar Award for Plant Science through Longwood Gardens Internship
*Pennsylvania Landscape Nursery Association from the Philadelphia Flower Show—Longwood
*Invitations to study abroad in Japan—Longwood affiliation

What the fuck is happening to my life?!

If I didn't intern at Longwood, I couldn't get invitations to study abroad or win prestigious awards. The trajectory in my field would crash and burn. I felt lightheaded, and my skin crawled as if a million ants marched up and down my body.

"I—I can't breathe. What's happening to . . ."

The last thing I heard was the thumping of big feet on the floor by my head. My last thought was my life was over.

My eyes began to flutter open.

"Get her some water. Where are the paramedics?" Dr. Abel's voice boomed over my jellified body.

Stuttering sounds seeped out of Olivia's shrieking voice, "I don't know. The dispatcher said five minutes. I'm sorry, Dr. Abel. I'll go downstairs to meet them." Shuffling sounds turned into clacking across the tile floor and then silence.

My head hurt. Was I on the floor? Why was it so bright? I closed my eyes, feeling nauseous. I tried to move my arms but they felt like weights. When I moved my head, the room spun. Was I having a bad-news stroke?

"Don't move, Seneca. Help is on the way. Thank God I reached you before you hit the floor." I opened my eyes again, only to see Dr. Abel looking like shit, pasty white with red lips that hung open as if he was preparing to give me mouth-to-mouth. *That wasn't happening.*

Olivia's shriek pierced my eardrums, announcing the paramedics as they rushed to join me on the floor. Similar to every medical show you've seen on television, they took my temperature, blood pressure, and pulse. All good. They shoved their latex-covered hands through my hair to be sure I wasn't bleeding or had a hematoma, as they called it.

A rather fine medic stared into my eyes as if he was attracted to me. Sadly, he was only flashing a penlight into my eyes blinding me. *Asshole.*

"Let's get you in a chair and see how you do." Mr. Asshole Medic hooked his iron muscled arm beneath mine lifting me gently into the chair I'd once been sitting in. His buddy went through all my vital signs again and proclaimed, "No stroke, and no other noteworthy symptoms. Just a scare."

A voice cleared the haze, "She was only out for fifteen seconds. I counted. I had just given her some bad news and she shut down," Dr. Abel said, panting. *No shit, Sherlock. What did you expect to happen?*

It was my turn to chime in. "About that. You'd better have a trick up your sleeve to get me a new one, or I'm fucked."

Mr. Asshole Medic smirked, "It seems she is doing much better. Keep hydrated miss, and don't hold your breath when you're upset. It never bodes well." He winked at me and I gave him a snarky wink back, then a prick of pain flashed behind my eyes. *Fuck, that hurt.*

"Hey, funny guy. Should I be having searing pain behind my eyes?" If I was going home to an empty dorm, I wanted to know if I was going blind.

He pursed his lips and looked up like he was flipping through a Rolodex for an answer. "That's not an uncommon sign of fainting. Is your sight blurry, seeing stars, or tunnel vision?"

I scanned the room testing each of those symptoms, nervous that I broke something that couldn't be fixed. "A little blurry when I look far away," I said, concerned.

"Then don't do that," he laughed hysterically. *Hilarious.* "No need to worry. That should clear up in the next fifteen minutes. Take it easy, okay?" For a brief second, I thought he might be interested in me again the way he scanned my face and my mouth. Just like me to turn a terrifying moment into a sex scene. *Geezus.* "Okay, then. We'll send you the bill. The secretary gave me all your contact information. Someone from the EMS will be in touch soon."

Shiiittt! Another bill I won't be able to pay without a job.

Olivia sat with me for another thirty minutes making sure I was of sound mind and body before pulling Dr. Abel out of another meeting. It's nice to know that immediately after my episode his life went on as normal. What the hell was mine going to look like?

I wished my head wasn't buzzing. I'd like to piece together my next steps but I hadn't a clue where to begin. If I pack up my single dorm room and moved into a quad, I'd save three hundred dollars a month. Maybe my dad would send me a few bucks so I could put gas in my car. I was suddenly hungry. *Crap!* I didn't get a meal plan because I was supposed to be at Longwood-fucking Gardens this year. I fell over my knees fighting back the sting of tears threatening to disfigure my face.

"Are you going to be sick?" Olivia bellowed. She really was a nice person. While I appreciated her desire to stand vigil while I got my bearings straight, it quickly turned to annoyance, and, unfortunately, I barked back at her sympathy.

Still bent over my knees, I craned my face to the side, "What do you think, Olivia? My whole fucking life has just turned inside out. How am I supposed to feel?" I think I sneered at her—based on her stepping away from me so quickly.

"I meant physically sick. I have a trash can if you need it." She pushed her peekaboo-toed shoe against the black can and slid it next to my leg. "Seneca. I can't imagine what you're feeling now, but please give Dr. Abel a chance to make this right for you. You have a week before internships begin. Other opportunities won't be as fabulous as Longwood Gardens, but it will satisfy your degree and still present other future opportunities."

Her earnest compassion was Oscar-worthy. Did she really believe her boss would pull a Hail Mary in a week? I truly liked and admired Dr. Abel, but this was a rabbit trick that would fail—epically. I sat up straight and took a deep breath, then did it again. With the help of the armrests, testing my balance, I forced myself to stand up tall. Still woozy, I listed to the right and Olivia reached out to steady me at my shoulder. I reached up and crossed my body placing my hand on hers, appreciatively.

"Thank you for your literal and figurative support. I only hope your words are heard on-high and a great miracle will fall down from the heavens this week, but I can't sit by and do nothing." Feeling more confident that I wouldn't fall over, I pulled my purse off the back of the chair and carefully crossed the room. I turned and gave Olivia a final wave goodbye as she moved her fingers up and down demurely, a pained look on her face.

When I turned around, I saw Dr. Abel storming down the hallway with a manila folder in his hand. I suppose I should wait, and say . . . what exactly? *Thank you* for crushing my dreams?

Though, in actuality, it wasn't his fault. *Thank you* for saving me from a head trauma? More his fault. Or, *thank you* for assigning me a babysitter so I didn't die alone? Okay, that was a little dramatic. I was a lost soul on a river going nowhere. Something needed to drop in front of me to jumpstart my life again.

"Oh, thank goodness you're standing; though, if you don't mind, would you please take a seat so I can go over what happens now?" He pointed to the waiting room black leather couch following me to the seating area. His long fingers held up the folder and shook it twice before excitedly placing it on the coffee table in front of us.

"All is not lost, Seneca. In this folder, I have three late entry internships that would not only secure your timely graduation but would offer you a life-changing experience. They might not be the direction you originally intended, or wanted," he muffled the last part, "but are solid horticultural and agricultural opportunities that would enhance your already vast knowledge and experience. Let me call them today to vet them out. I'll get back to you later this week. Okay?"

The contrite pursing of his lips and crinkling of his brow released the bow of my shoulders, and a jolt of serotonin was felt in my less fuzzy brain. Olivia was right. Things were looking brighter. Dr. Abel wasn't letting me drift out to sea. Hope was not lost, though the logistics of how and when this would all happen still left me a mess.

My fingers twisted in my lap and my knee began to bounce. I needed a concrete plan to feel at peace, and something had to be done today to make things right for me.

"I really appreciate you going to bat for me, Dr. Abel, but I need to make some decisions today about my housing situation. I can't afford to live in the room I'm in now, and, not knowing what these opportunities include, I'm going to be financially up shits creek if I'm stuck in a university boarding contract." Too tired to keep my head upright, I sunk back into the couch tucking my head into my chest resigned to fail. *Again, dramatic, but justified.*

He hummed a few times, then sighed a couple more, before the proverbial light bulb popped his head up. "I don't know what I was thinking. Of course, I'll get your contract waived and your deposit back, but I think you should know that one of these internships includes a private room on their property. You should also know it's over a hundred miles away from campus, but you wouldn't have to come in but once a semester, so it shouldn't be too bad. Can you give me forty-eight hours before completely freaking out?"

Freaking out was my specialty. "Sure." *What else was I supposed to say?* Today would be a good day to drop into Glenda's office.

My legs felt like stumps as I traversed the campus back to my dorm, ignoring all the things I loved about this campus. The giant broken button sculpture, the Atmosphere and Environment XII, and Ben Franklin sitting on a bench. This was probably the last time I'd see these amazing sculptures. I fought the urge to fall to my knees and scream, for fear of being locked up for hysteria. Glenda was out of town until Thursday, forcing me to suffer alone. Except, perhaps, if Abigail, my best friend, would talk me off a ledge.

I held my breath walking through the busy lobby of my dorm wishing I was invisible. I hated feeling this way, but I was spent. Someone called my name and I lifted my hand robotically hoping—it was a sufficient response—turning the corner to my hallway. Blessed peace was steps away when I heard another voice emphatically calling my name. *Leave me the fuck alone!*

It was my perky resident assistant, Ellie. *Ack.* Two people couldn't be more opposite than the two of us. She was porcelain white with ultra-blonde hair that hugged her Barbie-esque jawline. She had to be a size two draped in haute couture. Then there was me. Deep-tanned skin, compliments of my Native American mother, my Caucasian father notwithstanding. Long, straight black hair, that when allowed, reached down to the middle of my back. My wardrobe consisted of second-hand retro clothing that screamed, "This is the real me!" Most days I didn't know who the real me was, but, today, using a tomahawk to slice my door down came to mind.

I whirled around, forcing a grimace on my face. She didn't deserve my wrath, and I wasn't malicious enough to give it to her either. "Ellie. Hi. What can I do for you?" I stated, saccharine sweet.

She preened, twisting a curl in her long bob, whining out of her Botoxed lips. "Hi, Seneca. Our floor is having an ice cream social tonight, and it's come to my attention that no one on our floor has met you." *There was reason for that.* "Can you make it?" *I'd rather bite my tongue off, thanks.*

I flipped my hair like the cool girls did, "Gosh, that's so nice of you to ask, but I have to decline. I'm preparing for an internship I'm starting next week. Actually, I may not be living on campus this year. I'll know in a few days. Best not to get the girls too attached."

Was I for real? I cracked myself up. I was almost a decade older than the oldest girl in my dorm. Slurping ice cream and fawning over football players wouldn't even make my bottom ten things to do on a Thursday night.

Her eyebrows hiked up to her hairline, her pretty pink mouth went slack, "No! Really? Is everything okay? I mean, you're not in trouble, are you?" She sounded first concerned then quickly morphed into self-preservation. I thought about fucking with her, but decided I was done with the conversation.

"I'm not in trouble. My internship changed, and my living situation will change, too. That's all. Now if you'll excuse me, I have a raging headache."

I didn't wait for a response and jiggled my key into my door, walking in without looking back. Finally. Alone. I dropped my backpack, my purse-and my pants-and began dialing Abigail, as I made a beeline for my bathroom. She picked up just as I squatted onto the toilet seat.

"Hey, you! Are you so excited to be the next superstar gardener at Longwood Gardens?" A beat passed, then two, then three. "Sen? What's going on? Talk to me." And that's when the waterworks began.

Big, ugly sobs ripped from my throat, stealing what little air was in my lungs. I didn't know where to start, and, God dammit, I continued to pee nonstop throughout my initial sobs. If this internship situation didn't kill me, dehydration would. Abigail trusted me, believed in me to get a good education and complete my degree in four years. It wouldn't matter that losing this opportunity was beyond my control. The end result would be the same, I'd never get ahead. Whenever I had a great situation, something stupid, out of my control, would happen.

First, it was having to move from Michigan to Illinois to help my dad open a small grocery store after my mother had passed from cancer. No sooner did she get her diagnosis than she mysteriously disappeared, leaving a note she didn't want us to have to watch her suffer, except, three months later, she returned on death's door. So much for not wanting us to be traumatized. We still had to care for her painful exit from this world. I'd barely dealt with the trauma of losing the one person I thought would always be by my side, when my dad made an announcement the day after my high school graduation.

"Seneca, I'm selling the house and moving to Dolton, Illinois. You can join me if you want to, but I'm leaving as soon as the house is sold." He never asked what my plans were or if I had even applied to any colleges. When my mom left, it felt like my dad left me, too. The only redeeming part of that move was Abigail, my best friend in the world, decided to join me. The aunt who raised her was a real piece of work, barely providing the essentials a growing needed. Abigail's mom died when she was four years old, and her miserable aunt was the only one to step in and raise her. *Good riddance to her.*

Then, once again, just as I was starting to save some money and think about going to community college, my dad made another announcement.

"Me and Belinda are going back to her home town in Cincinnati. The store is up for sale, and as soon as it sells, I'm leaving. You'll have to make other living arrangements."

What the fuck was so important he'd move away again without a simple discussion? Sure. His business was failing, but not asking how I'd survive was despicable. Who does that to a kid? *Don't ask.* Again, never getting ahead. It seemed to be my mantra. Which was funny because Abigail's was "Always falling behind." What a pair we were.

So that leads me to four years ago. Abigail, never Abby, offered me an open invitation to join her in Mystic, Connecticut. I really didn't have much of a choice. I was homeless, with a thousand dollars in the bank and zero prospects for my future. The choice was simple. Perseverating on a future I couldn't see kicked me into action. I moved out of my dad's apartment a week before he left town, only seeing him twice these past four years.

"Seneca!" Abigail was screeching into the phone. "Do I need to call 9-1-1? Speak to me!" *Oh shit. Did I black out on the can?*

"Hang on." I set my phone on the tiny counter, wiped myself, flushed, and washed my hands. "Okay, I'm back. Sorry to freak you out, but, when I tell you what happened, your anxiety will be through the roof."

Twenty minutes later, I'd reenacted the whole conversation. From my Scarlet O'Hara faint to the hot EMS asshole, onto Dr. Abel's fix, which could land me on a damn farm for the rest of the fucking year. My energy drained, I dropped face-first onto my bed.

"Dear God! What the hell did you do in a past life that is breaking through the time-space continuum to bust your ass?"

I loved her sass and wonky way of thinking, especially when she talked to her chicken, Amy the Great. *Again, don't ask.*

I wailed into the fluff of my comforter, muffling my cry, "I. Don't. Know!" then rolled over with one arm draped over my forehead, still in Scarlett O'Hara mode. "But it better-the-fuck stop! I can't take the stress anymore. Abs, when you hang up, I'm going to spoon all the spoons, then move on to the forks. Every towel is going to be refolded, and I might bang on a neighbor's door to do theirs, too. I need one of your amazing hugs." My cries turned to gags as my snot plugged my orifices.

Abigail dropped her voice a decibel and spoke quietly to me. "Sen, you need to breathe with me. Come on. I'll walk you through it like we used to do in high school. Breathe in to a count of four, hold for a count of four, and exhale to a count of four. Focus only on your breathing. I can't hear you. Do it!" A soothing Abigail was a rarity, as was her patience, so I obeyed.

"Fine." We breathed through four cycles of four, and, just like always, I settled myself enough to speak without a hitch in my voice. "I'm better. Thank you, Abs. I don't know what I'd do without you." On the verge of crying again, I promised to call her as soon as I heard from Dr. Abel.

I needed to see this situation as a stumble on my road to success, not a complete collapse. At least, I think that's what Glenda would say. I'd received a text from her confirming an appointment on Friday when she returned, with strong verbiage not to do anything rash. *Define rash?*

I popped some popcorn, pulled out a forbidden on-campus beer, walked to the TV in a sports bra and boy-short underwear. I opened my computer to a movie app and typed in "Gone with the Wind." I needed to see if I nailed the fainting parts, scrutinizing how I would have dealt with Rhett Butler and his misogyny. *What an ass.* Which reminded me of a certain asshole I may or may not have taken a tumble with visiting Abigail a few years ago. He was a gorgeous asshole. Proud of it, too. His skills were epic. I just wished I didn't use sex as a means of dealing with my OCD. I could use a good fuck right now.

Chapter 3

SENECA

Visions of cornfields and koi ponds flooded my brain as I passed from deep-state sleep to awareness. You know the place where you aren't sure if what you're experiencing was real or imagined? My mother's face was outlined in the stillness of the water. I knew what seeing my mom meant. She'd come to my dreams from the moment she passed from cancer. Four years ago, when I was living with Abigail, I woke up the same way and began sketching gardens. Two specifically: a community garden with fruits and vegetables and a Zen Garden with meditative thoughts from the great masters that reflected the ascension of the higher self when completed. The first garden had been underway for over three years now. Abigail used her community to run, harvest, and replant each season. My job each summer was to hone the varietals, inspect the soil, and configure new ways to water it. Elias, Abigail's hot, mammoth husband, was an engineer, now restoration mechanic, manufactured our watering devices. I'd never seen a project he couldn't conquer.

My plans for the Japanese Zen Garden were on hold until I graduated. It was a monumental project that had taken years to design. Beyond the pavers, every rock, stone, pebble, and branch could be found on Abigail's one-hundred-and-sixty-acre property. Though I'm sure they don't have the right equipment to crush stone or a place to gather sand. Serene koi ponds with lily pads floating in bunches on still water added the perfect place to sit and reflect. Elias had already started carving ornate benches with his college buddy, Alex, around the community garden. *They could make a few more, right?* Elias built the pieces and Alex carved in all the details. Flowers, birds, swirls and more. I never really appreciated what he could do until he made Abigail's Bed & Breakfast sign. It was magnificent, with colored gem mosaics inlaid in the design. Who wouldn't stay at her place after seeing that work of beauty?

The reality of where I lived would pose a problem for the koi pond I wanted to make. We lived in a temperate zone. What did you do with them in the winter? Do you let them freeze in the water during the winter, like a cryo-bath? That sounded terrifying. *I needed to read up on that.* Regardless, I wasn't going to do any of that at Abigail's place, or at the Longwood Gardens. If I had been given the opportunity to go to Japan, well, that would have been the perfect place to learn from the masters. That was a pipedream now. Best not to perseverate on it. *Tell that to my cuticle's half eaten.*

I vacillated between getting my shit together and finding a cheap place to live off campus since I wouldn't be finishing my degree this year, or hiding under my covers and having pizza delivered at ten in the morning. Stuffing my face like a glutton was a hands-down preferable decision. My phone interrupted my ordering just as I gave them my debit card info and swapped the call to see my father's image pop up on the screen. Switching calls too quickly, consequently forced me to endure one of his utopian lifestyle conversations.

"Hey, Dad. How's it going?" I said cheerfully, straining my face. I didn't hate my dad, only his flakiness. He loved me, but his low self-esteem seemed to get the better of him. Which then led to bad decision-making. Which then gave me whiplash. I was perpetually up in the air with him. Glenda said that was the catalyst to my OCD. His inability to live a stable life conversely made me immovable. Once a plan was in place, it stayed—come hell or high water. I was the poster child for stubbornness once a plan was set. Before then, I was quite malleable. It took massive amounts of energy to create a workable plan. I detested anyone breaking it apart.

"Sweetheart! I couldn't be happier, which is why I'm calling." *I could hardly wait for the punchline.* "Belinda and I are getting married! Isn't that terrific?" *Excuse me while I puke.*

My silence prompted his concern. "Are you still on the line, Sen?" Another beat of silence.

"Yeah, I'm here," I mumbled.

"Don't you want to congratulate us? We're going to Acapulco for a beach wedding. Sunsets, champagne, and sandy beaches. I'm so happy." *I need a new bucket.*

I didn't begrudge his happiness. He deserved it. "That's great, Dad. Many happy returns." My fake sincerity fell on deaf ears. *Whatever.* He didn't know me. I'd only seen him twice in the past four years. Once at Abigail's wedding and the next when he met me for Parents' Day freshman year. A crappy pizza, a pat on the back, and a hundred bucks to "get you through the semester," was all he could muster. *That chump change wouldn't last a month!*

"We're leaving next Tuesday. I wanted to let you know if you called. Belinda's kids are meeting us for the weekend on Thursday. I'm sure you have plenty to do, so I'm sure you understand why I'm not extending an invitation to you. We'll catch up when we get back. I'll send you pictures. Yeah, this is terrific." His exuberant voice fell off at the end of his pitch like he was talking himself into this marriage. *You're in too deep, Dad.*

There was a knock at my door. I walked half-naked across the room, grabbing my wallet along the way. Phone in one hand and a tip in the other, I used my elbow to lever up the handle and kicked it open with my foot. The kid with the pizza bobbled the heating bag. It was then I realized the impact of seeing a scantily clad woman standing in front of him almost knocked him off his feet.

"Here," I smiled coyly and shoved the money over the box. It took him a minute to register we were making a transaction that didn't involve his dick and pocketed the money. He slid the steamy, hot, gooey goodness out and handed me my pie. "Enjoy the view," I cooed.

His bugged-out eyes didn't falter even when he stepped back from the door and squeezed his bulging pants. "Definite."

I snarked out, "Bathroom is down the hall to your left." I swung the door shut, blurring out all the details about the resort and what he was going to wear. I couldn't care less.

I placed the pizza on my desk and finally drew my line in the sand.

"Dad, I'm really happy for you. The details of your wedding aren't interesting to me since I won't be there. For the record, it would have been nice of you to offer me an invitation instead of assuming I wouldn't want to be there for you. I mean, I am your only daughter." My bitchiness was not contained. He needed to hear it. Every fucking word. I rushed him off the phone with an excuse and flopped onto my bed, outraged.

Fuck my life! I needed all ten fingers and toes to count how many times he'd humiliated me, ignored me, placated me, disregarded me, and failed to show me, not tell me, how much he loved me. For god's sake, send a fucking card on my birthday. Be a sport and throw in a fifty-dollar bill. Drive your goddamned ass out to campus once a year and see all the wonderful projects I've been a part of. Here's a thought. Invite me to your fucking lame wedding and pay for the airfare.

This week was becoming a tsunami of fucked-upness and I didn't think I could take another hit. I went to the bathroom and unrolled several pieces of paper towel, stopping at the mini-fridge for a bottle of iced tea. I cracked off the top and guzzled half of it before pulling out my chair, sitting down not-so-lady-like, swinging my leg up then thumping it on my desk, as I flipped open the pizza box. Double cheese Hawaiian pizza pulled like taffy as I extracted my first slice. This better fix my mood or Ellie, my resident hall assistant, would need to call campus security to hoist me off the roof. *I swear, I'll jump!*

I was kidding. I loved life too much to create that scene. I had friends. Okay, one friend. One that was more like a sister. She needed me. At that moment, I truly realized how much I needed her, too. She was the only family that mattered and I needed to let her know immediately.

I wrapped my hands into the paper towel and wiped the grease from my chin, feeling like *Jabba the Hutt* from *Star Wars*—the original—and speed-dialed Abigail to finish our conversation. Again, my call was interrupted by none other than Dr. Abel. I shook my head clear of inner dialogue and promised myself, whatever he said, I would deal with it. I wasn't a child. I could handle this. That's when the pacing started.

"Hey! Dr. Abel. What do you know? Will I graduate on time?" I sounded desperate, but I had nowhere to go but up today.

He chuckled. He knew my moods, and never told me to relax or calm down, which I appreciated about him. He respected me and my feelings, unlike another male figure who should have done that for me my whole life. *Moving on.*

"If I didn't know you better, Seneca, I would say you haven't fared well these past few hours. Though, I think you'll think better of me after you hear about the amazing opportunity I found for you. As I mentioned, three internships presented themselves after everyone had been assigned. While two of them are more up your alley, they are several states away and don't offer any accommodations for room and board," he said, unemotionally but empathetically.

I was burning a path on the vinyl floor, waiting to hear about Door #3. "Thank you so much for balancing my situation with my goals, Dr. Abel. It means a lot to me that you made that a priority." I tipped my head side-to-side as if I had a choice in the matter.

I could hear his smile through the phone as he acknowledged my appreciation. "That's what I'm here for, Seneca. I'm your dean *and* your mentor. We're a team. When I tell you about the third opportunity, I need you to stay calm. It's a little out there, but the benefits far outweigh the deficits." I could feel my ass clenching to the point I stopped pacing.

I cleared my throat of pizza grease. "Deficits?" I gulped.

He chuckled again. "I suppose it's how you look at it, but hear me out. We've sent interns to this location a few times in the past for agribusiness and animal science majors, but not specifically a horticulture major, like yourself. Eloheh Farms specializes in organic farming and dairy production. The owner, Mr. Valize, is having some trouble with his soil, and thought— if we could help him—he could reciprocate and help you fulfill your degree. Are you still with me?"

Eloheh Farms. Mr. Valize. Why did that sound familiar? Where did I hear those names before? "Uh, yeah. Still here. You're right. This is totally the opposite direction I was going in. Why did you think I would be a good fit? Can't he just do a pH test and handle the problem that way? This isn't brain surgery." My snarky attitude was getting old, even to me. I needed to chill out and let the man finish.

Tsking sounds pattered through the line. He was trying to save my ass and here I was being ungrateful. I thought I'd grown older and wiser, but, alas, I still had room to grow.

"Sorry, Dr. Abel. Please continue," I said with contrition.

"Thank you. Our first priority was finding an internship. The second was finding one that fell within our working parameters. Lastly, it pays a stipend, offers onsite room and board, and will teach you how to work the land in similar—but different—ways to achieve your goals. It may not come with an invitation to the International Gardening School in Japan, but it will illuminate best practices in both farming and food production. All worthwhile skills. So . . . do we have a winner? Or would you like to continue your college journey for another year?" His laugh wasn't so subtle this time. I was between a proverbial rock and a hard place. I knew firsthand that even plants can thrive in crags, and so would I.

Digging my fist into my eye as I pressed the phone to my ear, an eerie feeling came over my body. Inner voices sounded like tribal drums beating in my head when one of them pierced my consciousness Minotaagwazi . . . *My mother! She's watching!* My heart soared knowing she would be a part of this decision. I needed her so badly today. Whether still pond waters or tribal drums, she was making herself present, and I needed to let my stubbornness subside and listen.

I sighed deeply, then spoke confidently, "We have a winner. When do I leave?"

Chapter 4

SENECA

It took two days to get all the paperwork sorted out before I returned to Dr. Abel's office to sign off on my internship. Ten pages of fine print indemnifying the university, and ensuring I fall under their insurance umbrella should I get dismembered or other catastrophic scenarios. All of it was moot. I needed this opportunity to graduate in the spring, and if blindly reading and initializing paperwork got it done, so be it.

"One last piece of information, Seneca. You'll be living at Mr. Valize's home on Eloheh Farms. He has assured me that you will have separate quarters and will respect your privacy. He has a sink in the bedroom, but you'll have to shower one floor below. I hope that won't be a problem?" Dr. Abel didn't wait for my answer, pressing on.

"Mr. Valize requested you call him when you leave campus so he can plan to greet you. He also suggested that you bring snacks, toiletries, and personal items to last you a couple of weeks. The nearest town is forty minutes away. He only goes twice a month to stock up on necessities. I'm sure you can work that into your daily routine, right?" Again, not waiting for my response, he popped up from his seat and walked past his desk. "Here are the directions, contact information, and your first two assignments with due dates. Best of luck, Seneca. I'm sure you won't regret making this shift. Mr. Valize is a solid man with an amazing work ethic. You'll get along well. I'm sure of it."

I sat there dumb and mute, being given my directions. All consolations were gone. I was forced to move forward without question. If I didn't know better, I would think that Dr. Abel had a golf game to get to with how quickly he covered my assignment and motioned for me to get out of his office.

I shook my head clear of any doubt, forcing myself to buck-up and swallow my pride at the thought of working on a farm through the school year. This was not part of my plan. I stood to my full five-foot-five inches and raised my head high. "I'll do you proud, Dr. Abel. Thank you again for all your help pulling this together for me so quickly. I truly appreciate it. I'll let Olivia know when I arrive." My lips pressed together tightly as I dragged the corners of my mouth backward into a forced smile. It was the best I could do under the circumstances.

After his quick pat on my back and, "Do your best," I booked out of his office to take one last walk around campus before making the ninety-minute journey to East Stroudsburg, Pennsylvania.

Why did I get the feeling I was being exiled to Outer Mongolia? Could it be I won't know anyone? Or wouldn't be able to walk around town since it's forty minutes away? And who will I talk to all day? Surely, Mr. Valize had his own responsibilities, leaving me to my own. *Whatever they will be.* Farms are big places. I hope he has pigs or a chicken like Abigail's. I love those pink piggy tails and little snorts. They are adorable.

Know what else was adorable? Me trying to stuff my dorm room into a third-hand 2010 white Honda CRV. After learning about Abigail's car troubles on her way to claim her inheritance, I made it a point to have my car serviced. Old Betty here would not burst into flames before, during or after I arrive at my destination. She would be with me for the long haul—or until I had a steady paycheck. Whichever came first.

Two lamps, a twin XL foam bed topper, a purple, faux fur area rug, a box of knickknacks, another box of assorted kitchenware, including my microwave, and two big pieces of luggage full of clothes, and I was ready for my next adventure. I hoped Mr. Valize didn't mind helping me move all my crap up to his attic. Come to think of it, I hope he has air conditioning up there. I'm a cold sleeper. If I'm too hot, I'll be up all night. God help anyone pushing my buttons the next day. I'm a bear when I don't get my beauty sleep.

I said goodbye to all my favorite sitting spots and promised to visit again soon. I waved to the *Wings of Thought* sculpture on Mentors' Circle and finished my walkabout, shuffling back into my dorm to check out of my room with Ellie. *God help me.*

I knocked on her door and waited impatiently. When she opened it, she flipped her hair like she was expecting a guy.

"Hey, Wa . . ." Ellie stopped short. "You're not Walker." *Amazingly astute observation, Ellie.*

Forcing a dry laugh, I moved things along. "Nope. Not Walker. So, here is my room key. It's all tidied up, and I just need you to sign here that I am discharged from Williams Hall." I shoved my lease agreement and a pen in her face, not wanting another minute of being in her presence.

Her face fell. Her sigh was almost sincere. "Oh! So sorry you're leaving us. You'll truly be missed." She took my pen, held the document up to her door and scrawled her name.

I pointed abruptly at the page, "And date it... please." *Where are my manners? Wink. Wink.*

"Of course. Here you go. Be sure to stay in touch. Bye." She stepped quickly back into her room, leaving me staring at a closed rock star-studded door.

One step out of this hall and she'd be out of my mind forever. My friendships consisted of lab buddies, research assistants, and the facilities manager at the horticulture center. Remmy was an older man in his late thirties who could kiss me off my feet. He did it twice last year. Too bad I was moving on because he was a cherished distraction whenever I had to stay up late to log measurements of soil decay. Silver, tinged brown long hair with deep blue eyes kept an eye on me while I worked. I'd turn to record notations on my clipboard and he'd conveniently be fixing lights in the hothouse. It didn't take long to start a conversation, and, well, one thing led to another, and his jumpsuit zipper "accidentally" broke, and we added a few degrees to the already warm air in the greenhouse. It's amazing how two grown adults can maneuver themselves onto a five-foot wood bench without breaking a lip lock. This was the only time in my life I could work in the dirt in a skirt. Remmy took advantage every time he could. No wonder those Regency Romances were so hot. Who wore panties in those days? Women were ready for anything, anytime.

I considered swinging by one last time to cop a feel on his tight ass but figured that groping a grounds man in broad daylight might cause a problem for both of us. *C'est la vie.* Onward and upward.

My phone buzzed as I finished punching my destination into the navigation app on my phone, shoved my earbuds in to keep the conversation going without holding my phone, and buckled up. My heap of an ancient car didn't have fancy hands-free technology. I was lucky to have automatic seat adjustment and front and rear defrosters.

"Hey, Abs! I'm just getting on the road," I yelled, looking around to make sure I wasn't going to plow over anyone as I backed out of my parking place.

Gasps echoed through my earbuds. *I know. I shocked myself.* "Really? Sen! Are you so excited to be taking your first steps into the real gardening world?" I wish I felt as excited as she did. I was still clawing my way out of a depressive attitude about this assignment.

I smacked my lips together, working out the dry mouth I suddenly experienced. "I'm not sure excited is the word, Abigail. More like trepidation. Remember how I told you my original internship at Longwood Gardens fell through? Or did you forget?" I sometimes forgot how Abigail's ADHD sabotaged her.

"What?" she drew out the word, "That was your *dream* job! How are you even breathing right now?" *Good point. How was I?*

I replied with a dramatic sigh, "It's true. I've traversed a mental breakdown, shocked a pizza guy with my nudity, and suffered learning I was banished to a farm in Bum-Fucked Egypt. The only good news is that I, I mean you, don't have to pay for room and board this year. It's included in the internship."

When I decided to go to college, or Abigail had demanded I do, I'm still not sure how it happened, she paid for me to go to horticulture school to realize my gardening dream. My only payment was to build her an intricate meditation maze that I went on and on about when I first arrived at her newly acquired property. It was a small price to pay, and I was stoked about getting it done for her with my newly-acquired skillset. She's going to have a cow when I tell her I'll be working with—*cows*! When I took her through my conversation with Dr. Abel and where I was going and who I would be working with, she squealed.

"Oh my god, Seneca! I know this is a one-eighty from where you wanted to be but think of all the knowledge you'll acquire. Who knows, maybe the farmer will help bale your hay? Or milk your pussy?" She broke into hilarious cackles followed by raucous laughter. Abigail wasn't shy about her anatomical descriptions. She went right to crude, when given the opportunity.

I shook my head, appreciating how I got to be so lucky to have her as a friend. Money aside, she kept me laughing from the moment I met her. "You're a laugh-riot, girl. Since I'll be working with his soil problem, it would be more like mud wrestling. Not that I'm above that. You know I'm all for bizarre sports, especially toe wrestling." I laughed so hard that my eyes wouldn't open. Not a healthy way to drive. "Okay. Stop. I can't see the road!" Several moments later, we caught our breath and my mental status declined rapidly into panic.

"What if Mr. Valize hates me? Or I can't help him with his soil problem? Or I forget to shut a barn gate and his cows run for the hills? I don't know about farming, Abigail. I know flowers and architectural garden stuff. Okay, I know about soil, but nothing beyond pH levels and mulch . . ."

She cut me off. "Whoa. Slow down, sweetie. You're one of the smartest people I know. You'll figure it out. Tell me again where you're going?" Her voice shifted suddenly from consolation to apprehension. *Hmm.*

I tried to remember the place but couldn't recall the name. "I forgot, only that it starts with an E. A Native American name, I think. I'll let you know when I get there. I should pay attention to the road. Look for my text in a couple of hours. Love you!"

She giggled. *Yeah.* At twenty-eight, Abigail still giggled. Her husband Elias loved it, and it was kind of adorable. "Yeah, okay. This internship will definitely be enlightening. You've got this, Sen. East Stroudsburg, huh? Valize... hmm." *Why was she musing on those details?*

We said goodbye, and I cast my eyes on the horizon as the afternoon sun approached its zenith. I cranked up some country tunes on the radio, pulled out my earbuds, and adjusted my attitude. In ninety minutes, my life would either spin off its axis or the stars would align. I wish I had a crystal ball. Or maybe a Magic 8 Ball would suffice. This girl needed order in her life, fast. The alternative was to spend the first week rocking in my attic tower.

Chapter 5
ALEX

I was desperate. I regularly accepted interns each harvest season and throughout the rest of the year. It was cheap labor. Smart college students who needed life experience on a farm could be counted on to show up, work hard, and offer new eyes to problems I see every day. This intern, however, would either make me or break me.

I'd been living at and now running *Eloheh* Farms since my parents passed in a car accident twelve years ago, forcing me to retire after eight years in the army. Caring for my younger brother was more important than another insignia on my shoulder beyond my silver bars. The military called it a hardship discharge or dependency discharge. I called it a fucking relief. Since my last tour in Afghanistan, the constant stress caused me to feel that my mental health was slipping. As I looked back to when my dad and mom were diagnosed with cancer six months before my discharge, things didn't add up. They were still running through a battery of tests, but nothing conclusive was noted. For lack of anything substantive, the doctors put both of them on light doses of chemotherapy, hoping it would knock out whatever the cause was. Ultimately, a freakish car accident took their lives, potentially sparing them years of pain and suffering. Wallowing in shock and loss wasn't an option. I had a fifteen-year-old brother, Dane, to care for. At the time, he was too young and too inexperienced to run this farm. He needed to graduate high school. Not be a farm hand. He was a smart kid who could win a college scholarship in robotics or anything else, and make something of himself with a little effort. His life was just beginning, and mine was near a meltdown. I'd been shipped up north from Fort Eisenhower one day after the crash, and I never looked back.

Keeping the farm was never a question. This land has been a part of our family for over one hundred and fifty years. A Valize had always had a stake in this place, and my duty was to take on the yoke my ancestors accepted proudly. I'm not above working the land. I love it—mostly. While in the Army, my talents led me to the Intelligence Corp. My job was to know everything our soldiers would encounter in the field before it happened. I was intelligent, quick-witted, and processed information at lightning speed. My commanders depended on me intrinsically and our troops even more. Men and women would die if I got my wires crossed. It was a shit-ton of pressure. My only failure during my eight years of service was sending a battalion into a sandstorm that hadn't been predicted. No lives were lost, thank God, though it rattled me knowing I was at the helm. The storm wasn't predicted because it was too small for my radar to pick up. When a storm came up, they were forced to hit the deck, seek refuge, or find a ditch until it passed. The small patrol I'd been watching skimmed along the wire of our base. They didn't have a fighting chance against the flare-up, huddled for twenty minutes, breathing through their bandanas until it passed. You might as well be inhaling sawdust through gauze. Excruciating. Thank goodness I only got a knuckle swat for my fuck up and not hunted down and flogged by those six service people.

Our family farm flourished under my care, cultivating it into both an organic dairy farm and an organic provider of fifteen herbs and vegetables to the tri-state area. My soil was tested monthly, and I'd never had a problem up until now. I was losing thousands of dollars unable to sell products to our end-users for fear someone would get sick and completely put me out of business. I'd done some pretty asshole things in my life, but deliberately letting people eat potentially contaminated food would be heinous. I had integrity if nothing else.

Dr. Abel highly recommended Ms. Locklear as my intern. Thank goodness she became available when she did because hiring a professional company would cost me even more. If she couldn't identify the problem in the next two weeks, I'd bite the bullet and pay the big bucks. Who knows if I'd get any answers, but, most assuredly, I would lose this whole planting season. Or worse, my reputation. Or, the ultimate worst, be shut down permanently.

My phone buzzed as I rode my John Deere tractor back to the barn from the fields. I pulled the clutch and killed the engine. This thing sounded like a slow-moving train clanking down the track. Rhythmic and relaxing. I pulled my phone from my pocket, thinking it was a phone call, but saw a text from an unknown number.

"Hi. This is your intern. I'll be arriving in thirty minutes. I'm super excited to meet you and get started."

She sounded perky. Maybe even fun. My last intern was too serious. The one before that was aloof. Perky was sounding better every minute. I restarted the engine and parked the tractor next to the barn. I had a few minutes to wash up and make some iced tea. I wasn't a good host, but I'd put my best foot forward today. After that, all bets were off. I'd planned on barbequing burgers tonight, and, if she were up for it, I would make a bonfire so we could get to know one another. We'd set a plan in motion for the next day and get to bed early. It was imperative we worked well together. I wouldn't abide insolence or a poor attitude. If that text was any indication of her personality, we should be off to an easy start.

Soon, I heard her car crunching down the long gravel drive, a full quarter mile, to be exact. A white SUV puttered along until it stopped at the bottom of the ranch house stairs. I'd take a look at her engine sometime. It sounded like a cat was whining under the hood.

The sun was bright and cast a long shadow over her body. But when a mane of long, silky black hair exited the vehicle, I got tingles down my spine. She ducked back into her car to grab something, and, after she cleared the door, my jaw dropped. It wasn't her astounding beauty that made my stomach fill with bees. It wasn't even her deeply tanned, long-legged body that made my pants feel tight. It was those almond-shaped eyes with eyelashes for days that knocked me off my feet. But when she lifted her head and her bright smile turned sour, I knew trouble had fallen at my door. *Seneca.* How in god's name did this Tasmanian devil find me?

SENECA

You know that moment when you finally figured out how the Rubik's Cube needed to swivel to get each side one color? The tenacity of trial and error? The patience to see the problem through to the end? That had been my week. Flow. Patience. Trust. Perseverance. Those were the watchwords of my faith up until now. I was ready to put all the bullshit aside to make this internship a positive experience until I realized where I'd heard the name Eloheh Farms.

Alex. Not Mr. Valize. *Alex.*

If Dr. Abel had said Alex Valize, I'd have put together his name and farm a lot fucking faster, choosing a different internship. Two semesters of this narcissistic, pig-headed asshole. I'll say it again—Fuck. My. Life! Full disclosure, he did fuck me and rocked my world, but that was irrelevant. His ego was the size of Abigail's property. *That's a lot of ego.*

I gulped, swallowing my pride then covering my eyes from the sun. Be professional, Seneca. Put the past behind you. Do your job. Graduate and get on with your life. My mantra lost its pizzazz the moment I recognized the man I'd have to please to pass my internship. Life is twisted.

I rubbed my forehead and walked to the bottom step, taking in his broad shoulders, full, muscled chest and strong hands on his narrow hips. *Damn, he was sexy.* I let out a deep sigh regretting that one stupid night four years ago.

"Now, isn't this something, *Miss* Locklear," he said emphasizing my illustrious title. The hiss he added didn't go unnoticed.

I cocked my head to the side, annoyed. "Hello, Alex. Or should I call you, my new employer, Mr. Valize?" Keeping the snark out of my tone took a lot out of me and I sat down on the step, shakily.

His deep laugh peeled through the air, sending vibrations down to my lady parts without my permission.

I replied. "This sure is something." My eyebrows rose to my hairline of their own volition. "Isn't it ironic that when we vowed never to see each other again we'd meet up only a year later at Abigail and Elias's for Thanksgiving? Then, the year after that, again, at Thanksgiving. And the Fourth of July party, again, at their house the year after. I suppose it's only natural that we meet again, and me, at your mercy." My sardonic speech was meant to be satirical, but, after saying the words, it was downright hysterical.

The thumping of his boots down six steps, followed by the thump of his fine ass parking itself on the step above mine, said it all. We were almost equals, looking each other in the eyes. But I didn't forget who's the boss here.

"Should we call a truce before shots are fired?" The laziness in his voice was too much. Slow. Rich. Taunting. *Searing my panties off.*

I turned my body, lifting my eyes slowly, analyzing the crow's feet at the corners of his eyes and the slow smile creeping up his stubbled jaw. Snippets of close encounters of the incredible kind from years gone by zoomed through my brain. His shirtless chest. How he dragged his hand through his hair as he looked at me over the Thanksgiving table. His massive dick standing proud waiting to introduce itself to my pussy the summer we first met. *Yeah.* We had history, but none of that mattered this year. I wouldn't let him screw up my chances of finishing this assignment. I had one focus and one focus only. Fix the soil, put in my time, and get the hell out unscathed. *Or broken-hearted.*

I drilled my palms into my eyes, clearing out whatever I remembered from our past, not giving him a reason to question me more.

"The white flag has been raised." I conceded. "Let's work out our terms. Plan it, then execute it. That's what I'm here for. Nothing else. Are you good with that?"

I summoned up every ounce of control I could muster forcing myself not to blink. He wasn't going to play me figuratively or literally. I was the fricking dungeon master, the gatekeeper, and Zuul of Gozer. He wasn't getting anything by me. I wouldn't let him use his charm or taunt me with compliments to break through my defenses. I wasn't a kid anymore. I was a woman on a mission, dammit.

Smirking again, he said, "You sure have grown up, Seneca. But I see you. Make no mistake about it. I like your plan. We'll get it down on paper after dinner. Let's get you settled. I'll give you a tour, then you'll know what you're dealing with. Making plans with you will be the highlight of my day." He stood, offering his hand to help me up. It might have been an olive branch, but I was wise to his craftiness. I'd get up myself.

Brushing off my backside, I stood, stepped down, and walked back to my car with purpose. I opened the driver's door, popping open the trunk. "I have a whole dorm room in here to drag up to the attic. Would you give me a hand?" I rested my hands on my hips, watching his face contort.

"Attic? Why do you think you're living in my attic?" The way his hands jammed onto his hips put me on the defensive.

I was done with these games. "Dr. Abel was clear that your interns stay in the attic suite. Has something changed without his knowledge?" My exasperation was quite evident.

More chuckles reverberated through his chest. "The last time an intern stayed up there was two years ago. I couldn't get the HVAC to work properly, so I cleared out my office from the spare room and turned it back into a bedroom. It has its own bathroom so you'll have your privacy. Is that satisfactory, or would you rather suffer the extremes this winter?"

Again with the sass. I suppose I should be grateful for a temperature-controlled abode. I reached into my trunk and pulled out my first suitcase. "HVAC, please." This time, I reeled in *my* sassy attitude in exchange for appreciation. This girl does not sleep in frigid or scorching quarters.

Alex descended the stairs as if walking to his people with all the swagger of a god. Those cowboy boots lifted his perfect ass, giving a slight pop to his hips each step he took. Muscled arms stretched his tight blue T-shirt making me salivate. The smirk he gave, catching me gawking, made me turn, hiding my blush. I wanted to kiss him—no—smack him for using his charisma to disarm me. He stepped alongside me, lifting out the next suitcase. The static electricity that bounced between us mottled my thinking. I tried to warn him it was too heavy for one hand, but his arrogance got the better of him. His grunt made me wince, and I was sure he'd pulled his back out.

"Are you okay? I meant to warn you how heavy they were," I mumbled, mildly sorry.

"Uh-huh, I got it," he grimaced, his voice catching as he reached a second hand onto the handle of my way-overpacked suitcase. I should have apologized, but I took sadistic pleasure in seeing him suffer. *God knows he inflicted enough on me.*

"How many dead bodies do you have in here?" His chuckle wasn't so bright this time.

I bit my lip, stifling my laugh, "Just two."

Old Betty, my ancient Honda SUV, sure could pack it in. It took almost a half hour to empty her and lug everything I owned into the spacious bedroom I'd call home. Alex had already supplied a five-drawer dresser, a reading chair with an ottoman, a floor lamp in the corner, and two side tables on either side of the queen-sized bed. *No more living like a prisoner.* There weren't any shades, only sheer white fabric with small bees that fell gently from a pewter rod and floral finials. The hardwood floors looked original, with small pits and worn lacquer on amber teak boards. It was like walking back in time with contemporary accents. It showed how the thoughtful person who decorated this room wanted it to be inviting and special.

I flopped myself backward on the down duvet, luxuriating in its softness. I'd be tossing my old comforter the first chance I got. Most of my stuff would be trashed after I graduated anyway.

"I'd like to suggest that we put off everything else on your list so I can never leave this bed." *Oops!* Once the words left my mouth, I saw precisely what Alex's face insinuated.

He scrubbed his face, wiping off his lascivious grin, "I wish I could oblige you, but that is a different internship altogether. You have an hour to get yourself settled while I make dinner. I'll see you in the kitchen when you're done." He looked over, pausing for a moment longer than friendly, and spun on his heel for an expedient exit.

I suppressed a laugh, thinking of how we would torture each other all year. I'm not foolish enough to think either of us could eradicate our memories. Our mutual goal was all business, nothing else. I gave myself a little pep talk about not instigating.

"Behave, Seneca," I mumbled to myself. "Regulate yourself like Glenda has been teaching you for two years. You've kept Alex at bay for four years already. What's one more?" *Uh, you live in his house now?*

Chapter 6

ALEX

I didn't waste a moment storming out of my house, calling Elias. Not waiting for a hello, I dove into a tirade the moment he answered.

"I can't fucking believe who showed up at my door for her Y-E-A-R long internship?" I dragged out my shrieking words, punching the air. "Do you know how fucking impossible this is going to be?" I rubbed my forehead, tearing at the skin. "What the fuck am I going to do?"

A rumble sounded through the phone. "Let's see. This is Alex, right?"

"Yes, asshole." I cursed.

"And that was three fucks, right?" Elias snorted, deepening my anger.

I growled. "Listen, smartass, this shit is for real. Do you know who my new intern is?"

One moment passed, assuming he was pondering who it could be. Until the second moment passed, and the realization hit me. "You knew. You're a piece of shit. You knew, and you said nothing! I hate you!" My pacing stopped as I collapsed onto my front steps. This was a set-up. I should have seen it coming.

Uproarious laughter rang through my phone. Elias screamed across his house, "He knows!" followed by shrieks of laughter from Abigail. I hate my fucking friends. Where was their loyalty to me? Not even a morsel of suspicion was shared during our five conversations in the past two weeks. I smacked my forehead hard. I'm so stupid.

"Give me that phone," Abigail sniped. "Hey, Alex," she said sweetly.

"Don't 'hey Alex' me." I snarled.

"Sweetheart, I only figured it out this morning when she told me which farm she was working at. I can't help it she didn't know Valize is your last name, or why she didn't put two and two together. When you saw her name on her paperwork, nothing rang a bell for you?" *I really am an idiot.* Her sincerity was questionable, but she does have ADHD and could have forgotten to call me this morning. However, that didn't excuse my best friend, Elias, for not saying anything.

Grumbling some more, I muttered. "You're forgiven, but that mass of a man you call your husband is going to get his ass kicked next time I see him."

She made whimpering sounds, "Okay. You beat him to a pulp." We both laughed. The idea that I could whip a six-foot four monstrosity of a mountain man was ridiculous. He could wrap my six-foot ass around a tree with one hand.

I stood up, rubbed my hand through my hair, and turned for my front door. "I gotta go. Talk to you soon. Uh, and, if you think I should know anything else about this fiasco, how about you do me a solid and let me know?"

"Sure thing. Good luck, Alex. I believe in you." Abigail crooned as Elias laughed some more before the call ended.

Assholes.

With a deep sigh of frustration, I marched up the stairs, slammed the screen door, and began making dinner.

SENECA

"Wow. That smells good. I haven't had a home cooked meal in weeks." I marched into the kitchen and lifted the lid off a pot of bubbling, sweet smelling baked beans.

Watching Alex cook gave me tingles all over. I never considered him in a domestic way. I also didn't have the opportunity to see his physique from the side in a long while. His high, tight ass and shapely thighs mocked me from across the room. He pulled out all the fixings for the burgers he promised earlier along with a big pitcher of iced tea.

I leaned back on the counter, behind the refrigerator door, my arms under my breasts. "Anything I can do to help? Maybe set the table?" I chirped shocking him when he shut the door.

His jaw began to tic and my eyes widened at the possibilities he was imagining.

"Are you okay, Alex?" My concern grew as he stood there not saying anything like he saw a ghost. I pushed off the counter, stepping closer to him, removing the jar of pickles from his frozen body. "Here, let me take these. I'll just get the table set. Okay?"

He shuddered as he jerked back to consciousness. Shuffling over to a cupboard next to the fridge, he opened the cabinet, extracting two plates and setting them on the counter. He shuffled down to another set of cabinets pulling out two glasses without a single word. Handing me the glasses I stepped across the wide kitchen and placed them on the table, looking over my shoulder, waiting for him to come back from wherever his mind went.

On my second trip back across the kitchen, he made a strange sound in his throat before speaking. "Sorry. I blanked out there." He shook his head absently. "The way you stood there reminded me of a friend from a long time ago. Guess it kind of threw me."

Finding his bearings, he walked out the sliding glass door to the barbeque to flip the burgers. That friend of his must have been something special to grip him like that. I questioned the wisdom of pushing him for more information but decided to hold my tongue. Not an easy thing for me to do. Alex had always seemed to be a carefree, dancing-through-life kind of guy. Open, fun, daring and devilish. That's who he had always been to me. His rounded shoulders and slack expression were the antithesis of his persona. I sure hoped he wasn't a Jekyll and Hyde incognito. I didn't have the emotional bandwidth to deal with that.

By the time the table was set and the iced tea poured, he returned with the burgers and toasted buns. He smiled shyly, placing the platter on the table and turned back to the stove to dump the beans into a bowl.

"Uh, would you mind grabbing the coleslaw from the refrigerator? I must have forgotten to take it out." Smiling brilliantly, I did what he asked, opening my mouth to ask again if he was okay, then snapped it shut, reminding myself of my promise not to push.

I placed the bowl of coleslaw onto the table and we sat down.

Once I had my plate full and began to eat, I realized sitting across from him was a mistake. His eyes were on me, and I opened my mouth wide biting into the juicy burger. Droplets of juice ran down my chin and Alex stifled a moan. *Damn him.*

I stood up abruptly, grabbing my napkin and wiping my face. "If it's alright by you, I'd like to take my dinner back to my room. I need some alone time."

He swallowed hard, wiping his chin, too and nodded. "Sure. Please bring the dishes out when you're done. You know, ants." I nodded, scooping up my plate, snagging my glass, then offered a pressed smile as I exited the kitchen.

Entering my room, I decided my desk would be the safest spot to eat, though I'd rather eat in that comfy chair in the corner. I'd probably drip burger juice onto the chambray material and ruin it, and I didn't need any additional negative vibes from Alex. If leaving the kitchen wasn't a sign of dismissal, I don't know what was. Watching his jaw chew was sexy. I didn't know that was a thing, but it made my nipples twitch. I devoured my dinner alone as I pondered boundary options. One thing was crystal clear: when I wasn't working with Alex, I needed to physically distance myself from him.

Later, before returning my plates, I dug through my backpack for the assignment package Olivia put together for me. After sprawling out on the cloud-like duvet, I slid out a thick stack of papers, noting the list of assignments and due dates in bold on the horticulture department letterhead. Each week, I was required to submit a journal entry with every task assigned and completed. Any concerns or new information and how I handled each item should be explained in detail, offering full transparency. One copy would go to Dr. Abel and the other to Alex. Supposedly, he could improve his mentoring style as we navigated my internship and beyond. The word "transparency" was underlined two times. A list of derelict actions, knowingly or unknowingly, could revoke my internship. I was responsible for communicating any concerns or issues to Alex and Dr. Abel. Twenty-five percent of my grade specifically focused on this topic. Additionally, twenty-five percent of my grade hinged on learning new and improved techniques revolving around organic farming and organic dairy production. To my chagrin, gardening wasn't mentioned. *Wasn't that my major?* The balance of my grade would be solving the "Client's" soil problems. Did Dr. Abel think I could solely fix Alex's uncooperative dirt? Several issues could contribute to the problem, and, even then, Alex might not be able to fix them. *Who knows?* I'll do what I can.

My first assignment, due tomorrow, was a detailed itinerary of a typical day based on the farmer's needs. *I bet that didn't include gawking at the farmer's ass. But I digress.* I sketched an outline of what I assumed would happen and would compare that to what actually would happen. I pushed my papers aside, clutching the notebook I'd jotted my notes in a spiral notebook and sat up. I sucked in a big breath, padding over to my desk for my dishes. Quietly, I opened my door noticing Alex wasn't anywhere around. Maybe I'd get lucky putting my dishes in the sink without running into him. To be sure, I called his name, getting louder each time.

"Alex? Alex. Alex!" No answer. I didn't want to skulk around his house, so I pulled my phone out and texted him.

"Hi, Alex. Would you like to have that talk now?"

I washed my dishes and laid them beside his on the drying rack while I waited for his response. My phone pinged as I poured myself a glass of water.

"Head out the back patio and keep walking for a hundred yards to the red barn."

Berating myself, I probably should have been helping him with that chore.

"On my way."

I ran back to my room and grabbed my work boots. Tough, brown leather hiking boots that had seen better days, were a staple in my wardrobe. Unspeakable bacteria had to live on these things, and I thought better of putting them on in the house. I took a moment and swapped out my jean shorts for some cargo shorts, stopping in the mirror for a quick inspection. Besides my dark purple tank top, I looked pretty bland. Nothing to look at here. I slid through the back door and tied up my boots, trying to remember what I knew about milking cows.

A black and white blur whisked by me as I walked through the barn door. Teetering on my heels, big, strong hands pulled my shoulders backward just as the animal thrust itself into my chest.

"Benny! Stop attacking the lady." Alex chastised him, then righted me back onto my feet. "Are you okay?" He should have let go of me once I was back on my feet, but instead he lingered, allowing me to enjoy the warmth of his breath on my neck, giving me shivers.

"Yeah. I'll survive." It appeared as though Benny was a well-trained dog since he sat two feet away from me, panting with a sweet smile on his face. Reluctantly, I pulled free of my savior and knelt eye-to-eye with the pooch that would need to be my best friend at Eloheh Farms. I held out the back of my hands, letting him have a good sniff. If he gave me his approval, I'd love him up so much he'd never leave my side. It sounded like a good plan. And it was working. I cupped his sweet face and scratched behind his ears, rewarded with a sloppy kiss in my eye socket. Border collies were the best companions. Steadfast and true. Unlike his owner. The last time I'd sat across a table from Alex was two years ago, with his final words being, "I'd like to stay in touch with you. Would that be all right?" Except he never did. Did he think I'd be so smitten with him that I'd follow him around like his dog? Hardly. He was a distraction. One I didn't have time to entertain. I chalked it up to another empty promise. *Men.*

"Are you done corrupting my dog? I want to introduce you to my girls." *Of course, he had a harem of women nearby.* "We can have that talk on the patio after they've been milked." *So, we're talking about cows.* Duh. "I'd planned on a bonfire if that suits you."

He stared at me, presumably waiting for a response. Relieved to know his *girls* referred to cows, I took that moment to catalog the contours of his chiseled jawline, long, lush eyelashes that looked like he wore eyeliner, and baby blue eyes making the blue sky pale.

"You said you were milking your girls? If we weren't standing in front of your cows, I'd slap you for another of your lewd comments." I loved toying with him. After he made that sexist remark in Abigail's kitchen when we first met, I knew how to keep him on his toes.

Alex rolled his eyes, jamming his hands on his hips. "Are you ever going to let that go? *Hrmph.* Moving on." He marched forward, pointing to each cow, calling off their names.

"Emma. Bernice. Eunice. Belinda. These are my bread-and-butter producers of organic milk. Ten cows in total. One day, I'll branch out to other dairy products, just not until my soil problem is resolved." He hung his head, rubbing his palm over his brow.

I hustled to keep up with him, almost smacking into his back when he stopped abruptly.

"Did you say Belinda? My father has a girlfriend named Belinda. This is priceless." I burst into laughter, my eyes watering at the resemblance of the two Belindas. Big feet, big ears, and both chewed on their cud. I'll never look at her the same way again.

He shook his head. "Ironic. Moving on."

Alex walked me through the milking process from teats to refrigeration. Since his milk was organic, there wasn't pasteurization or homogenization to deal with. It seemed he had a sister who was artistic and designed both the farm logo and the carton design. Several points of interest were identified around the barn's interior, along with a large tin sign stating procedural warnings.

I stopped, pulling my chin between finger and thumb pondering each warning. Alex had wandered over to another cow stall on the opposite side of the barn to milk his other cows but still was within earshot.

I yelled, "I get the rules about closing each stall, not leaving the milk out, and turning off the lights before nightfall. But could you help me understand what you mean by "Pay attention to the udder?"

The click of a pail handle hitting tin was the only response I got. A large figure walked down the center of the barn, the sun behind him making it impossible to make out his face. Big burly shoulders and a barrel chested man draped in overalls and a ripped T-shirt stopped between me and the sign. I gasped, my heart nearly stopping.

My eyes travelled skyward searching for his face, finding his big black eyes staring back down at mine. "It means, pay attention. Pay attention to the cows' teats. If they are red or chaffed, we need to treat them immediately. It also means, if you see something that doesn't look normal or looks right with you, say something immediately. We aren't one of these big farms who can afford to keep a vet on retainer." Mystery Man's gravelly voice sounded more like a cautionary tale with mild threats than a pep talk.

A rustle behind me made me whirl around. "It also means that if you see someone needs help, offer it. We don't have time for egos and attitudes. You get me? Let it go," I said sternly as he finished his explanation. "Seneca, this is Tiny. Tiny, Seneca. He's my right-hand man. You'll listen to him like you're speaking directly with me. Got it?"

Why did it seem like I was being spoken to like a naughty child? Had Alex divulged our tenuous past to Tiny? More importantly, how did a mammoth of a man get the name Tiny?

"I'm picking up what you're putting down. And, you," I stared down Alex, turning to point a finger at Tiny, "I'm not a derelict. Big-mouthed at times, but not to the detriment of a project or anyone's safety. Let's roast some marshmallows!"

Chapter 7
SENECA

This place keeps surprising me.

First, I was expecting to live in an attic loft. Simple, functional, and private. Now, I'm living in respectable luxury twenty feet from my boss. Awkward, you say? I couldn't agree more.

After lengthy discourse of dos and don'ts around the house and farm, we continued to our precarious relationship. We agreed that putting our past in the back-forty, as it were, would be best for our professional relationship. Additional boundaries included: how long showers would be, (no more than 15 minutes), food preferences (no tofu), and duties required to complete my internship (extensive). We also agreed that continuing this discussion after I had a sufficient amount of sleep would bode well for our oppositional personalities that crept into our discussion.

Secondly, I kindly asked Alex to disclose any other farmhands I might encounter, or them, me, without being shocked to death. When Tiny appeared out of the ether, it felt like a giant rat slid up my pant leg. Creepy-crawly and reminiscent of a Freddy Krueger character in *A Nightmare on Elm Street*, horrifying. After he finished choking on his saliva, he listed his sister, Annalise, who helped around the house and watched the farm when he was gone. He mentioned he had a part-time weed picker, but let her go the week before I arrived. "Seasonal help," he stated.

Today's surprise was the unexpected cuddling in my bed. It felt good, and whoever was there gave long, wet kisses. When I turned, reaching for my morning snuggler, I screamed when I felt long, silky fur. *The rat was real!*

"Holy shit!" I sat up abruptly, shoving myself up to the headboard. "How the hell did you get in here?" Benny sat up smiling, if that's possible for a dog to do. He lifted his paw, and, like a sucker, I reached out and shook hands—paws—whatever. Satisfied with our meeting, Benny rolled onto his back going belly-up. I loved dogs. I wish I hadn't moved around so much growing up so that I could have had one of my own. When a soft underside of a pooch presented itself, I baby-talked a whole conversation on my own.

"Aww. Who's da cutest boy? Do you want da scratches? That feels good, right?"

Of course, that's when my door swung open and a shirtless Alex stepped through without warning.

"There you are. Bad boy, Benny. You stay out of here."

I'm sure Alex said some words. Maybe used a reproachful tone. Though all I heard was the thrum humming through my chest as he stood in the morning light, his sun-kissed skin rolling over taunt muscles and deep cut abs.

Alex gulped hard, ignoring my swoon. "Is that what you sleep in?"

What? I looked down at my light blue tank top and boy short panties and realized why he was transfixed.

"Always," I said as I pulled Benny in front of me like a shield.

His brows knit and a typical scowl etched its way along his handsome face. "No! You do not get to use my dog as a cover up. He's mine. Benny, go!" Alex pointed to the door angrily and Benny looked at me for help.

"Sorry, buddy. Your dad's in a mood. Time to go." I reluctantly let him go, pulling my pillow over me. My pathetically demure pout was enough to send Alex out the door, too. He turned less aggressively before pulling the door shut, saying, "He can open doors. Sorry." The door clicked and I relaxed onto my other pillows. My mind wandered back to his low-slung grey sweatpants revealing his deep V. I licked my lips like a woman starved, wishing we'd met up again in other circumstances. My body tingled, yet my head throbbed with the abrupt awaking. I tried quieting myself through deep breaths. *Useless.* Instead, I crawled out of bed and stood in mountain pose, reciting an ancient poem my mother taught me when I was young.

Bring us peace to all our souls, O Lord. You who connects all beings. You give us light and strength. You teach us the importance of reflection. Your circulation supports our living."

I once knew the Ojibwe words, or at least some of them. Now, I only remembered the first word *Nana'isanishinaam*—Bring Us Peace. God knew I needed that. My mother knew I needed that, and took measures to ensure I wouldn't forget that there was a higher being all around us. I chanted the prayer quietly several times until I felt my feet strongly supporting my body on the earth. That was my sign I was ready to move on.

I quickly got myself together, dressing in jeans and a meme T-shirt—*I can either be on time or wearing pants. Pick one.* It seemed appropriate given how my day started.

I padded through the living room into the kitchen, surprising Alex.

"Can I help?" He bobbled the coffee mug in his hands, the hot liquid sloshing over the top making a puddle at his feet. "Sorry," I grimaced, reaching for the paper towel.

I could feel his agitation slither across the room directed at my face. The distinct lyrics regarding "loathing" from the *musical, Wicked* ricocheted through my brain. "I'm going to change my shirt and socks and I'll be right back. Instant oatmeal and cereal are in the pantry next to the fridge. Help yourself. Bowls and plates on the right of the sink," he growled, carefully setting his mug on the counter and shuffling out of the room.

Things were really looking up this morning. I'm sure by three o'clock I'll have burnt his house to the ground. He'll be chasing me with the only surviving knife from the inferno. We've got to get into a groove or this will never work out. I'm just not sure what needs to be done to make that happen.

Opening all the drawers and cupboards making myself familiar with his kitchen. I grabbed a bowl and spoon as directed, for the noticing the napkins in a square woven basket on the kitchen table. With a Froot Loops box tucked under my armpit, I waffled about where to sit. Feeling closed in, I opted to sit on the deck, soaking up my surroundings appreciatively.

The sun was still stretching her rays when I curled up on a bench pillow. Her friends, the clouds, danced through a powder blue sky making shapes that mimicked Benny, and I even found a

Belinda the Cow cloud. Between slurps and chews I smiled deeply, appreciating the gentle breeze, acres of green grass and trees, and the sounds of a slow-moving creek in the distance. This place was heaven on earth.

The mood on Eloheh Farms in Pennsylvania was so different than at Abigail's estate in Mystic, Connecticut. In Mystic, there was a current of elitism and entitlement built on the backs of the indigenous people over two hundred and fifty years. Eloheh moved slower. It felt thoughtful. Settled. Less divisive. Both were amazing in their own way, though I could appreciate why Alex chose to run his family farm. It settled the soul.

"There you are," Alex said, poking his head out the sliding glass door. "Ten minutes and you get the grand tour beyond the barn. Work gloves are mandatory. If you don't have your own, we'll grab some in town later this evening. Always wear your work boots. No tennis shoes or those fashion boots. They're both useless in this terrain. We'll be spending all day outside, so bring a hat. I'm making sandwiches. Do you have a water bottle?"

So many directions all at once. Hiking boots—check. Gloves—gardening only. Hat—wide brimmed to hide the sun. That left water bottles. I had two. Which one should I bring? A gallon-sized jug or a quart-sized version? *Argh! OCD rears its ugly head, again!*

I collected my dishes and meandered over to the sink to wash them. I was a tidy guest if anything.

"Will we be able to refill anywhere along the way? If not, I'll grab my big jug." He looked at me like I was from outer space.

"Didn't you see the creek running through my property? You practically stared at it eating your breakfast." *I thought we were dropping the attitude.*

Pressing my lips together, I steadied my voice. "Yes. I did see the creek. I also remember you saying we were going "Way out beyond the barn." What you didn't say was if there was water "Way out there.""

At that moment, Alex gave his best raging bull impression, complete with snorts, and steam coming out of his ears. "Bring whatever damn bottle you'd like." *Is that one stomp for small bottle or two for the jug?* This man was so infuriating!

I marched my ass back to my bedroom, swiping up my hat, gloves, and J-U-G. Only, upon returning to the kitchen, noticed he was gone. I heard his voice outside on the front porch, though, and redirected myself. With a sharp retort on my tongue, I stopped short when I saw a beautiful strawberry blonde woman; older than myself, and younger than Alex. There was a similarity that beckoned familial. She had a big smile on her face, while Alex looked like he'd drank coffee rinds.

"She's right there," Alex snapped, gesturing to me as I walked out the door.

The woman cocked her head to the side doing a slow nod. "I now see the problem." She walked over to me with her hand held out. "Hi, I'm Annalise, Alex's younger, smarter sister."

I fought to keep from laughing. I liked her already. "Hello. I'm Seneca, Alex's pain in the ass. It's a pleasure to meet you."

"Oh my god!" she said swiveling her head back and forth. "You've met her before?!" she shrieked. "No wonder you're freaking out."

Alex growled, crossing his arms. "I'm not freaking out. And, yes, we met several years ago at Abigail and Elias's house. She's her best friend."

Annalise's eyes bugged out. "The gardener girl you . . ." She smacked her hand over her mouth.

He shut his eyes, grinding his molars. "Shut up! Listen. Do the shit you always do around here, and please take the chicken out of the freezer. If you have time, could you make some cornbread? We'll be getting back at sunset and won't have time for baking." Giving me the stare of death, he pointed to the golf cart parked next to the barn. "Go. I'll meet you over there in a minute."

Not wanting to start a war between him and his sister, I obediently headed in the proffered direction. It seems that big bro and little sis swap dating stories. *Interesting.* I'd better keep my mouth shut around her, or I'd never get a break from either of them.

ALEX

I gently grabbed my sister by the elbow walking her up my porch stairs away from Seneca's peering eyes. It's times like these I wished I didn't share my love life with my sister. Shit like this always boomerangs back making me the fool. I'd never learn.

"Anna. I'd prefer if you didn't spew out my past to this girl. My *private* conversations with you are just that—private. Also, don't get too chummy with her. She's like a wild mustang that will rip your heart out sooner than wearing a saddle." *That didn't sound right.*

Her eyebrows shot to her hairline. "Really, Alex? She's a horse you'd like to saddle up? No wonder she ran away from you. You're a god damned pig." She yanked open the screen door leaving it to slam in my face.

Women! I can never say the right thing. I need to take a vow of silence before I lose my nuts to one of them. "I'm leaving now. Thank you for coming over. Have a lovely day, little sis," I said sarcastically. I didn't wait for her reply. I had one minute to get my game-face on, and acting like a raging asshole wasn't going to make this day any better. I was Seneca's boss. Not the asshole she made me out to be. What do I care anyway? It's not like we'd ever be in a real relationship. She's too young and obstinate. Wild dogs got along better than we did.

How did my parents stay together for forty-five years? What did my dad tell me? "Practice saying 'yes, dear.'" That wouldn't work now. It was too condescending. My mother had slightly better advice, "Don't go to bed angry." Words meant for declared partners. *Though an idea came to mind.*

I jumped into the driver's seat of the golf cart driving us out to the first rows of rhubarb, kale, broccoli, and cauliflower. I turned the key, powering the vehicle off when we arrived, and shifted in my seat to face Seneca. She looked back, concerned.

Clearing my throat, I softened my voice like a good friend would when breaking bad news.

"I had an idea I'd like to run by you."

Her eyebrows arched. "Sure?" she questioned.

"I've been beating my head trying to find a way for us to work together that doesn't instigate bad feelings or aggressive behavior. What if we start over? Pretend we know nothing about each other? We'll ask questions, getting answers from the horse's mouth without shadows of the past casting shade. No preconceptions. What do you say?"

I waited patiently, scanning her face for a quick dismissal of my idea. When her almond-shaped eyes lifted to mine, hope shone brightly. "It's funny you said that. I'd been feeling the same way. Nine months is a long time to argue. I'd rather learn and help you figure out your soil problems. I accept your scheme with one proviso."

Feeling elated at her agreement, my balloon burst with her one demand. Hesitantly, I asked, "What's that?"

A slow smile reached her eyes. I knew that face. Naughtiness laced with excitement. "We have to have fun."

Air burst through my lungs, and my pants became tighter. This woman would be the death of me if I let her. "Indeed!"

I marched her through row after row of vociferous vegetables, then onto the next set of rows of fruits. We were known for our extra sweet strawberries and gigantic blueberries. We offered U-pick options on Sunday mornings in the summer to help us extract the over abundance of crops. (We just couldn't afford to pick them all.) Kids from four counties would trek over and help their parents find their perfect berries to make into jams, pies, and bread. I didn't think about having kids until those little rug rats shoved tiny handfuls of blueberries into their mouths staining their lips and cheeks. They were truly adorable. Some fathers planned to have enough kids for a baseball team. Not me. I wanted enough kids to chase through the rows of berries listening to them squeal with laughter, tackling each other and shoving juice into their hair. *Three ought to do it.*

"Hello?" Seneca's voice pierced my daydream.

I scrubbed my face back to the present. "Sorry. Do you have any questions?"

She shook her head and jumped back into the golf cart. I took her way out to the far north corner of my property, allowing her to see the serene vista that overlooked the creek and down into my neighbor's meadow. Elias and I would come out here with a six-pack of beer and shoot the shit, unraveling the twists and turns life threw at us. We planned our future. We dreamt of our perfect women. The night we drank to my disaster of a short-lived love affair with Meghan, the high-powered saleswoman who traveled extensively, gave me the worst hangover of my life. It seemed I drank more of the relationship "Kool-Aid" than she did, resulting in me—in love—and her—loving only my cock. Unfortunately, she found Pierre in France to sate her pretentious style of living, and I found Benny at a dog shelter. He made up for her lack of loyalty, tenfold. Though long licks on my face—while I slept—wasn't what I'd call an intimate relationship.

We reached the crest of the hill and rolled to a stop. I fought every urge in my body to thread her long, silky black hair through my fingers. She had no idea what that one night four long years ago did to me. We were animals with each other. Unhinged and unleashed. This was why ultra conservatives said dancing leads to sex. *Bingo!* I switched off the engine unable to keep my eyes straight ahead.

Her lithe body slid off the seat wandering off as she pulled the brim of her hat down protecting her tanned face from the long, summer sun. The weather was surprisingly comfortable for a September morning. Soon fall would be upon us, tamping down the urge to sit in its warm rays.

"Sure is pretty up here," she uttered. She crouched down sifting soil through her long fingers. I watched as she pushed the dirt around feeling its texture, smelling its earthy, musty scent. I liked how she took the initiative to make herself acquainted with her surroundings like she lived here her whole life. However, when she stiffened sharply, I became concerned. Seneca's face blanched and I didn't know what happened.

The uneasiness in her voice whined out, perturbed, "Tell me again. When was the last time you soil tested?"

I crouched down beside her. "I do a home test every month and contract a third-party company to test quarterly. I can't afford to have any problems on an organic farm. We don't use pesticides or any other harsh chemicals. We mostly use organic Neem Oil, peppermint and thyme as pesticides. In addition, at the beginning of the growing season, we make two applications of a chrysanthemum-based nonsynthetic pesticide and one more mid-season to ensure we don't have bug infestations. I've had good luck with that system for over ten years. What are you sensing?"

Today was supposed to be an easy drive through the property. No problem-solving or distractions, just allowing her to get the lay of the land. I should have known Seneca's sixth sense of gardening would find its way out. She'd displayed her talents many times at Abigail's estate in her plant groupings, trimming techniques, and animal deterrents. She was clever and creative. I had to believe her college education only enhanced those gifts.

She stopped sifting through the dirt, wary eyes lifting to mine. "I'm not one-hundred percent sure, but it has a tinny smell to it." She scooped up another handful and pushed it toward my face. I cupped her open hands in mine and inhaled carefully, keeping the dirt a safe distance from my nostrils.

My eyes shot to hers. "Oh my god, Seneca. It does! You have an incredible nose." She had an incredible everything. Cognizant of holding her hands, I let them go and stood. "How did I miss this? I test every month for impurities. Now, you have me doubting my abilities."

A slow gust of wind emptied from my lungs, feeling disgusted with myself. I should have known to smell it. Damn it! I *do* smell it—regularly. I suppose me kicking the dirt was unmanly, but I felt I couldn't help it. I felt inept. Here I was summoning an intern to help me fix my soil problems, and I completely missed this profound detail. *What a fool.*

Seneca stood, placing her dirty hand on my forearm. Her compassion emanating through my body. "Alex. I believe you when you say you smelled the soil as part of your testing ritual. But do you test it as far out as we are now?" *She had a point.*

She paced up and down, twirling the ends of her hair around her dirty finger, staring hard at the ground. I joined her, wringing my hands in front of me. Several minutes later she stopped in her tracks and yelled. "Shiitt!"

I knew the feeling. I tried not to allow my emotions to rule me, though I was this close to having a fucking tantrum. Everything I'd worked for. Every plan I'd made was based on my land cooperating with me. I'd never considered something wrong this far out on my property, or at all. We were a quarter mile away from my crops. The only action this part of my farm saw was cows, then only once a week since I rotated them from field to field. I whipped out my phone hoping I'd get enough reception to make a call to my chemist friend, Leo. His reports had always been reliable, but now I'm questioning his aptitude for soil testing.

The phone rang. I held up one finger just as Seneca was preparing to speak. The line clicked over to voicemail. I kept my finger held up silencing her while I spoke.

"Hey, Leo. It's Alex. We have a huge problem with my property and I need you to get in touch with me the moment you get this message. The soil over by the creek smells tinny. And before you ask, it doesn't smell like that around my crops. Give me a call." I clicked the phone off and shoved it in my back pocket.

Seneca walked over to me, bumping my shoulder. "We'll get to the bottom of this. Dr. Abel taught us specific protocols to rule out most problems. If your friend goes through them, we'll know exactly what we're up against. I think he should also test your cows' milk and take some plant samples to be sure they aren't infected in any way."

My brows knit together as I fought to maintain my composure. I hadn't even considered my cows being contaminated. That's when Vesuvius erupted from my mouth, again.

"God damn it, Seneca! Why did you have to tell me my cows are fucked up, too? Don't I have enough to worry about with my crops?" I shifted from foot to foot, confused about what to do next. "Should I recall my produce? Send a Public Service Announcement to the locals radio station telling the whole friggin' county to come and get a refund? I'm sure everything purchased has been ingested already. What if those people get sick? I don't have that kind of insurance." I buried my head in my hands. "How long has this been going on?" I wailed.

Yeah. I'd lost it. Panic choked out any reasonable thought left in my body. I felt faint. All these years building my skills and confidence evaporated in two minutes. *Fuck!*

A hard fist to my deltoid stopped my doomsday rant. "Slow the hell down, Alex. Freaking out isn't going to help your situation. We don't know *if* your cows *or* your crops are affected. Save your hysteria until after the test results come back. In the meantime, I suggest we get back to the house and make a trip to a grocery store for bottled water for ourselves and jugs of it for your cows."

What did she just say? Water poisoning?

She grabbed my elbow, shoving me back into the golf cart passenger seat as she ran around to the driver's side. Time and space fell away as shock coursed through my body. I don't know how we got back to the house, but when Seneca flicked my ear, I snapped out of it.

"What the hell, Sen?" I said, rubbing my ear and exiting the vehicle. She was off and running up the steps, charging into the house before I could catch up to her.

"Hi, Annalise. Sorry to disturb you, but where does Alex put his truck keys?" I entered the house behind her, slamming the door for effect, agitated she thought I needed assistance.

"I've got this. Go get in the truck." She stared at me belligerently. "Now!"

Seneca had perfected the eye roll. Every year at Thanksgiving when I tried to make small talk, she'd roll those big black eyes into her perfectly arched brows. She was maddening. This was *my* house and *I* called the shots. So what if I had a mental breakdown in a field? I was entitled. The idea that my parents' and grandparents' legacy would end with me being caught off guard drove me near to hysteria. I'm only human, you know. This whole thing better be a sorry mistake, because, if it wasn't, I was literally up shit's creek.

I snapped the keys off the cow-head shaped hook and snapped at my sister. "Do you need anything from town?" I growled.

She threw her rag onto the coffee table, squeezing her eyes shut, lips pressed tightly together. "What in Holy Hell is going on here? What did you say to that poor girl? Do I need to remind you...?"

I cut her off, annoyed. "I'm not the problem here. The problem is that we may have a soil contamination issue. Which means we might have a water contamination problem. Which means don't drink any more of the fucking water! Now do you need anything from town or not?" She fell into a chair.

Yeah, I was harsh. I didn't mean to direct my helplessness at my sister. It wasn't her fault Armageddon was hailing down upon us. I sucked in a deep breath willing my heart rate to settle. "Anna. I'm sorry for yelling at you. It's just all too much to take in. Seneca had the forethought to feel the soil up by the creek and noticed a tinny smell. Leo's been called, and with any luck he can come by later today and test everything. In the meantime, please do not drink the water. Boil any you need to cook or clean with and I'll be back with a truckload of bottled water soon."

Her bewildered face said it all. I stepped closer, pulling her up into my arms, needing her comfort and giving her some. "We'll get through this. Let's try to be patient, okay?" I pushed her away gently and turned toward the door.

"Alex," her voice cracked. I turned and looked over my shoulder. "Be brave, sweetie."

I forced a pained smile for her benefit. "I'll do my best."

Chapter 8
SENECA

Driving in silence gave my mind plenty of time to ruminate. When did Alex decide he could call me Sen? That was for close friends only. I may have technically known him for four years but he'd pissed me off more times than not. He didn't have the privilege of using my shortened name.

The modest town of East Stroudsburg, Pennsylvania, was better than I'd expected for a rural community. Google said it has under ten-thousand people, and, judging by the ten people I saw in a name-brand grocery store, I believed them. I suppose any town that claimed a fast-food restaurant was a growing community. My brain did a little dance knowing that I could get my favorite shampoo and some decent french fries whenever I wanted.

With my anxiety abated, I dared to look across the truck, studying Alex's visibly concerned expression. In the years since I'd met him, he'd only gotten more handsome. He was twelve years older than me looking sexier as his blond silver-tipped hair sprung out when he tucked it behind his ears. Longer than before, it made him look younger. Deep grooves had formed over his brow, presumably from the pressure of his farm and raising his younger brother and sister. He wore a beard now, trimmed close to his skin with flecks of blond and grey peppered throughout. His mouth was every woman's desire. An inviting, bowed upper lip, sardonic and sexy, sitting above a full suckable lower lip. I'd thought about that smile for years. It mocked me, taunting me with desire yet telling me I'm not good enough.

This morning, I felt the pull between us as we stood looking out over his property. It would have been the perfect scenario to have him wrap his strong arms around me pulling me to his chest, kissing me along my neck. But he didn't. The feeling was momentary. My mind must have been playing tricks on me. Except, the tremors in the air were palpable. I could smell the soap he used, and the peppermint he had been sucking on before we left the house. It was there, and then it was gone. All for the better because messing around with Alex was akin to wildfire, and the grass was dry around here.

He caught me staring at him. "Like what you see?" And there was that panty-melting smile.

"Yes. McDonald's. Can you drive through for me?" I stifled a laugh as his smile faltered. If I gave him a cheeky comment, we'd be going down the same road to disaster we'd always traveled. I adjusted my professional façade and stared at the chain restaurant.

"Sure," he muttered.

We both placed an order, then pulled into a parking spot to eat. "You didn't have to pay for me," I pointed out, shoving my debit card back in my wallet after he pushed it aside.

He scrubbed his face. "Seneca, I know you're on a tight budget. You have been since I've known you. While you're working on my farm, at my request, you're not spending your money on food. I've got this."

His jaw was set, and I was too hungry to argue with him. I wasn't broke, but I couldn't afford to eat out often. "If you insist," I snarked.

Alex ate like he was in prison. He scarfed down his Big Mac in two minutes followed by guzzling his soda in almost as fast. I'd only finished half a bag of fries when he burped.

"In a hurry?" I taunted. He shifted in his seat, sending a deadpan stare my way. "Okay, I'll shut up." *I get it. Shut up shutting up.*

Minutes went by and I forced myself to finish, eating quickly. Sitting in his vehicle in silence was uncomfortable, and his foot began to bob. I looked at it, annoyed. Then my stare shifted to his face.

"It's a habit I picked up while in the Army. I can't seem to break it," he blurted out, sheepishly. "I'm sorry for freaking out back there. Panic attacks are another habit I can't seem to shake when I'm under a lot of pressure. Though anyone in my situation might have acted the same way. Regardless, I appreciate you keeping yourself together."

I didn't know what to say to that. I wasn't as affected by panic attacks. Seeing Alex out of control was unsettling, though. He always presented himself as confident and unflappable. To see him flustered and fretting rubbed off on me. I'm not sure I wanted to know this side of him. It made him feel more real. More human. Not someone I could objectify any longer.

I leaned over the console, folding my elbow underneath me. "You don't need to explain yourself to me. Anyone in your shoes would feel the same way. Leo will come by soon and in a few days this scare will go away and all will be forgotten."

He rolled his shoulders back, exhaling heavily. It appeared my soft voice and calm demeanor helped him to relax. I wanted him to see past the first wash of terror. Everything felt bigger when it first hit. My OCD was proof of that. Glenda helped me name that inner bully who tries to get its way.

"BOB got you by the short hairs?" I pulled my sunglasses down my nose, sarcastically.

He mirrored me, smirking, "Who's Bob?"

"B.O.B. isn't a person. It's an acronym I use to settle myself when I'm stressed. It means Blow Off Bullshit. The method doesn't fix my obsession, but it does give me a chance to synthesize what is important and what isn't so I can let it go instead of flipping out. Get it? B.O.B?"

Alex sat unaffected for a long time before bursting into laughter. "That's the dumbest thing I've ever heard, and the most incredible thing I've ever heard. Where did you dig that up? Your therapist?" My elation at him underestimating my acronym turned to scathing hatred.

I sneered back, "I did, actually. You should try it sometime. You're A.S.S. could use some sensitivity training." I grabbed my garbage in one hand and yanked the door open with the other, slamming it behind me. I marched over to the closest waste can and shoved my trash into it. Every time I let my guard down with him, he shits in my face. Why does he act that way? How are we supposed to build trust when he continues to belittle me when I'm trying to make our situation more pleasant? *Fuck him!*

A truck door slammed behind me, encouraging me to start walking. He could fuck off while picking up a few cases of water while I'd take a walk around Center Street for some window shopping. This was precisely the kind of time out I needed—shopping therapy.

I heard his boots closing in on me, and I looked both ways quickly before pulling open the first door I came across. Immediately I headed for a display case closest to the register. Why I felt that provided safety was ludicrous, but I did it anyway. I picked up a lotion tester and squeezed out a few drops when his hot breath blew down the back of my shirt.

"Don't run away from me. I'm sorry. I'm an ass. You know I'm an ass, but I don't do it intentionally. I come by it naturally," he chuckled. *He wasn't wrong.*

I couldn't turn around. I'd be looking at his muscled chest, and I couldn't trust myself not to reach up and touch it. "Alex, don't make me make a scene in this store, because I will. Back off," I hissed. He didn't move. Was he smelling my hair? Seriously. You don't piss off a woman then sniff her hair. Not cool.

"What about "back off" don't you understand?" I slid to the left around his bulk, rubbing the lotion into my dry hands. The woman behind the register tracked us as we moved around her store like a chess game. I'd move and look at a knick-knack, then he'd step either in front or behind me. Either was too close for a friendly shopping trip.

"Can I help you find something?" the nice, elderly clerk offered, concern lining her brow.

My eyes became laser beams as I locked onto Alex's eyes willing him to leave the store. "All set. Here, I'll take this."

I rolled to the right taking a ginger-orange candle I'd been sniffing and set it on the counter. *Checkmate.*

"How much is this?" I said, smiling brightly.

She relaxed and smiled back, though she kept eyeing Alex as if he'd rush the counter. "Eighteen o' one with tax."

"Great. I'll take it." I breathed a sigh of relief as the bell on the door jingled finally as I watched his fine ass leave the store. The nice woman rolled the glass into several sheets of tissue paper and set it into a floral bag so it looked like a present. She accepted my debit card and slid the package across the counter proudly.

"It's so pretty. Thank you for your patience as my—friend—hovered around your store. You've arranged it really well. I hope to be back soon." I looked over my shoulder making sure Alex wasn't lurking about, took my bag, and turned toward the door.

"Please do, dearie. We get new shipments twice a month." I had to smile back. She was too sweet. I wish I had had a grandmother like her. *I wish I had a grandmother. Period.*

Exiting, I found Alex relaxing, his back pressed against a brick wall.

"Ugh! I thought I got lucky and got rid of you." Whining was a cheap way of having an adult conversation. Good thing today I didn't feel like adulting anymore and crossed the street.

Alex took my disgust to heart and headed for his truck.

"Be at the corner in thirty minutes or you're walking back to the farm. And, in case you think you're so smart, there aren't any cabs, Ubers, Lyfts, or bicycles to rent." The corner of his mouth turned into a snarl. *Fine by me!*

I didn't realize how much I needed to be alone until he pulled away. When I'm at the farm, I felt claustrophobic. Alex was too close, either in the bedroom next door, sitting next to me in a golf cart or eating at his kitchen table. My dorm room was quite different. Even though there were twenty other girls within seventy-five feet of me, I could close my door and feel solitude. Even if the witches above me were blaring their Sex Song Playlist on Spotify, it was better than Alex crooning the best of Thomas Rhett on our too-long drive into town. I swear he knew his whole discography.

East Stroudsburg wasn't too bad as long as you didn't require high couture. They had a name brand discount grocery store, three fast food restaurants, a dry cleaner, and interestingly enough a Native American History Museum. My mom came from Michigan, The Ojibwe Tribe I later learned in school fell under the Chippewa Nation umbrella. I had thirty minutes to kill and the door was open, so I went in.

I paid the nominal entry fee and thanked the reception person for the docent audio device. The detailed depictions of the new Pennsylvanians meeting with the Lenape Tribe of Delaware, also called Lenape, were a disgusting facade of how the White man, in less than one hundred years, virtually made the Pennsylvanian Lenape extinct. I gasped at the indignity they must have felt. For god's sake, the sign said this tribe had been alive and well since 500 B.C. Strange vibrations traveled up my spine and my ears began to ring. I wasn't scared so much as feeling connected to the past. For a moment my head became dizzy and my stomach cramped. Then they were gone. *So strange.* My mother would talk about dreams she would have. More like visions with a message that were open to interpretation. If having them was a gift, she passed it down to me. Fortune telling wasn't my specialty, but garden creations were. Periodically, when I was engrossed in designing or planting a tingly sensation would hum through my body and my mind would travel to pristine woods or prairies of tall grass. Those visions were so calming and reassuring, I took comfort knowing I was doing what I was made to do.

I continued the tour, finishing within thirty minutes. As directed, I walked back to the designated spot I was told to be at. The serendipity of finding this museum felt more like destiny than accidental. I'm glad I spent the time getting to know the indigenous people of this area. Their artwork was incredible, and I promised myself one day I'd learn to bead the way my ancestors did.

As promised, Alex was idling off Center Street and Dean Street. I pulled open the cab door to his thumb thumping against the steering wheel to the beat of the music.

"You're late," he chastised. *Unbelievable.*

"Then why are you still here? Aren't I supposed to learn my lesson and walk home like a naughty child?" I sassed. His eyes sparked, making his eyebrows quirk.

"I'm not your jailor, Seneca. I looked at the clock and saw you walking from the Pocono Indian Museum and decided you were expanding your education and therefore needed leniency." His highbrow judgment wasn't lost on me.

"Is that so?" I hitched my lip up like he did.

He cocked his head to the side, not giving up. "Yes. It is. Are we done here?"

Still needing to needle him one more time, I cattily shouted, "Yes, Warden, Sir!" and saluted him.

Laughter peeled from both of us and Alex put the truck in gear. "I got enough bottled water for a month. I'm looking into some kind of filter to keep our feeding water clean until we get an answer on its quality. I'll probably have to sell a kidney for it. Though I might need it if I get cancer like my parents did."

My jaw dropped. His comment was no laughing matter. I hadn't considered Alex already ingesting poisonous water for months. Curious, I probed deeper.

I pulled my seatbelt forward so I could turn in my seat. "Can I ask you something personal?" I inquired softly.

His jaw stiffened, "Maybe. What about?"

We'd reached the last stop sign in town, and his eyes closed dramatically.

"You can breathe, Alex. You can take a pass at answering if you want. I only wanted to know more about your parents and how they got sick"

The truck didn't move and his thumb began to strike the steering wheel again. A nervous habit I'd begun to notice. I looked behind me through the side view mirror and saw another vehicle approaching, yet still we weren't moving.

"Hey, Alex. We have to move. Listen. Forget I asked. It's not important. Let's go." *I think I broke him.* The car behind us beeped and he floored the gas. Leaning forward, he switched stations, rock and roll now, keeping his eyes on the road. He didn't talk or look my way. I followed his lead and kept my mouth shut and my hands in my lap. Why did I always have to know everything? My directness was a blessing and a curse. Today it was definitely a curse.

Alex's phone buzzed as we were pulling into his circular driveway. He threw the truck into park before stopping completely, throwing us forward like ragdolls. He looked at me, frightened.

"Sorry. You okay?" The air was thick around us in anticipation. I could hardly breathe.

I reassured him I was fine and pointed to his phone. "You'd better get that."

"Hey, Leo. Thanks for getting back with me. Yeah. Uh-huh. Three days! What do I do? Ask my cows not to drink? Let my crops die on the vine? You can't come sooner? Fine. I'll be waiting. Thanks again." Alex punched the red phone icon and threw the phone onto his dashboard, yelling. "Fuucckk!"

I didn't have to be a genius to figure out what the conversation on the other side of the phone went like. DelVal, as us students called it, didn't offer a class in the horticulture curriculum about managing potential poisonous chemicals or handling the affected farmer. *Humm?* Wait. That's not completely true. We did have a speaker from a waste company that came to discuss garbage dump decontamination. I couldn't be sure, but perhaps some of that information could be applied to our situation.

"I take it you'll have to wait until he can come out?" His disgusted snort said it all. "I was thinking, I could email Dr. Abel and see if he has any resources we can tap into in the meantime. What do you think?"

My experience with men, especially older ones, was that they didn't think a young woman could have enough knowledge or experience to solve complicated problems. Thankfully, those instances were few and far between. Even with Alex's bravado, I didn't think he'd discount any help in these circumstances

His right hand cupped the back of his neck, giving me a front row seat to his gun show. Those powerful shoulders and delts were captivating as he replied. "Thanks, Sen. That would be great. Now if you are done checking me out, we have animals to care for before dinner." *Busted.*

Chapter 9
ALEX

If yesterday was a shitshow then today was Armageddon. Leo arrived, conducted some preliminary soil testing starting from my house to the creek every two-hundred yards, and took a milk sample from Eunice. That turned out to be over fifty samples. *This would cost me a small fortune.*

Leo flipped the tailgate down on his pickup and spread out his test strips. "It's going to take me the better part of an hour to spot check a few of these samples. My results will only tell part of the story but will give us a starting point to work with. If you have other things to do you might want to focus on them instead." His voice was deadpan as he held out a sample cup of soil.

Seneca stepped forward like I knew she would. She wanted to know everything and wouldn't stop bugging you until she got what she wanted. *It's like she has OCD.*

"My mentor said that the pH and nitrogen levels could be the problem. Is that what you're testing for?" *Good question.*

Leo's eyebrows lifted, "That's correct. Satisfactory levels would be between six and seven-point-five for the soil and between six-point-five and eight-point-five for the water, if you're following EPA standards." He seemed excited to talk shop with her. What I needed were the exact levels of my soil and water so I could save my farm.

"I've studied that. How soon will you have the official numbers back?" Seneca queried argumentatively. "We have livestock to protect, not just our plants." She was closing in on the poor man.

Carefully, I shifted, placing a hand on her shoulder holding her in place. In my most soothing tone, I tried to placate my intern. "Seneca. Leo knows what he's doing. He's been working with me for years. He knows the ramifications of these results. Let's give the man some space to do his job."

You could hear her molars grinding inside that pretty mouth of hers. I removed my hand almost as fast as I placed it there, pivoting to one side. "Let's," was all she said and yelled for Benny.

Tiny exited the barn with a playful Benny bolting ahead to meet his new best friend. I tried many times over the years to let Benny follow me around the property, but he always got into trouble. He never met a squirrel he didn't want to eat or a potato he didn't want to dig up. Frankly, I was concerned the Department of Natural Resources was going to fine me for killing the squirrel population in Monroe County. After the sixth murder, I put Tiny in charge of keeping him either in the barn or on an extended leash attached to a zipline from the house to the edge of my crop line. Lucky for us today, he came directly to Seneca, saving me from chastising Tiny in front of her.

"Hey there, big boy. I think it's time for me and you to have some cuddle time." Her coos and baby talk to that big lug was adorable. "Would you mind if I took Benny in the golf cart over that hill?"

She pointed to the first swell on my property. The only thing she'd find was a giant maple tree and grass. An obvious place to sit and think. It's funny that she chose that place because it's my go-to spot when I needed a "think," too.

I nodded. "Would you mind if I joined you? I need the distraction. We don't have to speak, but, if you're going where I think you're going, I could use a time-out." I half expected her to make a fuss, but she only pulled her sunglasses down slightly, eyeing me.

"Sure," she deadpanned.

"Tiny, grab me a leash. You do still remember where it is, don't you?" I chided him. I couldn't resist giving him a hard time about Benny's leash.

A low rumble emanated from his throat as he spun on his heel to jog back to the barn to fetch it. I looked at my watch. Fifty-five minutes of pure torture starting now.

Seneca drove, Benny rode shotgun, and I enjoyed the view sitting backward in the rear of the cart. Minutes later we'd pulled up near my favorite tree. Benny did a downward-facing dog, and Seneca did some sort of windmill thing. Me? I moseyed over to the far side of the giant tree listening to her and my dog getting friendly on the other side.

Beyond my troubles, it was another beautifully warm fall day. The nights and mornings were cooler now—my favorite time of year. Autumn was a three-layer dressing season: the first layer for cool mornings, the second for steamy afternoons, and the third for the chilly nights. It was a constant fluctuation of warm to cold and back again. It had a rhythm to it, beckoning a farmer to plant and sow. A gentle breeze played with the green, yellow, and orange leaves. Another week or two and they will turn to scarlet. That's when I knew there was a god. My appreciation of nature grew tenfold when I went to Afghanistan. The barren tan sand stripped me of humanity. There was nothing to denote season changes helping your mind anticipate change. I was positive that the desolate climate induced my first signs of PTSD. There was no hope in sand, only death. There was nothing to grasp onto. It was miserable. My first day back on the farm, even having to bear my parents' passing, was better than any day I'd served on the other side of the world. I made sure my parents were buried under a tree and beside the creek close to where I'd taken Seneca the day after she arrived. The shade, and beauty of the spot would care for their souls for an eternity.

"I can hear you breathing over there," Seneca chirped, annoyed.

Silently I breathed out. "And I can hear you, too. We had an agreement not to speak to one another. I think you need to be punished." *Now that would be entertaining.*

Her gasp was satisfying. I let her stew on the threat. We'd made several agreements—hers actually—our first evening together on the farm.

1. Stay professional at all times. *She put her hand on my arm first.*

2. Be respectful of each other's privacy. *Okay. I broke that one when I walked into her room unannounced.*

3. Clean up your mess. *So far, so good.*

4. Dress appropriately at all hours of the day and night. *She broke that every goddamned day. Cleavage. Pajama shorts. Sexy hair blowing in the wind. Why does she keep standing there in the breeze?*

I had a clear case, but, unless she advanced on me, I'd have to control myself. Having a good reputation with the local colleges was paramount over my dick finding a new home in her pussy. *Damn! Now I'm thinking about her pussy!*

Time to recant. Still not encroaching on her side of the tree, I attempted to restate myself. "What I meant was that I-I . . . forget it. I'm going for a walk," and stormed away.

SENECA

Benny was a terrific distraction, at least for a while. He was a pushover, literally. I scratched behind his ears for ten seconds, then he rolled to his back effectively demanding I continue his massage. Dogs were so lucky. They got full body rubs every day without the expectation of sex. Long licks across my face were my payback, and I loved them. Once he was satisfied with his care, I pushed myself up against the giant tree trunk, and he laid half his body over my legs pinning me to the ground. My eyes closed easily while thoughts of the meditation garden I would soon create danced in my head. I'd have lots of sculptures of varying sizes representing frogs, fish, and birds. Buddhas to meditating llama sculptures. A full scope of visual representations of relaxation and calm for every taste. It would be eclectic and memorable. I couldn't wait.

Calm settled easily, with Benny as a weighted blanket lulling me into a nap. Until Alex exhaled loudly like a child needing attention. *Can't a girl get some quiet around here?* He had his whole property to chill out on. Why did he have to come with me? And, what's with punishing me? What did I do? I've been a fucking perfect angel since I got here. What's his problem?

I was gearing up to tell him off when he tried to rephrase his statement. Letting him suffer with an apology was worth keeping silent. Although, when he stormed off, I wished I had asked *how* he wanted to punish me. But that would be counterproductive to our agreement. The reality was we both kept toeing over the line of propriety. It wasn't that I was entirely opposed to the idea. It was what the repercussions of going too far might create. I surely didn't want to feel uncomfortable for the next nine months. We were adults, more so him. He was forty and I was only twenty-eight. Not the biggest age gap conceived but enough for a boss and his subordinate to be called questionable.

My watch showed we had fifteen minutes to go and I was getting antsy-pantsy. Gently shoving Benny off me, I watched him roll to his back again. He was so adorable and manipulative, I couldn't say no to more puppy love, though, we needed to go.

"No more lovin' for you, big guy. We need to get back to the house for our results. Now, where did your daddy go?" I looked all around the tree then toward the next swell finding him staring off into the distance.

"Come on, boy. Let's go fetch him." He thumped his tail along the front of the cart as I led him back and tied off his leash. Alex was in a tough spot. He didn't need me agitating him any more than he was feeling now. I resolved to be a better, more respectful employee moving forward. I was here to help him with whatever he needed—mostly.

We pulled up to the house just as Leo was closing his tailgate, a sheet of paper trapped between his teeth.

Alex rushed forward as I trailed behind, respectfully, holding Benny's leash and keeping my mouth shut.

Managing his panic, Alex stared at Leo, and Leo stared back. *What did that mean?*

One minute went by, then two, and neither man spoke. Eyebrows raised and lowered. Knitted brows came together and relaxed. This must be what they call "Man Speak." No sounds at first, then lots of sighing, grunting—from both of them—and muted cries in Alex's throat.

Leo retrieved the paper from his teeth, shoving it into Alex's hands. "I'm sorry, Alex. I'll have the final results and remediation protocols for whatever we find in about ten days. From my preliminary testing, it could be worse. I'd start with a nitrogen-reducing fertilizer immediately. Hopefully, it will make enough of a difference when I test again. Keep your animals close to the barn. The pH levels were higher the closer you got to the creek. I wish I had better news." He hung his head and opened his truck door. "I wouldn't sell any crops until you hear from me." His ignition sputtered and he drove slowly down the dirt driveway leaving us literally in the dust.

I didn't know what to say. How to comfort him. Anything. He turned first, his eyes turning to azure. My eyes bore into his chest watching the small heaves you get right before you cry. My heart broke for him and I couldn't look up. Instead, I stepped closer, sliding my arms around his trim waist, resting my head on his heart, and willed his to keep beating. A small wail tore from his throat as he tightened our hug. Compassion became a life raft destined to save him. I projected whatever positive energy I could into his body, wishing it would take his pain away. A teardrop fell on the top of my head tearing my heart in two, making me cry, too. We held each other as hues of orange and pink streaked across the sky. Anyone looking at us would think we were lovers watching a sunset instead of watching a legacy fade away into the night sky.

Chapter 10
SENECA

It had only been three days since I arrived at Eloheh Farm when tragedy struck. Alex was inconsolable, instructing me to complete my first assignment which was given before I left Delaware Valley University. He became mute and unapproachable staying out in the fields applying nitrogen to counteract the issues with the plants Leo specified. Alex's rationale was, "There's nothing you can do to help." Of course, I could help! I could cut his efforts in half. If he added Tiny to the project—into thirds. Instead, I'm sitting on the couch with Benny curled up on the floor beside me, him licking my foot as it hung off the cushion.

"I know, big guy, but, until your master gets his head out of his ass, I'm stuck here doing homework." He got up and laid his snout on my thigh, forcing me to pet him. "I'll try talking to him tonight at dinner. I'm not making any promises he'll budge, but don't let me stop you from trying to talk some sense into him."

Great. Now I'm talking to a dog. Expecting him to understand, offering commiseration. Is this what Abigail did with her chicken, Amy the Great? I see the allure. I reread my responses to the three essay questions.

    1. Describe your workspace/environment in detail. Include

possible points of interference and/or challenges you could encounter during your internship.

Response: Alex. Alex. Alex.

2. Describe your daily duties and rough timeline when they are required.

Response: Babysit Alex before and after work hours. Be a playmate to Benny, his dog. Indeterminate timeline.

3. What recommendations would you submit after your first week at your internship?

Response: Find a new internship. Get Alex mental health services. Get a dog.

I suppose I should elaborate on my answers. Perhaps even remove the snarky tone. Though unless Alex changed his attitude, I won't have anything to do but babysit Benny. I promised myself I'd let him take the lead and be the boss-man, but I have a good feeling I'm going to have to break that promise and open a can of whoop-ass to make this internship worthwhile.

"Come on, boy. Let's find something to eat. I'm done with homework for today."

I gathered my papers in a pile and left them on the coffee table to forage for food. Benny veered me over to the pantry no doubt for his treats, of which I was happy to oblige. While there, I snagged the peanut butter and jelly, a bag of kettle chips, and three sodas. Since we were in a forced drought, alternative beverages were going to be our standard fare.

Being the kind, sweet woman that I was, I prepared three plates: for me, Alex and Tiny. PB&J all around with a generous helping of chips. *Hmm.* "How about some pickles, Benny?" I spoke absentmindedly. The fridge was well stocked by Annalise and I hoped dill pickles were on the regular shopping list. *Looking. Looking.* Ah! There they are. Thank goodness. The other option, bread and butter pickles. *Gross.* Dill or die. Nothing in between.

Finished with my task, I texted Alex and Tiny lunch was ready. Benny stared at me, insinuating he needed lunch too. "Sorry, buddy. Nothing for you." Looking left and right for any sign of Alex, I slid my finger down the side of the knife cleaning off the remnants of peanut butter and jelly and held it out for my new friend. What's a sandwich without having a friend to share it with? I think I'd spent too much time alone today. First, talking to a dog like he would answer me. Then, rationalized sandwich etiquette. I needed exercise after lunch.

The front screen door slammed followed by several heavy steps clomping just inside the door. Tiny entered the kitchen first, smiling. It was his first since I'd arrived. I guess all I needed to do was feed him to get that response. Alex, on the other hand, still looked like someone had pissed in his beer.

Breaking the silence, I said sweetly, "Making any progress?" Both men looked at me with scowls on their faces. "Dumb question?" I countered, humbly.

No reply. Whatever. We sat in silence, chewing and crunching to a choir of birds outside the open sliding glass door. Twice I tried to speak but thought better of it when Alex clearly heard me, breathing in deeply and snarled. He was being an ass. Tiny tried to save me by shaking his head to keep me quiet. Did he know who he was talking to? Definitely not. Fifteen words between two people in five days wouldn't constitute familiarity. He'd learn, starting now.

"Have you considered changing your attitude for the next ten days so you don't lose your ever-loving shit?" My direct comments hit exactly where I wanted it to land—square between his eyes. If I weren't such a strong woman, I would have taken my plate and locked myself in my room after the curling of his upper lip. A vein I'd never noticed pulsed at his temple, tempting me to push him again.

He jerked his head to look at me straight on. "Do you ever keep your mouth shut?"

My eyes went wide. I bit my tongue all day long with this guy. No more. I lashed out, "No. Not when I see someone who needs an attitude adjustment. You have no control of this situation. I got it. We need a new plan. One that lasts exactly ten days. I have a job to do and you're not helping me figure it out. Be the damn mentor you signed up to be."

Alex stood up abruptly sending his chair skidding across the wood floor. He grabbed his can of soda and walked out onto the deck, whipping the sliding glass door closed after himself. *That didn't go at all like I'd planned.*

Tiny grumbled as he popped the last bite of his sandwich into his mouth. "You two have issues. Figure them out . . . now!" He pointed to the deck, hissing. *Fine!* I collected my plate, putting away the pickles and potato chips as Tiny tracked me with his eyes around the kitchen. *Was he just going to sit there until I went outside to beg Alex's forgiveness?* I stood looking outside for several minutes waiting for Tiny to leave so I could hide in my bedroom. He didn't leave. He did stand, though, crossing his arms over his chest, grinding his teeth. *Geezus, buddy. Give me a break!*

Rolling my eyes, I slid open the doorwall and walked outside, Benny in tow. I said nothing, finding a bench seat to sit on. He wouldn't look at me, nor I him. My manicure, or lack thereof, was more interesting than watching him grind his molars. Even irritated, his straight nose and squared chin were sexy. It wasn't fair to be mad at someone while feeling all tingly inside. I hated myself when I mixed anger with sex. That's probably why the groundskeeper at school was the perfect release for me. No commitment. Only pure lust unleashed. Unfortunately, walking away wasn't an option today—or this year. I had to play the long game, and, so far, I'd been benched.

Think carefully, Seneca.

I rolled my lips together, breathing in slowly. "I'm sorry, Alex. For giving you a hard time and for the circumstances we're in." The statement alone should have been enough. Except I felt a lesson percolating. One that needed addressing immediately. "The only way to get through this holding pattern is to find something to do."

Sage words.

Alex sat up, pursing his lips, leaving me unsure where he stood on what I'd said. He shook his head slowly. "Unbelievable. You never stop. Can't you see that this isn't your problem? There is no *we* in this situation. *I'm* the one who will suffer the consequences of this situation no matter what you do. I don't even know why I need you here anymore. Tell me, Miss Know It All, what do you bring to the table that is essential for you being here any longer? You found the soil problem. You've pointed out I'm a piece of shit with a bad attitude. You even stole my dog's affections. Tell me where to go from here, Seneca."

I palmed both sides of my face, forcing my eyes shut. I needed to be here to graduate, I wanted to say. I wanted to learn—anything. I've known him, kind of, for four years and hated seeing him suffer like this. If he could take one step forward, we could find a solution together. With the exception of Annalise and Tiny helping him all these years, he's had the burden of this farm and dealing with his parents' deaths by himself. He was pushing me away. I understood why but felt let down he wasn't trying harder to work through this crisis with more dignity.

His hands were clasped between his knees as he rested his elbows on his strong thighs. He broke his stare, letting his head fall limply as if he gave up completely. I'm not sure why I got up and walked over to join him on the lounge chair. Maybe because I needed comfort as much as he did. Rules be damned. Our solidarity was more important. I pressed my left hand between his shoulder blades and rubbed it side to side. I did as he asked, keeping my mouth shut, letting my hand speak for me. His shoulders stiffened, then he exhaled slowly, releasing the tension built up these last few days.

For several minutes we sat companionably. I dropped my face to his shoulder, extending my other hand down the length of his arm relishing the sinews of his corded muscles. I didn't intend on making an overture. I did it to comfort him without speaking. So, when he pivoted toward me clasping my face in his hands and devouring my mouth with his tongue, I was shocked. He turned my head to allow him deeper access and all sense of consciousness was lost. My hands grasped his neck holding on for dear life as he ravaged my mouth. I felt his silky, soft hair with my fingers while tasting the saltiness from his lunch. He tasted delicious.

We moaned into each other's mouth, each tongue chasing the other's. I could have stayed like this all day, but Benny had other ideas, putting one paw on each of us unceremoniously dipping into our two-person huddle. I smiled into Alex's mouth, driving my tongue once more before pulling back. His hands didn't leave my face even when Benny whined trying to get our attention.

Intoxicating, whispered words slipped from his bruised lips, "Can we do this for the next ten days?" *Please!*

"Hmm," I moaned. Drunk on his words, I concurred. "That's the best solution you've offered since finding out there was a soil problem."

My stupid words yanked him back to reality. *Fuck!!*

His breathing slowed as he dragged his thumb across my swollen lower lip. I wanted to cry, "Please don't stop," but instead chastised myself, again, for opening my big mouth.

Being the bigger person, Alex suggested reason. "This was an excellent distraction, but we should stop before we do—you know."

He kissed my forehead like I was a child and stood up. "I'll put on a pot of coffee, and let's see if we can find a more productive way to spend our time." He pulled a quick smile and walked back into the house with his buddy, Benny, knocking his tail against his leg.

I could think of lots of productive ways to spend our time, even reproductive ways if given a chance. *With a condom, of course—so not too reproductive.* This was progress. Our silent agreement to move forward was the most important thing we could do today. My training was solid. I knew there was more to be done in the short term to mitigate his crops, but he needed to trust me.

When I picked up my phone to call Abigail for a pep talk, Annalise appeared carrying a bottle of wine and a comforting smile. *Excellent. Afternoon drinking!*

She handed me a glass, taking stock of my disposition. "I'm going to assume that today didn't go so well." She unscrewed the brown bottle and poured out a crisp chardonnay.

"Not even slightly. Your brother likes to sit in his head-cave for a long time, doesn't he?" I said annoyed.

She pulled a large swig from her glass. "Like a bear in winter. I wish I could say it was stubbornness, but I think it comes from his time in the service. Being ever vigilant against enemies is nerve-racking. One wrong decision and lives are lost. I wouldn't doubt he's thinking the same way right now. He won't only lose this season's crops, Seneca. He could lose his livestock, or, worse, human lives. That's a lot of pressure on a man who is devoted to keeping his family's legacy alive."

Of course there was more to this than a minor inconvenience. This could be life changing. "Well, when you put it like that. . ." I stared at the bubbles floating to the top of my wine glass and a light bulb went on.

In an instant, I slammed my glass to the side table and ran into the house. "Alex! My gut is telling me this is not a soil problem. This is a water contamination problem. What I mean is, you didn't do anything wrong. This problem has to be percolating up *through* the soil from a contaminant in the water—your creek!"

I stood looking intently at his frozen features, realizing I'd just made his problems infinitely worse. *Fuck!* This wasn't a small ammonia problem that some nitrogen therapy could fix. This was epic! I grabbed the countertop—feeling lightheaded from the realization. "I'm so sorry, Alex. I could be wrong. I'm praying I'm wrong. But, if I'm not, it would explain why your soil issues took so long to identify."

He didn't move as his chest heaved uncontrollably. My problem blurting things out might be fine for me, but the receiver then has to digest my obsessive need to be correct. Knowing what to do with that information was paralyzing. Thank goodness Annalise came inside. She'd help me contain this situation—wouldn't she?

Each of us stared from one person to the next as if one of us had the winning answer to our problem. Alex fisted and unfisted his hands. Annalise's eyes shifted like she was watching a tennis match across the kitchen. And me? My mouth opened and closed like a fish out of water, gasping for air.

Alex chucked the mug he held in his hand against the wall, shattering it into a multitude of shards. "Why would I entertain an even worse situation, Seneca? Better yet, why can't you keep your fucking opinions to yourself? If ammonia in the soil was the problem, at least we'd have a solution. Not an organic one, but a solution, nonetheless. Can you imagine what a fucking water contamination in my creek could do to me? My animals? My community?" He didn't wait for an answer and began to pace. Annalise broke eye contact with me and bolted outside, returning with her bottle of wine. She handed me my glass, refilling both of ours to the brim.

After downing half her glass, she stepped forward, settling her hand on Alex's shoulder. "Hun. If Seneca is right, it could explain why Mom and Dad got cancer." *Oh, my fucking god! Could this story get any worse?*

From the moment Dr. Abel told me about losing my dream internship, to then having to work on a farm for a year, frustration festered deep within me. Then, finding out Alex was the owner of said farm, to the farm being contaminated, had I entered the Twilight Zone? No one has that kind of bad luck. I thought I was feeling depressed because my college career was winding down and adulting would be hard. There's no way I could have imagined the magnitude of this life and death shit. This was all above my pay grade. Especially since I didn't control any of it. My heart rate soared, making my head woozy. Nothing was happening as planned. My airway felt cut off like in Dr. Abel's office. *Not again!*

I tried to speak. The words on the tip of my tongue . . . then everything went black.

Chapter 11

ALEX

I saw Seneca's eyes roll back and I dove to keep her from hitting her head on the table. Catching her in mid-air like a football, I rolled her to the right, clipping my hip on the table but saving her a worse injury. I'd never pegged Seneca for a fainter. She was always in control. Always calling the shots.

"Sen! Are you okay?" Panic sizzled through my body. She didn't respond, but Annalise did.

"Call 9-1-1!" The chicken dance she was doing wasn't helping at all.

I countered, more calmly than I thought I could, "I'm calling her friend, Abigail, or at least her mentor, Dr. Abel." She was in my care and nothing bad was supposed to happen to her.

All thoughts of me and my problems evaporated as I cradled her in my arms, carrying her over to the living room couch. Her coloring was pale, which scared me. The contrast from her normal hue was drastic, making my heart palpitate. My only saving grace was her breathing slowed and smoothed out. If we weren't in a crisis situation, I would have kissed her pillowy dark pink lips like Snow White, awakening her like Prince Charming. *Yeah, that seemed laughable even to me. Charming—yes. Prince–no.*

"Annalise, hand me my phone." I hardly recognized my motorized voice. My previous life rose to life. I was a captain giving direct orders to my battalion expecting them to perform as trained warriors. Cadre were tasked with staying calm under fire and caring for Seneca as my sole assignment.

Annalise scurried over to the entry hall, then rushed back, holding my phone. "Here you go."

I pulled the couch pillow under Seneca's head, keeping her on my lap. It was the only way I could think of touching her without getting myself into trouble. Elias's number was first on my favorites' list, and I touched the screen to call him. He would know how to break the news to his wife.

Keeping the worst of my concerns at bay, I said, "Hey, Elias. Listen, Seneca passed out. She's okay. Unconscious, but okay. Do you—" he cut me off.

"Wait a minute. Did she pass out? What did you do to her?" I could feel his scrutiny through the receiver.

I chewed the inside of my mouth, struggling to stay calm. "For your information, it wasn't *me* who did something to her. She did it to herself. Will you get Abigail on the line so she can tell me what to do?"

Using the Universal Communications System known to every family in the world, he screamed across the house. I pulled the phone away from my eardrum, sparing my hearing. Elias cleared his voice and announced, "She's on her way. For the record, I still submit you did something that made her brain explode." He chuckled, happy with himself. Wiping that smirk off his face was priority *numero uno* when I saw him next.

"S.T.F.U., asshole," I snarled.

"I will not shut the fuck up. Someone has to hold you accountable for putting a young woman in peril.

"You know who's going to be in per—."

"Give me the phone," Abigail screeched. The Kraken had been released, which was why I always left the room when she was ripping into her husband. "Is she okay? Did she hurt herself when she passed out?" The sincerity of her concern was sweet. She and Seneca had been friends since middle school and they knew everything about one another, which was why I called her first.

"Hi, Abigail. She's resting peacefully. Have you known her to have these spells in the past? Do I need to get her to the hospital?" My questions were rapid fire. I didn't want to waste any time if she was in danger.

"No. She's not in danger, just tripping out. It's like the circuit breaker in her head switches off when it's too overloaded. It will reset when she wakes up. Have a glass of water at the ready, and maybe something sweet to get her blood sugar up. How long has she been out?" Abigail's unaffected words gave me hope Seneca would bounce back quickly. I rubbed my brow easing the headache lurking behind my eyes.

I looked at Annalise to confirm our timing. "About three or four minutes, I guess. Is that too long?" Seneca better wake up soon. I need confirmation she would be the same person when she awakened. My nerves were shot.

"Wait. She's waking up," Annalise squawked. I looked down to see her for myself.

A deep sigh from Abigail echoed through the phone. "Thank goodness. I'll call to check on her later. Make sure she drinks that water before doing anything else. And Alex—thanks for calling and taking care of her. I can't have anything happen to my best friend in the whole world." Abigail's voice caught in her throat, triggering my own response.

"Me, too," I croaked.

She disconnected the call, allowing me to give Seneca my full attention. Annalise was running back with the glass of water and a big box of cookies. I brushed the patient's face with my thumb with care, "Hey, pretty girl. Are you doing okay? You passed out."

I waited while she pushed her tongue around her mouth finding purchase with her words. "Drink this, Sen." I brought the glass to her lips as she lapped up the liquid like a kitten. It was hard to imagine this sweet little thing was also the big-mouthed drill sergeant from earlier. The juxtaposition of her two personalities was confusing and unsettling. I never knew who I was talking to.

Dark brown eyes stared into mine, searching for what, I didn't know. I could only stare back. It was like I could see into her past and her future all at the same time. I knew so little about her except what Elias had told me. The one unforgettable drunken night we shared left an indelible mark on my soul I still couldn't decide if it was holy or hell. She felt things in the air that average people couldn't even clock. Her Native American roots were prevalent in everything she did outside of four walls. That was how she knew to scoop up the earth and feel it on her fingers, smelling it like it breathed. I should have listened to her instincts. It shouldn't have mattered that she had only a few years of book learning. She was wired to the earth with more information than I could provide. *Who was the mentor now?*

Her hand lifted and fingered through my long hair. She pushed a lock behind my ear and I fell a little further. Such a complex creature. Would I ever really get to know all of her?

"What happened, Alex?" She didn't try to sit up. I didn't encourage it either.

My calloused hand rubbed her upper arm, enjoying her softness while I could. At any moment Seneca could revert to a Tasmanian devil ruining this perfect moment. "Abigail says you short-circuited yourself and fainted. It makes sense since everything around here is out of control." I closed my eyes recalling how I'd been losing my shit for the past twenty-four hours. "I need to be a better example and mentor to you. I'm sorry, Seneca, for adding to your worry."

My sister stepped forward. "If you don't need anything else, I'm going to head home. It looks like the two of you will get on without me."

She kissed my forehead and did the same to Seneca like she belonged to our family, then walked out the front door. *Wouldn't that be something?* I chuckled, imagining how that would look.

Seneca wrapped her hands around my neck gently, "I'm sorry, too. I have a bad habit of saying what's on my mind without thinking about how it will be received." She was quiet, looking at my lips. Tempting me to pull hers into my mouth. Her lips were perfectly bowed, plump, and delectable. Having tasted her earlier made it impossible not to sip from her mouth again.

I leaned forward pressing my forehead to hers, tenderly. "You scared the shit out of me. Please don't do that again." She nodded slowly. The endorphins that coursed through my veins were pooling in my gut and they were telling me to seize the day. *And I did.*

I tipped her chin up with two fingers and slowly leaned within a breath of her mouth. "I need this, Sen. I need you." She closed the gap, pressing our lips together in the most erotic kiss I'd ever had. Her tongue skated over my lower lip pulling it every-so-slightly when she came back to center. I moaned into her mouth when she pulled even harder.

"I need you, too," she cooed. Never had a woman given me permission to devour her mouth like Seneca did. The push and pull of our tongues, sharing control, was a well-synchronized dance. Darting in and out, then stilling when a deft hand found a breast or nipple. Mine and hers. Her touch scalded my skin to the point that I told her to stop flicking my nip, or I'd flip her over and spank her. Her wide-eyed gasp told me everything I needed to know.

With little effort, I shifted her legs to straddle mine so she could feel how much I wanted her. Seneca moaned as she began grinding on me like her life depended on it. My hands dove into her long, silky strands, pulling lightly at first and then harder, increasing her moans. I could see her breast pebble into tight buds begging me to suck them. I slide my hands under her tank top stopping when I found her nipples. Rolling them between my fingers and fabric, her back arched, as she rode me to her climax.

"Alex," she squeaked, when I caught her pebbled bud through the delicate fabric with my teeth.

"You like that, baby?"

"Yes! More, please." *God, I loved it when she begged.*

Ensuring her other bud was given all the attention it deserved, I unclasped her bra salivating at how her breasts spilled out. Full, and pert, and milky like a latte. I shifted my mouth, enveloping as much of her breast as I could fit in my mouth. Touching and tasting her didn't seem to be enough to sate my desire for her. I wanted more, too.

Her hands cradled my head, pushing my head down toward her heat. I liked how she was thinking and shifted her down to the couch cushions. Seneca was no wall flower. She knew exactly what she wanted, pushing my ego to new heights. We needed a bed—now.

I shimmied my ass to the end of the couch, pulling her back up, cupping her ass-cheeks tightly and stood.

"Tell me to stop now, or I can't be responsible for what happens next," I said breathlessly.

Our eyes met and locked. Hers hooded, but wary. Mine laser focused. The moment of complete surrender came to a screeching halt. It was as if an imaginary wall dropped between us, shielding our desire against destruction. Even in her semiconscious state her ability to separate lust from reality was impressive. She kissed me sweetly, tucking my hair behind my ears, sagging against my shoulder.

"You, we . . . we're working together. I was confused after fainting. We need to stop."

She unwrapped her legs from my torso and slid my off body until she stood wavering like a willow branch. I didn't let her go, whether from needing her hands on me or to help her stay upright. Why did she always have to be the adult in the room? Of course, she was right. An intimate relationship would most definitely affect our work together. I might be an insensitive pig sometimes, but I wasn't an abuser. This internship would end one day, and, if our relationship was meant to be, then I'll fucking *carpe diem* on her that very moment.

I kissed between her eyebrows, smelling her sweet lavender shampoo, wishing I could fall asleep with her hair fanned out over my chest. *One day.* Concern seeped into my horny brain, I was supposed to make sure she drank lots of water and ate something immediately. Thinking with my dick wasn't helping her get better. Though I'm positive she *felt* better.

Gently, I spun her around and sat her sexy ass back onto the couch. Shoving her glass back into her hands, I said, "Drink. Then eat as many of these as you can." I placed the chocolate chip cookie box in her hands not waiting for an answer. Having Seneca in my arms again ignited feelings in me I thought were gone for good. My thoughts sounded stupid. Even when I was in the Army, I'd never longed for anyone. Not for my mom, or dad, or my brother. And recently, not even Meghan. Sure, I wanted the feeling of home when I was away, but not desperately. Somehow this girl got under my skin and I knew exactly when it happened—the grease from the pizza she was eating across the kitchen island at Abigail's over four years ago. So sexy. So expressive. The way her tongue flicked the cheese into her mouth not able to capture the trickle of grease gliding down her chin. Yeah. That's when it happened. My sick imagination of her tongue lapping the end of my dick like she did with her food fucked with my mind. That was also the moment my mouth moved before my mind engaged and said, "Bite off more than you could chew? I've got something else you can choke on if you're interested."

If a man wanted to be shunned for the rest of his natural life, no finer words could be spoken. I was—
am—a fucking idiot. My self-awareness of who I am now versus who I was then was distorted. It took Seneca ten seconds to figure me out and ten seconds more to stuff those feelings down to enjoy an alcohol-induced fuck-a-thon two weeks later. Passion was a cruel master. Today, though, I would reel the bastard in and silence my dick.

Seneca finished her snack then slid backward into the couch cushions, draping her elbow over her eyes.

"You look tired. Are you feeling better?" She whined her displeasure and rolled to her side looking at me like a sad puppy. Ironically, Benny took that moment to sit up and lick her face. *Lucky dog.* She grimaced and scratched him behind the ears telling him he was the best doggie ever. Satisfied, he looked at me, then pushed himself closer, daring me to intervene. *Bastard.*

"I'm a little nauseous," she croaked. "I don't know why this keeps happening. I need to sleep. Help me to bed?" Her sad, plaintive eyes begged for my help. I may not have been a prince years ago, but I'd be damned if I didn't help this damsel in distress. Nudging Benny away, I stood and bent to lift her behind her knees and back, kissing her forehead like the sweet girl she really was.

"I've got you, baby." Having her in my arms, even if it's to be her nursemaid, was heavenly. "Let's get you into bed. You'll feel better when you wake up." My term of endearment hovered over my head, reminding me that she wasn't my baby or anything else. She was an intern and I was her boss. I'd be smart to remember that from now on.

Chapter 12

SENECA

The sun peeked through the blackout shades, defeating their purpose. It was a relief though to know what time of day it was. It felt like I'd been asleep forever. My dreams were effusive, flitting from colorful, rich gardens to steamy breath along my neck that aroused every cell in my body. Disturbing feelings of helplessness buzzed in and out of my dreams leaving me agitated when I awoke. How strange. Was it possible to have so many contrary feelings in a matter of moments? It must be, since my head felt one thing and my body felt something entirely different.

I pulled myself out of bed, focusing on reaching the door without falling over. My stomach gurgled obnoxiously, forcing me directly to the kitchen before using the bathroom. Last night was a blur. If I'm being honest, I am embarrassed more than concerned. I'd never had this problem in the past, so it was disconcerting. Making an appointment with a doctor sounded prudent, if I had one.

A large glass of orange juice and a granola bar were on the table, waiting for me to appear. My gratitude for Alex rose immensely with the knowledge he had thought of me and my health beyond my fainting spell. Trusting my stomach and head would clear after eating, I plopped into my seat gobbling up my breakfast.

I needed a shower and a plan. I searched for a pad of paper in the junk drawer next to the sink. Collecting a pen as I pushed around a myriad of odds and ends, I found what I needed and plopped down at the table to create a detailed outline:

- Research: Surrounding businesses, water remediation protocols, resources from Dr. A

- Salvaging crops: organic and nonorganic options (nitrogen therapy, alkalines, etc.)

- Safe water source for the animals and us – filtration and treatments

- Long-term options: Eloheh for Alex and me, to complete my college requirements for graduation

I didn't realize starting college at twenty-four and finishing at twenty-eight would be such a blessing. Trying to figure out this puzzle—when I couldn't figure out who the hell I was as a woman—would have sent me to a mental hospital. I just wasn't equipped then. But I am now.

"Hey! You're up." Alex announced emphatically.

I jumped up, knocking my chair over, startled. "Geezus, Alex. Not fair sneaking up on me that way." I brushed my hair out of my eyes, deciding what to do first: pick up the chair or collapse from the adrenaline rush. Alex smiled his devious grin; he got off on keeping me on my toes. He made the decision for me, righting the chair while I braced both hands on the table, getting my bearings straight.

"Sorry. Here, let me help you." He stood next to me, guiding my tush to my chair. Once tucked under the table, he patted my shoulder like I was Benny. Where was the warmth of last night? Did I dream he kissed me? There was no mistaking his strong, tanned hands running up and down my arms; his caress was a piece missing in this puzzle. It was time to find out what it was.

Alex took a step to the other side of my seat, noticing my list. "What's this?"

I swung around in my seat, annoyed he sat there with a smug look on his handsome face knowing what he did to me. In any other scenario, I'd have loved his mouth on my tits. But when I was asleep without my consent? *Uh-uh*.

Pursing my lips and crossing my arms, I attacked.

"Since I was out of it last night, tell me again what happened when you brought me to my bedroom?" I stared him down, not giving him a chance to avoid the question.

"Let's see," he hummed deviously. You yanked off your shirt and bra showing me your fantastic rack. Then, I reached across your pillow to grab your pajamas, sliding your tank top over your luscious body." He leaned forward over the table adjusting his chair so that our mouths were inches apart. He continued, his warm breath on my face.

"I may or may not have grazed your creamy breasts in the process. A hazard of the task," he winked seductively drawing me closer to his red, pillowy lips. "Finally, I had you put your hands on my shoulders to steady yourself as I held open your pajama bottoms while you stepped into them, pulling them slowly up your toned, tanned legs. That's all!"

Alex leaned back in his chair watching me gasp at his smug retreat. *Damn it! So close.*

Exasperated, I smacked his knee. "Then what? Because, if you hadn't noticed, I have these small bruises on my chest." I wasn't stupid. Alex always checked out my tits. I could be wearing a burqa, and he'd find a way to ogle my breasts.

He leaned forward to get a better look. "Oh, yeah, those. Clean out that panicked mind of yours. I didn't maul you in your sleep. When you were falling, I caught you under your arm and my hands held on for dear life. I was saving you, woman. Not copping a feel. Give me some credit, would you?"

I uncrossed my arms, falling back into my own seat. I suppose his explanation was plausible. Alex was a slippery fish, and I knew he wouldn't waste an opportunity to touch me. Though the way his forehead ruffled and his mouth pouted, I gave him the benefit of the doubt."

Attaching his hands to his hips, he inquired about my list again. "Are we good?"

My eyes rolled back in my head, "For now."

I watched as his eyes scrunched slightly as he reviewed the list in front of me. The small jut of his chin followed by a sigh had me perplexed. They were all tells he was what? Frustrated? Annoyed? Or worse, angry?

I sat unmoving waiting for him to speak. He had thoughts. I could see the wheels in his mind moving as his eyes scanned the page carefully, "You know exactly what you're doing, don't you?" I nodded.

"I don't have any answers, Alex. Only a path to find them. These were just a few thoughts on my mind. We can do this any way you want. It's your farm, and your future. You make the call." I prayed he accepted my surrender. I reluctantly figured out my place in this puzzle. All decisions would be his and his alone. Being an intern was the same as being any other kind of employee. Until given responsibility, stay in my lane. Sometimes, I was a day late and a dollar short, but I always got the lesson at some point.

Shock overtook me when he closed the gap between us, falling to his knees and holding the paper between us. "I'm so sorry I didn't trust you, Seneca. You have a good head on your shoulders, and I shouldn't have lauded my position over you. You are a valuable part of my farm—my team. It won't happen again. There won't be any more inappropriate advances. Clear responsibilities and expectations will be outlined to remove any questionable actions. Okay?"

A slow smile crept up my cheeks. "So, no more finger bruises on my breasts?" I taunted him, wanting to know how serious he was.

His deceptive grin gave me hope for more than he'd offered. "Sadly, not. Promise." He crossed his heart like a Boy Scout. "Even if you beg me. Or at least until your internship is over." He licked his lips, a jolt of electricity coursing down my spine. *I'd never get tired of those sexy lips glossed over by his tongue.*

He'd drawn a line in the sand. For better or worse, I'd follow his edict to the letter. We had work to do. A farm to save and a legacy to salvage. Alex stood up, offering his hands to pull me from my seat.

"Get cleaned up. I'll meet you back here in fifteen minutes. Bring your computer and a bigger pad of paper."

Alex and I explored the internet from A to Z for every option available to remediate his situation. The bottom line, we needed those test results, stat. Our short list included keeping the animals and ourselves safe. The crops would live or die. On the downside, we couldn't sell them or eat them. They'd be bagged and analyzed later. On the upside, surrounding weather reports assured rain would be coming in the next two days giving us time to set up rain cisterns to capture safe drinking water for the animals. We would continue drinking bottled water and boiling ground water in the meantime for cooking. By two o'clock, we sagged back in our seats, exhausted and hungry.

"I'm starving," I cried. "I'm making tuna sandwiches. Is that cool with you?" Remembering my oath to let him make the decisions.

He nodded. "Let me check on Tiny in the barn. Make two for him, please. I'll be back in twenty minutes.

I went through the paces of making lunch when my phone rang. "Hello, Dr. Abel. Thanks for calling me back so quickly."

His usual jovial voice was somber. "I'm so sorry for sending you to Eloheh Farms, Seneca. If I'd known you were in danger, I'd have dug deeper for another opportunity."

My heart broke for him. He'd only wanted the best for me. His contrition was very much appreciated. "Oh, Dr. Abel. It's not as bad as that. I'm fine. We're drinking bottled water and boiling the rest just like I'd been taught at school. I'm following all the preliminary protocols prescribed in our Health and Safety classes. Alex, Mr. Valize, has learned to rely on me for my resources, which makes me very grateful." *Wow! Seems I had already learned something as an intern.*

He sighed deeply. "While I'm happy you're making progress. I'd like you to consider taking one of those out of state internship options. I'll get you a grant or scholarship to cover your expenses. I can make the call and have you up and running again by the end of the week." His pleading made me anxious. I didn't feel threatened staying on the farm. We'd made some adjustments and everything would be fine. *Right?*

"Dr. Abel. It's not necessary to go through all that. I'm fine. We'll have answers to both the soil and water situations by the end of the week—hopefully. I'm sure we'll find a reasonable solution and everything will work out." *Was I selling him or me on if I should stay?*

I wanted to stay. Not because I liked Alex. I mean, I did. *Though he was off limits.* I wanted to stay to make a difference. For his farm, his family, his community. This internship would pay off if I could make even a small impact on this problem. I owed it to myself and my boss not to bail on him when times were tough. I was stronger than that. It was in my blood to work hard and treasure the land I loved. I wouldn't betray it that way.

For once, I carefully chose my next words, hoping I wasn't screwing myself in the end. "Dr. Abel. If it's all the same to you, I'd like to stay. I made a commitment and I intend to see it through. Mr. Valize has shown himself to be responsible, and protective of my health and well-being. Let's give it to the end of the semester, okay?"

The phone was silent for a long time. *Was he still there?* He cleared his throat and sniffled. "You are one special lady. If I didn't know you as well as I do, I'd pull this internship from under your feet without hearing another word. My gut trusts your decision to stay and try to make a difference. However, my experience also tells me this is a long-term problem that could take years to resolve satisfactorily. I will honor your request to stay but only until those test results come back. I will not endanger your life one day more. That's my final word on the matter. I will send Mr. Valize my decision when we get off the phone. Be safe and have a good day, Seneca. We'll talk again soon."

My lungs burned with the thought of another setback. My legs became wobbly. I needed to sit down. I swear, if I pass out again, I'm going to cry. I might cry anyway. *Shit! Shit! Shit!* I dropped my head into my hands forcing myself to think logically.

"Stay in the moment. Don't think about tomorrow or the next day. Be present, Seneca. Take control of what you can and let the rest go." My positive self-talk eventually did the trick, allowing my head to clear. Alex didn't need an insecure student to babysit. "I've got this," I internalized with gusto.

I felt him before I saw him. He had a unique vibration that purred within him. Not a buzz. More like a lion that hummed, if that's possible. It was warm. Comforting, yet put me on alert.

"What's wrong? Are you feeling lightheaded again?" He rushed to my side settling his hand on my back. *I must I remind him that his touch is verboten?*

My head was too heavy to lift from my chest, let alone remind him of our agreement. "I might need to leave the farm if the test results are bad. Dr. Abel will send you an email this afternoon. He's protecting me." Each word was another dagger to my heart. How could I be so unlucky?

Labored air blew through Alex's lips making them bubble. "I can't say I didn't see this coming. I almost sent you away this morning. The stress has obviously unhinged you to the point of passing out. I can't—my farm can't—be the reason for your bad health."

My head whipped up. The daggers—once sunk into my heart—went to my eyes. "I don't have bad health—I'm OCD! I obsess when I feel out of control. Frankly, I've never been this out of control before. The circumstances are out of control. I just need a nap to reset. If taking an occasional rest is what it takes to get the job done then that's what I'll do!" If ranting got him to let me stay, I'd rant daily.

"See! This is what I mean. You're not choosing to take a nap, Seneca. Your body is revolting against you. And, like usual, you're not listening. You cannot control this situation. It's not possible. Every fucking thing on this farm is out of control. Unfortunately, you're the only one whose body can't tolerate it!"

Alex shouted as he stomped back and forth around the kitchen, working hard to make his point. He grabbed the pad of paper we'd collected our data on, shaking it aggressively. "Figuring out what the hell to do next has to be our only focus!" His eyes locked onto the page, rolling his eyes at what looked like a light bulb going on. He shifted his eyes to mine, then back again to the page. He flipped through to the next page, returning his fiery eyes back at me; all the while, Tiny slipped into the room, making his presence known, reminding me it was time for lunch.

"Seneca," Alex continued, "the answer is right here. It's what you had said. The cause of our problems isn't on the farm, it's outside the farm! Look," his pained voice switched from despondency to possibility. "On the map," he pointed. "Three companies could potentially be leaching into the water system. Knowingly or unknowingly isn't the issue right now. The question is are we affected, and if any of their hazardous waste is being dumped into the creek? I don't know a thing about FDA-approved levels of whatever bullshit is in our water. However, I do know that they have very specific soil specifications for me to advertise organic products, and hazardous waste isn't listed anywhere."

He dropped into the seat across from me, slapping the pad on the table like he'd saved the world from a nefarious being. *He may be doing exactly that!* All three of us were silent as we marinated in what heinous acts those companies could have created. Tiny pulled up a seat, speaking quietly.

"I wish I was able to express myself well in words, but I can't." Instead, he opened up his arms, palms up, inviting us to hold hands in solidarity. For such a big man, who proclaimed he couldn't speak his truth, his gesture spoke volumes. We were in this together for the long haul.

Chapter 13

ALEX

The next forty-eight hours were a race to erect as many vessels as possible to capture today's anticipated rain. Tiny and I visited our friends at a grainery for giant plastic containers, hauling them home and positioning them next to the barn for easy access. The animals were our main concern now, and devising a water distribution system was crucial.

Seneca tended to the ten cows and dozen chickens. They needed milking and collecting regardless of whether we kept their milk or eggs. Tiny set aside a milk vessel for testing. We would pump and dump as long as necessary until we knew what we were dealing with. Annalise kept the house efficiently running, as usual, and at night we researched each of the three possible contamination perpetrators.

We pulled as many federally-mandated reports as possible off the web, including annual stock reports for the biggest possible offender. The smaller ones required us to visit county offices, and we weren't doing that until Leo visited on Monday with his results. Two more days and everything I've come to love will either live on or die a painful death.

It felt really good to do something positive around the farm today. I desperately needed the distraction. Moving forward, it made sense to have a redundant system for emergency purposes. I'm embarrassed that I didn't think of it long ago. Seneca had shed a light on so many things in the short time she'd been here, making me feel like an idiot. Here I was, sitting on my small farm in mid-America thinking I was the top dog in my field, only to learn the big world was shitting down my throat without me knowing it. I should have been more aware of potential hazards. I should have created redundancies for hard times. I should have kept myself on a continuing education path to learn new and innovative ways to work more efficiently, not harder. I can't believe it took a crisis to wake my sorry ass up.

Tiny strode out of the barn, waving me off early today with the excuse he had a dental appointment. *Ha!* I think he found himself a woman and was going on a date. Thinking about that giant man with a tiny woman—
or any woman—seemed comical to me, or dangerous. I suppose there is someone for everyone. Who was I to judge?

Entering the barn near sunset was a sight to behold. Stacked hay looked on fire when the sun caught it right. Bright beams of sunlight pierced through the old slats in the attic, reminding me my parents were looking down on me, encouraging me to keep their legacy alive. Thoughts of my parents faded when I saw Seneca patting Eunice on her nose as she chewed her cud. They looked at each other like they understood completely each other's feelings. I couldn't help overhearing the sweet things Seneca had to say.

"You're going to be okay. Alex's got your back and I have your—nose? Milk? You know what I mean. Whatever happens, we love you and will do everything to keep you a happy cow." She laid her head on Eunice's snout and turned, catching me out of the corner of her eye.

"Whoa. When did you come in?" Her eyes shifted from left to right figuring out what direction I may have come from.

I chuckled, "About the time you pledged your undying love to a fifteen-hundred-pound side of beef." I thought my comeback was funny. Unfortunately, Seneca's hands jammed onto her tiny waist popping her hip to the side.

She glared at me, "Laugh all you want. Side of beef, my ass. Animals respond positively, like plants, to affirmations. When was the last time you opened your heart to your girls?" she said emphatically, waving her arm in Eunice's direction. *Two weeks ago. The night you arrived.*

That was the end of me. I burst into laughter. Not because what she said wasn't true, but because I could picture her as a five-year-old girl with pigtails frustrated getting her point across. *Adorable.*

Ignoring her attitude, I stepped next to Eunice's stall and patted her neck. "To answer your question. Recently. Though I wanted to talk to you, not Eunice." Her face softened, her hands slipping into her front pockets. "I can't thank you enough for pushing me along this week. I was in a bad place a few days ago, and, while I can't say I'm farther along, at least I have a partner to share the burden with." My declaration sounded appreciative in my head. But hearing it out loud, I realized it sounded like we were an item.

She smirked, shifting her weight to the other foot. "Happy to be of service. Ready to call it a day?"

I nodded, turning off the overhead lights, closing up the entrance doors, double checking they were secured, and met at the big sliding door where she waved to her befriended cows, wishing them sweet dreams. *Silly woman.* We walked to the house in silence scuffing our feet at the bottom of the back stairs off the kitchen getting the muck off our boots. I was starving but didn't feel like cooking. I wanted to find more middle ground with Seneca. We worked well today. My heart felt calmer when I was with her. If only my dick felt the same way.

Motioning her to walk up the stairs ahead of me gave me a gorgeous view of her curvy ass. I've got to give it to Seneca, I haven't seen a pair of shorts, jeans, yoga pants, or pajama bottoms that didn't provocatively outline her small waist, full ass, and toned thighs. She was all woman. If I kept thinking like this, I would have her on her back fucking the life out of her and in jail the very next day. *Be a professional, man!*

As she walked into the kitchen she spun around with big, bright eyes declaring, "I would love some barbeque chicken. I saw that smokehouse restaurant in town. The smells coming from it made my mouth water. Would you like to join me?"

Well, damn.

I stalled, pondering my options for a nanosecond, "I was thinking the same thing. Let's get washed up and head out." My enthusiasm made her smile demurely, with a two-thumbs-up.

SENECA

After pocketing the remaining hand wipes the waitress dropped on the table after our meal, Alex went to the men's room and gave me a few minutes to take in the place. Up until now, he had encompassed my view. Worn wood rafters crisscrossed the ceiling with old, tarnished chandeliers fitted with tiny bulbs. Whoever designed the place in 1964, when it was established, wasn't thinking about aesthetics. Dark, heavy wood banquettes lined the side walls, resembling horse stalls without doors. Each center table was adorned with a fake sunflower in a tiny colored vase and four mismatched chairs from various decades. It's such a classic place. A diamond in the rough, if you will. But the food! Oh my god. It was glorious. I had my heart set on barbecued chicken, but the menu had other suggestions—and I'm glad I listened. The sweet, succulent brisket that fell off the bone came with three dipping sauces, one tastier than the next. Thick steak cut fries, and creamy coleslaw made this meal tops in my book.

"Still licking your fingers, I see." Alex snarked, staring at my fingers in my mouth. I slid my thumb in and took a slow suck from bottom to top just to remind him of days gone by. "You can stop that now. Behave yourself." He waved over the waitress, signaling for the bill.

"Wait!" I wailed. "I want a piece of the apple pie to go. And we need to stop at the grocery store for some vanilla bean ice cream—apple pie a-la-mode. Better get two slices. One for each of us. Oh, hell. Get the whole damn pie. We can snack on it all week. Comfort food is the only real cure to what ails us. And we are sick. Right?"

He scratched the back of his head, "I suppose we are." He caught up with the server and added it to our bill. We headed to my car, swinging the carryout bag between us. The grocery store was nearly empty when we got there, allowing us to get in and out quickly. Food planning wasn't my forte, but Alex knew what staples we needed, and grabbed those few items as well.

We had twenty minutes to pass the time, the silence uncomfortable. I needed a distraction, so I dived into his past.

"So, tell me, are there other Valize children besides Annalise?" I glanced at his face, hoping this was a safe topic, realizing I knew so little about him. He smiled proudly.

He looked straight ahead confidently. "Yes. There is. I have a younger brother, Dane. He's away at the University of Pennsylvania studying software development. He followed in my footsteps and did a six-year stint in the Army to help pay for his college tuition."

Interesting. "Wow! I thought I knew the answer to that question."

"So why did you ask it?" he said, annoyed.

"Well—I just thought—you'd never mentioned him. What's he like? Does he ever come home?" I sounded like a parent asking twenty questions.

"Slow down, Sen," I caught the wink he gave me illuminated from on coming headlights. "He's thirteen years younger than me. Dane was an oopsie baby long after my parents thought they were through having kids. My dad's vasectomy wasn't as successful as he thought it was." He hummed, thinking about it. He went on.

"He's the reason I left the Army. The farm was secondary. He needed a guardian. Annalise was still in college, and we hadn't any family in the tri-state area. Moving him to Georgia near me, wasn't an option, so I took a hardship retirement and came home. It would have been a hardship if he wasn't such a sweet kid. He's actually super smart and has a promising future. I couldn't deny him that, especially since our parents died abruptly in a car crash."

"I'm so sorry to hear that. How tragic. Do you see him often?" *What else could I say?*

He hummed some more. "Not as often as I'd like. I drive over for parents' weekend in the fall, in two weeks, and then again in the spring. He takes extra classes in the summer but helps me for six weeks or so. He's looking for an internship this summer, though I'm unsure where he'll do it. We'll see."

I pulled into the driveway, killed the engine, and unbuckled my seatbelt. He did the same. Both of us hesitated leaving the cocoon of the car. "You're very supportive of him. You're a good brother. I don't have any siblings, but I imagine it's hard to stay close with the distance and all. Abigail is the closest thing I have to a sister without being blood."

The moon shone brightly, allowing me to see his face clearly. "Why are you looking at me that way?" I said softly.

He fidgeted his fingers, head hung heavy over his broad chest. "I wish you had a sibling. You're a very caring person. It's hard not being able to share that love with someone who wants it and needs it."

I bit my lip, impressed by the depth of his statement. "That's kind of you to say. I guess that's why gardening is my passion. I get to care for things that truly need it—thrive on it." I giggled. "I'm so weird."

Alex shifted uncomfortably. His mouth twitched, presumably finding a nonthreatening response. "Not so weird, Seneca. You're different, sure, but more unique than weird. It suits you."

My jaw dropped, and my heart palpitated. "That has to be the nicest thing anyone has ever said to me." Tears welled in my eyes and I tried to hold them back. This was the first time a man had looked beneath my exterior and found me special. I was floored and speechless.

I grabbed my purse and bolted out of the car, slamming the door behind me. He followed closely, catching my elbow before I ran up the stairs and into the house. The tears I tried to hold back now flowed freely. I felt like a blubbering fool.

"Hey," he said compassionately. "What's wrong? What did I say? I didn't mean to make you cry."

I sniffled, rubbing away my tears. "You didn't do anything wrong. It's just . . . just that even my own father hasn't said anything like that since my mother died. It seemed like, when she left, so did my father. Physically, he was present, lying around in his La-Z-Boy and sipping a beer. But, in actuality, his fatherly instincts evaporated. You just hit a nerve. I'm all right. I'm going to go to bed. Please put that ice cream away, would you?"

He released my arm, nodding slowly, watching me enter the house. How could a grown-ass woman be so strong one minute and fragile the next? Is this why men called us the "fairer sex?" Because we had a deep, overpowering emotional center, and they didn't? After watching Alex traverse all his emotions about his farm and brother, I didn't believe it. His emotional quotient was equal to mine, only he hadn't tapped into it completely. How manly would he feel if he did? *Humpft. A big baby, for sure.* This big baby needed to brush her teeth, braid her hair, and pick up the romance novel Abigail gave me for my birthday several months ago.

While snuggled into my bed, I heard the door open, and Benny barged in. I loved this big guy. He knew exactly when I needed some love, and I spooned him into me while holding out my book on my side. I'm unsure when it happened, but I heard my book hitting the floor and then sensed a tall figure standing in my doorway.

"Come on, Benny. Let's go," he whispered.

Benny lifted his head and then laid it down again, determined not to leave.

I groaned. "He's mine tonight. Get your own dog," I muttered.

Alex walked in, pulled my covers up around Benny and me, and walked out the door, mumbling. "I thought I had."

Morning came quickly. I awoke refreshed and ready to take on the day. But where was Benny? My door was open again and I could hear the clicking of his nails on the hardwood.

"Come on, boy. Let's get you fed. Your new friend is having a leisurely day."

I didn't appreciate his sarcasm. "I heard that!" I said, grabbing a change of clothes and heading for the bathroom. Today was going to be a great day. I'm sure I slept well because we did a bunch of physical labor followed by a great meal. I couldn't wait to conquer our next obstacle.

I walked into the kitchen as Alex stared at his phone, frozen.

"What's wrong?" I pleaded, rushing to his side. He tipped the screen so I could see it.

Leo: I've received most of your test results. Are you home this morning? We have a lot to discuss.

Oh, shit! "That could mean anything, right?"

I looked back at Alex, hoping he'd respond to the text, but he stood transfixed. I pulled the phone out of his hand and responded.

Alex: We're here all day. Should I start drinking now?

I thought a little levity might help, but his response weighed heavily on my heart.

Leo: Yes.

Alex finally looked down to see what I'd typed and bellowed, "Fuuck!"

He slammed his palms into his eyes like a fist had struck him, and my heart broke. He screamed again and beelined to the pantry, returning with a bottle of Jack Daniel's. In all the years I'd known him and all the holidays we'd sat glaring at each other, there had only been one night I could remember him turning to hard liquor, and that landed us in bed together.

Not bothering with a glass, he unscrewed the cap and took two long slugs. Pain etched across his face. His shoulders bowed forward; I couldn't watch him lose himself, not knowing how bad things might be. There was plenty of time to get wasted after Leo made his presentation. To his chagrin, I swiped the bottle from his hand and slipped the cap off the counter, screwing it back on.

"Give that back," he snarled.

"No!" I countered.

"It's my fucking house. I'll do what I want!"

"You sound like a big baby. Go to your room!" I barked, pointing my finger down the hall toward his bedroom.

Unbelievably, he did. *My god.* All the sweet things I thought about him last night turned to dust this morning. He was a fucking man-child. Someone had to be an adult today. I guess it's me.

I stalked down the hallway, Benny at my heel, and banged on his bedroom door.

"Grow the fuck up, Alex, and pull yourself together. I'm going out to feed the cows, and, when I get back, you'd better be ready to act like a man in control, or I'll beat the shit out of you with a pitchfork!"

That'll teach him.

That didn't sound very employee-like. Or even respectful. But if I'd learned one thing in my life, enabling people to wallow in their shit only led to deeper shit. He could have his moment of catastrophizing, but that was all. We didn't have a day he could take. Once we heard the results of Leo's testing, every moment counted. Look at me. A big-mouthed, curvy, Chippewa princess leading her tribe into battle. *I want the fucking headdress!*

Chapter 14

ALEX

I've often admired the ostrich and its ability to bury its head in the sand without a fucking care in the world. The invisibility cloak concept was all too compelling. I avoided speaking with Seneca by sneaking out of the house, jumping on my golf cart, and riding up to my thinking tree. Leo texted that he would be here in an hour, and I wasn't moving from this spot until then. Being a coward wasn't my *modus operandi;* quite the opposite. Being in the thick of the action had always been my preference in the service, with my friends, and running this farm. Everyone knew who was in charge, never challenging me—EVER! But then I never had a Seneca front and center poking the bear. She was relentless. Banging on my door, telling me to get my head out of my ass. *Ha!* Little did she know my head wasn't in my ass, but in the god damned sand!

My watch beeped, alerting me that I had fifteen minutes to face the music. If I never have a monumental crisis like this again, I'll vow to be a better man. Be more charitable. Less irritable. *You know what I mean.*

Big grey clouds floated low in the sky, blocking the early morning sun. Fall was beginning in full swing, and, by the looks of it, it wasn't leaving. The barometric pressure threatened to deliver a rare migraine—a perfect way to greet the Reaper.

As I pulled up to the house, Leo was exited his truck. Tiny signaled that he was on his way, and Seneca bounced down the front steps like any other day, having company over. Did she bake, too? Little Miss Sunshine was always ready with a sweet treat for anyone other than me.

I closed the distance to Leo, sticking out my hand like a gentleman. "Morning, Leo," I grunted unintelligibly.

"Alex," he said matter-of-factly but perked up when Little Miss Sunshine greeted him.

"Good morning, Leo. Why don't you come in and we'll talk. I just made a banana bread. It's still warm. Coffee or tea?" *See what I mean?*

We all settled around the kitchen table, pushing the napkin tray aside. Seneca frowned at me, and I pulled it back into place while she set a small, colorful serving tray filled with her treat right in the middle like we were her children. *Maybe we were.* Like a good hostess, she served Leo his hot Morning Breakfast tea, asking if there was anything else she could get him, and then sat down.

"Where's our tea?" My sarcasm was in full bloom, pointing from me to Tiny. She shrugged her shoulders and jutted her chin to the tea kettle.

"Help yourself," she said smugly. She was going to get it later. Boss or not. So disrespectful.

Leo nibbled on a slice of bread as he spread out all of his findings, pointing to each one as he went.

"See here? You're well aware fertilizer seeps into the soil, eventually reaching groundwater and then the water supply.

Any contamination follows the same path. It's the nitrogen that primarily builds in excess along with phosphorus, which can lead to harmful algal blooms in water bodies, impacting aquatic life and potentially affecting drinking water quality if the contamination is severe; this process is often referred to as "fertilizer runoff" or "leaching."

That was a mouthful. I rubbed my temples, overwhelmed. Chemistry wasn't my strong suit. I understood all his technical jibber-jabber, but what did it all mean to me and my farm?

"That all sounds fascinating, Leo, but could you break it down for the simple folk." That migraine bloomed again.

He rolled his eyes as he took a sip of his tea. Remarkably, Seneca said nothing, and Tiny looked like a giant teddy bear stuffed into a tiny seat, understanding unknown. "Look here," he pointed to a detailed report with bar graphics, pie charts, and columns of < or > levels I couldn't follow.

"This report contains all the information about your property, including identified contaminants, which remediation methods will work best, and the specif—"

That's it. I cut him off. I knew what was in the report. I needed the bottom line of what to do about it.

"Sorry, Leo, but I can read the report later. Tell me precisely what the hell is in my soil, and is it in my damn drinking water." I tried to shake clear of my attitude, but it wouldn't let go until Seneca slid her hand onto mine. I stiffened, not expecting her touch.

She smiled at me, then at Leo. "I think Alex is saying that we already know there are contaminates. We need to know the extent of the damage—where it resides—and a way to go about fixing it. Which of these pages say that?"

She was good. Really good. Even Tiny relaxed his shoulders. I stared at her unabashedly.

Leo cleared his voice, effectively breaking the silence. "Yes. Well, your radon levels are unusually high here in the house. Your nitrogen levels in your fields, we suspected, were high, too, but not treatable in an organic way."

He stopped looking to see if we were all following. "You see, some of these contaminates are usually found in crops that use synthetic fertilizers, but you don't use those on an organic farm, which causes me great concern."

I was paralyzed. There had to be a reasonable solution to this problem. There had to be.

"Without getting too technical, atmospheric nitrogen combines with hydrogen to create ammonia. Your levels by the creek are forty percent higher there than at your fields. That means your creek is the carrier of the contaminant, not an unstable soil balance."

A collective whine went around the table. I ran to the bathroom, losing my banana bread and tea. I'm not sure what happened after that, but Leo and Tiny were gone when I came back. The sliding glass door was open, and Seneca sat on a lounge chair, a fleece blanket wrapped around her shoulders, as rain began to fall. Benny barked at her from inside the opening, begging her to come in. She wouldn't. I tried as well. I watched her from the kitchen window. She was sitting like a statue as cold rain whipped at her face. She didn't blink an eye, only looked as bad as I felt.

I couldn't watch her anymore, so I went to my bathroom to run a hot bath with lavender Epsom salts. I took a clean towel from the hall closet and laid it on the counter, then grabbed her robe from her bedroom to lie beside it. Determined to get her inside, I kicked off my cowboy boots at the front door, walked over to collect my girl in my arms, and carried her like a baby into the bathroom.

We didn't look at each other. Neither of us spoke as I slowly peeled her out of her wet clothes. She let me pull her sweatshirt over her head, unbuttoning her tight jeans and slipping her long-sleeved T-shirt from her saturated body. Even then, she didn't move. I unwrapped her lower half, yanking them to her feet and pulling her socks off. I didn't bother with her bra and panties as I lifted her again, setting her slowly into the warm water. She gasped as the temperature change enveloped her, bringing her back to consciousness. I kissed her gently on her head, headed for the door, and left her to thaw in peace.

"I'll be right here if you need me," I whispered, leaving the door cracked so I could hear her if she needed me.

My phone rang as I moved to the opposite side of my bedroom, answering the call. It was Leo.

"Hello, Alex. I'm sorry we didn't finish our conversation, but I spoke to Seneca about your next steps. You cannot sell your crops or dairy until the EPA clears them. I'm very sorry for your financial loss, but everyone's health is paramount. Seneca didn't look too good when I left. Is she doing all right?"

Seneca was not all right. I'm not all right. Nothing was right about this disaster.

"She will be. Who do I call to start the remediation process? And who can I sue to pay for the damages?"

His choked chuckle didn't add to my mood. "While I can't give you a name at this time, the two tests we're waiting on should give us more clues as to what kind of companies produce these contaminants. Try to focus on keeping you and your animals healthy. I'll call in a few days with more information. In the meantime, you'll need to find an environmental lawyer to guide you through this complicated process." *More money I don't have.*

I ended the call, flopping backward onto my bed. A volcanic surge coursed through my body, ripping me apart. I grabbed a pillow, stuffed it into my mouth, and screamed my lungs out, praying I wouldn't have an aneurysm. This wasn't happening. I had to blame someone. I had to kill someone! My rational self was nonexistent, leaving my primitive, caveman brain to plan a mammoth hunt. A corporation had to be behind this, and I'd be damned if they'd got away with it.

"Alex?" A soft voice permeated my rage. "Are you okay?"

Was I okay? No. Was she okay? I prayed to God she was.

Chapter 15

ALEX

Wrapped in the robe I'd left for her on the bathroom counter, she padded across the bedroom, hair dripping down her back. She held a towel, drying off a few locks of her silky black hair at a time, looking defeated.

"Come here." I motioned for her to climb on the bed. I needed her comfort, her heat, her sympathy. "Would it be too much to ask for a hug? I know what I said before about being professional, but I'm breaking apart here." She searched my eyes, looking for an ulterior motive, but I didn't have one. Thankfully, my pathetic plea was enough.

Now was not the time to gawk at the curve of her breast at the gap of her robe. Nor was it appropriate for me to appreciate the smoothness of her thighs as she crawled across the mattress to lie down beside me. Being tempted by her beauty made me feel like a neanderthal. *I was embarrassed with myself.*

Fuck it! "Roll over and let me hold you." Her eyelashes fluttered, registering that we'd be spooning. "Don't look at me. I'm hideous."

As she rolled her sexy ass in my direction, I tucked her into my chest. Her damp head rested on my bicep, as we both relaxed, syncing our breaths effortlessly. I smelled the lavender of the

Epsom salts in her hair and shoulder. The touch of her hand covering the one I'd wrapped around her waist had me glowing. Nothing outside this room mattered anymore. I couldn't almost forget why I was upset.

Her thumb gently stroked the skin between my thumb and forefinger, waking my semi-erect cock to full staff. I moaned when she slid her thumb into the palm of my hand with feather-light strokes, stoking the flame within me.

Mmm. "Your hands are very deft," I whispered behind her ear. I used my chin to push her hair back, breathing another deep whiff of her scented hair, cursing myself for wanting more.

When she rolled herself deeper into my arms, my hand grazed the underside of her full breast, causing additional angst to my mottled mind.

"I need to tell you what Leo said after you, uh, departed," Seneca said apologetically.

I flattened my hand along her belly, hoping to distract her for a few more minutes. Relenting, I responded flatly, "Let me have it."

She tried to turn more but I wouldn't let her. "Well, he warned us that the contamination might be irreversible." She spoke the words one at a time like she was in pain having to utter them.

I squeezed my eyes tightly, absorbing her words like shards of glass cutting through my skin. "I know. I've been trying not to allow myself to go there, but the truth is I'm finished here. It would take decades for the land to heal, and, even then, I couldn't in good conscience call it an organic farm. This is so fucked up."

The damn broke for both of us. My chest convulsed, then hers followed. Choked cries evolved into open crying, and, I swear, if Seneca weren't here, I'd be lost. Cast into a petrified state no longer able to feel or function. I buried my face in her neck, praying that something good would come from this.

Her hands grabbed hold of mine, pulled them tightly to her chest. I couldn't get close enough to her to relinquish my pain or hers. She opened my fists, balled under her own, pressing them to her breasts, cupping them tightly. An offering to wash my anguish away. That sweet ass of hers pressed into my thickening cock, awareness of what she offered, tore me apart. It would be so easy to get lost in her. To cast away my pain, if only for a few minutes would be a gift. I wanted her so badly. My body demanded her badly.

"Please," she begged softly. Everything we agreed to went right out the window with that one word. She wanted me—and I was desperate. *Consequences be damned!*

My one hand slid down her outer thigh, relishing her toned, shapely leg, returning to her inner thigh in a loop. Sweet gasps huffed out of her delicate throat, emboldening me. Slowly, I traced her body, enjoying every curve and swell. She shivered each time I touched a sensitive spot, moaning her approval, insisting she wanted more.

"You're so beautiful. So sexy, Sen." My words stumbled out of my mouth, not caring if I said too much. "Are you sure this is what you want? I need you too much."

She reached between us, grabbing my cock firmly. "Yes, Alex. I want this. I need you, too," she whimpered between affirmations.

Fuck! A wildfire grew within me. I grabbed her hip, rolling her back to lie down flat. I shifted over her body letting her feel the hunger between my legs. Everything about her was stunning. I'd dreamed of this moment. Her long, beautiful hair fanned out on my pillow, begging me to take her. Her tongue swept over her soft, pillowy lips, inviting me to taste them. This was a dream I never wanted to end. Fuck the farm. It could burst into flames for all I cared at this moment. Nothing in this world or the next could replace her.

Pushing her robe open fully, I groaned, "So fucking beautiful."

Lifting my knee between her luscious thighs, I spread her open, swallowing hard at her wet, glistening pussy. "Stay right here. Do not move," I commanded, rolling off the bed to reach into my nightstand for a handful of condoms. I shed my pants and underwear quickly as our eyes locked. My heart raced watching Seneca scan chest, then down to my abs, tracing each one until she reached my rock-hard cock. When she wet her lips hungrily, I damn near lost it. *She was so fucking sexy.*

My smile hurt, knowing how badly she wanted me. When Seneca let her guard down, she went from being a pussy cat to a wildcat. I tore my T-shirt over my head, pressing my chest to her tits, loving how her buds pebbled under my skin, and body squirmed in anticipation.

Tearing her eyes from my engorged cock, she took my chin in her hand, forcing me to look her in the eye. "I'll do whatever it takes to empty that head of yours, Alex. And, you'd better not fucking stop!" Fireworks exploded in my head. *She didn't have to ask me twice.*

Growling into her mouth, I pulled her lower lip hard. "You won't get an argument out of me." I licked her belly from her bellybutton to her tits staring her down the entire way up.

"Jesus, Seneca. You're killing me." I latched onto her right tit desperately as my opposite hand kneaded her other sumptuous globe. I rolled the delicate nub tightly between my lips, flicking my tongue upward repeatedly. Electric pulses shot through my body as her hands threaded viciously into my hair, screaming my name.

"Fuck, Alex. You're a beast!" she said, throwing her head back further.

Damn, straight I was. She wouldn't forget it either when I put my cock deep into her pussy. I released my mouth from her tight red bud, giving her other bundle of nerves the same treatment. Her hips squirmed underneath me, her mouth gasping each time my teeth slid over her peaks.

Sensing her discomfort at my lusty mouth on her breasts, I slid upward to devour her lips. Our tongues chased each other, teasing, darting deeper and deeper, sharing promises of more to each other. I didn't know what "more" meant, but I wanted it with her.

I lined myself up between her thighs, my pulsing dick dragging my head through her slick folds.

"This is what you want, isn't it, baby."

She sobbed, "Sooo badly."

My mind raced with all the dirty possibilities of what and how I wanted to take her, every one of them filthier than the last. Remembering the first time we fucked had been emblazoned on my mind for more than four years. We were drunk, but beyond remembering. Temptation bloomed on the dance floor when we went out with Abigail and Elias, which turned into an engagement party at someone else's wedding. Her black hair flowed in soft waves well past her shoulders. Those tight, blinged-out jeans hugged her curvy ass driving me insane. Her blouse hung low, and, for the life of me, I couldn't imagine not seeing her tits for the rest of my life. It didn't matter if the music was playing fast or slow, we ground against each other, moaning into each other's ears, begging for more. I wanted her so badly I considered fucking her in a bathroom stall. I was an asshole for thinking it but a prince for controlling my desire for her. I had plans to lick, suck, and fuck every inch of her body, and a bar wasn't feeding into my fantasy.

She'd said then, "Call me a ride-share. I'm going home," then slid her tongue into my smiling mouth for a deep, sensual kiss that left me with bite marks on my lower lip. After that, it was a blur. I must have called for a second ride because I found her back at the inn, draped over her pillows on the blow-up beds we were sleeping on due to some upstairs construction. We rolled over each other, her clawing my back, and me gripping her long tresses as I drove myself deep into her until we both exploded with the release. My ego assured me it was right to flip her over several moments later and fuck her again from behind. Her moans of pleasure, and filthy mouth taunting me to ride her harder sizzled my brain to dust. I'd never felt that out of control and aggressive during sex. Flopping back onto the mattress, I rolled my head to the side to look at her swollen lips surrounding a serene smile. Understandably, she was blissed out and happy. I was, too. By the following week, I'd ruined it again by not calling her like I said I would. We didn't talk about our feelings every time we met year after year. My feelings simmered underneath the tension between us each time I set eyes on her. There was no doubt I wanted her. I could feel her desire, too. But in our case, stubbornness vs. stubbornness didn't cancel eachother out.

Today, though, my carnal lust couldn't be contained any longer. I became the beast she claimed I was, emotionally and physically. I'd make sure the past would be forgotten, replaced with new ones of desire. We were establishing a new, stronger foundation destined to stand the test of time, and, this time, I wouldn't fuck it up saying something stupid.

I sat back on my knees, straddling her silky thighs, my cock thrumming with pent-up desire. I patted around the mattress, looking for the condoms I thrown down beside me, and ripped the packet open with my teeth. Placing the latex on the head of my dick, Seneca lifted her head, crying, "Please! Let me." *There's my greedy girl.*

Granting her wish, I removed my hands, allowing my sweet temptress to sheath my aching cock, desire pooling in her eyes every inch as she covered the eight aimed at her wet core. Her hooded eyes shifted to mine. If she were looking for approval, she'd get it in the devilish smile I beamed down at her face. I slid a finger through her seam, testing how wet she was, overwhelmed at how beautifully it glistened.

"You're soaking, baby," I crooned. She nodded, dropping her head back to the pillow, dazed. "I bet you still taste like honey. So sweet. Warm and delicious." Her hips bucked up, reminding me of my intended goal. I hummed my pleasure at her desperation. "Yeah. I've got you, Sen. Relax."

Time stopped as I dipped my head to her wetness, staring intensely into her eyes on my way down to her sex. I kept watching her as I flattened my tongue, swiping it through her folds, her black lashes fluttering like a butterfly. Tonight, I'd imprint my face in her brilliant brain for all eternity.

She arched her back, screaming, "Fuck, yes! Alex, yes."

I smiled, watching her body writhe from my mouth with satisfaction. It had been over a year since I'd been with a woman, and, even then, Meghan couldn't hold a candle to Seneca, no matter what I tried with her. My ego grew seeing how deeply Seneca responded to my hands, tongue, and, in a moment, my cock. I grabbed hold of her knees, pushing them up to her shoulders. "Hold onto these, and don't let go," I demanded, my captain's voice booming from where my face commanded her pussy.

Shifting myself higher, slowly, my cock penetrated past her folds into her wetness. She was tight. So fucking tight. I groaned, pushing deeper until my balls slid over her pussy.

"You feel incredible. So wet. So tight." My eyes never left her face as I withdrew my dick, only to slam it back even harder. She gasped at my urgency, but her face said it wasn't very pleasurable. I pushed her legs higher and slammed her again, relieved that the new angle was what she needed to enjoy herself. I felt like a fifteen-year-old boy fucking a girl for the first time the way I drilled into her. I was guilty of wanting to bring myself to orgasm first, then corrected myself by sliding my fingers between us, pinching her bundle of nerves to bring my girl to orgasm first. I watched her body convulse, feeling her inner muscles squeeze my cock like a vice. Unintelligible words spewed from her mouth like an incantation. Watching her pussy accept everything I gave her was the most erotic thing I'd ever seen. She was my new religion, and I promised to pray to her body every day, twice a day.

Her eyes shone with tears and appreciation; arms flung out in surrender. "I'm speechless. How could I not know how much I needed that?" I wasn't sure who said it, but I knew we both felt it equally.

Chapter 16

SENECA

The expression "rocked my world" took on a whole new meaning. Otherworldly was more like it. Alex's proud expression was well-earned, and I couldn't take that from him.

"Well done, Mr. Valize. Is there anything else I can help you with? I am at your service, you know."

He climbed up my body, grabbing the flesh at my hips, mumbling praises as he moved to my breasts. He stopped, struggling to take a whole one in his mouth. "God, I love these tits," he cried, then stopped like he didn't realize I'd been attentively watching the reverence in his eyes.

Frozen in place like a transparent adhesive bound us together, we stared, transfixed. A tingle traveled through my body. It felt like two ghost-like arms wrapped around us, blessing this moment. *Was it my mother?* Through the window, I caught a glimmer of a rainbow emerging from the cloudy sky and I knew my life would never be the same.

Alex's thumb brushed the side of my face, getting my attention. "How are you doing, baby?"

I pushed his hair back, examining every inch of his face. Every scar, freckle, and crinkle of his deep, sapphire eyes. "Is this just sex?" I probed carefully. Several moments passed as concern formed on my brow awaiting his reply. I knew I was being too direct, but I needed to know.

He lowered his face, a breath away from mine, planting a soft, sexy kiss at the corners of my mouth before touching them with his calloused fingers. "Never."

Never?

He kissed me deeply, possessively. Expressing what words couldn't describe. I gave him everything I had in those kisses. My desire. My needs. The dam I tried holding back all these years burst open, flooding my heart and my head. This was the moment I knew we had a chance to make our relationship whole. We'd work out the details. I only wanted all of it with him.

"Alex, please. Fuck me—hard," I begged. I craved him so badly that I pulled up my knees showing him all of me. Willing him to fuck me like I'd never been fucked before. I knew he wouldn't let me down.

"God damn, woman. Be careful what you wish for."

His cock barely fit in the condom anymore, the tip already catching his pre-cum. Lining up his dick he slowly drove himself in, inch by inch. He pulled out when he saw me hold my breath, waiting for me to exhale, then drove back in further. He had mastered my body and what I needed from him. He was talented. *No.* Gifted.

"You will never make me wait this long again. Do you understand me?" he said unsmiling.

"Yes, sir," I replied, humbly. I shocked myself. I'd never called a man "sir" before. Was it because he sounded so stern? Or because he was a captain in the Army? It just came out of my mouth, but somehow, it felt right to be commanded by Alex.

His slow smile filled me with anticipation of what he'd do next. He pulled out entirely, driving back in again so hard he forced me higher on the bed. "I like the name sir," he hissed. "I certainly earned it in the Army, and I hope I'm earning it now."

I giggled, realizing I'd never shared this kind of dialogue in bed before. "You most definitely are."

Alex unapologetically plowed into me impressively for a long time. When suddenly, he pulled out, leaving me deprived and peeved. "What the hell, Alex? I'm so close!" I whined.

Smirking, he watched me writhe on the bed, trying to get him back inside of me, "Put that back in. Now!" I cried desperately.

"Greedy girl," he taunted. "Will you recognize that Benny is *my* dog? Not yours. And even if he seems to like you more, I'm still his master." *Are you fucking kidding me?*

"This! This is why you stopped me from having the best orgasm of my life. Fine! Yes, Benny is your damn dog. Always and forever. Satisfied?" *Benny still loves me more.*

His smile became evil. "Very. Now take my dick." He plunged into me so fast I winced. I grabbed his shoulders, carving nail marks into his back as I hung onto him for dear life.

"Touch yourself," he barked. His instructions were crystal clear, and, when I did, I immediately shattered into oblivion. The wait he inflicted on himself must have heightened his release because he exploded into me, making this union undeniably otherworldly.

"Seneca! Fuck, baby, yes. You are incredible."

Coming down from such an incredible height was like a balloon spinning in circles as the air whooshed out. It didn't take rocket science to figure out he felt the same as I did. But because Alex was Alex, I didn't want to feed his ego. He had enough for one day. Though, honestly, he earned every stroke I'd given him. He rolled to the side, pulling me with him, flipping my hair off the pillow to avoid getting caught between us as we spooned. Lusty, blue eyes twinkled when he smiled at me, giving me permission to melt into his touch even more. One hand rubbed my shoulder and bicep, kneading the tissue delicately, while the other reached for my hand, massaging between my fingers. I whimpered, not realizing how many nerve endings were tucked between each valley. This was all new to me. No one had explored my body as Alex had. It's as if he was memorizing every cut and curve from my face to my toes. I reveled in his mind-body connection that most men couldn't seem to find. He knew precisely how to pull an orgasm out of me and I bowed to his mastery. When his eyes again became hooded, and heavy with lust, I thrilled at the promise of another orgasm. Seeing him this way was intoxicating, exhilarating.

I turned my head, desperate for his lips not to be disappointed, as he allowed me space to kiss him. I pressed my tongue into his mouth, searching for him—needing him. Finding what I wanted, I sucked and teased tongue until he rolled me on top of his broad chest. He was hard as steel again. His big hands gripped my hips, lifting me on top of his long, thick cock and slammed me down ruthlessly. I screamed at the intrusion, and continued screaming until he slowed my pace down. He guided me as we moved as one. He'd claimed me, then owned me body and soul as he controlled each pump with a level of desire I could barely comprehend. Weren't fucking. We were making love. The tempo increased as I chased my release, riding him the only way I knew how—wild and deep.

"I'm coming. Buck those hips, baby. Please."

Alex didn't disappoint. Three thrusts later, we reached our summit together. "Sennn. Fuck, you feel so good. Clench down on me. I—I... fuucckk, yes!" he choked out.

"My god, Alex. I can feel your cum shooting inside me. Damn." *Yes, damn. Where was the fucking condom?*

Chapter 17

ALEX

You've never seen two people so deep in denial that they forgot to hate each other. Then again, I didn't hate Seneca, and, judging by the way she rode my cock, I'd say her opinion of me had shifted, too. That was until I realized I hadn't put on a fucking condom this round of play.

Her eyes blew wide at the exact moment mine did. "Alex. We forgot protection. I mean, I'm on the pill, but still, no protection." Not panicking, she pushed her damp hair behind her ears, biting her bottom lip.

I needed air. I took a big breath, letting it out slowly. *Keep your cool, man.* "That was my bad. I'm so sorry, Seneca. Do you think we'll be okay?" I didn't wait to find out. I slid her to the mattress, sat up, and scrubbed my face.

My nightstand clock read four o'clock. *Geez.* We'd lost our sorrow in each other's arms for almost six hours, three of which were a nap and the rest pure bliss. It took every bit of courage to not rush to leave the haven of my bed, shower, and check on my animals.

She never answered my question. I stood, forcing thoughts of a theoretical baby out of my head.

"Where are you going?" Seneca croaked. She followed me out of bed, looking like the native princess she was—lithe, stunning, and powerful.

I held out my hand like a stop sign. "The shower. Playtime is over, and my girls in the barn want their daddy." I cracked myself up. I knew it sounded lewd, but, damn it, I couldn't help myself. My mood had shifted. Dark humor boiled to the top when I was overly stressed, today notwithstanding.

She eyeballed me. "You're a sick, perverted man, Alex Valize." She swayed her hips, sauntering across the room until she could put her hands on me again. She was insatiable. The next time I had her in my bed, she'd be on all fours with her ass glowing red—and me, wearing a condom.

A sinister grin emerged, my voice going husky, "A very perverted man, but you already knew that about me years ago. You must be a naughty girl to keep coming back for more." I smacked her ass, taking her open mouth in mine as she gasped. "Keep poking the bear, baby, and you'll see firsthand how naughty I'll make you."

I winked at her as I turned toward the bathroom, leaving her dazed and wanting.

Seneca met me at the barn twenty minutes later, carrying a bottle of water, which triggered my contamination issues. Was this going to be my existence forever? I needed to start making plans for the long term, whether I wanted to or not.

"Can I help? Maybe figure out how to hook those water containment bins to a hose?" She looked around as if she was scouting out an apparatus to help her.

I liked how she wanted to do her part. She was already getting an A+ on her internship, but this was asking too much. "Thanks for offering, but Tiny rigged something up this morning while we were, uh, working other things out," I said, giving her a sexy wink.

She closed her eyes tightly, hanging her head. "I guess everyone deals with grief differently. I prefer our way," she added, smarmily. "I'll start boiling water and storing them in pitchers. We'll figure something out for dinner."

She spun on her heel and walked out of the barn. I stood up from milking Bernice, arching my back from the bent position milking required Rested my hand on her haunch, I called after Seneca, "I have a whiteboard in a storage cabinet at the back of the house. Why don't you search for it and the markers? We'll brainstorm our options after dinner."

It sounded like I was giving up, though I was being practical. This problem wasn't going away now or in twenty years. It's best to reel in my expectations and figure out a new future. I didn't have the heart to call my brother, Dane, and tell him the bad news about the farm. I'd be visiting his campus next weekend, and this bullshit would keep until then. Annalise, however, needed to know immediately. Before finishing with the second-string cows, I pulled my phone from my back pocket and invited her and her husband to dinner. This was a family decision; everyone needed to participate in the process. Dane made it clear he didn't want anything to do with the farm, so I didn't feel bad excluding him from the conversation for now. I'm sure he'll be shocked when we cancel our annual Christmas celebration. *This years' would be more like a funeral.*

When I'd entered the house, I realized I hadn't texted Seneca that we were having company. I'm so used to making decisions and doing things independently that I forget someone lives with me now. I kicked off my boots on the rubber mat by the front door changing my routine with the seasons of leaving them outside in the summer months.

I shuffled into the kitchen, my head held low. "I, uh, forgot to text you. I invited Anna and her husband, Steve, to dinner. You know, more brains, more brainpower?" I gave her my best puppy dog eyes. Deflecting, I commented, "This pasta sauce smells great. I can fry up more hamburger if you like?" I hoped my help would lessen the hardship.

A flash crossed her face. I couldn't tell if she was upset or planning to screw with me. I'm betting on the latter. "I suppose I should give you a hard time, but your sister," she paused for effect, "called and asked what she could bring. See Alex? Women are much more civilized. We look out for each other." She doubled over in hysterics like a cackling hyena.

"Your Highness. Once again, you have taught this lowly peasant he isn't worthy. My deepest apologies." We were making memories without even trying. Judging by the speed of my heart, there wasn't anything I'd forget about this woman.

She vigorously tapped her wooden spoon along the pot's side, flicking and swishing it like a wand pointed at my head. "Arise, lowly peasant. You are forgiven. Now get me a damn glass of wine before I clock you with this spoon!"

Yes, ma'am.

The dishes were cleared, and the family room was set up as a war room. Two computers lined the coffee table, one casting Google Maps of the area off one screen and the other in a split-screen view with remediation options. The whiteboard Seneca found was balanced on the fireplace mantel, below which I stood on the hearth to post our ideas. Seneca handed out pads of paper and pens to take notes, along with a cooler full of beer and two bottles of wine ready to go on the corner bar. Assembled and prepared for battle, I called the meeting to order.

The front door slammed shut, and Tiny appeared. "Sorry. The traffic was terrible." He smirked, knowing we didn't have a traffic problem around here. Benny rushed to him in welcome, then settled back at Seneca's side while she worked.

Ahem. I unfolded the paper I'd stuffed into my back pocket, "Ladies and gentlemen, friends and family. The great Winston Churchill once proclaimed, 'We have before us an ordeal of the most grievous kind. We have before us many, many long months of struggle and suffering. You ask, what is our policy? I can say: It is to wage war' . . . and kick the ass of whoever fucked up our farm and our lives!"

Maybe that was overkill? Never! "Whether the last two tests come back in our favor or not, we can no longer call Eloheh Farms organic. To remediate the land properly, as noted here," I pointed to the first cast image on the television, "every possible resolution involves planting new crops and laying extensive amounts of mulch to pull nitrogen out of the soil including copious amounts of water. Here's the real problem. Replanting won't help make our farm organic again for over twenty years. Additionally, we can't use the area water system for irrigation because it, too, is tainted. That leaves us up shit's creek without a paddle. All thoughts and ideas are welcome at this time."

While delivering our life-threatening circumstances comedically, that's where the fun ended. I stepped down from the hearth planting my ass on the cold brick. You could have heard a pin drop by the semiconscious looks of everyone in the room. "I guess now would be a good time for everyone to grab a drink. I know I need one." I pressed down on my knees and looked at Seneca, who seemed deep in thought.

A few minutes later, alcohol at the ready, Steve clicked his tongue and offered, "How far out does the contamination go? I know we live five miles away, but does our neighborhood need to be concerned?"

Every moment I didn't answer, he became more petrified. Annalise took his hand, rubbing her thumb across the back of it. "We should have the county run some tests. Maybe a ten-mile radius around your farm?" Her creased brow broke my heart, and I rushed to her side, rubbing her back.

"Write that down. That's a great idea. We can get on that tomorrow." I kissed her head, patting Steve on the back. The ripple effect of what had happened created a new source of pain and guilt. This problem started on my land. The repercussions of contaminating a whole county gutted me.

I had a lot to process. My ego aside, I returned to the whiteboard, drawing a target from the edge of my property abutting the creek to a dashed line representing the ten-mile mark, and played around on the map application to see how far this problem could reach, then took screenshots. "What else?"

Seneca clicked on her keyboard several times, and then the image on the TV changed to a regional map. She jumped up and used her finger to identify three locations upstream from us that were under suspicion. Her face was animated, and her body moved like she needed to pee.

"See, here! These corporate hazardous material monsters would be the source of our problems, not an abundance of nitrogen in the soil we once thought was the culprit. My problem, our problem, is the manifestation of dumping and leaching into the water system. If we hire a lawyer to investigate their compliance reports, we'd know whom to direct our ire to."

With arms spread wide and her convictions apparent, it sounded like a reasonable course of action. Except, who was going to pay for that? And how long would it take to get a judge and jury to proclaim a verdict? I couldn't break her heart with all the effort she put into researching the source of contamination. She wasn't wrong, only naïve that we could march into their offices pointing a finger and them cutting us a check. *Not in this lifetime.*

Reading the room, I could see glimmers of hope in their bright eyes. They were looking at the long game when I needed a first down. "Excellent work, Seneca. Let's investigate where and how much an environmental lawyer would cost. Maybe they'd pity us and take it pro bono because the ramifications would run far and wide."

Her lip quivered, seeing the juxtaposition of her suggestion. "Sure. I'll look into it. What are we going to do in the short term, though?" Looking defeated, I offered her some hope.

Stoically, I led the charge. "We have some big battles to fight, but please don't be discouraged. Seneca is right. We have to develop a short game that will protect our livestock and our name. Don't worry. If one of those motherfuckers poisoned my farm, they will pay big-time."

My head began to throb, thinking of all the details that needed addressing. Taking on a big corporation was the last thing on my list. I sat down on the hearth again; our brainstorming screeched to a halt.

Tiny's gruff mumbles pierced through our veil of despair. "Can your friend, Elias, house your animals while we get this all sorted out? You said he lives on some acreage in Connecticut, right?"

Big, Bashful, and brilliant!

Both Seneca and I jumped to our feet, locking eyes on an idea as big as he was. "I'm calling Abigail. You make an inventory of what needs to be transported. And you, Tiny, get a gold star *and* cape because you are our superhero!"

I crossed the room and attempted to hug my friend, but his immense size left me looking like a rag doll hung from his shoulders. He finished the hug, squeezing tightly. I felt my spine pop appreciatively after the unplanned chiropractic adjustment.

"Thanks, buddy. I needed that. Organize food and supplies to make our move efficient. Write up feeding and vet schedules. I'll arrange transport as soon as I strong-arm my friend into lending us a hand." Tiny's flat-lined smile was a sure sign we were moving in the right direction.

Annalise and Steve picked up the stray bottles and glasses and moved them into the kitchen, Benny following closely for crumbs. *Who needs a Hoover?* We had a plan. Not one for the long term, precisely, but one that would sustain us in the short term.

Chapter 18
SENECA

In retrospect, my aggravation at having to shift my internship was a microcosm of what happened in real life. I sounded like a whiny bitch who wasn't getting her way. Everything became crystal clear this week. Being a horticulturalist wasn't just playing with plants. My scientific training was being put to the test. Knowing what caused soil or water problems wasn't enough. I needed fortitude, patience, and a sense of humor to handle the magnitude of moving chickens and several half-ton-plus animals two hundred and fifty miles away. We didn't know how far the contamination spread, so moving them to a nearby farm wasn't an option. Now that I'm thinking about it, Alex and possibly his family could no longer live in this area.

This whole situation was depressing. It's not my usual funk. This depression was more culturally induced. I was half Native American and part of the Ojibwe tribe, which fell under the Chippewa Nation. My cultural trauma came from centuries of brutal suffering that somehow permeated my being and plagued me when I had big decisions to make. It felt like a boulder pressing down on my chest, making breathing hard. Shadows of the past haunted me at these times. The irony of Alex and me having to pack up everything and move hundreds of miles away triggered past indignities, I'd learned as a child, was called the Trail of Tears. Our situation looked the same, must have felt the same, and was caused by the same thing—White Man Syndrome. Greed, power, and disdain when others didn't accept the way the White man said it should be. From a distance, our problem didn't appear the same. But, make no mistake, oppression in any form has no expiration date. Disregarding Mother Earth was the root cause of Alex's troubles. Getting restitution for his suffering would be an uphill battle, but I wouldn't create more by walking away when things became difficult.

Annalise, Steven, and Tiny left a few minutes ago, promising to do whatever was needed to make the move. Alex and I, however, had a conference call with our friends in Mystic that couldn't wait.

My phone pinged. *Ready when you are,* Abigail responded. Alex finished letting Benny out, locking up, and turning off the kitchen light when I motioned for him to join me on the couch. He took my hand possessively, tucking mine into his other one.

"What will we do if they say no?" His voice quavered, his eyes misting. My stomach turned, knowing it was a possibility, though not a big one.

Leaning forward, I kissed his pouty mouth, giving him my best supportive smile. "They won't let us down. I won't let you down. Ready to make the call?" He nodded, and I pressed Abigail's screen icon, set it to speaker mode, and set the phone between us on the coffee table.

"Hey, girl. It's late. Is everything okay with you? Is Alex being an ass again?" Even in a crisis, she could make me laugh.

"Hello? I'm right here, so stop disparaging me to your friend," Alex blustered. "Is Elias with you? This call affects him, too."

A rumble echoed through the receiver, "What exactly is affecting me?"

I jumped in, setting the stage for what we'd been experiencing these past two weeks. Alex then took the wheel for the punchline.

"We already told you about the contamination issues at Eloheh, which brings me to my next pickle. How would you feel about renting me a few acres for my cows and chickens to live on until we figure out how to remediate the problem?"

Alex looked pale and a little green around the gills, asking for such a huge favor. It may have taken a lot out of him to humble himself this way, but it needed to be done. We sat quietly while Abigail and Elias chatted, the anticipation making us sweat. A few minutes later, Abigail spoke.

"What about you two? Would you like to come and stay with us, too? We have the room, and the tourist season is almost over. We won't have many visitors staying with us in the inn for a few months."

Oh my! I hadn't even thought about both of us staying there. I usually stayed with them when school was closed, but having Alex across the hall? That could be dicey. This was too big an imposition.

Alex swiveled to face me. "Would that work for you?"

I blurted, simultaneously, "Depends on my internship reassignment."

Alex fell back against the cushions, confused.

"Seriously, Sen. You'd bail on me?" He sulked deeper into the cushions, looking assaulted.

The corner of my mouth hitched up, "No! But the college board might insist I'll need a new one if I can't finish this one. Let me speak with Dr. Abel and figure out my options. I'm committed to you, but I still need to graduate; the internship is my last requirement. Let's put a pin in this and get you and your animals to Mystic first."

Surprising me, Alex pulled his head out of his ass and sat up slowly. "I'm sorry. I'm being ungrateful and selfish. You have your life to live, too. I have no right to shackle you to my problems." *Impressive.*

Forgetting we were still on an open line with our two best friends, we were startled when Elias chirped in.

"Did you hear that, Abs? In the history of my friendship with Alex, he has never admitted to being selfish. Will wonders never cease?"

Everyone but Alex chuckled. "Ha. Ha. Take your potshot, Big Man. I can take it. So, is this a go?"

Abigail squealed, "Absolutely, yes! When should we expect you?"

My heart thumped loudly in my ears. Everything was moving fast and getting faster. Again, Alex took the wheel.

"I'm heading out to see my brother this weekend. If I'm not mistaken, Seneca, you're going back to Delaware Valley to meet Dr. Abel. How does next Wednesday look? I'll need to transport ten cows and a dozen chickens. Elias, are you sure your barn is big enough for all of them?"

Geez. I didn't think about all those logistics. Thankfully, Elias was all over it.

Gruffly, he replied, "We'll make it work. Plan to drive over after your visit with Dane. We'll move stuff around and put up temporary fencing for a pasture your girls can use. With any luck and a few extra hands, we should be able to finish before the first snowfall."

Abigail blabbered on next, "I'll make up your old room and move my stuff around my barn office, so Alex will have a place to work. Sen, you'll hang with me in the house. Be sure to tell Dr. Abel we would love to continue your internship here. It's not like you haven't already built our gardens. You already have plans to build your zen meditation garden once you graduated. That is comprehensive enough to call an internship, right? You can start earlier to complete it before graduation. He has to agree, or I'll become his worst nightmare." She taunted. "I'll give Mr. Brickner a call about legalities and financial stuff. You know he's the one whose family has been overseeing the family trust since 1832? He's incredible."

Overwhelmed and breathless, I conceded. "It would make sense for all involved. I'll pitch it to him, but, if you could send him your invitation and a commitment letter, it would go a long way toward moving this along. He'll need details about your property and you'd need to let him explain the program to you. He'd be a fool to turn it down. I can't thank you both enough for your big hearts and incredible friendship. I have no words . . ."

A river of tears slid down my face, making my shirt damp. Some were in gratitude. Some in hope. But mostly, relief. Even Alex, who had been so stoic in his resolve to keep it together, choked on his tears.

After brushing off a few tears, Alex made arrangements with Elias. My mind whirred with everything that needed arranging in the next week. Usually, I'd be a pig in mud, making lists and cheering on my OCD. But now . . . I could feel my mind shutting down. Closing my eyes, I listened for the guys to finish their plans. " . . . Dammit, those chicken coops are brand new. I'm not leaving them," Alex sputtered, annoyed. Though I missed most of their conversation, hearing him lose everything built over the last two centuries became increasingly painful.

During our time of misery, a comical image inserted itself of Amy the Great, Abigail's chicken friend, who would have several new friends to "play" with. Breaking the tension, I shared my break from reality with the group.

"Abs? Tell ATG company is coming." We both burst into tears at the thought of her pet chicken "sharing" her excitement about meeting new chicken friends. On more than one occasion, Abigail had assured me her chicken spoke to her and, in this case, would be "happy" to play hostess.

Alex looked apoplectic while Elias moaned exasperatedly, "Come on, you two." I carefully shifted away from Alex to the other side of the couch, knowing my sense of humor wasn't shared. Thankfully, he didn't reprimand my *faux pas*.

Alex signed off the call, exhausted and annoyed. My head throbbed; my limbs were too heavy to move. The thought of packing up all my shit was daunting. Selling Dr. Abel on an alternate internship felt improbable, if not impossible. My life was out of control, and the only thing keeping me from caving in was seeing Alex and his family safe.

Chapter 19
SENECA

It was Friday, and Alex had already left to visit Dane at Parents' Weekend as planned. He carried on about having "too much to do," but I reminded him he had four others who would help him. Benny would go with him for emotional support and then stay on with Annalise and Steven when he returned to deal with the farm. It was enough to deal with livestock, even if Alex would be lonely without him.

Tiny agreed to keep working on the farm and to keep it safe from looters or other horrible things that could happen while Alex was away. He lived several towns over and felt confident that he would be safe from contamination. Swinging by once a day wouldn't be an inconvenience.

Alex confessed last night, "I feel like a heel leaving him like this. He's been a great employee and friend." I agreed, but what else could I say? "As soon as this all settles down, I want to do something special for him. Maybe send him and his "special" friend away for a sunny weekend in Aruba." *Tiny on a beach towel sipping daiquiris was laughable.*

I spent the day packing up my things and stuffing them back in my car. It had only been three weeks since my internship began, and it's a good thing I hadn't unpacked everything. I suppose that's a blessing now. My hopes of completing my program were minuscule at best. I spent the rest of my time completing whatever assignments I could, composing a comprehensive presentation for Dr. Abel for the Eloheh situation, and packing up the linen closet and kitchen pantry for Alex. Dr. Abel needed to know every detail of what I had learned practically and professionally. That was a slippery slope. *I'll leave out the sarcasm, yelling, chastising, and awe-inspiring sex. Definitely—leaving that out.*

After lunch, I joined Tiny in the barn, and packed up food tack to move the small herd of cattle and cleaned up the chicken coops. I'd called the vet to inquire about sedation for the move and best practices for a safe journey. Schedules were made, food and supplies were tallied, and everything else was packed up for storage until decisions about the future could be made.

Before Alex left, he went into town to collect as many boxes as possible that would fit into his pickup. The barn wasn't the only building that needed packing up. There was no reason for all of Alex's personal belongings to stay at the house; God forbid it was ransacked. Anything that wasn't necessary to eat and shower with was boxed up and made ready to move when the time came.

By Sunday morning, my car was packed, and sandwiches were made with the last of the lunchmeat to keep me sustained for the drive back to school. As I turned the key to lock up the house, an minivan pulled up, and Annalise hopped out with a basket.

"Oh! Thank goodness I caught you. Please take these with you. Have some for the ride but save a few for Alex. They're his favorite." Annalise was one of the kindest people I'd ever met.

What I would have done to have a big sister like her. I would miss her so much.

I peeked under the red gingham napkin to see a gallon Ziploc bag full of lemon squares. "Oooh, those look good. Maybe keep the basket for now. I barely have room for me in the car as it is."

She laughed and pulled me into a huge hug, making my heart swell. This woman was one-of-a-kind. I got in my car, ready to start the engine, when she motioned for me to roll down the window. She leaned her elbows in through the window, conspiratorially pleadingly, "Take good care of yourself. Alex won't tell you, but he needs you more than ever. Stay in touch. We'll do whatever we can on our end. Hell! If word comes down that our community is affected, we might join you sooner than a Christmas visit." A nervous chuckle slipped from her tight grimace.

For her families sake, I hope that wouldn't happen. I thanked her again, started the car, and pulled through the circular drive for a ninety-minute drive to campus. My meeting with the Dean of Environmental and Horticulture Sciences, aka Dr. Abel, was set for nine o'clock, Monday morning. By noon, I'd be on the road to Abigail's, starting what I'd hope to be my last stop on my internship rollercoaster.

My meeting with Dr. Abel was twofold: It was wonderful to see him and be back on campus, but I dreaded waiting for my internship determination.

"As much as I'd like to grant you this change of venue, the Board has final approval on your friends' estate as a viable substitution. Otherwise, the integrity of our program would be compromised." Dr. Abel intoned, sipping coffee from a chipped mug. It was Olivia who stopped me on my way out that gave me hope.

"Seneca, I heard your presentation. It was direct, concise, and rationally sound. You know the Dean has to follow the school's rules and protocols, right? If there is any way to sway the Board in your favor, he'll do it. Oh! I almost forgot to tell you that Abigail Burton-McGinnis emailed over the specifications of her property and her expectations of what she wants you to accomplish to achieve your diploma. After seeing the pictures she included, I might have to schedule a weekend getaway this summer and see it for myself." Olivia tittered at the thought.

In my life, I've been let down by the people I've loved the most—the ones who should have had my back unconditionally. My mother bolted after hearing of her cancer diagnosis, only to return days before she died begging for forgiveness. My father chose a new girlfriend over me instead of ensuring I was settled before he left; no regret or forgiveness was given. Even Abigail bailed on me when she took off to claim her inheritance. I was an island floating alone at sea. It took her two weeks to realize what a horrible friend she'd been, and she begged for my forgiveness. This was followed by an offer to join her at her new home for however long I wanted to stay. Abigail's only stipulation to joining her was to get my degree, with the caveat to return and build the garden of my dreams. *She was a tough negotiator.*

Surprisingly, Olivia, who had no stake in my life, descended like *Tinker Bell* to sprinkle her special brand of fairy dust with a kick-in-the-pants to keep me moving forward. For four long years, whether I wanted her help or not, she had my back without asking for anything in return. Perhaps there was something I could gift her for her kindnesses.

I pulled her into a hug, thanking her for her support. "I truly appreciate everything you've done for me. When you have a free weekend, please contact me, and I'll make sure there are complimentary accommodations for you and a friend for a long weekend at Abigail's estate. I'm sure she'd love to have you." If there was one thing my mother taught me, it was that showing your appreciation was as important as doing the good deed itself.

My phone sounded with an odd series of beeps. I thanked Olivia again and stepped into the hall to see a weather warning of high winds and torrential rains this afternoon. Being the responsible adult I was, I skipped visiting a few professors and got back on the road. Because I'm neurotic, I replayed every sentence exchanged this whole weekend as I drove. One, in particular, from Annalise, made my chest ache. *Alex needs me more than ever.* What did she mean by that? Did it come from Alex? She must have meant since I arrived at Eloheh Farms, but I was picking up something more than that. *Hmm?*

Picking up where I left off— over thinking—I perseverated. I pondered our room assignments at the inn. Did Abigail have guests staying this week? Would I be putting her out? Or worse! Would I need to share a room with Alex?

I quickly yelled at my phone, engaging the accessibility feature, and immediately dialed Abigail.

"Hey, Abs. Me again," I didn't wait for a response. "Question. Do you have paid guests staying with you this week?" Powering through my questions, I stopped abruptly, holding my breath, trying not to overthink this.

She snorted what sounded like snot down her throat, "Not immediately. Friday and Saturday, the inn is having a Fall-Out Party. Get it? Fall. Out. Never mind. Three of our four rooms are booked. Why are you concerned?"

How could she not put it all together? "Sweetie, do the math—five rooms total. Three rooms are rented, that leaves one bedroom for me, and you live in the last one. Where will Alex sleep?" My indignation was misplaced; we'd already done the dirty deed multiple times, all on the same night. Though, she didn't need to know that.

She gasped. "The horror of it!" *Said with typical Abigail dramatics.* "Of course, I can do the math. Can't you be adults and enjoy your side of the bed? The alternative is sleeping on a blow-up in my bedroom, listening to Elias snore. Trust me when I tell you, Alex is a much better choice." *Instead of never getting ahead, it's never catching a break!*

I wailed my despair, "Fine. I'll deal with it. Hopefully, he'll go back to the farm, and we won't be in a situation like that. Anyway, I'm twenty minutes out. Need anything from the grocery store? I'm stopping for sandwich stuff and some snacks. I bet you'd like a carton of strawberry ice cream, right?" I plied her with her kryptonite. I needed her weakened when I asked for another favor later tonight.

"Oh, yes. Definitely, and a couple of cartons of skim milk. I'm on a diet." *Seriously?*

"Then why get the ice cream?" I countered sardonically.

Humpf. "Because I'm getting the skim milk! Duh?"

"Right. See you soon. Text me if you think of anything else."

Abigail was my best friend, but trying to follow her logic was like waiting for water to boil—frustrating. Pulling into the store parking lot, I saw she had texted me.

Don't forget to get a big box of condoms. (eggplant emoji; various heart and winking emojis)

I didn't respond. If she thinks I'm fucking Alex two bedrooms over, she's on drugs.

Chapter 20

ALEX

"God damn it, woman. I've missed you!" I said, hissing into her neck. My cock throbbed as I pressed my steel rod into her soft, wet pussy. Every part of her smooth, tanned body molded to mine each time I pumped into her, relieving me of my built-up stress.

Of course, I felt weird fucking my intern two doors down from my best friends, but I got over it as she walked into the kitchen in tiny cotton shorts and a thin sweatshirt that read, "Try Me." *Fuck, yeah, I'll try you.* Two pizzas were laid out on the long, center island just like they had four freaking years ago when this all began. So help me, God, if grease slips down her chin again, I will hike her up on the island and fuck her on the pizzas that mocked me.

Sadly, she blotted the double cheese and pepperoni pizza, effectively cock-blocking me. *Touché Madame!* Elias sauntered in. His hair was wet, his beard longer than I'd ever seen it, stopping in front of me with his hands on his hips.

"Do I need to remind you how to behave in front of a woman, ass-wipe?" *Aww. Hear those words of endearment?*

"Do I need to remind you that you're the ass-wipe that seduced a young girl who *only* needed a ride to Mystic and not a permanent fixture in her life?" *I loved this game.*

Elias chest-bumped me, grabbing two slices of pizza and a paper plate *because he was housebroken now*. Piling on the salad, Abigail walked in, also looking squeaky clean.

"Hello, boys and girls. How are we tonight?" Her condescending tone alerted us to her sassy mood. "No one is leaving this room tonight until we agree on the sleeping arrangements this weekend. My guests are arriving Friday, and I need to plan accordingly." Little Miss Innkeeper pointed her finger first at Seneca, then at me. My eyes blew wide, hurt.

"I'm not your problem, innkeeper-lady. She is," I said, pointing to Seneca, who started choking on her pizza.

I jumped off the stool I was perched on, rushed around the counter, and pressed my chest against her back, prepared to do the Heimlich maneuver when she spit out a wad of melted cheese.

"You can step back, Alex. I'm fine. Ugh! I hate it when half the cheese is down your throat, and the other half is still in your mouth." Her face was red and getting redder when she saw us all looking at each other at the innuendo. "Fuck you all!" she berated us and stormed into the dining room with her plate.

That's why we got naked after Elias and Abigail were fast asleep. It was a great bedtime story I'll look forward to telling our children one day. *Children?*

Elias banged on Seneca's bedroom door before the sun came up.

"Princess! Get your ass up, and I'm not talking about Seneca. We have fences to erect. Not your dick. I'll see you downstairs in fifteen minutes."

The sass in his voice brightened my day only slightly less than running my hand down Seneca's curvy ass. I smacked her cheek, watching her flesh ripple to a stop. *Yeah. Mornings with Seneca—the best!*

Her eyes snapped open, and she reflexively clubbed me in the chest. "What the hell is going on here? First, my door, now, my ass. What's a girl got to do to get some sleep around here?" Dark brown eyes bore into my blue ones. I waggled my brows, insinuating something altogether too dirty for her. Her eyebrows rose to her hairline, supported by a snarky retort, "And I don't mean giving you a blow job!"

She shifted her body to the edge of the bed. Petulant and provocative, this woman had it all. "Aw, come on, Sen, you know you want to," I crooned, reaching out to touch her velvety skin.

A not-so-ladylike growl sounded in her throat. "Touch me, and you die." *What a way to go.*

Seneca was a mercurial creature. A lesson I've learned the hard way. The trick to not getting steamrolled by her was to know just how far to push before getting out of the way. I'm going to assume I reached that line and rolled off the opposite side of the bed to safety.

I took one more pass up her exposed ass right up to her delicate neck, lust exuded from my eyes like a bullet train to my dick. "I'm off to save the planet. You are an inspiration and a worthy opponent in life and bed. I loved every minute of it." I didn't wait for a reply, gathered my pajama bottoms, and streaked across the hall to my room for a shower and change.

Abigail was frying up eggs and bacon as Elias made coffee and set the table. Watching these two move around each other in a perfectly synchronized dance reminded me of my parents. Each had their morning responsibilities that were accomplished without a single word being said. Small smiles and gentle touches were the only words needed to feel close and appreciated. I wanted that, too, more than I thought I did.

Being the humble guest that I was, I offered assistance to my friends. "I'll be over here if you need anything," I sang, scratching Benny's ears. I'm ashamed that I didn't know where he slept last night. At home, he bounced from my room at night to Seneca in the morning. But this was new territory for him, and I hoped he hadn't gotten into trouble.

Seneca emerged dressed in tight jeans, a turquoise turtleneck that outlined her perfect curves, and her hair pulled into a high ponytail. I forcibly had to restrain myself from reaching out and hauling her ass to my lap for a deep kiss. My desire didn't matter because she only had eyes for Benny.

"Come on, big boy, let's get you outside for a walk." He smiled and thumped his tail against the center island, waiting for his leash to be hooked to his collar. "Maybe Amy the Great will introduce herself to you today. She's playing bashful." Benny panted, clueless as to what she was talking about. *I want a video of that meeting. Chicken vs. Dog. Feathers everywhere, and ATG, hanging limply from his slack mouth.* Seneca was right. I'm a sick fuck.

When she left the house, the door slammed behind her, and the proverbial music began.

Abigail: When did the two of you start fucking? *Does four years ago count?*

Elias: I knew you two would figure it out. *Thank you, friend.*

Abigail: If you hurt her, I'll break your dick off, fry it up, and force-feed it to you for breakfast. *Harsh!*

Elias: How did you get her to come around? *Grief sex.*

I interrupted the interrogation abruptly. "Boy, you two have a lot on your mind. All you need to know is that it's consensual, and our terms of engagement change daily. That's all."

My dear friend Elias erupted in a barrel-chested laugh, pointing at me, "You got that right. She's a tough nut to crack." *She almost broke my nuts last night.*

Abigail flipped off the gas stovetop, sliding eight eggs onto a platter and collecting a dozen pieces of toast stacked right next to them. After placing them on the table, she lifted the bacon from the grease-soaked paper towel, piled it onto another plate, and handed it to Elias to set on the table.

"You know she has OCD, right?" Her accusatory tone wasn't appreciated.

I rolled my eyes, annoyed. "Yes. She told me."

"So, you know, then, it isn't the kind where she knocks on a door three times asking if you're there? None of that repetitive stuff. She does, however, need order. A plan, like I do. She gets anxious if you switch things up on her, especially without warning." Again, with the finger pointing.

I stood up, collected a mug off the counter, and poured my coffee, with a drop of milk. "Listen. I'm fully aware of how Seneca's brain works. She's made it abundantly clear what sets her off. But what I can tell you that you might not know is that she uses sex as a release valve. Not that I'm complaining. On the contrary, I'm happy to oblige."

My two good friends' jaws hung in shock. Their eyes moved back and forth without moving their heads until both landed on me. "She's a s-sex j-junkie?" Elias sputtered out. Followed by Abigail, "She's a slut?" No stuttering attached. They were so cute.

The side door slammed, and all eyes focused on Seneca. "You better not be talking about me," she accused, releasing Benny from his leash.

I stood up abruptly, grabbed my plate and coffee, and moved to the guest dining room. I was done with this morning's interrogation and needed to confirm Tiny's arrangements with the transport company. Choking down a forkful of eggs, I made the call apprehensively.

A deep grumble echoed through the phone, "Yeah, boss?"

I chuckled, knowing that was half a day's worth of words for my right-hand man.

"Good morning, Tiny. I got your fax. Everything looks like it is in order. It's killing me to spend five thousand dollars to transport my cows. It's only three fucking hours to get them loaded and moved. Highway robbery!" I yelled, sipping my coffee too fast, burning my tongue.

More grumbles. "I thought so, too, but only three livestock transports are available next week. Our hands are tied. Sorry, boss."

It wasn't his fault, and he knew it, but that didn't stop him from absorbing the rejection and consequences of the people he cared for. His heart was bigger than his brawny body. "Are you ready to receive them?" Tiny interjected hesitantly.

That's a good question. Elias and I had made good progress setting up a temporary pen that would allow them to move about, but it was a tight fit. The barn stalls were also snug, but it would have to do until I could figure out how to house them better. This whole cluster-fuck of a situation was wearing me down. Since I arrived late Sunday evening, Elias and I worked non-stop to get everything prepared. He even hired two friends to lend a hand, allowing us to complete both projects simultaneously. It's Wednesday, and our water supply at the farm was almost depleted. The pit in my stomach turned sharply, and I dropped my fork to my plate. I forced myself to breathe, but panic gripped my chest, creating more panic.

"Ship them now!" I barked, running out of the dining room into the back hall bathroom. Dropping to my knees, I shoved my phone out of the way. Painful heaves launched my breakfast into the toilet. It took several minutes to figure out if I'd hurl again until I heard Tiny yelling my name, distracting me from my abrupt evacuation.

Swallowing back more bile, I forced myself to respond. "I'm f-fine. Ship the cows and chickens. Tell me when they'll arrive. And, Tiny? I couldn't have done this alone. I can't thank you enough for your hard work and care. It means the world to me."

Dead silence permeated the ether. Surprisingly, that said more to me than any words he could have mustered—another reminder that actions speak louder than words. The line went dead as I scrubbed my scruff, facing another symbol of my circumstances—a toilet bowl. How was I going to get through this? Better yet, how was I going to overcome it?

Knuckles knocked lightly on the door, breaking my lament, "Are you okay?" Every day, someone asked me that. And every day I had a harder time keeping a strong façade. I didn't have it in me anymore.

"No," I whispered. I stood holding my head, burdened with an encroaching headache.

The door creaked open, and a soft hand touched the middle of my back, calming yet supportive. Making my breath hitch. A towel appeared before me offered by her other hand. I didn't deserve her. I'm a dumpster fire with no chance at being extinguished. "Alex?"

My eyes jerked up, catching my tired, bloodshot eyes, sallow cheeks, and disheveled hair in the mirror. Abigail stood behind me, not the woman I thought would save me. It was a punch to the gut. Seneca was done with dealing with me. I wasn't her responsibility. I'd obviously failed her miserably.

"We've got you, sweetie. You're not doing this alone." She pushed the towel into my hands and backed out of the room.

I watched her in the mirror. Eyes down. Lips pouting. She was a beauty. Too good for my asshole friend. An asshole who took me in, bent over backward to help me, and did everything in his power to make this move successful. I should consider a new pet name for him. Just not now.

As promised, my girls and the rest of the crew arrived two days later. When a beat-up pickup pulled in behind the livestock trailer, I almost cried. Tiny emerged carrying a thermos in one hand and work gloves in the other. We stared at each other, strengthening our brotherhood and recommitting ourselves to one another.

Elias thrust out his hand, "Good to see you, little guy," he said amusingly. *That was the joke of the century.* They shook hands,

Elias clapping him on the shoulder. "Sure could use your meat hooks. We need both indoor and outdoor troughs assembled immediately. I'm sure the herd will be thirsty after their trip. Lumber and supplies are behind the barn to make stands. Troughs are arriving any minute, and—here's the feed truck. Right on time."

I appreciated Elias taking the lead today. Once my girls are unloaded, they'll need milking and washing down. Before dinner last night, I laid the hay in their stalls, leaving the feed to be divvied into plastic barrels we'd cut in half earlier. Winter was upon us, and planning ahead made the process much easier later.

A long tail of silky hair flashed in my periphery, distracting me from helping the truck drivers unload their cargo. Seneca's curved ass swung side-to-side in tight, dark-washed jeans. She was mesmerizing.

A hard smack clunked me in the back, mocking me. "You're looking at the wrong behind, my friend." He turned me by the shoulders, pointing me to the hauler. "There, those are the pieces of ass needing you today. Go!" *I changed my mind. I'm still keeping the name asshole.*

Seneca smiled at me coyly, but I was still salty she hadn't come to my aid earlier. Where the hell did, she go? I tipped my dusty red ball cap to her, recognizing her loveliness. She was a showstopper. It would be several hours later before the mystery of her disappearance was solved.

Late October brought early sunsets, forcing an early stop to productivity. Abigail made up a room for Tiny for tonight. He'd have to settle for a motel if he stayed longer. Farm duties were done for the day, and Elias commissioned me to hang twinkle lights around an extended firepit patio. The estate's Annual Fall-Out Party was another way for Abigail's community to gather after a long summer maintaining the community garden she'd begun when she first arrived four years ago. It seemed the townsfolk weren't too excited to see a new Farnsworth family member in the area. After so many decades of inferred espionage, Abigail won them over with her sincerity and grit. It didn't hurt that her inn attracted countless visitors, increasing tourism in the area. It was fascinating how a simple garden changed years of bad feelings. It was truly remarkable.

Even before I met Abigail, I knew I'd do anything to aid her in her vision. Then, after meeting Seneca and learning everything she created at the inn, I sought out other reasons to visit. We didn't keep a tally of who did what, though, after this past week, I was sorely running in the deficit.

"What's next?" I asked Elias.

He pulled on his beard, searching for something around the space. "Firewood. It's over by the barn. We need to keep this fire roaring for three hours. Cut enough to meet that criterion. I will hook up the hay wagon to the John Deere." In typical fashion, we walked together, commenting on how dry the season was or the cost of fuel to run our equipment. Our *Man-speak* was strong.

Elias walked along the path to the back of the barn, and I peeked in to check on my girls when I almost passed out. My fifteen hundred-pound beauties were rubbing their behinds against a tall post in the middle of the pen. A dozen long, stiff scrub brushes were drilled into the post, giving them the best rub they'd had in weeks.

When I'd gained awareness, I saw rows and rows of red gingham cloth attached like a shower curtain running between the pens. W*ho did this?* I leaned over a stall, watching how cute Eunice looked, scrubbing her ears back and forth against the post, humming in delight. Bernice sidled up to the other side, rubbing her back haunch like her ass was on fire. Emma and Belinda patiently awaited their turn grunting and bumping each other. I burst into laughter, enjoying the view, finally finding something to be happy about. I swear my shoulders dropped three inches, and the crick in my neck disappeared. After so many days of keeping myself together, I felt a moment of peace.

Soft boots rustled in the hay until they were right behind me. "So, you like it?" Seneca's voice sang like an angel who answered my prayers. I looked at her dumbfounded, unable to believe she cared so much about my cows' happiness that she'd make them freaking curtains.

She stopped short and bumped her hip into mine.

I grinned until my cheeks hurt. It was a good thing my hands were stuffed into my pockets, or I'd have grabbed both her hips and slammed them flat into mine groin. "I've never seen such happy heifers," I said, feeling higher than a kite.

"I'm working on getting rubber mats for the winter. Our girls need to keep their hooves on Cloud 9 if they are to pick up their milk production. The supplier couldn't get them here until next week. Each cow-lady will have her own."

Cow-lady. That was cute, like her.

Breaking my own rules, I swung her around into my arms, pulling her tightly against my chest. Her hands slid around my neck, pulling my hair forward until my lips were a whisper away from hers. "I told you I'd have your back, Mr. Valize. Did you doubt me?" She taunted me with her mouth, though my dick felt the pain more acutely.

Did I doubt her? Maybe? She disappeared for two days. I saw her at dinner. Then she was gone again. I tried her door late last night, but she wasn't there. After two nights, I became seriously worried something was wrong. When I asked Abigail where she was, she replied, "Busy." Women were so infuriating. At least she knew Seneca was alive and well. *So, this is what my little firecracker had been up to.*

I traced my tongue along her bottom lip, missing its sweetness. "More like concerned," I murmured, sucking that lip inside my mouth. *Hmm.* She tasted like apple pie. *I loved apple pie.*

A big bark called into the barn, and it wasn't Benny. "Stop fucking with the help, Alex. You have wood to chop; yours might be next if you don't finish it quickly." Elias had a unique motivational style I couldn't deny.

"Baby, I need my wood. Thank you for everything. My girls, thank you, too." I pressed another hot, wet kiss to her pouty lips, squeezing her luscious ass tightly.

Tit for tat, she smacked my ass as she turned toward the house. "Our girls have a date with their new vet in two weeks," she hollered over her shoulder. "She'll test their milk for purity, and you'll know if you're back in business." Those big, brown eyes winked at me as she sauntered away. That ass was mine tonight. No excuses.

Chapter 21
SENECA

Good news came at a cost today. Leo scheduled a conference call this morning to share the final test results. The radon test he ordered for the house was positive and at dangerous levels, making our decision to drink bottled water immediately an excellent one. However, I'm terribly concerned about Alex's long-term health. The second test was, thankfully, better.

Leo shared the test results on his shared screen, stating without emotion, "Radon is fairly simple to rectify, though it costs a pretty penny. An aeration unit will be installed at the water supply to the house, not in the house, and, depending on where that connection lies, could cost up to four thousand dollars. Without getting too technical, the radioactivity will be halved in about four days. *Radioactivity?!* Given the high levels, I suggest keeping it going for two weeks to be sure your system is crystal clear. Professionals will safely remove the filters from the aerator unit and resecure new ones each week. Radon is a very volatile material and requires special training to handle it."

Alex and I gasped, but Leo continued unfazed. "I know it sounds scary, but it's done effectively all the time. I recommend this company for a quote," he said, pushing a sheet of paper across the table. "They are very reputable, reliable, and competitive in price. Next, let's talk about the outlying areas of your farm. We know nitrogen levels rise exponentially the closer you get to the creek. The good news is that the sample I took on the opposite side of your property only had traces of ammonia residues. That means your family and neighbors shouldn't be affected, provided remediation begins quickly."

Another duet of gasps turned to shouts of joy and hugs. I hadn't realized I was holding my breath—and felt lightheaded with the good news. Finally, something good to celebrate.

Alex asked a dozen more questions about logistics, but I grabbed my computer to research how these toxins can affect a human, specifically Alex's. Additionally, I trolled The Johns Hopkins Hospital toxicology department, identifying a doctor I could hunt down to do some tissue sampling on Alex. His local doctor would be useless in this scenario, and I wouldn't let his body fester like his mother's did without receiving the proper treatment as soon as possible—not on *my* watch.

When he got off the phone, I slammed my computer shut. Today we would celebrate good news only. His mouth contorted from smiling to pain to hope. I felt every emotion deep within me, wishing I could do more for him. Happy cows or not, it wouldn't fix his heartbreak or pad his bank account.

I reached for his hand, needing his warmth. He took mine, pulling me into his lap on the couch where we had taken the call. His lips found my neck, feathering kisses behind my ear, sending shocks of electricity between my thighs. His arms hugged me so tightly I could barely breathe. Wrapping my arms around his broad shoulders gave me the security I've always wanted in a relationship.

We were forming a bond that elevated me to a place I hadn't felt since I was a child. I fought the idea that he wouldn't need me anymore when this mess was over. Was the reason we came together only because of grief and fear? Did he like me enough to fight for our future? Did I want his smart-assed mouth in my future? All those thoughts were put on hold as he looked around the room to be sure we were alone.

Alex wasted no time wrapping my legs around his muscled body, lifting me by my ass, and walking me over to the grand stairway at the front of the house. I kissed him deeply as he dodged lamps and side tables, then dropped me to my feet on the first stair. He pulled my high ponytail back forcing my chin even higher, growling into my mouth.

"Get that sweet ass up those stairs—now! I want you on my bed naked by the time I get there." He bit my lower lip gently, palming my breasts through my bra. "Go!"

I loved "Demanding Alex." Any doubts about his strength as an owner, provider, friend, or leader went out the window when we were together. He's the only person in my life I have handed over control of my body and mind. I had to be strong, independent, resilient, and humble every day. Surrendering to anyone, let alone a man, hadn't been fathomable. I was a survivor. Survivors don't surrender. They fight and claw for everything they want. I was the personification of a survivor until Alex sent me to his bed. Then I turned to jelly. Not because he wanted me to, but because he's earned the right to turn me inside out.

He carried an uncorked bottle of wine and two glasses when his door swung open. My heart sang at his thoughtfulness. *Had he always been this way and I was too stubborn to allow him to be himself?* I laughed, *Hell no.* That sexy, mouthy asshole showed his true colors long before today. I suppose it made this gesture even more worthy of my attention.

"Hi, Honey. I'm home!" he cackled, slamming the door closed with his foot. "I see you've been a good listener *for once,*" he mumbled.

"I heard that!" I replied with feigned insult, fighting off a smile.

"Don't get me wrong, Sen. I love fighting with you, though sometimes I want the low-hanging fruit—like your ass in my bed when I ask for it."

He was beyond funny and adorable. He was a smooth talker and sexy as all get out; I couldn't deny him anything. "Then why don't you bring that fine ass and bubbly over to the bed and let me fix you a snack," I purred, spreading my legs wider. His eyes blew wide as he licked his lips, moving quickly across the room.

He set the glasses on his nightstand, immediately unzipping his pants in one hand while bobbling the wine in the other. What he was trying to do was almost comical, but laughing wasn't what I wanted from him. I wanted serious Alex. Dark romance Alex. The one that made me burn and beg for more. I wanted his cock so deep inside me I would choke on it. I couldn't wait any longer. Rolling to my side, I relieved him of the bottle, freeing his hands to remove his clothes faster.

Left only in his boxer briefs and shirt, I took control. "Here. Let me," I pleaded, licking my lips. His eyes locked onto mine as I motioned him between my thighs. He stopped as his face hovered over my sex, licking his own lips.

He stared at my pussy in reverence, clit pulsing and glistening with wetness. I watched as he flattened his tongue licking my slit, humming as he went. My back arched unable to hold still. Sparks ignited all over my body wanting him more. Needing him more. His tongue made tiny flicks all around my tight bundle of nerves but never directly on it. It maddened me.

"Alex, please!" I was not beyond begging. That mouth of his brought me right up to the edge and left me hanging. My eyes pierced his as he looked up. "Do not do that to me," I begged.

He ignored my pleas in place of hot, wet kisses traveling from my pussy to my belly button up to between my breasts. He purposefully ignored my aching breasts to find my pouting lips, where he devoured me like a man starved. I tasted myself on his lips and tongue, reveling in my musky scent. It wasn't that I hadn't heard about women tasting their essence. It was taboo. So when I finally had the opportunity to do it for myself, it blew my mind how erotic and palatable it was. I now knew why men loved it so much. He was leading me down a dark road I didn't know if I wanted to go down. Every minute with him brought my desire to greater heights, and there wasn't anything I wouldn't do for him at that moment.

"I have something special for you," he growled into my ear.

"W-what is that?" Never a shy woman, my anticipation was killing me.

Slowly, he climbed higher over my body, presenting his taut six-pack over my face as he moved. His body rose even higher bringing his big, red crown that peeked out from under his briefs, directly to my mouth. My mind reeled at his devious plan, loving what would come next.

"Pull my underwear down, Seneca," he challenged me. I did what he said, working them down his body using my feet when my arms wouldn't reach any further. He chuckled, "You really are a clever girl. Now suck me like you mean it."

Fuck! His dirty mouth lit another furnace inside me, threatening to incinerate me. My arms were pinned tightly between his knees and my sides, leaving only my mouth for his pleasure. Saliva built up in my mouth seeing his pre-cum seeping from his tip. My heart raced as I looked up at Alex, watching me with an appreciation for the gifts that he was about to receive. *God bless, Alex.*

Without humility, I opened my mouth wide, accepting his pulsing cock deep into my mouth, then pulled it out with a pop. His legs tremored and his hands grabbed the headboard to steady himself. Without my hands to keep control, Alex guided himself deeper and deeper until he reached the back of my throat.

"Fuck, Sen!" he groaned, loving my mouth. I had plans for this cock tonight, but this—this was off the rails. "Do that again," he pleaded, slipping my hands free and grabbing his ass cheeks. I needed to touch him, feel him, and claw into his skin, making him mine.

He pulled back, letting me breathe deeply. He may have had the upper hand though I knew, beneath it all, I was the one making his every dream come true.

I hummed, licking my lips and challenging him to enter my hungry mouth again. He guided himself back in, rocking gently, bumping past my uvula, making me gag. I wanted more, and the next time he pulled his rigid staff back I told him.

"More," I cried out, saliva dripping down my chin. I didn't know when I became a dirty girl. I'd never wanted to let a man have complete control over me. I didn't trust they would know how to play with me without hurting me, and I hadn't wanted to take that chance until now.

"Fuck, yeah. Keep breathing through your nose. Relax your jaw because you're going to take every inch of my giant cock."

His filthy mouth spurred me on, especially when I'd already taken him past the back of my throat. I struggled to take his length and his gentle thrusts. He kept his eyes on me. Watching, gauging, exploring every inch of my throat. I wasn't sure if it was lack of oxygen or a spiritual awakening, but my mind floated effortlessly to a place of surrender and calm. I was so lost in this experience that I almost didn't hear him screaming.

"Fuck, Sen, I'm coming, baby. Swallow every fucking drop of me. Take it all. Yes, baby. Like that. Yessss!" He praised me through every spray of his creamy cum dripping down my throat. I did as he said, and swallowed like my life depended on it, and it most likely did. A moment later and he slowly extricated his spent cock from my sore, red mouth. I was mute, unscrambling my emotions and feeling relief at having survived my first deep-throat experience. *Shit! I didn't want to love it, but I did. I really, really did.*

Alex lowered his body carefully. His face glowed with perspiration adoringly. It appeared I wasn't the only one having had an out-of-body experience. He captured my face in his calloused hands, searing my mouth with his own. Claiming me. It felt like a promise, but I wasn't sure. The kiss ended with him rolling to his side and pulling my hips close to his. We didn't speak; we didn't need to. His eyes said everything I needed to hear; his fingers threaded through my hair lulling me into his orbit. For someone who didn't have an orgasm, my mind sure felt like it had.

"Sen, that was the most erotic experience of my life. That mouth is not only sassy, it's gifted. Incredibly gifted. It felt like an aura surrounded us the whole time. I can't explain it. More like a spiritual journey than a mind-blowing blow job." He kissed me gently, rubbing his thumb across my cheek as he held my face to his.

My fingers traced his bottom lip from corner to corner, studying the tiny smile lines that crept up his gorgeous face. I could see his life etched into this face. It was a work of art distinctly his own. My appreciation of every chapter he shared with me made tonight ethereal. He was right about the aura surrounding us. I could feel it wrapping itself around our bodies with love and safety. It was beautiful and undeniable. But was I ready to declare my love for him? If he knew how much he meant to me, would he guilt me when I left to explore my future? I wanted to say the words so badly.

"I felt my mind let go and my body flew away, Alex. It was an exquisite feeling I've never had before. You're trying to turn me into a submissive, and we know that isn't going to happen." I laughed off my feelings, knowing I was a liar. If I was ever to be submissive to a man, it would be to him.

He grimaced, breaking eye contact. His hand left my face and slid down to my hip, pulling me closer to his growing erection.

"You can't blame a guy for trying," he said lightly, covering up what looked like disappointment. His hand snaked between us, using his fingers to burrow deep inside my folds. "Let me try again. I'll try not to disappoint."

I pushed back from his chest in protest. I didn't need to come. *Did I?* I'd mentally rejected what our moment together meant, what it meant to both of us. My excuses were real, practical, and appropriate for our situation. He's still my boss, and we still have boundaries. *Another lie, I tell myself.* Why does sex fry my brain? It's supposed to relieve stress, not create more.

Alex studied my face, unsure of my response. He pressed my knees wider with his knee, hooking his fingers into my pussy, confusing my brain even more.

"Shit, Alex. That... we should... more!" I screamed just as he hit the right spot. Fuck if I didn't need this release. I'd deal with my weak, fickle, confused self later. "Oh god, Alex. Yes! I'm afraid to admit your hold on me—but those fingers!"

His devious smile was infectious, and I smiled back, leaning in for one more kiss. I had to get out of this room. It was a trap. One I was sure I'd never be able to leave if I stayed.

"Greedy girl," he playfully chastised me followed by a panty-melting kiss.

There was a loud knock on the door. *Saved by the bell.* "What!" we both shouted.

"Jesus Christ, you two. Are you fucking again? We have things to do. Alex, I'm sure you can finish up in ten minutes, so you'd both better be in the front parlor in fifteen."

I tucked my head again as he hummed happily into my hair. "We need our own place," he grumbled, sliding his hands down my hips to my ass. *He loved my ass. I loved his hands, and his fingers, and...*

I dipped lower, sucking his left nipple, pulling another appreciative moan. "Right after we save the universe, your farm, and your life." *The truth hurt?*

His hands moved so fast to my shoulders that they were a blur. "What do you mean by my life?" *What's wrong with me?*

My big, fucking mouth struck again. "Nothing. Nothing. It's, just that, I'm concerned about how long you've been drinking radon-infested water. I'd like you to get tested," I said encouragingly. "Just to be on the safe side." I bit my lip knowing how OCD that sounded. He wasn't my husband, brother, or even my boyfriend. I had no jurisdiction over him, yet I couldn't let something dark and sinister grow inside him.

His whole body recoiled, sitting up on the side of his bed. I moved beside him, threading my fingers into his long, dirty blond locks. "I'm sure you're healthy as a horse, Alex. I'm a worrywart. I perseverate over everything—especially you." My voice faded, knowing I'd, again, said too much.

He shook my hands free of his hair, wrapping his arms tightly around my torso. My heart broke for him again. Our lives were becoming too scary. "Thank you," he whispered, then began dressing silently.

Abigail had spread four sheets of paper on the antique wood coffee table, one for each of us. Alex sat in the brocade cloth winged-back chair, and I sat on the floor between his thick, muscular thighs. I still felt his musk in my nostrils and had trouble focusing on my friend barking orders.

"I have taken the liberty of assigning each of you a list of responsibilities before, during, and after the party. We have one more day before my guests arrive, then one more until the town arrives." Her tone was even, but she shifted in her seat like it was on fire. It appears her anxiety was getting the best of her.

"First, Seneca, move your things into Alex's room, he has more space. And, frankly, by the way, you two hump each other like rabbits, it shouldn't be a hardship." She winked at us fondly. Second, Alex, stack all that firewood you *haven't* split yet behind the cider stand Elias will be building today." *Passive aggressive was one of Abigail's strong suits.*

Unable to sit anymore, Abigail skated around the table to stand before us. "Lastly, Seneca and I will be baking and setting up the dessert table. Saturday afternoon, we'll lay everything out, and our guests can enjoy themselves. Oh, one last thing. Nelson Jenkins and his band will arrive this afternoon to set up and get a sound check. Elias, please make sure he has access to electricity before then." Exhausted, she fell back onto the sofa.

I clapped supportively. "Very organized, Abs. Props to you. Where are the beer and cider coming from?" This was *my* passive-aggressive response to all the things Abigail left out of her plan. She always did. ADHD could be a real bitch at times.

Her hand smacked her forehead. "Son of a bitch!" she screamed. "I knew I was forgetting something. I'll call the apple orchard immediately and have them deliver cider jugs on Saturday morning. Elias, would you collect the kegs from Anderson's Liquor Store in the morning?" Red blotches appeared on her cheeks, and my heart squeezed as I saw her plans almost turn to dust.

Elias got up and walked beside her, slinging his canon-sized arm over her shoulder. "Don't worry, princess. It's already done." He kissed her on the head and looked at her master list. At first, I didn't like Elias's choice of pet names for my friend. I guess it's fitting to watch how he bows to her demands and paves the way for her successes.

Studying the list, Elias set his princess at ease some more. "The bar is built; it just needs placing. The hay and the blankets you collected from the Goodwill are already on the wagon. And you can cross off fairy lights. Alex and I have already started hanging them. If only he wouldn't get distracted." Elias pierced a stare at him, tutted, and shook his head at me.

"Don't look at me!" I feigned innocence. "He made me go upstairs against my will." My theatrical show of indignation had us all laughing our asses off.

"Whatever," Abigail interjected. "I'm happy to hear all is going well. If you think of anything else we need to attend to, please let me know immediately. I can't thank you enough for supporting me. It's the one thing I feel I owe this town for allowing me to serve them this way."

Abigail took on more responsibility for her ancestors' questionable history than was necessary. Frankly, she didn't have to own any of it. She'd walked into a past she wasn't responsible for. When Mr. Brickner, a lawyer, called to inform her that she was the last living member of her family inheritance, dating back to 1832, she freaked out. Who wouldn't? Except the town wasn't thrilled with the possibility of another Farnsworth ruffling their feathers.

Alex wasted no time running to the barn to chop the wood, which he was rightfully accused of not cutting. I excused myself to call the local hospital to set an oncology appointment for Alex next week. *He could thank me later.* I had a nagging feeling that his parents suffered from radon poisoning that went undiagnosed. I could be wrong. *What the hell did I know about medicine?* For all I knew, the real culprit to their cancer was toxic dumping into the water system. My research and good intentions weren't going to bring his parents back from their car crash, but I would have moved heaven and earth to keep Alex from suffering from cancer.

Chapter 22

ALEX

Chopping wood was incredibly cathartic. The physicality, combined with heavy metal music, emptied my head faster than getting drunk. I don't recall how many splits I'd made, but the immense pile of firewood was enough to stack six feet high. I chucked wheelbarrow after wheelbarrow full of wood to the designated location. Unfortunately, Tiny left early this morning to rip out the fields of my precious contaminated crops. Annalise and Steve offered their help cleaning the fields and closing the house, too. I didn't know when I'd return to Pennsylvania, now that the place was uninhabitable. My heart broke again thinking about all the catastrophic things happening on my land. I wouldn't be surprised if there were a desecrated Indian burial ground beneath the earth for all the crappy things that plagued it. I'd have to ask Seneca if she knew of any incantations to heal it.

I hung the axe in the barn and walked to the other side, preparing to milk my girls before washing up for dinner. To my pleasure, Seneca was milking while having a full-on conversation with Emma.

"Are you liking your new abode? It's cute, right? I know the move was a pain but look at your new scratching post and pretty curtains to help keep the draft off you in the winter. I'll take them down in the summer so you get a nice breeze. Does that sound good?"

My cows mooed their appreciation as I stifled a laugh. Seneca was an enigma. One minute, she was a hot and feisty woman, the next, a playful girl talking to cattle. How she kept her cool throughout these past weeks shone a completely different light on her that I was too stubborn to see. For someone stuck in their ways, I was sure being schooled on the benefits of flexibility.

I swept up an empty tin pail and set it beside her as she pulled Emma's teats. Although she was the youngest cow of the bunch, she was a big producer. She deserved to have a heart-to-heart with the woman stealing my own.

"Hey, pretty lady," I said seductively.

Seneca looked over her shoulder and chuckled, "*Humpf.* Don't hit on my cow, mister. She's a lady and deserves your respect." Her shoulders shuddered, laughing.

I pulled off my ball cap, wiping my arm across my sweaty brow, letting my girl enjoy how it clung to my abs. *I saw her eyes on me.* "Oh, I respect the crap out of her. She does her job very well and never complains. She's a keeper." *A keeper? Who am I talking about?*

Considering my double entendre, she pressed her lips forward. "A keeper, huh? We'll see. That is if we're still talking about the cow?" She waggled her brows in challenge. I wasn't taking the bait. It'd just cleared my head, and I didn't want to talk about the future and whether she was part of it or not. As it was, Dr. Abel still hadn't yet approved the transfer of her internship, making Seneca skittish about the future.

I pulled up a stool, helped her finish all ten cows, and fed the chickens.

The illustrious Amy the Great emerged as if on cue, moving out of the bushes and into plain view. I'd seen Abigail talking to this bird dozens of times. It seems she's quite the "listener."

"Seneca, you've met ATG, right?" It was a dumb question. She'd lived here for months at a time. "Do you think it's time to introduce her to the new chicks on the block?" I said, chortling.

She rolled her eyes at my reference to the singing group. *I couldn't help it. It just presented itself so naturally.* Haughtily, she proclaimed, "ATG, ignore him. He knows not what he does." *Great! Now she's quoting the Bible.* "You should know better than to talk down to her. She'll tell Abigail, and you'll get it for sure." That's when she cracked a gorgeous smile. Her hand slapped me on the back, "Come on. Let's see if she'll play nice. All the other chicks will be jealous, though. Only ATG gets to lay eggs in Elias's crocs."

As it was, ATG did enjoy meeting the other chickens. Strutting herself past each nest like she was inspecting the rank and file. It was impressive; however, she bolted when the doors to the coop started to shut. *No one puts baby in a corner.*

These were the little things that kept me sane. Chickens with attitudes. Cows that scratched. Best blowjobs of my life. And being surrounded by people who genuinely cared about me. In all this bullshit, I could still say I'm truly blessed.

My dinner was interrupted by a call from Leo. I hadn't expected to hear from him since he'd completed the radon project. I excused myself from the table and walked out to the front porch, pacing up and down the wood slats that made up an extended sitting area.

"Hey, Leo. What's up?" I fought the bile rising in my throat. Leo calling could only mean one thing—bad news.

As usual, Leo's words were deadpanned and uninspiring. "I've heard back from the Monroe County Commissioner. He has reviewed your case and sent it to the County Commissioner, as well as the Governor's office."

Wait. What? "Why the Governor's office?"

"There have been several anonymous reports over the last two years of unethical cradle-to-grave disposal by a few manufacturing plants up north. It seems that they start the waste disposal process correctly, but when no one, like EPA inspectors, are looking, they take shortcuts, and the waste doesn't make it to their final resting spot."

I sat down with a thump. This was too much. Under the EPA's nose? *Come on!* "What the hell does that mean for me?"

There was so much dead air that I thought he'd hung up. "It means you have a case that warrants careful review and possible, considerable recompense. Someone from the state will contact you shortly. The County Commissioner is looking into all reports related to contamination since before he was elected. Keep your phone close by. And, Alex. You'd better find a lawyer, quick."

I scrubbed my face, wrapping my head around this new turn of events. "Thanks for the call, Leo. I'll keep my phone on me at all times. Take it easy."

I reached for the off button when he called through the receiver. "You're very lucky, Alex. That girl saved your life and your livelihood. Talk to you later."

The bottom dropped out of my belly. Seneca literally saved me. I thought only having her around to be supportive was her enough. She never once complained about the situation beyond moving her internship from one place to the next. She jumped in and researched the shit out of all aspects of water and soil remediation. She befriended every person, animal, and crop she met at Eloheh Farms. She'd even scheduled me a doctor's appointment to check me out. It's true she's been a pain in my ass for four years, but now—now she's . . .

Pulling myself together, I stuffed my phone back in my pocket, reminding myself to keep it close, as Leo said, and returned to the kitchen, hoping I could finish eating my chili without crying.

"You look like shit. Who called?" *Elias. My dear friend. Always quick with his wit and eloquent command of the English language.*

"I'm better looking than you, especially when you squirrel away cracker crumbs in your beard. You're an embarrassment to mankind," I snarked back. "For your information, that was Leo." I made a quick retelling of his remarks, then settled my gaze on my angel, Seneca. "You, my dear," I said, pointing my spoon directly to her stunned face, "literally saved my life and the lives of everyone and everything at Eloheh Farms. I'll forever be in your debt."

Her tanned skin blushed to a velvety rose, making her more beautiful than ever. I got up and weaved around the island counter to her spot at the table, and offered her my hands, face up. Tentatively, she took them, staring at me appreciatively. I opened my mouth, pushing my tongue against my cheek, then closing it. I tried twice more to utter a sound, only nothing came out. I scanned her face, memorizing every freckle and crinkle near her eyes to the sexy, red pout that challenged me daily. I sniffed, feeling a gush of emotion bubble up inside me, a whimpering sound traveling up from my chest through my throat. I yanked her to her feet, albeit roughly, and pulled her to me, burying my face in her hair and finally letting all my pent-up feelings flow freely.

In my peripheral vision, I saw Elias cradle Abigail on his lap, creating another bout of tears of how my future might look like if my relationship with Seneca could survive. After hearing all the bad news two weeks ago, I thought I'd purged myself of tears. However pathetic I thought they were, these tears felt more cathartic. Gratitude bubbled up, choking my words. I was well and truly humbled.

Seneca pushed me back, cupping my jaw and wiped my tears with her thumbs. "Hey, hey. Any intern would have done the same. I'm happy I could serve you when you needed it most."

Any intern? Was she really buying her bullshit?

"Stop it!" I barked at her, pulling my face from her hands. "I hate when you do that. Do not minimize your role in this whole tragedy. You're wrong if you think any intern would step up like you did. It didn't matter that you knew me or was pissed off at me for all those years. You stayed. You helped. You cared. You matter so much to me. I'll never be able to repay you. Do you understand that?"

Her eyes welled up, and she began to shake. I was torn between hugging her to death and spanking her ass red. Didn't she know her worth? In the end, I sat down, pulling her into my lap while my friends sat watching the whole fucking show. I couldn't wrap my head around how a strong person could have such low self-esteem buried deep within them.

Abigail chimed in. "Seneca has been a part of my life for a long time. She only knows how to give unconditionally. That's why it hurts her so much when her generosity is taken advantage of."

Abigail's soft, supportive words permeated my being. I now understood that, when I'd asked to stay in touch all those years ago, then did the complete opposite, I hurt her so deeply. Our first sexual encounter was off-the-charts incredible. It seemed, at least to me, a sympathetic vibration ran between us. That's what possessed me to want to stay in touch with her. Again, I was the idiot. No wonder she won't trust me.

"*Debwe*," Seneca whispered into my chest. "It's an Ojibwe word meaning steadfast and true, like a tree. My mother showed me how to speak to the them. Relationships are *debwe.* Their roots are deep and vast, growing big and tall when they're properly watered and fed by sunshine. She'd tell me to be a tree, give a sheltering hug when needed, and stay flexible in a storm. That's all I was doing, Alex. Being a tree."

I could picture a beautiful native woman and her equally beautiful young girl standing under a huge tree, like the maple we sat under at my farm. Handing down the best of her people's heritage, establishing Seneca's connection to the earth, her mother cleared a foundation for her to grow strong and proud. The act wasn't only poetic. It was respectful and wise. The levity of her message rang true, hitting the mark precisely where it needed to be—my heart. There were so many facets to this diamond in the rough, I could live a hundred years and still find more sparkles shining brightly.

Elias cleared his throat, sliding his wife to her feet. "We should call it a night. It's been a long day, and we have guests arriving early tomorrow. Abs, what do you need us to do before we go to bed?" He kissed her on the head and began cleaning up the kitchen while she looked over her To-Do list.

Seneca ran into the laundry room, returning with a basket full of sheets and towels. "Let me get these folded and upstairs. I'll help get the guest room looking sharp. One less thing to do in the morning," she said, out of breath, breezing through the kitchen to the front parlor to work.

I humbled myself, announcing, "The firewood is chopped and stacked as directed. I also dragged out those banquet tables from the barn and set them up so you can start decorating as soon as you'd like. What else can I help with?"

Abigail smiled gratefully, "Thanks, Alex. You've done so much already. There is one more big job you could help Elias with, though." She smirked like she held a secret. I knew I was in trouble when Elias returned her devilish grin. "We have a tradition our guests look forward to every year. Elias usually takes the lead, but I need him to be the hayride driver for the evening."

This all sounded so cryptic. "I'm afraid. What am I being volun-told to do?"

She shifted awkwardly, rolling her lips, stalling. "Okay. It's a pie-throwing contest. I need you to be the target." She threw her hands over her eyes and peaked through her fingers. "It's for charity!" she added exuberantly.

Well, if it's for charity...

I stroked my chin between my finger and thumb, considering my options: humiliate myself in front of all my new neighbors or humiliate myself in front of my friends by being an ungrateful guest. "I'm in," I said, placating them. "It's for the kids or whatever charity you're giving the money to."

Abigail walked over, planted a sweet kiss on my cheek, then stepped away to wipe down the counters. "Half the money goes to buying new supplies for the community garden, and the other goes to underprivileged children needing quality meals throughout the whole year. You're doing a good thing. It's only for an hour or so."

I grinned, taking it on the chin. Elias walked past me, smacking me on the back. "You're a good man, Charlie Brown."

My friends left the kitchen together, retreating up the backstairs to their bedroom, leaving me alone in the kitchen with my thoughts. My world was changing like a bullet train crossing the countryside, a blur. In the past, I knew what I wanted and how to get there. My training supported those aspirations, and the death of my parents forced me to accelerate my learning curve. Dane was a great brother who offered his support and friendship. However, he didn't need to feel the burden of my circumstances. Protecting him from this hardship was paramount to everything I would sacrifice or suffer through. He had to stay at school and chart his future without a noose around his neck. The farm was an albatross; one he didn't have to fight. That was my job as his big brother.

I gulped in a big breath, letting it fizzle out slowly. I needed more time to work on every aspect of my life. Sadly, the farm situation stood front and center before anything else. Scrubbing my face, I turned, bumping into Seneca.

"Hey," she whispered.

"Hey," I replied, sliding my thumbs through her belt loops and resting my forehead against hers. "I haven't asked you about your life. Is there anything I can do to make it easier?"

"Mmm," she hummed, sliding her hands up and down my biceps. "You're doing a great job keeping me relaxed. That's not easy for someone like me," she teased.

I nuzzled her nose, "I think your internship is making you restless. I'm concerned. Have you heard anything from your mentor?" Releasing one hand, I lifted her chin, looking carefully for signs of distress.

She pressed her lips together, fighting my stare, "Nothing yet. I suppose that's a good thing. It's the weekend. I doubt I'll hear anything. So, I decided to forget about it until Monday. No sense ruining my weekend." A nervous laugh trickled from her pretty mouth.

Here's the thing. Seneca always worries. It's her trademark. When she's not worrying about something, I become worried. She's the queen of stuffing down her emotions—not wanting to explore them. I thought I was bad, but she excels at it.

Chapter 23

SENECA

I think it's time for another session with Glenda, my therapist. It's been a few weeks, and Alex has pushed me out of my comfort zone with all his questions. I had a dumpster full of emotions needing to empty—the sooner, the better.

He's being so sweet. When he puts his hands on me, I forget there's a world around me. The euphoria I yearned for came when his mouth blissfully descended on mine. It was life-altering. Soft, pillowy lips that set my belly on fire when he smiled into my mouth. Had there been a way to bottle that feeling, I would be rich.

Our evening last night was filled with snuggles, whispers, and something I didn't want to put a name on. I'd never been in a real relationship for a reason. Whenever I gave my heart away, the person left me devasted and adrift. My mother. My father. Abigail. Even the facilities guy from DelVal. Though Remmy didn't make promises for the future, he only made plans to meet up, then ghosted me. I'd never felt lower when he did that.

Sleep came easily for me last night. I reached behind me, expecting to run my hands down Alexs' tight abs only to feel cold sheets. *What time was it?* I reached forward to his nightstand and turned the clock jerking the covers off. Nine o'clock! Half the day was gone. I slipped into a pair of leggings, a long tee and a DelVal sweatshirt skipping down the front stairs to an older couple and their bags.

"Hi!" I pivoted quickly. This was Abigail's business, and blowing by them wasn't an option. "I'm Seneca, Abigail's happy helper, does she know you're here?" I bit my lip, hoping they'd tell me she did.

The sixtyish man with broad shoulders and short brown hair tinged with silver offered, "Not yet. The front door was open and we figured it would be all right to come in. Were we wrong?" His concern was unfounded.

"Absolutely not!" I chirped. "It's an inn. The door is always open, unless it's between the hours of eleven and seven. Let me take your coats. Stow anything you like next to the grandfather clock, I'll take care of them shortly. Please follow me into the kitchen. I'm sure you'd love some tea or coffee."

His wife handed me her coat kindly. "My husband, Seymour, forgot to introduce us. I'm Fran, and we're exhausted lawyers from New York. We look forward to this weekend every year. Abigail is so warm and refreshing. She keeps us feeling young."

Wasn't she delightful.

"Abs! Look who's here. Seymour and Fran . . . Sorry, I don't know your last name yet." I hated not having all the details.

Abigail cut me off, "The Roses! Welcome back, friends. Just call him Sy," she said, scooting across the kitchen, divesting herself of her apron. He smiled so sweetly at Abigail like she was his own child. It's hard to think of him as a big-time lawyer when he pulled her into a hug. "Can I offer you something to drink? You know

I have everything, so don't be shy. I have your favorite pumpkin muffins coming out of the oven in a few minutes. Let's get you a nice spot in the front parlor. Touch anything. Read anything. You know the drill. It's so good to see you."

She rambled on, stringing all her thoughts together as she was prone to do. Leaving her to her guests, I found my escape. "Which bedroom can I drop their bags in?" I pointed toward the front stairs.

She dropped her head and closed her eyes; clue enough that she either forgot or still hadn't given it any thought. "I've prepared the blue room for them," she winced, remembering she needed official names for each suite.

I nodded emphatically, "Great choice." I looked at the sweet couple, "Have you stayed in the blue room before? It has a beautiful view of the gardens." I don't know why I was rambling. They seemed perfectly happy toodling around, looking from surface to surface. "I'll just . . ."

I took my leave, vanishing up the curved grand stairway, past the pastoral mural, and deposited their luggage in the appropriate room. *Tonight, we will name these damn rooms.*

The Roses left for sightseeing after their snack. Downtown Mystic had so many boutiques and historic sites to see. They should be busy for a while. This was my moment, to reenact the Great British Bakeoff, making enough pumpkin and zucchini muffins to feed an army. Next came four giant-sized iced chocolate cakes and ten dozen mini apple strudels with powdered sugar icing. The cider mill promised to bring twenty dozen donuts when they dropped the cider, and, so help me God, these people better finish every crumb. My ass can't take eating the leftovers.

It was well past noon before I could walk to the place where I would build my Zen garden and meditation pathway if my internship was granted. Regardless, I would return here in the spring to create the garden of my dreams. I sent Dr. Abel the sketches I'd made long ago and a manifest of costs, required materials, and specs. Over the years, I'd made several improvement while learning new techniques and materials to incorporate.

I'd built a quarter-acre community garden between the garage off the driveway and the barn. A butterfly garden filled with an array of purple asters, bee balm perennials, Egyptian star flowers, deep purple catmint bushes, and fuchsia cone flowers in the front yard by the property line. By mid-June, guests would be treated to a fairyland of hummingbirds, butterflies, and more while sitting on stone benches on either end. Abigail and I would go antiquing throughout the years, finding curious statues, fairy creatures, cherubs, and jeweled ornaments to enhance the whimsical sanctuary. Last year, we added four bird houses that attracted more more than birds from four states. Abigail's estate had become a favored destination for ornithologists, and I couldn't be prouder of her and what we'd accomplished as a team. *If only she'd decide on a catchier name for the inn than the address. The 441 Inn. Boring!*

Beyond the community area, there was a peaceful glen near a cluster of willow trees. This space would be my next creation. Woodpeckers could be seen banging their beaks, deer nibbled on soft roots, and every form of flora and fauna came alive. I envisioned a glorious stepped-down water feature lapping in a river of stones of all sizes. To the keen listener, the sounds would create a calming effect on the soul. For now, I sat on the scrub grass, my arms wrapped around my legs, lost in thought to the outside world.

My studies covered manicured gardens and mazes that were revered throughout Europe. Arctic tundra gardens were cleverly filled with specific varietals, while Eastern culture gardens favored gentle winding paths and meaningful statuary. My vision is a little of each with an emphasis on Zen styles. Winding paver paths ending in a concentric circle surrounded by water features, inspirational, discreet signage, and hardy plants that could survive the northeast winters. Guests would be encouraged to read an inspirational sign and think introspectively about life, their moral compass, or new possibilities. At the end of the maze, another sign would offer positive affirmations, congratulating them on being present and worthy. The effects of this prospective treasure brought tears to my eyes. Abigail offered a considerable endowment, and I had a lot to deliver when it was finished.

Sweet notes of sandalwood and patchouli caught my attention, filling me with dreamy desire. "There you are," the voice said, my eyes still closed, enjoying my final moments of envisioning. Alex dropped to my side, draping his warm, strong arm over my shoulders, and pulling me in tightly. He sat quietly letting me emerge from my dream state, not realizing how immersed I was in my thoughts.

I rested my head on his shoulder, smiling as if I had the most incredible orgasm. "Here I am," I sighed.

His throat hummed, warmed my belly, and sent tingles down my spine. "You look—sated. What have you been doing out here alone?" His insinuation illustrated his true character—sex focused.

"Just meditating on my Zen Garden project. I can see it so clearly; feeling the energy it would provide our guests. It's inspiring even to me."

Capturing my face in his hands, he looked as if cataloging every freckle there. "*You* inspire me." His husky voice lured me over to straddle his legs.

I bit my lip, grinding my hips into his crotch. "What else do I inspire, Alex?"

He rolled me to my back so fast I squealed. "This!" he said, driving his shaft against my jean-clad pussy. His sapphire eyes turned dark, as they locked onto mine. "I'm taking you here. Right now," he growled.

Without warning, he unbuttoned my pants and had them half down my thighs before I realized how painful crabgrass on your ass could feel. "Fuck, Alex. Give me your jacket." Needling pain scratched my tender skin every time he moved me.

He huffed out a breath, pulling his fleece over his head and shoving it under my backside. "You are prettier than any flower you've planted, baby."

That was the second most sexy thing he'd ever said about me. My confidence in this relationship grew, as did my libido. I responded unapologetically, "Are you saying that because I gave you a mind-bending blow job yesterday?"

Was I trying to minimize his compliment? I did it again.

He stopped his onslaught, face red with aggravation. "See? You did it again." *I know! I'm so sorry.* "If I say you're the most fucking beautiful flower in the god damned universe, then you'd better fucking say thank you. Do it again, and I'll tan that beautiful behind so hard you won't forget it. Understand?" *Yes, sir!*

I knew I fucked up. He had been working hard at not being an asshole, and here I was picking up where he left off. When would I learn?

I whispered what he needed to hear, "Thank you, Alex. That was one of the most beautiful things you've ever said to me. I-I . . . "

Did I want to say the L word? He must know I already like him. I couldn't be sure he felt about me the same way I was growing to think about him. Love seemed too soon. We were only beginning to be nice to each other. There were so many hurdles to overcome before saying those. . . irrevocable words to each other. Sex was not love, even if it transcended this dimension.

He pushed back to his knees, spreading my legs farther apart. He shook his head in what seemed to be confusion. He pulled me from my back, not so gently, I might add, then up onto my knees. I could clearly see the strain on his face, more than in his tight jeans.

"Open your mouth, Seneca," he demanded, and I opened wide.

"Get my fingers wet," he commanded, and I did.

"Do not take your eyes off my face," he hissed, as he pulled two wet fingers from my mouth and slid them under my panties.

"Ahh." His thick fingers entered my pussy without concern. "Damn! You have such long fingers." I wasn't complaining. Only I kept forgetting how they hit my special place so perfectly.

He growled again, "Then maybe you'll need another two fingers to help you remember to be gracious when given a compliment."

As he inserted two more fingers, half his hand in me, as he attacked my mouth, his tongue dueling with mine. He wanted to teach me a lesson, and I couldn't think of a better way for him to make his point.

"Ouch!" I cried as he bit my lip.

He did it again. Softer, though. "Are you going to forget, Sen?" He curled his fingers upward, making me gasp. My inner muscles clenched tighter around the intrusion loving the sharp pang between my thighs. "Fuck, beautiful. You're crushing my fingers."

Umm. I took great joy from that comment. "Then put your magnificent cock in me instead." He wasted no time unzipping his tight jeans, releasing his engorged cock, and shoving his boxer briefs and pants down to his ankles.

Alex roared as he pushed me back to the earth.

"You drive me crazy, woman!" He ravaged my mouth as he hovered over me, his bulging arms holding himself in precariously over my much smaller body. I could see the wheels turning in his head. He wanted to fuck me, though equally wanting to finish my punishment. He was kinky that way.

Without care, he lined up his dripping cock and slammed it into my wetness, eliciting a deep groan from both of us. He gripped my wrists, locking them tightly above my head, making promises of pleasure on his delicious lips. I watched his exquisite face as he pumped his rock hard shaft deep within me. Every slide of his cock was a punishing blow. His anger was evident in his body, but his kisses said otherwise. This was his love language, and it spoke volumes.

I did as he said; my eyes never leaving his face. His eyelashes fluttered each time I clamped down on his thick cock, giving me the most incredible sight I'd ever seen. Alex's vulnerability made me feel powerful and in control. Yet, when he took control over me, I dissolved into supplication. It was a give-and-take with a rhythm of its own, strengthening our relationship each time we allowed it. He continued his onslaught driving his tongue between my raw lips, sucking hard and muttering between breaths. He slowed his rhythm, taking our lovemaking to another level, then sped up as if driving home his earlier point. He was still conflicted.

His tempo slowed to a complete stop. *What was wrong?* He didn't move or pull out. He stared unblinkingly into my eyes, breath jagged, as he struggled to find his words. I waited as he gathered his thoughts. I was moments away from coming and hoped he'd find them soon.

Decided, he pulled his cock out excruciating slowly, then drove back into me hard and fast, stealing my breath and my orgasm. I arched my back, desperate to touch him, until he drove in deeper roaring, "Mine!"

My heart soared hearing his proclamation. *I was his!* My world shifted on its axis as my mind skidded across the Milky Way. He let my hands go as he fell to his elbows, keeping me close without crushing me. Was this the moment *like* met *love*? It had to be. It felt so right.

I cupped his jaw and tipped his face, noticing a tiny scar above his eyebrow. *Why had I not seen that before?* There was so much I didn't know about him. I needed time to explore everything about this man. Time that wasn't promised. Smothering my anxiety, I made the conscious decision to let my heart decide what to do.

And, before I knew it, words I could never take back flew out of my mouth.

"Alex Valize, please be mine." My scratchy words were given freely. I watched the tiny crinkles at the corners of his eyes ignite again with desire. Even after punishing sex, he wanted more—from me, his woman. I wanted so much more and he took me again slower, sweetly even. Our bond was solidified today. Nothing more needed to be said.

Sated and chilled, we dressed quickly and then huddled together, watching the puffy white clouds float by until late in the afternoon. Today would become a cherished memory for the rest of my life. But if we didn't get going, it would become a horror of epic proportions if Abigail had to wait for us.

Chapter 24

SENECA

By early evening, two more couples checked in—a young couple on their honeymoon working their way through the East Coast and another older couple from Michigan. My phone buzzed in my pocket, but I didn't have time to check it. Normally, I'd jump right on it, but I had to fight off the urge and focus on our guests.

Abigail's custom was to offer a light snack of pastries and assorted beverages when guests arrived in the afternoon. I happily took over so she could attend to preparing dinner. Guests were offered a special incentive for booking early: a happy hour of beer, wine, and appetizers before the sumptuous dinner included with their room fee. Overhearing conversation around the room reminded me that we all have our baggage, talents, and preferences, and we should not judge others so quickly.

By seven thirty, Elias began clearing dishes while Alex wiped down all used surfaces. Abigail was a bit of a germaphobe. Back in the kitchen, she had Elias seal the remaining food in containers and set the table for our staff meal. I was excused because, "I'd been an enormous help meeting and greeting my guests." Abigail's praise always made me smile. Her gratitude made her glow. Besides, Alex and I had cows to milk and eggs to steal from his chickens.

"Don't wait for us," Alex called back, winking at his buddy. I slipped on my down vest, then slid my hair tie off my wrist, securing my long locks for milking. I forgot to do that once and suffered through combing fatty, dried-up milk from my hair for the next two days. *Nasty!*

Finally, remembering to look at my phone, I saw Dr. Abel had called. My stomach flipped and nausea gripped me. I dropped myself onto the first bench I saw to catch my breath. This was it. Go or no-go. Launch or failure to launch. Every movie cliché ran through my head like *The Polar Express.*

Alex turned, noticing I wasn't with him and frowned. He walked back to sit next to me, eyeing my phone. Gently prying it out of my clutches, he understood my paranoia.

"This is it, huh?" He handed me my phone and kissed me on the cheek. "Whatever happens, I support you and your decision." He rubbed my knee in small circles, reminding me I wasn't alone.

Another niggle from my past zipped through my consciousness. I don't recall my father ever saying that to me. Not when joining him on his move from Michigan to Illinois. Not when he left me for his girlfriend. Not about which college I'd chosen to go to. Never. I didn't need Alex to be a father. *No.* He did, however, sound more and more like a committed boyfriend. I was starting to believe we might truly have a chance to make this relationship something more permanent. My heart warmed at the thought. Shifting on the bench, I gently leaned in to kiss his ruddy lips, whispering, "Don't go being the wind beneath my wings unless you plan on taking on the job permanently." *Was that a threat or a wish?* "I mean, as a friend, or . . . something."

He chucked my chin, grinning, "Or something?" he teased.

I was really happy it was dark outside because I could feel the heat rising up my neck and cheeks. Thank goodness the weather was cool. I needed something to balance out the wave of warmth traveling up my body. "Yeah, or something."

His strong hands lifted my face, angling me the way he liked it when he wanted a deep, long kiss, and I readily obliged. "Do you want that 'something,' Sen?" he said, his voice raspy, but serious.

Did I? My thoughts flipped like an old-time Rolodex. Every obnoxious thing he'd ever said and done over the years was measured against every kind word or action he'd made in the past month. Scales never lie. The latter far outweighed the previous. I needed to lay down the past and stop revisiting it to move forward.

I outlined his perfect mouth with one fingertip, drifting to the deep smile grooves that bracketed it. It was time to take a chance, to let fate and faith do their thing.

I kissed him softly, speaking to his soul, "Yes. I want it. I want you, Alex. Please don't let me fall. I'm not sure I can take it again." An errant tear slipped down between our lips. He licked it immediately as if solidifying his promise to protect me, if only from himself.

He kissed each eyelid, my cheek, and my nose before engulfing my mouth with his. It would have been so easy to take a literal romp in the hay until a low scratching sound fluttered around our feet. A proud, brown chicken with a bright red plume bobbed her head, flapping her wings and strutting back and forth.

"ATG. Really? We're kinda busy here, girl." My disappointment of having to break our kiss was replaced with the hilarity of this busybody chicken giving her approval dance. "Yeah. I'm excited, too."

Alex looked at me, then the chicken, then back to me. "I'm going to cook that chicken if she interrupts us again." His mock scowl wasn't lost on the bird. She squawked loudly, not liking his tone.

I threw my head back hysterically. ATG was, in secret, a cock-blocking mother-clucker. I cautioned him, "Better watch it, Alex. She'll shit in your shoes if you piss her off." His eye roll looked like he was going to take his chances.

I stood up, and pulled him with me. "Let's get the girls situated. I'm starving, and it's not only for dinner," I winked and ran down the path to the barn with Alex closing in fast.

It wasn't until after dinner that I realized I hadn't listened to Dr. Abel's message. Maybe, subliminally, I wasn't ready to hear what he had to say, though I needed to prepare myself for the worst.

I told Alex I'd like everyone to listen to the message with me. We crept up the backstairs, which was initially used by servants, to Abigail and Elias's suite and knocked on their door. Hearing quick movements and creaky floorboards, told us we were interrupting. *Too bad. This was important.*

"Abs? Elias? Can we come in? I need your help tonight," I begged quietly. Whispers hissed through the door while Alex and I giggled like children on our side.

"Hang on!" they both hollered in unison. Several moments later, the door whipped open, and Abigail hung onto Elias's arm, looking like parents caught in the act by their children. "What's up?"

I looked at Alex, needing his encouragement. Instead, he pinched my ass. "Tell them," he prodded.

"Can we come in? We have some news to share with you, and it can't wait."

Elias eloquently brokered the deal, "Hurry up," he said, ushering us into their sitting area across from one of many fireplaces in this historic home. Many of the original pieces were kept for posterity and their value, not my friends' décor preferences. Queen Anne chairs with brocade cloth, matching drapery, antique lamps with crystal bobeche dangling around the tapered retrofitted candle-like bulbs, were nothing Elias and Abigail would have ever picked. There were enough end tables, musty books, and floral wallpaper to choke a horse in this room. When she took ownership, Abigail insisted that all historic items stayed, removing all the dollar store, retro, kitschy seasonal décor the previous owner had strewn about. *It was despicable.*

Once seated, I pulled out my phone, preparing to call my voicemail. With trepidation, I continued. "I have an answer to my internship request and wanted you both to listen to it with me. Everyone in this room will be affected, and I'll need your consent before responding. Okay?"

They looked at each other approvingly, "Anything you need, Sen. We've got you."

A wave of relief hit me from head to toe. I settled myself before pressing the button, turned on speaker mode, and announced, "Oh, and Alex and I are officially dating."

Smooth, Seneca. Smooth.

Abigail went to reply, but I held up my finger to pause her. Dr. Abel's voice came through the phone.

Hello, Seneca,

You are the luckiest woman I've ever met. He definitely had that wrong.

The department board of directors reviewed your petition to change internships and agreed, given that circumstances were beyond your control and you shouldn't be penalized for them. However, that being said, your proposal for the new internship has several stipulations: both for you, your current sponsor, and your new sponsor. I'll email you everything now, but I wanted to congratulate you on your excellent work at Eloheh Farms. Mr. Valize sang your praises several times in the past few weeks. We have his reviews on file, which contributed positively to the board's decision. We will advise him and Mrs. McGinnis of our decision, but you should know Mr. Valize will have to sign off on these changes and evaluate your final project at the 441 Inn.

All right then. Please check your email this weekend. Olivia will send a video chat invitation for late Monday afternoon to discuss all the specifics.

Happy weekend.

I stared at the phone, processing every word Dr. Abel said. Shock, not at his message, but his perky tone, wigged me out. *Since when did Dr. Abel sound perky?*

Alex pulled me into his lap, whooping, "You got it, Sen. I'm so happy for you."

Elias shushed him, "We have guests, dipshit. Quiet down." Whoops turned to whisper-screams and happy dances. Abigail locked eyes with me and began bawling like a baby. I peeled out of Alex's arms and threw myself onto my dearest friend.

"This is surreal, right? I get to stay! We get to work together again. I mean really work together. You're going to be my boss, review me, and check all my work." I stopped abruptly, thinking about the downside to this arrangement.

"Oh shit, Abs. I'm going to be taking up one of your rooms. You're going to lose income. I'm going to take you away from your guests." *Oh, no!* I quieted my voice and carefully told her she'd have to fulfill her worst nightmare–homework. "You're going to have to write reports and turn them in on time!" Her brow crinkled and widened wildly. Writing papers and turning them in on time wasn't her forte when we were in school. She'd rather take an algebra exam than find dangling participles in her essays. My part-time job in high school was turning her outlines into documents. Even if she did her homework, there was no guarantee she'd turn it in. It could sit in her backpack for weeks before her noticing them there. *The joys of ADHD.*

She wrung her hands looking at Elias, her protector and kink daddy. Like the man I knew him to be, he gave her his devilish smile, coaxing her to make eye contact with him. "Are you going to let a few short reports keep you from helping your bestest friend in the world?"

I loved that he used "bestest" as if he invented the word. *I'd used it for decades!* Her frown turned to a pout before looking him in the eye. Sulking, she said, "No?" like she had an out.

He pulled her hair back, forcing her to focus on his face. "You'll do your best, and, if you ask nicely, I'll help you make all your deadlines and ensure they are on your calendar," Elias reassured her like a father would a young child. Most people didn't understand this aspect of their relationship. Most people didn't know it existed. Elias didn't want to be her actual father, even though she'd never had one she'd known of. He wanted to protect, support, and encourage her like a daddy. It was sweet. *And, hot as fuck,* overhearing their dirty playtime talk.

I leaned over her back, resting my chin on her shoulder, "We'll do it all together. Okay?" She trembled, presumably with the added weight of being responsible for my success.

"Thank you, bestest friend ever. You won't regret it." I kissed her cheek, stood, and went to Elias for a big bear hug. It was a beautiful moment until Elias shoved us out of his room and into the hallway toward our bedroom door. I could only imagine how he would tend to his overwhelmed wife; it could be an all-night adventure. My lady parts tingled wildly.

Chapter 25

ALEX

*F*inally! Something good is happening for Seneca. My problems had been a fricking weight around her neck since she walked back into my life. She'd get her degree, some invaluable experience, and an additional opportunity to build Abigail a unique, awe-inspiring Zen Garden that would attract new visitors. Elias would continue his work as Abigail's *Oz*, making Abigail's dreams come true while focusing on his own, restoring cars. However, I was taking up valuable space from my friends' businesses—both of them. Elias gave up half his workspace to accommodate my chickens and cows. I needed a plan and perhaps a mentor of my own, to get me to the finish line of a new place.

Tonight was the Inn's Second Annual Fall-Out Party. Donations poured in as guests paid to chuck pudding pies at my head. One hundred and fifty visitors mixed, mingled, and shared stories and anecdotes of this season's community garden. These people embraced what Abigail had offered, creating new relationships and opportunities for all involved. We'd collected five thousand dollars through generous donors by the night's end. Half would go to a children's farm-to-table program Abigail worked out with Elias and the local school system. The other half would cover the spring community garden prep and materials. *Water and fertilizer weren't cheap.* Any monies left over would cover the Inn's web advertising. It seemed Lindsey, Abigail's webpage designer, figured out how to use SEO to the Inn's advantage. When the young lady came over on Sunday, I got schooled in Search Engine Optimization and why "No organization can afford to live without it." I liked how she slowly coached Abigail, using metaphors to help her understand. I won't lie; I listened to every word, knowing I'd need to hire her soon. Eloheh Farms needed a new look for a new start.

Monday morning was a rough start. I got up late, and, sadly, threw out my trick back. It hadn't happened in years, and, of course, it added to the pain in my ass of everything else I had to do. I wormed my way to the bedroom floor, slipping my pillow and comforter with me as I moaned in pain. Staying flat for twenty-four hours, alternating between heat and ice, always did the trick for me. Eight hundred milligrams of ibuprofen every six hours didn't hurt either. The bigger problem was that Annalise wasn't here to be my nurse, which put Seneca on invalid duty.

Ironically, my timing couldn't have been better. Seneca needed time to work on her new internship, detail her plans for her new internship for Abigail, and do all my chores. She'd milked the cows before breakfast and collected eggs afterward. When she was finished, she'd set up her office on my bed, and tended to me when needed. Beyond me having to suffer to get up to pee, it felt good to have a day to lie around and do nothing.

Now, rubbing my temples on the floor, she questioned, wistfully. "Hey, babe. I have a call with Dr. Abel. Do you mind if I put it on speaker? It'll save me from recapping with you later."

I replied groggily, my narcissistic side slipping out, "Does that mean you're stopping my massage?" *Enough about me. Let's talk about me.*

She kissed me upside down between my eyes, deadpanning, "Yes." Rolling to her side, she swung her leg over my face, and stared at my pathetic face, as she rolled her eyes. "Poor baby," she cooed, then jumped on the bed, waiting for her chat to begin. I couldn't see her from this angle but listened intently.

"Hi, Dr. Abel. Thank you so much for going to bat for me. I truly appreciate it."

"My pleasure, Seneca. Did you get the email with the new program outline? I can't sign off on it until we resolve some stipulations. I hope you understand."

"I do."

My girl was professional and focused if not a bit jumpy. Dr. Abel continued, "Based on Mr. Valize's letter, he still wants you to assist him with his livestock and reestablishing himself in Mystic. That means you'll not only be completing one internship, but also starting another."

Her hesitation caused me to stiffen. I hadn't wanted her to be pressured with two projects, but I still needed her help. I hope the pressure wasn't too much. A troubled Seneca was like a bull ride at the height of rodeo season—dangerous.

Dr. Abel was the key to her happiness. "It shouldn't be a problem. Mr. Valize is a reasonable person, and so is Abigail. We'll work it out."

"Terrific. Item number two," he trudged ahead, "Until your meditation garden is completed, your internship can't be cleared. Of course, you know what that means."

"I don't graduate," she murmured. The hitch in her voice pulled a whimper of pain from my throat. I desperately wanted to hold her and tell her we wouldn't let her fail.

"Exactly. The Board recommended a focus group of no less than twenty people who will experience your garden and fill out a survey. They all need to be completed, compiled, and summarized a week before the end of the semester."

"That's only five and a half months. I can't start building until the ground thaws in March." Her voice trembled, making my blood boil. My hands fisted, preparing to move, when a bolt of pain shot from my foot up to my mid-back.

"Hang on one minute, Dr. Abel." I heard her shuffle herself off the bed. I might as well have been a helpless baby seal washed ashore the way I felt. My eyes fluttered, and my stomach felt nauseated at the pain.

"Oh my god, Alex. Are you okay? What happened?" She crouched beside me, her silky black hair sliding over my chest. *My back wasn't the only thing in agony now.*

"I'm fine," I grunted. "Only frustrated for you." *In many ways.*

She kissed my lips tenderly. "Please don't worry. I'll plan it all out. Mother Nature willing, she'll keep the rains to a minimum in March. It will be what it will be, Alex." Planting one more kiss on my eager lips, she returned to her call.

"Sorry, I had to let the cat out of the room. It was mewling too loud." *Nice save, sweetheart.* "Dr. Abel, do you think this internship will benefit me in the long run? I know it doesn't have a big name, or big money attached to it, but I'd like my project to make a difference in the world."

I'd never heard insecurity in Seneca's voice. Was she wavering because she was questioning her abilities? Or was it because it was too small-town for her bigger dreams? My last girlfriend felt that way. It wouldn't be outrageous to think Seneca wanted more, too. Though seeing her working with the soil and her garden designs, I could see her doing that as well. I've only begun to open my heart to her, and now I see she could leave me the day after her internship is finished. I don't know if I could handle another breakup. Meghan hadn't been in tune with me or my business, but Seneca knew me almost on a molecular level. My instincts in relationships weren't good. Trusting them was even worse. I suppose time would tell if I had enough courage to let things take their due course.

Seneca wrapped up her conversation, getting Dr. Abel's support, though I missed his exact words through my drug-induced haze. I heard the snap of her laptop closing, followed by a deep, cleansing sigh. Things must have gone well. The bedsprings creaked as she rolled off the bed and back onto the floor, returning to my feet this time. She drove her thumbs into my arch, humming a tune and focusing on her task.

"That feels amazing," I moaned, sounding like I had a mouth full of marshmallows.

Hmm. "I'm happy to hear that," she said, contently. Your feet are so tight. No wonder your back is out." There was tenderness to her words without judgment. More pity than annoyance. I knew she cared about me. Wasn't that enough? Was needing more so important? I was too messed up to know.

My limbs felt numb. My tongue thick and heavy. I should have known that taking so many ibuprofen would knock me out. I never took drugs. I hated this feeling of being out of control and helpless on the floor. I suppose that's why I hadn't any inhibitions about blurting out my fears.

"You're. Going. To leave me when you graduate," I croaked out. "I'm just a pawn." I couldn't shut myself up. *What an idiot.*

An unidentifiable sound split the air, ending my foot massage. I pried my eyes open, searching for any signs supporting my accusation. I found tears dripping from the corners of her beautiful almond-shaped eyes. Her face became contorted as an ugly screech peeled out of her throat. *What had I done?*

She stood, rubbing her hand over her worn jeans, then eyed my door. She was running. I could feel it. I wasn't sure what I wanted to happen. Leaving now would save me so much heartache later. Then again, I could feel the fissures cracking through my hardening heart like an earthquake breaking through concrete. My heart signaled to my mouth, "Please, Seneca, stay," but it wasn't fast enough.

She was out the door in a flash, leaving me aggravated at both of us and helpless. I shut my eyes, resigned our relationship would be over in five months, if not now. When a cold drop of water dripped between my eyes, a painful jolt of pain shot through my head. Another drip and my teeth chattered, my anxiety shifting into high gear. When the next drip came, I saw it and fought to roll out of the way. Then my back spasmed, forcing me to take the drip in my ear. I screamed my frustration through the searing pain.

"Stop! What the fuck, Seneca? Why—"

"Because you are torturing me, so I'm torturing you!" she said, punctuating each word. "Do you think so little of me that I would use you to get ahead? Who the fuck gives everything she has to save your ass, to leave you high and dry at the end? Only you! Elias is right. You are a dumbass." She flicked another drop into my eyes.

I tried to speak up. I tried to get my voice to call out to stop her. To get her to . . . what? What exactly did I want her to stop? Stop yelling at me? Stop calling me out on my self-deprecating tone and insecurity? Or telling me to stop being a piece of shit boyfriend? I was all those things and more. As soon as I could get my sorry ass off this floor, I'd get back down and grovel at her feet. Frustration streaking her face, she strode out of the room, slamming the door behind her. *Dumbass.*

Chapter 26

SENECA

The King of Self-Saboteurs had struck again. Determined to make his life a living hell, Alex had deliberately manufactured obstacles to his detriment. If he thinks provoking me will drive me off, he'd better think again. When I say I'm all in, damn it, I'm all in!

"What crawled up your butt," Elias teased.

After sketching out my exact plans for my project, I wandered into Elias's workspace in the barn. He was restoring a faded 1954 dark blue Corvette. I'm not a big car person, but even I could see this beauty coming to life. Elias was an artist as well as a gifted mechanic.

I rolled my eyes dramatically, "The usual. Your dumbass friend." I dragged my feet, circling the car.

He harrumphed, wiping a silver thing with a red cloth. "I think you need to lower your expectations or cut him some slack. As much of a jerk as he can be, he'd give you the world if you gave him the time of day."

Cut him slack? "I don't think you understand, Elias. He's the one who needs to give me a break. He's already got me packed up and out the door before I even have a chance to figure this all out." I felt a headache coming on from defending myself. My expectations were simple—I had none. Only that he treat me with respect and be was honest with me. *And orgasms. Yes, those, too.*

"Seneca, sit down," he demanded, pointing to a stool by his workbench. Walking slowly toward me, he stopped and placed the silver-colored car part—or was it a tool?— on the wood top. "This is not a tit-for-tat scenario. For as long as I've been friends with Alex, I have never seen him wrapped so tightly. He is beyond overwhelmed in every aspect of his life, especially *you*."

My mouth gaped at his emphasis on me. Elias continued, unusually animated, "Frankly, Sen, I don't know if he would have found out about the contamination issue until he became sick or died of radon poisoning. Those things aside, that man has been a fool since he met you. Okay, a bigger fool. It didn't matter if he was a captain in the Army, raising his brother, or saving the family farm; he takes his relationships with people very seriously. When his last girlfriend dumped him, he was inconsolable. Whatever he felt for her was minute compared to what he feels for you."

He scrubbed his tidy chestnut brown beard with his inked mechanical arm, and it dawned on me how mesmerized Abigail had been when she described how the cogs seemed to move together when he worked his arm. *It was fascinating.* In his calming parental voice, he concluded, "Give him time, Sen. Try not to take everything he says literally. He's about as good with words as I am. And I suck at communicating. Let's get everyone settled here and worry about what it all looks like in the spring. Okay?"

Why does he always have to be right? I breathed an audible, pained sigh.

Elias was telling me to be patient. *Ha!* That's like telling a dog to sit and setting a steak in front of him. Nearly impossible. The truth was a hard pill to swallow. I'm choking on it but forcing it down for my sake and his. Even though I felt entitled to speak my truth, Alex had his, too. I suppose neither one was more important than the other, but my need to be *righter* was my problem to own. We had this insatiable, animalistic draw to one another that permeated through our souls. He said it himself. Sadly, that feeling alone wouldn't be enough to make this relationship last. I had more pondering to do.

Reluctantly, I wandered back into the house to find Alex still on his back, his phone on speaker mode, resting on his muscled chest. His eyes glazed a deep azure blue as he focused on a spot on the ceiling. Given what the person on the other end of the line was saying, I couldn't tell if the drugs had him spaced out or in suspended animation. I waited outside the open bedroom door, listening.

"Your cooperation is highly appreciated. We have a team of environmental scientists arriving at your farm tomorrow. The preliminary testing your friend, Leo Tucker, performed was excellent, though we have more advanced technology that gives us exact levels. Pinpointing the precise location of the containments will help us halt and remediate each toxin completely."

If I were to make an educated guess, I'd say the Governor's office finally got back with him. Alex didn't say much about having to wait an extra three days for them to call, but, given his condition, I'd say the stress caused the back strain, not moving stuff around for the party this past weekend.

Alex chanced lifting his arm above his head to shield himself from pain. His groggy words still held a hint of appreciation. "I can't thank you enough for following up with me. Taking the lead on what to do next is a load off my mind." He winced, bringing his arm back down to the floor. "I know you can't say for certain, but do you think I'll be able to move back to my property anytime soon?"

His voice cracked, spitting out the words. My heart broke, too. I held my breath, waiting for the verdict.

The voice on the phone clucked his tongue, "Nothing is for certain, Mr. Valize. If the issues you've been experiencing match up with the two other complaints logged this year, I wouldn't plan on farming on that land for several years. The half-life of some of these chemicals is twenty years. At best, you're looking at five only to clean up the problem before inhabiting it again. I'm afraid to say that organic farming is out of the question."

A sound akin to a wounded animal erupted from Alex's body, sending his body into a pained fetal position. I ran into the room, panicked. "Alex, baby, I'm here. I'm here." He was visibly sweating. His hands grabbed clumps of his hair, yanking at the strands. I didn't know what to do.

I heard the man on the phone calling out, "Mr. Valize. Mr. Valize. Are you all right?"

I grabbed the phone off the floor that had slid off his chest. "Hello. This is Seneca Locklear. I'm Mr. Valize's intern who found the problem. What can I do to help?" I was out of breath, shaking my loose hand, then jumped up to pace the room. Alex was inconsolable, and this man was the only one who could help us now.

The man cleared his voice, "Nothing can be done now. We'll get back to Mr. Valize once our results come in."

Oh, hell no! There was always something to be done.

Reason needed to prevail. I recalled all the data I had collected about the industrial businesses upstream and what they manufactured. There were primary disposal processes: capsulation, ground injection, and incineration. There had to be something wrong with them. One of those processes had to add up to something. "Mr.? I'm sorry. I don't know your name."

"Sorry. I'm Sebastian Malcolm. The Lieutenant Governor of the State of Pennsylvania," he said contritely.

"Okay. Well then, Mr. Malcolm. In my research, I found three companies in particular that had annual reports stating there had been minor spills or infractions. I highly suspect one or all of them have been skirting the EPA and dumping into the water system via the creek that runs through Mr. Valize's property. And, if not directly dumping, their containment systems leach into the soil and down to the groundwater. Please. I'm begging you. Follow up on those businesses. If you give me your email, I'll send my data immediately," I pleaded. Every stone had to be turned. "One other thing, if I may. Mr. Valize's parents both suffered from an unknown cancer some time over twelve years ago. Could they have been affected, too? Unfortunately, they passed together in a car crash and their health concerns went with them. Would it be probable these contaminates were the cause of their illness?"

It was a long shot. One that had to be taken. My dumbass boyfriend needed all the answers he could get. And, when he got them, I'd find the biggest, baddest lawyer to extract every ounce of justice out of those bastards. *Ugh!* I'm so aggravated with the whole thing. *Wasn't there anything we could control?* This was not something someone with OCD should be spearheading. *Then again, maybe it was.*

"I'll take that data and give it to my team to dissect. We must first figure out what we're dealing with before determining who is to blame. We will get to the bottom of it as quickly as possible. Please email my assistant and give my regards to Mr. Valize. We'll be in touch."

I took his information and thanked him for his time, hanging up the phone, somewhat relieved. Hearing the complete demise of Eloheh Farms overwhelmed me, and I fell to my knees beside my broken man.

Alex needed hope. Hope that he could rebuild here in Mystic, on Abigail's estate. Hope that something could be salvaged from his farm. And, hopefully, our relationship will stand strong through it all.

I gently pulled his arms away from his face, replacing them with soft kisses on his tear-stained cheeks. "Are you able to sit up?" I brushed his wet hair back behind his ear while he contemplated his physical state, whispering words of encouragement to coax him out of his stupor.

"Baby, how about I get you into a hot bath? You deserve to relax. Allowing your emotions to come out takes great courage, and I'm so proud of you for working through them the best you know how. I could join you in your bath, if you'd like? I'll wash your hair," I said, tempting him to move.

He whined like a sad child, "You're just trying to placate me. Leave me here to die and go have a good life." He pulled his hands up too quickly, causing another spasm.

I chuckled. So, he wants to play the self-deprecating, poor-me card? Fine. Two can play that game.

"You know I can't have a good life without you being happy, right?" I milked my sarcasm to cream. Positioning myself next to him, I grabbed his wrists. Without caring about his poor ego, I pulled them away from his contorted, tear-stained face so he could see me taunting him with waggly eyebrows.

"Go away, Seneca. I'm not in the mood," he snarled.

I pulled harder on his powerful arms. "I heard your conversation. I know it feels like all is lost at Eloheh, but there is a silver lining in all of this. You first have to want to see it," I pleaded.

Err! "Fuck your silver lining. I'm done with the farm, my future, and with you. Get the fuck out of here!" he screamed with more vitriol than I'd ever heard out of his mouth.

Stunned, I released his wrists, falling back against the bedframe. Did he mean it? He wanted me gone? Here I was, trying to soothe him. Get him to laugh. Turn him on. All the things that typically got Alex to react. But this? Screeching for me to get out of his life, forced me to consider the authenticity of his feelings. Did he want me to go forever or only for now? *It sure felt like forever.* My confidence in our relationship took a deep dive straight into the dumpster. I knew he'd hit bottom. He even knew in the pit of his stomach that he might not recover from this disaster. He could take a day, a week, or even a month, but the bottom line was, if he didn't face his problems head-on, he'd lose himself possibly forever. Elias said to give him time. Fine. He could take all the time he needed, but I couldn't. I was his intern. And if there was a way for me to earn my degree and jumpstart his future, I'd take that challenge.

Keeping myself from being an asshole back to him, I took the high road. "I'll check on you later. Do you need anything before I go?" I waited a full five minutes, then stood, grabbed my computer and research data, and left the room, closing the door softly.

Chapter 27
SENECA

After peeking in on Alex several hours later, and him still lying flat on his back asleep, I crept out of his room recharged and ready to put my plan into action.

"I've called this meeting to aide and assist a man in need. While all of us have given generously, we need to do more. Our friend has hit an all-time low, and time is of the essence. With that said, I have a plan in place, but I have no authority to execute any of it without your approval." My friends sat sipping hot cider at the formal dining room table where all major decisions had been made in the past. Elias raised a single brow, tapping his thumb on the table, waiting not so patiently. Abigail, however, was bouncing out of her seat waiting for the next big adventure we'd take together. My five-step program was off and running.

"First, my plan comes with a rather large price tag. One that you'd both need to shoulder until Alex's business can begin to repay you." I waited a beat, expecting hesitation, but there wasn't any.

I continued. "Secondly, here is an aerial map of your estate. One that needs a proper name, Abigail. Not an address," I reprimanded her again. "Your one-hundred and sixty acres is perfect for expansion. There is a service drive here. And another, here," I pointed on the screen. "My plan, should you accept it, would be to build another barn, house, and fenced-in pastures for the girls. Eloheh Farms would be reestablished on a land contract on the far northside of your property. In contrast to the community garden by the estate home, Alex could carve out a large enough area to start his organic farm and dairy without even being seen from your second floor." I stopped short, holding my breath. I'd dumped a lot of information at their feet and prayed they'd be on board. Elias, Alex's best friend, looked at Abigail, sharing an annoying secret look I wasn't privy to.

"What? What's going on? What are you two hiding?" I jammed my hands on my hips, aggravated they were keeping me in the dark.

Elias chuckled. "We aren't hiding anything. We've spent every night in bed, not sleeping but conjuring up ways to help our friend. Your plan falls right in line with some of those ideas." I guess he didn't want to outshine me. "There is another tiny bit of information you may not be aware of," he said tauntingly, not proceeding with his statement.

"Like?" I sassed back.

Abigail interrupted, "Like we bought the farm next door last year. They were bankrupt, and, at Mr. Brickner's encouragement, we bought it for a steal." She bit her lip, grinning at her husband. *God only knows how they celebrated that coup.*

I jumped from my seat ecstatically, "That's amazing! Un-fucking-believable that you withheld it from me the past month, but go on."

Elias ran his hand through his hair, showing off his magnificent mechanical tattoo and boulder shoulders, "We haven't done anything with the property except demolish the rundown buildings and clear the land. We wanted Alex to use it. The only reason we bought it was so we wouldn't have to look at an obnoxious building behind us." He leaned forward, brushing his lips across Abigail's lips, delighted.

I was in shock. This plan was working better than I thought it would. I ran around the table, catching my hip on the corner in the enthusiastic process and throwing my arms around each of them, wailing my gratitude into each of their necks.

"You are both getting awards for being the best friends ever. I'll fill out an application for you somewhere soon." I returned to my presentation. "Let me finish, and then we can hash out the details, okay?"

Abigail looked at me with puppy-dog eyes. "You know you don't have to do this? We'll handle the financing and building, in addition to supporting if you, you . . ."

I cut her off. "Yeah. You do that, but I'm in this until it's done. This intern takes her job very seriously, which brings me to my next point, number three." I flipped the screen, revealing a detailed preliminary timeline.

"As you know, I need to start building my senior project mid-March when the ground thaws. I will need all hands on deck, especially you, Elias, to lay the stone path. At the latest, it has to be done by April 5th so I can bring in a focus group and get their surveys compiled into a final document by the following week. Since business is slow for the next few months, can we raise a barn for Alex?"

Abigail bounced in her seat, clapping her hands and blurting out, "I'll call Mr. Brickner to arrange for funds to be transferred to my account by the end of the week. He'll draw up the necessary papers for the land contract and we can get this party started."

By the press of Elias's lips and jut of his chin, I could see the cogs of his mechanical brain putting this all together. "I have a restoration to finish, but it should be completed by next week. Let me do some networking to get some quotes for everything we'll need. Abs, get hold of Derrick and see if he's interested in throwing his hat into the ring. He could do all the finish work once the building is erected."

My excitement jacked up another notch, and I leaned in for my last point. "Step number four involves Lindsey's help. Alex needs a marketing plan. He'll need tons of exposure and hype to get people ready to show up and start buying his produce and milk at the beginning of the season. I was thinking we'd start small with a produce stand out here on Route 34. We could use billboard marketing to bring in travelers, people from surrounding towns, and the city locals. We also need business research demographics so we aren't pissing on someone else's fields—if you know what I mean." They nodded.

"Awesome! That brings me to step number five, a new home for Alex. In the barn blueprint, I'd like to create an office big enough for him to have a loft area to rest and relax without having to leave the area. Nothing fancy. A mini fridge, desk, file cabinets, a futon, and a nice rug. Something cozy and calming for my wound-too-tight boyfriend," I winked, knowing they'd understand.

"Or to have a quickie midday," Abigail supplied, shaking her noggin like a bobblehead. I opened my hands in supplication.

"Or that," I said coquettishly. *I'm not ashamed of being a horny girl.*

"The reality of getting his business off the ground was more important than building a home. If all goes well after the harvest next year, he can get that project off the ground somewhere else. We all know the only obstacle keeping this from happening will be Alex's pride."

We were all in agreement, but first, "Elias, your first assignment is to get my sorry-sack of a boyfriend off the ground and into a hot bath. When he's done, do what you can to get him to stretch his legs and hips. He'll feel more like himself."

His eyes shot up, "Me? Why me? Why don't you do it?"

I jerked my head at his indignation, slamming my hands onto my hips. "Do you think he'll accept it better from his big-mouthed, annoyingly beautiful girlfriend that pities him? Come on, man. Get real." I air-pointed a finger at his chest.

He sighed. "Point taken. I'll try tonight."

"Excellent!" I clapped. "My last big ask is that we don't tell Alex what we are up to. I want it to be a big surprise, but I also want him to be a part of the process. His pride is frazzled, and being weak in front of me, I think, is killing him." I crossed my arms under my bust, thinking of how to do all these things discreetly.

I didn't wait for their reply and slapped my laptop shut. "I'm going to get ahold of Tiny to see if he can join us for a barn-raising party after Thanksgiving. With any luck, we can have it up and roofed before Christmas."

Abigail looked to Elias again, then back at me, concerned. "Do you really think it's his pride getting in the way? He's had a lot thrown at him. Maybe he's just overwhelmed." *I wished that were the case.*

I twisted my fingers, contemplating sharing his last words with me. After pacing back and forth, I blurted out, "He said he was done with me." They gasped in unison. "Of course, he said he was done with everything and wanted to be left for dead, too. When did he become so dramatic? That's *my* wheelhouse."

Later that evening, Elias did what he'd said he would do. However, he had to deadlift Alex off the floor and dump him in a pre-drawn hot tub of water fully clothed. Abigail and I heard shouts promising "death in your sleep" and "I'll duct tape your ass when you least expect it." *Such violence.* We giggled like schoolgirls, envisioning the looks they shot at each other. Elias emerged shortly thereafter, his face serene.

"I haven't had that much fun with him in months. Thanks for assigning me that task. Mission accomplished." His smug expression was priceless.

My concern for his pain overrode my elation. "Was he still in a lot of pain when you threw him in the tub?"

He rolled his eyes, "I didn't pay attention. He wasn't focused on his pain. Instead, he was busy fighting for his life. He's fine."

Laughing at Alex's expense was bittersweet. I promised myself right then and there I'd let him come to me. I would play the dutiful intern behind the scenes until he got his head out of his ass, but I wouldn't be the cause of any more emotional damage. I excused myself and went upstairs to my own bedroom. Sleeping with Alex was over. I'd collect my things tomorrow when I knew he'd be out of the room.

Today, though, I spent my time enhancing my PowerPoint deck with notes, organizing my tasks and assignments, and forwarding a copy to Dr. Abel, Elias, and Abigail. If ever there was a time to pull our talents together, it was now. We had the time, resources, and ambition. What could possibly go wrong? *Famous last words, I know!*

ALEX

It's almost a week, and my friends haven't said anything about my sullenness. Every time they saw me, they smiled and asked if I would like to join them in some activity from cooking to mucking out stalls. It took too much out of me to do more than wave them off with a grimace. I couldn't take it anymore. I threw on my boots and down jacket and stole the golf cart I'd given them for their wedding years ago. I needed wide-open spaces without familiar faces. Somewhere I could empty my brain and reconnect with the earth.

Abigail took me on a grand tour of her property soon after she inherited it. Her pride and awe at what was now hers inspired me to start anew. I had a great reputation in East Stroudsburg. Quality and friendliness were my trademarks. I would miss providing for them. Joking around at weekend markets and fulfilling their suggestions of new vegetables or varietals they would enjoy. We were a symbiotic ecosystem helping each other not to survive, but to thrive. I suppose reaching out to them with a notification would be appropriate. But what would I say?

Dear Friends,

By some fucked up turn of events beyond my control, my farm and your community have been poisoned by assholes upstream. Find yourself another supplier outside a five-mile radius and get your blood tested.
Best Always,
Alex "The Idiot" Valize

Yeah. That's not happening.

There was a time when I imagined living in Abigail's back forty, having a secondary organic farm. Or maybe a horse ranch, though I don't know much about horses. I don't know. Something I could play at while visiting a week at a time. I drove around the fence line, determined to revisit this line of thinking. What if Abigail let me move my cows and chickens out here? Start a new version of Eloheh Farms, organic dairy and eggs. It wasn't much of a living, but it was something until I could expand or find my own property nearby.

My head hurt from all the thinking I'd been doing. Not to be outdone by the ever-growing tightness between my shoulder blades, I stopped by a small pond adjacent to a large maple tree, reminding me of home. Fighting back the emotions I'm working hard to ignore, I wandered the area, thinking of all the good times I'd experienced growing up on the farm. Rolling hay bales that fed our cows doubled as a jungle gym. The swing my dad hung from my favorite maple tree pushed us higher and higher. My mom baked pies, bread, and countless other goodies to sell with the milk they sold roadside. Their tagline said, "Baked goods and milk. Is there anything better?" They even made T-shirts and sold coffee mugs for decades before they got sick. I had a great childhood with strong family values and appreciation for every human life. Another saying popped into my mind, something my grandma used to tell us: "People who love the land will grow in your heart." Isn't that ironic? Seneca loved the land. Without my knowledge, she embedded herself in my head and my heart. She cultivated the land. Her heritage revered the land. *Geezus!* Why did I tell her to go away? I'm a fucking fool.

It didn't matter. I needed to get my head out of my ass. She had her life to live. A life with a person who wasn't so mercurial and insecure. How was it that I spent my whole life feeling strong, in control, and secure in myself, only to have one disaster, albeit a colossal catastrophe, shake me to the core? I needed that guy to come back. I needed a new purpose. I deserved to follow my dreams even if the woman I was beginning to love needed to follow hers.

I jumped back into the golf cart and followed the fence line to the house. There had to be a way to convince Abigail and Elias I was worthy of a second chance at their farm. Plans were for people who wanted security. It was time to get back to work. I couldn't wait for a master plan unfold. I'd figure it out along the way. My goal required wire, a posthole digger, and work gloves. By tomorrow morning, me, myself, and I had a date with a new destiny.

❧☙

"Why are you two laughing at me?" I didn't think my idea was funny. It was ambitious. I only needed their permission to get started. *Were they shutting my idea down already?*

Elias laughed mockingly, "We're not laughing at you. Is it a coincidence, Abigail, that we were talking about starting a similar project a few nights ago?" *He was mocking me.*

"Why, no, husband. Not a coincidence at all." She fought a titter. *Okay, Abigail was definitely mocking me.*

"Stop mocking me!" I stormed around the room. "Is that a yes or no? I'll buy the land or rent it. I have some savings, but you'll have to wait until I have an income for the rest. I'm a sound investment." I pounded my chest emphatically with my ability to follow through.

They did that telepathic married couple thing, saying in unison, "It's a yes." *They were becoming more annoying every year.* I continued my upset toddler march around the dining room and into the front parlor when it finally registered what they'd said. I bolted back to the table, my heart pumping erratically.

"Yes? As in, go ahead and start?" It felt like an anvil had been lifted off my shoulders. The race of endorphins to my brain sent me staggering backward. "I can't believe it. You are both so . . . incredible," I stammered out. "I don't know what to say." I rubbed at the sweat pouring off my brow.

"Say you'll get your sorry ass out of my sight. I want to fuck my wife." Elias waggled his brows as Abigail raced up the back stairs like a scared rabbit. Those two had an exciting, twisted love life I'd only hoped to find in Seneca. I hadn't seen her all day. I told her to go away—forever—like a brat. She'd made herself scarce at my demand and was doing a great job of it, too. If anything, I'd owed her an apology, including some direction to get her back on track.

The trip upstairs was arduous. Every step meant I would have to expose a little more of myself. Sharing my feelings had been a last resort in all my relationships, which was why I kept fucking them up. Until now, holding back didn't hurt like this. Seneca mixed up my molecular composition to the point I'm not the same man she'd met four years ago. The problem was that I didn't know this "new" guy, and it scared me. What if I did open up, and she shun me anyway? How long *would* it be before I turned back to my old ways? Why did love hurt so damn much? *I loved her? Oh my god! I love her! Now, what would I do about it?*

I'm not sure how it happened, but all of Seneca's things disappeared from my room over the past couple of days. She didn't show up at dinner and evaporated after leaving me a basket of eggs she'd collected from the coup each morning. I was perplexed to say the least.

By the beginning of the third day, I was back to work and out of my stupor. I was time to get some answers.

I chucked off my work boots in the mudroom and hung my coat on the chicken hooks arranged in an array on the wall. Abigail sing-songed to the sizzle of eggs being fried. Bacon wafted through the air, and strong coffee made me want to sing along with her.

"Hey, Abs," I said, entering the room, her back to me. I walked around the long island and tapped on her shoulder. She turned, swinging her spatula at my face. "Whoa, there. It's only me," I smiled apologetically, my hands help up like a cactus. "Where's Sen?"

Abigail pulled her wireless earbuds out, setting them in a small bowl under the backsplash. "What the hell, Alex? You scared the shit out of me. What were you saying?" Her annoyance was justified. I shouldn't have come from behind. It was another of her ADHD quirks. Anything that resembled a ninja, needed swatting.

She flipped the eggs and turned off the heat. "Where is Seneca?" I stared her down, waiting for any sign of being gaslit.

"At the library doing homework," she said without so much as an eyelash flutter.

"Homework? I didn't assign her anything. Did you? Dr. Abel? She never mentioned anything to me." *Why would she, asshole? You sent her away—forever. Remember?*

She gave me a side look, "She's a student, Alex. She's studying. How the hell am I supposed to know? Sit down and eat." A heaping plate of eggs, bacon, and toast was shoved into my hands, effectively forcing me to sit down and shut up. *Fine.*

"Where's Elias? He wasn't in the barn when I left and he isn't here eating with me." I aggressively stabbed my eggs, knocking the fork against my teeth, eating too quickly.

Abigail filled her plate and slowly walked it to the table, then quickly retreated to the coffee station to pour two scalding cups of coffee. It wasn't ironic at all when she placed the cup in front of me, taunting me with the phrase, "Life doesn't wait for you. Go get one."

She sipped her cup, eyeing me over the rim, "Tell me about Eloheh Farms. What kinds of crops did you grow? The kinds of people you met. That kind of thing."

I cocked my head to figure out her angle. I didn't recall ever having this kind of conversation with her. She knew most of what I did, generally speaking. My website said it all. "Ah, the usual stuff. Kale, romaine, lettuce, carrots, radishes, different herbs. Why?" She was up to something.

She sipped again, followed by a snarf sound. "Alex, it might come as a surprise to you that I have a community garden outside that window. My gardeners plant all those things. Occasionally, a member will ask me if I would consider making it an organic garden, but I've declined due to the excessive cost and attention it deserves. I've encouraged them to bring any organic materials they'd like to use, but most don't follow through. More to the point, I'd like to better understand which specific crops flourish better in an organic environment."

I paused, running through all the crops I've grown. "Everything grows better in an organic climate, specifically peas, beans, and clover top the list. I've noticed kale and broccoli make good ground cover. Some studies say daikon radishes break up the soil better, allowing nutrients to flow more evenly. Overall, it's like dating. Crops act like personalities. They grow better when paired with a complementary personality."

Her coffee mug hit the table hard. "That's incredible, Alex. It makes so much sense. I can't believe none of my tenured gardeners didn't share that with me. Is this a super-secret only shared in ancient cultures?"

I couldn't tell if she was being sarcastic or sincere. Abigail had never gone to college, though she was brilliant in her own way. Any woman who could get my friend to do her bidding should have been a psychologist or circus trainer—more likely the latter. Chuckling to myself, I murmured, "Maybe a bit of both."

After Abigail's confused look, we ate in companionable silence and, when finished, cleaned up together. I liked her warmth and opaqueness. Abigail wasn't a woman with a hidden agenda. Meghan was, and left me traumatized. I think I attracted the wrong personalities. Like my plant example, this time I chose a different personality to help me grow in ways I never thought possible. Seneca was broccoli to my kale.

"Be honest with me, Abs. Is Seneca avoiding me?"

She stepped forward, pulling me into one of her fabulously warm hugs. "I'm always honest with you, Alex. You used some pretty harsh words on Seneca the other day. The kind that lasts a long time. My guess is she's feeling raw about it. Moreover, she has responsibilities to look after and does not have enough time for either. Licking her wounds has never been her style, Alex. On the contrary, she's the queen of stuffing down her feelings."

I pulled on the ends of my too-long hair. My brain hurt. I was out of RAM. Nothing was processing in my clogged head. I needed to let something go, or I'd go crazy.

I plopped down on a barstool, defeated. "Abs, you're her best friend. Tell me what to do?"

She patted my shoulder, "Breathe and be patient. Focus on what you can control and let the rest go. Go on now and dig your holes. Rope off what you need, then let Elias and I review it. Be generous with your estimations. Hopefully, the weather will hold and we can cart out to look it over in a few days. As for Seneca, that's the patience part. Give it some time. She'll come around—maybe," she muttered the last part.

If Abigail didn't think I had a chance, I would be doomed.

Chapter 28
SENECA

Micha, the Mystic archives librarian, set me up in the law library section of the public library. She'd pulled volumes of environmental law for me to scour through. I figured the differences between Pennsylvania and Connecticut law wouldn't be so far off and would provide precedence for any lawsuits Alex needed to file. There wasn't a dollar figure large enough to make up for losing his family legacy. However, a hefty settlement would help him reestablish himself without claiming bankruptcy. I wasn't naïve. I knew these kinds of cases could take years to settle. Hedging my bets on the Lieutenant Governor of Pennsylvania's involvement gave me hope for an expedited resolution. I'm crossing my fingers, toes, and chest for divine intervention. I'd take any help I could get.

"How is it going, Seneca?" Micha should have been a ninja the way she snuck up on me.

"Geezus, Micha! I almost had a heart attack," I cried, clenching my ass. "I'm, uh, finding some good stuff. There have been several similar cases around the country that are pertinent to Alex's case. I'm no lawyer, but finding these cases will save him thousands of dollars in research. He'll need every penny he can to raise a barn, set up shop, and build a house." I slumped back in my seat, exhausted from days of research.

I should have told Alex where and what I was doing. I was still his intern, and following his instructions was my job. If only he could see the forest through the trees. He could thank me later.

"I'm happy I could help. Have you spoken to Lindsey about remodeling his website to reflect his move? That will also be important for his past and future clients." I smiled appreciatively. Her genuine interest in Alex's success was touching.

I touched her shoulder, "I have her scheduled for next week. You'd be surprised how important making a timeline is for someone like me. Focusing on too many tasks at one time makes me anxious."

She chuckled. "I hear you there. Let me know if you need anything else. I'm heading out for the day." I waved and dug through another thick volume, dreading looking through four more.

Dear patrons, the library will close in thirty minutes. Please make your selections and move to the check-out desk as soon as possible. Thank you.

I noticed the time on my phone. Startled, I'd been at this for eight hours. That's probably why I barely jumped when two large hands landed on my shoulders. "Thought you could hide from me, huh?"

His deep, resonant, husky voice made my belly flutter when he whispered in my ear. It took three days for him to find me. I tried not to take it personally, doing my best to put an end to my emotional rollercoaster. I couldn't let our attraction to each other get in the way anymore. He was a mess, and I was fighting not to become one. Unfortunately, when his dulcet tones permeated my eardrums, I battled against my oath.

I sat up straight, shutting the volume before me, and began packing my things. The void in my heart at shutting him down felt awful. I had to hold firm. There was too much at stake for both of us to bend even a little.

"I wasn't hiding, Alex. As your intern, I've been researching precedent law to help you file a lawsuit. They will need these to make a case once the Lieutenant Governor calls back with their final results." My mini-monologue was clear, concise, and unaffected—at least I thought it was.

Alex pulled up a chair, shifting mine to face squarely in front of him. He held my shoulders tenderly, his expression morphing from stern to pained to understanding. He had never been shown me this depth of expressiveness with me. Usually, it had been hot lust, disdain, or frustration. I was lost.

I tried to look away, not wanting him to break down my walls any further, but he surprised me and leaned back in his seat, releasing me from his hold. "I didn't think my life would be so complicated, Seneca. You appeared from my past, sending me into a tizzy. You've proven yourself time and again by being there for me. You went above and beyond, day in and day out, without being asked. I should have listened to you more, respected your approach, and never treated you so abominably a few days ago." He shifted in his seat, leaning forward to rest his sinewy forearms on his knees. *Not fair. Leading, my head shouted. Overruled, my body shuddered. My brain had been in these law books far too long.*

My hands twisted in my lap, unsure how I felt. I understood his apology. He had never voiced those words before. He shouldn't have said the things he said. I was his equal, internship or not. Didn't he know me well enough to know my intentions had only ever been benign? I couldn't look him in the eyes. It would have been a sign of defeat, and I couldn't give him that. It was my last defense.

It didn't matter. Two long, thick fingers lifted my chin, forcing me to look him straight in the eye. "I'm sorry for everything, Sen. That's all I wanted to say."

He leaned forward, kissed my forehead softly, and lingered by my face longer than necessary. Fissures of anguish shot through my body, splitting me open, desperate and vulnerable. I should have been happy and even elated that he finally said the words I needed to hear. Except I wasn't. My mouth stayed sealed; my body frozen in suspended animation.

Alex silently stood, lines of contrition carved into his forehead—taking away another piece of my heart—and walked out the door. *Where would we go from here?*

ALEX

Thanksgiving was next week, and, after Abigail and Elias approved the square footage I wanted, they pointed to another section of land they acquired last year just beyond their own. Since then, I'd plotted out and installed sixty post holes along a wide-open piece of hilly land to run wire through, delineating my new pasture. It couldn't be used for farming, but it was perfect for my girls to roam. They'll love to eat all the delicious varieties of grass next spring. Herding them over before I had a place to house them was ridiculous. This led me to my next problem: how would I afford a new barn? It wasn't that I was poor. I invested my earnings well, had money in the bank, and a pension that paid enough to feed me and my animals every month. Nevertheless, erecting barns costs tens of thousands of dollars in materials and labor. Not to mention where would I find the manpower? Adding a bank loan to the long list of tasks accumulating on my nightstand required a project manager and a flow chart. The more challenging question was asking Seneca for assistance. It would be a great learning experience that would aid her for life.

A knock on my bedroom door jolted me out of the small settee I'd used as a workspace in my room when I didn't want to be interrupted. You'd think a giant house like this would have tons of nooks and crannies to be alone, but it didn't. My only other option for solitude was in the dank basement storeroom, which I would have seriously considered if it weren't for the cold and musty smells. Besides, the lighting sucked, and I didn't need to feel like a naughty child needing a lesson.

"Who *is* it?" I sing-songed.

"Little Red *Riding* Hood," the voice replied in kind. "Is the Big Bad Wolf decent?" *This definitely wasn't Seneca.*

"Never for you, Red. Come in," I joked.

Abigail bounced into the room, hoisting herself on to the elevated bed. "Elias and I are going over to the hardware and tack store the next town over. Wanna come?" She tucked her tiny hands under her chin, looking adorable.

I rubbed my chin, noting her timing was spot on. "It does sound tempting. I'm compiling a materials list for the new barn I want to build next year. I'm unsure if costs are the same in this part of the country, so, yeah, I'm in." I smiled appreciatively, gathering the piles of papers strewn around me.

She popped up like a kid at Christmas, "Sweet! We're leaving in ten minutes. Get it together and meet us outside." She slid off the bed on her belly and, dare I say, skipped out of the room. She was up to something. That gleam in her eye meant I was in for a surprise.

I slung on my Carhartt denim jacket and popped open the backseat cab of Elias's F250. It was a beast of a pickup, though, similar to his personality, the interior was detailed in black and camel leather that screamed sophistication inside a rough exterior. That's my friend in a nutshell. Stepping up on the running board to climb in, I almost stumbled upon seeing Seneca in the backseat as well. Her long, silky hair was braided so it fell off to the side of her delicate shoulder. Her hair alone left me breathless. It'd been far too long since we touched each other. When she bit her lip, it sparked a deep sense of need that, unfortunately, made my cock uncomfortable during the short ride to the store.

"Uh, hey, Seneca. I didn't know you'd be joining us," I stammered like a dumb teenager on his first car date.

She was stifling a laugh. "Maybe it's because you're the one joining us?" She cocked her head to the side with more sass than necessary.

I fought the urge to roll my eyes at her petty statement. "Sure. Anyway, uh, good to see you," I deadpanned, feeling if I released any of my true emotions, I would embarrass myself. We pulled out of the driveway aiming towards the Mystic River and into the next town.

Abigail turned a shiny, bright smile on Seneca, "I think it's time to go wild in that retro store we went to a few years back. What do you think?"

Seneca's head fell back, exposing her long, delicious neck. She'd always tasted like vanilla cream no matter where I licked her. *Fuck.* I was one tick away from conjuring up the sweet taste of her pussy, when she purred back at Abigail. "The magic that sexy purple dress had over Elias was priceless. He didn't have a choice but to crawl his fine ass back to you!" Elias snarked, knowing she was right.

"I wasn't *that* pussy whipped," he retorted, unconfidently.

Sure. The two women tittered while Elias stewed. These women thought they were so clever and cunning. These two were thick as thieves and forces to be respected. On the contrary, their wrath was legendary—at least in my experience.

The low hum of Jelly Roll singing "I'm Not Okay," wound around my body tightly. I'd been living every word in that song. It was like it was written only for me. I wasn't a child with grand illusions of life. *Okay, maybe when I was young.* But, shit, life got harder every goddamned day I was alive. If it weren't for my good friends and an awesome dog, I'd have walked away from being a farmer and found a comfortable ditch to live in until I died. I suppose this was why everyone says each of us needs a village. If not to lift us up but to save us from ourselves. *Mine was working overtime.*

A few minutes later, we'd pulled up to a massive barn, touting, "If we don't have it, it doesn't exist." *We'll see.* As we entered the store, Elias suggested we split up for a while and meet back at the hotdog stand in the middle of the store. I looped my arm through his tree trunk bicep, pulling him with great force, "Come on, sugar, you're with me." I waggled my eyebrows for effect, being met with a dramatic eye roll. "See you ladies in forty-five minutes."

I had a laundry list of materials I recorded on a notes app on my phone. "Let's check out lumber costs." Elias stopped in his tracks, crossing his massive arms across his chest.

"Did it ever occur to you that I also have a list of things to get? We're starting in *lighting*." He pulled me by the back of my neck, "Let's go!" he said too emphatically. *I guess we're looking at lighting first.*

We walked silently, looking at all the clever displays and discounts offered when bought in bulk. Elias picked up a hedge trimmer and held it out with two hands. "I bet your bush needs some manscaping, huh?" *What the fuck?*

"Seriously? You look like the Texas Chainsaw Massacre guy. You scare me sometimes." I waved him off, appalled, "And for the record, I'm good down there. Everything is nice and tight. You, on the other hand, need a weed whacker, especially for those nostril hairs."

His face fell. "You cut me deep, Alex. I may not recover," and skulked away.

"Oh, come on, pretty boy. Even the best of us need a refresh now and again." I cajoled him like a child.

He scoffed. "I don't need your pity, dumbass. That's my wife's job. I only look as good as I do because of her. You don't like what you see? Then fuck off or talk to Abigail."

I was goofing around! Maybe he did have a hang up about his hygiene. It was hard to believe someone that size could be so sensitive.

This place was quite spectacular. Each department was broken into residential and commercial. Giant-sized chandeliers, from lit-up wagon wheels to crystal drop styles hung from rafters, along with fans and a huge array of LED lamps. My old barn didn't have anything this nice, and not knowing if or when I got a settlement I couldn't splurge on fancy lighting. All my purchases would be functional until I had a steady income.

"What do you think of this Mercury LED chandelier? A couple of these would light up a whole barn." Elias nodded his approval.

"Elias, my cows don't need to read at night. They can moo in the dark. Besides, they're over fifteen hundred dollars each. Try again." I knew chastising him was petulant, but the enormous cost of this project was crushing me.

He put his big paw on my shoulder, "Breathe, Alex. Don't spend money on junk. You'll only have to buy it again. This is a wish list shopping trip. No dollars spent. Live it up." His smile would have been reassuring if I wasn't panicking at how quickly my money would be spent.

We played his game, moving from lighting to plumbing, then finally to the lumber yard. He wasn't wrong in suggesting I shop with my eyes and not my wallet. I could dream about my new barn with a few upgrades. My current wood barn needed a new paint job and better drainage, and, if the money fairy would drop an extra fifty thousand dollars down from the sky, I'd buy a multi-unit milking system to improve efficiency. Since I don't need to paint next year, I should consider a more cost-effective alternative. *Maybe a steel or a prefab unit?*

"Hello?" A smack on my back brought me out of my musings. "Time to meet up with the girls. I'm starving. I have to show you all the awesome junk food they sell. Fresh fried mini donuts, dairy-free ice cream (*never*), and grill-cooked corn on the cob. If

Abigail ever throws me out, you'll find me living in aisle seven. I love it here."

I knew Elias was joking. Those two were made for each other. "Noted," I said, pretending to type that into my phone.

Seneca and Abigail were already sitting at a table for four. It seemed hundreds of people were doing the same thing this Saturday afternoon, and we scored finding a table. "Hi, babe!" Abigail squealed when Elias deadlifted her to his shoulders, kissing her soundly. "I guess you had a good time," noticing our full buggy. "Look what Seneca and I found?"

Elias chimed in. "Eat first. Talk later." He pointed at each of us, asking if we wanted a brat or hotdog. Corn or chips. Water or soda. He barely waited for our answers before sprinting into line. Ten minutes later, he motioned for me to help haul our food back to the table. After stuffing a whole hotdog into his giant mouth, he sighed contentedly as if in post-coital bliss. "So good." He chugged half of a sixty-four-ounce soda before pointing to the girl's buggy. "Continue."

Seneca animatedly pointed at each item like Vanna White, starting with a thick brown and cream-swirled wool area rug folding in on itself. "This four-armed black patinaed floor lamp is perfect when you want to shine light in lots of directions. Oh! And, isn't this the cutest picture?" *Sure, if you like a giant cow with a daisy behind its ear.*

I interrupted. "Now, this beauty," I crawled out from the picnic table, entranced. "This is your best choice of the day." I ran my hand over the box on the flatbed trolley beside our table. A camel-colored boss chair with brass studded nails had my heart pumping. *My ass would look great in that chair.* Sadly, it reminded me of a similar one my dad had when I was younger. He loved that chair until my brother and I raced it with another chair down the hallway, with Dad's rifling down the basement stairs to its total demise. *Obviously, I survived, having gone to parachute school.* Regardless, I had a million things to bring from Eloheh once I figured out where to put it all.

I cocked my head warily. "Are you redecorating your barn office, Abs?"

"Actually, it's going into a workspace for Lindsey. She's been spending upwards of six hours a week on my business, and now, yours. She'll need a place she can feel comfortable."

"That makes sense, but haven't you run out of rooms? You need all five of the inn guest rooms. Your barn is stuffed with Elias's reno business and your art studio. Once my cows leave, where would you put it?" The more my puzzlement grew, the more they snickered. "Okay. What gives? What am I missing?"

Roars of laughter bleated from my friends' mouths. I must have been in my room recuperating too long. "Didn't you notice the side garage has grown since you last were here?" Elias said through a mouthful of corn.

Abigail tossed him a stack of napkins, pointing to his scruffy beard; a corn mosaic threaded through the strands. "After the community garden was planted, Derrick came over with the help of a few gardeners and built a four-room building that houses supplies and a small cashier room. Lindsey will work in the last space doing web design and marketing for me. At some point, I'll rent her the space to run her own business." She beamed.

For someone without a higher level of education, a stable home life, and a history of poor planning, she certainly understands the value of people—not the resources they bring, but simply the inherent goodness most people have if given the opportunity to let it shine through. Her picture should be in the dictionary next to the word philanthropy.

"You're something else, princess," I crooned, stealing Elias's pet name and giving her a huge hug.

"Hands off, Alex. She's *my* princess. You don't get to call her that. Right, princess?" Abigail soothed her wild beast into submission by running her hand up his massive chest with a gleam in her eye.

"Ow! Hey, why did you pinch my nipple?"

"Because you sound like a Neanderthal. He's just teasing, Alex. Relax," she chided.

Ironically, Seneca barely said nothing, which made me uncomfortable. We'd never sat in silence. Our jibes and jabs were standard fare. Without them, the air felt flat. I gathered our garbage, brought it to the bin, and contemplated our last conversation.

I apologized as sincerely as I could. Every natural inclination to touch her was shoved down, respecting her wishes. I hated every damn minute of it. Things couldn't go on this way. Seeing her today and not being able to touch her was torture. It had even affected my sleep. Once able to sleep through a tornado, I kept waking up to every creak of the floorboards, hoping she'd finally decide to visit me in the night. After praying for a reprieve for the first week, I forced myself to get over myself. Abigail's wisdom of me needing more patience would prevail. As of tonight, I'd double down and keep the lines of communication open while keeping my thoughts and body on a short leash.

Chapter 29

SENECA

Today was email day. The first went to Dr. Abel, giving him an update on both my Eloheh Farms research project and what I'd accomplished so far on the garden project. The second email went to Abigail, bringing her up to speed on material costs for the winding pathway and water features I'd need to order before the end of January so they'd arrive in time to inspect them before installation. After copying each person on my efforts, I double backed to send Dr. Abel a private message sharing my duplicitous actions loft we'd build in Alex's barn. Thank goodness, Alex still hadn't any idea about our plans to raise a barn the day after Thanksgiving. I was surprised with my mentor's quick response.

Dear Ms. Locklear:
You've done it again. I'm not sure if it's your stubbornness not to fail or your resilience to overcome obstacles that keep you turning life's lemons into lemonade. Brava!
I'll expect to see a floor plan of the loft space by next week. I may want you to add one to my own farmhouse at some point. Haha.
Best to you,

Dr. Abel

Best to you? Dr. Abel joked again? Is he going senile? Will emojis be next? I'd better send Olivia a message to check on him.

My internship task lists were finally updated and on track. By ten-thirty in the morning, I'd finally felt like I could take a full breath. I'd already collected a basket of eggs and deposited them on Abigail's counter, making a notation of the count on a chart I kept in the mudroom. I was pleased to see the only reduction in egg production was the week we'd moved them. Once a week since October, I had a local chemist sample the eggs for purity, finding only traces of contaminants for the first two weeks. His suggestion was to wait a full three months before, in good conscience, selling them. Abigail said she'd handle the disposal of the unusable eggs, and I went on with my day.

Thanksgiving was less than a week away, and I was thinking about Tiny, Annalise, Steve, and my dad. As an afterthought, only because I hadn't yet met him, I remembered Alex's brother, Dane. I sent private messages to each of them with an invitation to our Thanksgiving dinner and to stay the weekend for a surprise barn-raising weekend for Alex. Afterward, I texted both Alex and Abigail for a brief meeting in the kitchen at lunchtime. Abigail pinged my phone first with a smiling emoji, but there was nothing from Alex. Mystic Valley was notorious for bad cell service and was out of range from the house cell coverage. I knew for a fact, though, Alex wouldn't miss a meal unless he was stuck in a well. He'd be back soon enough.

Lindsey was coming over today with a marketing mockup for Eloheh Farms. The real issue was how Abigail and Elias wanted to incorporate that nonexistent name of the inn. Once we had that worked out, it would be full steam ahead. One of my brainchild ideas was to have an inn group calendar to coordinate times and dates for each of us. It would help us plan and prepare for upcoming events. So many of our decisions moving forward must have management's approval. *Hence, now and forever more, the entity Abigail and Elias shall be named "management." Again, too much time in the law library.* Every sentence I typed now sounded like legalese.

"Yoo-hoo!" A sweet young voice sounded from the foyer. "Anybody here?" That must be Lindsey, but she wasn't scheduled until later this afternoon. I closed my computer and left my room to get the door.

"Coming," I hollered, loping down the curved staircase.

It *was* Lindsey. Her happy face peered at me through black-framed square glasses that looked a bit too harsh for her fair complexion. *The girl was pure porcelain.* The blonde, messy bun on top of her head suggested she didn't know how to create a stylish messy bun or she'd just rolled out of bed. I'm going with no girlish inclinations. Not a drop of makeup rouged her flawless skin. *Bitch.* Plus, her clothing said, "I'm only wearing clothes because nudity in public isn't allowed." Saggy, grey sweatpants hung from her sleight frame, not to be outdone by the pilled full-zip fleece that the eighties wanted back. This girl was a mess. I'd have to ask Abs if she could join us on our next vintage clothes outing. At least she could leave that nasty fleece in the store for another unsuspecting patron.

"Wow! You are not what I was expecting." Once those words were out of my mouth, I knew I'd hurt her feelings. "Wait, let me rephrase that. From what Abigail has told me about your skills and amazing attitude, I had you pegged as an older person for some reason. But, hey, you are better than my imagination. I'm going to shut up now. Follow me."

"Abigail!" I called too abrasively. "Look who came early! It's Lindsey." I expected a look of surprise but none came.

"Hey, girlfriend. Thanks for coming early. Things are happening at lightning speed around here and I can barely keep up." *She knew? The time hasn't changed on the calendar.*

Lindsey snapped her wrist forward like it wasn't any big deal. *It. Was. A. Big. Deal.*

"Gals, can we have a serious chat about the calendar? Abigail, I thought we discussed the importance of using the calendar to make us all more efficient. You had Lindsey down for one o'clock, and it's only eleven in the morning. Care to explain?" My sassy, patronizing tone was not lost on her.

Ahem. "Well—I had a few things canceled and wanted to get other things moving this morning. I'm sorry I didn't change your precious calendar." *She did not just mock me.*

I choked on my saliva, "My precious calendar? There hasn't been a day in your life you've remembered to go to the grocery store, do your laundry, or call your boss to tell him you've moved out of town without my help and planning—and you *still* forget. Abigail, you know I love you to the moon and back, but your ADHD is the worst! I'm only pushing for your benefit. *And, my own.* Four people live and work here. It's not a judgment or that we care; just give us a heads-up." Pressing my hands together in prayer, I pleaded for her compliance. *I know it's a stretch!*

Lindsey looked back and forth between us like a tennis match. Then graciously stepped in like a tiny ninja mouse. "Girls, while this isn't my lane, I'd like to offer some comfort to you both." I knew she'd say something profound. I could feel it.

". . . you're both being ridiculous." She pointed to Abigail, "You're ADHD." Then, she redirected her increasingly judgmental stare at me. "And, from what Abigail has told me, you're OCD. Hello? You're polar opposite thinkers. You get that, right?" She nodded, trying to sell us something we didn't need. Neither I nor Abs flinched. "Let me try it this way. Each of you needs to work on deliberately taking a step forward to provide the other with what they need. Abigail likes serendipity and whimsy. She is creative and light-hearted. Seneca, your are tenacious, righteousness, organized, and focused on task completion. You look toward the end game. Abigail enjoys the journey. This is what attracts you to each other." A smile spread across her face, imparting what she thought was immutable wisdom.

Maybe. Probably. Fine.

"How old are you, Lindsey?" I countered, clearly zigging in another direction.

Her brows knit together, "Twenty-two. Does it matter?"

I tilted my head, reassessing her. "Either you have a hidden psychology degree, or you've recently finished one of those love language books. Your analysis hits too close to the mark. Well done, and noted. Abs? You on board with working harder to keep this ship from sinking?"

"As long as I don't have to raise the dosage on my meds, then, yes. That shit is expensive," Abigail moaned.

"Tell me about it. I can only afford one of the two drugs my therapist suggested," I mirrored her distress.

"Are you kidding? Try being dyslexic! There are no drugs for that. I only got diagnosed before I graduated high school. My parents sold their timeshare to pay for my therapy to help me get my head on straight. The guilt is killing me!"

We stood frozen, listening to Lindsey's confession. How could someone so brilliant be dyslexic? Either she's a good faker, or her therapy has worked. Not that it mattered. It didn't change how amazing she was and her incredible work for Abigail over the past couple of years. We weren't letting her go.

Abigail rushed to her side, "Holy shit, Lindsey. If you had never told me, I'd have never known."

Feeling left out, I joined their hug, squealing, "You really are a genius. You should feel so proud of yourself."

She replied unaffected, "Thanks, guys. I never meant to deceive you; it's just something I have to work around every day. Just another to-do on my long list of to-dos."

I smacked my head. "Why didn't I look at my neurodivergent brain that way? Up until I started therapy with Glenda, people would tell me I was obsessed; like it was a disease. OCD is a condition. Like yours, it never goes away. It's just something on my I deal with or around it. Priceless, Lindsey. I'll put that in a book one day." Her face blushed, and she smiled as we finished our hug.

The side door slammed, informing us one of the guys was back. "Nice. Girl-on-girl time. What did I miss?"

Each of us pivoted, drawing our arms under our chests, giving Alex our best stink eye.

Me: "You never change, do you?" I said, accusingly.

Abigail: "Do you think your perverted comments are *funny?*" Abigail's smack talk was laughable.

Lindsey: "You missed deep tonguing, boob twisting, and crotch grabbing. If you stick around, I'm sure we can whip up some body origami for your viewing pleasure."

His jaw gapped open. *She hooked that fish the first time she met him. You go, girl!*

Dumbfounded, he continued to stand there until I not so discretely pushed it shut. "Dumbass."

Abigail patted his shoulder, moving past him to the refrigerator. "There, there, Alex. Now, you have something new for your spank-bank. Say thank you to Lindsey, your new web and marketing associate."

Lindsey, ignoring the interruption, ran through the inn's stats for the past quarter, sharing her thoughts on next year's plan. Abigail flattened her hands on the counter, pressing her lips together, "You're saying we increased community garden production by eighteen percent and inn income by twenty-five? How is that even possible? Nothing has changed."

Lindsey giggled. "On the surface, nothing has. It's your efficiency that has made the difference. Data analytics show a variety of trends in market research. A lot can be learned from them."

Perplexed, Alex asked, "You're one of those savant-types, aren't you?"

His compliment sounded more like an accusation, but, in Lindsey's style, she shut his attitude down quickly. "More like a wizard." *Oh, my god, I love her so much.*

Elias walked in at the end of her slam, winking at Lindsey in admiration, "You're a girl after my own heart. I should have you review my portfolio and tell me where I can diversify. I'm sure there is untapped financial genius in that big brain of yours."

She blushed. The fact that she was so unassuming and genuine gave me hope she'd find a way for dumbass Alex to get ahead sooner than later. Any money she could find or save helped all our projects. Of course, none of it was my money to spend—only to ask for.

"What's next, Lindsey?" Abigail moved this meeting along.

Her eyebrows knitted together, and we all stiffened. "Before we talk about next year, or Alex's business, we have to solidify a name for this place. It's uncomfortable for me to speak to sponsors for your garden and other ventures when I can only give them the address." She bit her bottom lip, embarrassed.

"Exactly!" I yelled. "I've been saying that for years. Since Alex's business is setting up shop a mile away, we need boundaries, or an org chart, or something." Finally, I could share my angst about this topic." Lindsey would make this better or we'd be in deep doo-doo. "Can I ask one more thing since we're on the topic of naming stuff? We need names for the guest rooms, too. Blue Room sounds so . . . boring."

Alex took a stab at speaking again. *Brave man that he was.* "My farm back home was called Eloheh Farms. It means harmony, wholeness, abundance and peace. It's a Cherokee name." He looked at me with sad eyes, "Seneca is half Ojibwe from the Chippewa Nation. I want to carry the Native American heritage of the Eloheh name to my part of the property. I-I mean if you and

Elias would allow it." He turned to them with pleading eyes. He was impossible to say no to. *Trust me. I'd tried.*

I sighed deeply, putting my insecurities aside. Alex truly cared about me. Why would he have said all that stuff? Without thinking, I stretched my hand over the table in his direction. A peace offering, as it were. When we touched, an eagerness of desire hummed through my body zeroing in between my thighs.

"None of us will forget your people's hardships. Promise," Alex said, raising my hand to his lips for a gentle kiss.

If this man wanted back in my pants, he'd said and done all the right things. My mouth salivated thinking about that mouth and his trail off kisses down my . . .

"What do you think, Abigail? This is your ancestors' estate. It runs farther back than Alex's farm," Elias asserted.

"More importantly, you don't want to confuse your brand with his," Lindsey said preemptively. "Let's toss some names around."

Everyone threw out their best suggestions as Lindsey recorded them. After ten minutes, the unanimous winner was *The Farnsworth Inn and Eloheh Farms*.

"Long but classy. Distinctive, yet inclusive. Nice job, everyone." Elias crossed his arms, looking smug, "Yeah, that little jewel was mine. I'm not just a pretty face." A round of slow claps began. The one person with authority to give the go-ahead had shoved her tongue down his throat.

When they came up for air, Abigail fanned herself. "O.M.G. I knew I'd married a genius. I love it!" She launched herself at him again like we weren't standing there looking at them. *Yeah, he was getting laid as soon as this meeting was over.*

Lindsey cleared her throat, "While you two are re-consummating your marriage, the rest of us need to move forward. I know I'm young, but I've researched hundreds of inn sites, and none offer what you have here. Identifying your inn with your legacy's name will align with all the other Farnsworth buildings in town, increasing your SEO. Eloheh Farms won't suffer by brand, only by location. However, Alex, if you're feeling extra entrepreneurial, you could form a separate company that creates and ships your organic dairy products nationwide. It's a leap, but doable."

Stars formed in Alex's eyes as he followed the trail Lindsey supplied. He'd mentioned this to me on a local level but never commercially across the country. That might be more than even he could handle alone.

"Let's not get ahead of ourselves. Alex doesn't even have a barn, let alone enough cows to handle that kind of capacity. Let's put a pin in that idea. Moving forward?" I waved Lindsey on.

"Regarding the meeting I called for earlier, could you all stick around after Lindsey leaves? I need to run something important by you. It won't take long."

Lindsey quickly packed up, giving hugs all around, "Keep those good ideas coming. Talk to you soon. Happy Thanksgiving." Abigail walked her to the front door while everyone else cleaned up.

Alex sidled up alongside me at the island bumping my hip. I fought my growing grin chancing a glance up at his high cheekbones and sexy as hell full, red lips. "Hey," he whispered. *When did that word become synonymous with sex?*

"Hey. Thanks for respecting my people. It was... cool." I bit my lip not knowing how our attraction was going to keep this now platonic relationship from returning to our base animal instincts.

He rubbed his lower lip with the tip of his long, thick thumb. *Not fair. Baiting, my head yelled. Overruled, my ovaries cried.*

Tipping his head down, he spoke quietly into the shell of my ear, "I do respect you. Your genius. Your heart. Your abilities and feistiness. But I especially respect everything from here to here," he said, pointing from my head to my feet. He nipped the top of my ear with his teeth and sat down at the table leaving me swooning and speechless.

Elias blurted out, "Are you two back to fucking again?"

Argh! A long list of expletives zipped through my brain like a frustrated cartoon. "I'm not even going to dignify that with a response." Abigail picked up where I'd left off.

"What's on your mind, bestie?"

"Right. Thanksgiving is in ten days, and I thought we should include our friends and family. We've all been through so much this year. I'd like us to share our gratitude together. What do you think?" No one spoke, so I pressed on. "I was thinking I'd reach out to my dad and my step-monster. More than likely, they'll go to her precious family, excluding me," saying the last part under my breath. "Alex, what about Tiny, and your sister's family? Is Dane coming?" I was hopeful at least Tiny would come. He's single.

I closed my eyes, realizing I had hijacked Abigail's home and holiday again. "I'm so sorry, Abs and Elias. I'm so comfortable here that I keep forgetting I'm a guest. I should be asking if you are open to us inviting strangers to your home for Thanksgiving." My bottom lip rolled down ever so slightly. I'm pretty sure my puppy dog eyes would seal the deal.

"Oh my god, you're pathetic. Of course, you can invite *anyone* you want. You're family. God knows, I don't have one, and Elias's has all but disowned his. But please don't have high hopes for your dad, though. It's a lovely thought to include him, even if he always disappoints you."

Abigail hit the nail on the head. She was number one on my gratitude list, always. "Is there anyone else you can think of from town? Lindsey? Micha? Derrick?"

"Yes, to Derrick. What a sweetie but Lindsey is going to her Aunt Micha's for the weekend. May Derrick and Lindsey . . .he is almost old enough to be her dad. Like Elias. "

"Hey! A very young dad. Never mind. Fuck all of you. I have a ba—" I cut him off quickly before he spilled the beans about the barn. "That's right, your back-thing to fix, I spurted out.

"I'm taking your car, Abs." Elias stormed out of the kitchen before he said another word.

"Sure, babe. Grab milk on your way back!" He waved in acknowledgment.

"What was that about?" Alex exclaimed.

Me and Abigail shared a look. "He's got a little sciatica. My big man still thinks he can lift cars by himself. Not anymore." Abigail flitted across the kitchen like her explanation was sufficient, stopping only to answer my question.

"Do you need anything from me, Abs? Otherwise, I'm going to start staking my brick path. Elias needs to look it over and make sure it's Americans with Disabilities Act safe. It sure is convenient your hubby is a mechanical engineer."

"I'd hurry up. It's going to rain any second," she cautioned, leaving the room.

"It's only water. I'll wear my galo . . ." A giant crack of thunder flashed purple outside the kitchen windows, and my shoulders slumped. I really did have to accomplish that task before the end of the week. "I guess I'll have to go to Plan B. Plan Boner."

Abigail stifled a giggle. "How tragic."

My dear Alex sat there watching the whole exchange and bolted out of his seat without even a wave. You could hear his feet clomping on every other stair leading to his room. "Like a dog with a boner," she said, cackling. *She's got that right.*

Chapter 30

ALEX

I *must have done something good.*

Those words from the *Sound of Music* were pounding in my ears. Old movie musicals shouldn't be in my head right now but damn my parents for playing that shit all day, every day, when I was a kid. Disappointing, but true, I finally said something right to Seneca, and I'm happily going to get laid like the good man I am. She punished me long enough with her adorable fluttering long eyelashes fanning her flawless, tawny skin. The way her stare ravaged me when I cut firewood, forced me to fuck myself in a cold shower.

Today, though, I almost came in my pants when she said "Hey," like a seductress. When she bit her lip as though I was sucking her nipples, I grabbed the counter to keep from collapsing. She was a siren, an illness in my head I couldn't stop. Everything good, bad, and ugly about her I've come to love. There! I said it. I'm a man in love.

Seneca padded into the room wearing a short, silky kimono covered in pale pink flowers, like those on a lily pad. It wrapped around her, loosely dipping lower in the front every step she took.

Her swaying hips pulled me into a trance as they carried her across the room.

She hummed, amused. "It will be raining the rest of the day, Mr. Valize. I know we've already had our morning meeting, but I was hoping we could, uh, catch up on those, um, less important but necessary tasks. I know we agreed to let them go for now, but we shouldn't forget they need our attention at some point. What do you think?"

Standing next to my bed with her robe exposing the curve of her ample breasts and baby-soft belly, all rational thought evaporated. My girl came to play and I wouldn't disappoint her again. This was my moment to show her what she meant to me.

Mmm. "Your request is very compelling. Though, if you are completely sure of cleaning up our old list and starting fresh with a new one, I would be most happy to honor your request."

She smiled coyly. With the slightest wiggle of her shoulders, the flimsy material slid down her arms, catching at her elbows. "You're becoming a very wise man, Mr. Valize. You've been paying close attention, and I respect that about you. Let's let the past stay in the past. That list doesn't need to apply here anymore, does it?"

I saw her pouty lips moving but had difficulty comprehending her meaning. "You mean my petty behavior? Or my quick temper?" I asked sincerely. Any wrong answer and this whole moment would end us for good.

She crawled across the sheets, tucking her full length tightly to my side. "Both are right answers. However, there are a few more we should let go of. Such as my compulsion to micromanage everything you say and give you the benefit of the doubt because words aren't your forte." I breathed a sigh of relief. She dragged her pointer finger down my midline, never taking her eyes off me. When she winked at me, I fell even harder for her.

"Sure. That sounds reasonable," I stuttered out. I knew we were missing a few poignant issues in our relationship discussion, but my brain shifted to low as the rest of my body revved up to high.

Like a ninja, Seneca rolled herself flat on top of me, pressing her breasts into my hard chest. She kissed me softly, speaking nonsensical words like "niineta" and "gaagige." They were words with no meaning to me, but they sounded right coming from her sweet lips. I could feel the passion in her voice as she stretched each word out between her ever-powerful kisses.

Her tongue tangled with mine, staking her claim over me like she'd never done before. She wanted this, me, with every fiber in her body. Maybe I was stupid to assume these things, but I've been studying this woman for years. She was intricate and delicate, like a spider's web. Yet also, she wielded her will like a sledgehammer. I'm slowly learning her tells, meeting her in the middle, and together we're improving our relationship daily.

Her kisses traveled behind my ear, sucking the tender skin that made me quiver. She distracted me with her mouth, sneaking her free hand to my peaked nipple, pinching and rolling the oversensitive nerve bundle until I moaned. Her relentless torture forced me to push her hand to the other side, where she began the process again in earnest. Learning more through actions, not words, I witnessed her using my moves on me. *Clever girl.*

Done with her onslaught, I grabbed both her ass cheeks and attempted to roll her onto the mattress, only to have her drive her knees into my sides.

"Uh-uh," she tutted. "This has been on my to-do list for several years now, and quite frankly, it can't wait any longer."

"To-do list?" Concern bloomed across my face. Seneca must have seen my concern because she dangled her heavy tits over my face to soothe my fretting away with a kiss. Opportunity was dangling over me. Snatching a nipple into my mouth for a deep long suck was the only proper thing to do.

"Oh, God, Alex. You're so greedy," her wanton sounds echoed in my ears. "Yes. Fuck. The other one. Do the other one," she demanded. I replaced my mouth with a hand shifting my focus to her other peak. My woman loved nipple play, and, if she'd let me take control, I'd have her tied to the bed, giving it to her hard.

She pulled back abruptly when I finally released my mouth, returning her mouth to my chest. "I can hear you thinking, Alex. You better let me have my way with you or you'll be back on the bench for the rest of the year."

The year?!

"Fine. What am I thinking now?" I sassed back.

She painted slow circles around my areoles, pursing her lips in deep thought. "You're thinking I should tie you to the bed instead of me, right?"

Doh! She can read minds.

I lied. "I was not! I was-was thinking you'd better jump onto my steel cock before it falls off from neglect."

She chuckled. "Falls off? Seriously?" Instead of doing what I wanted, she pressed a finger to my lips. "I'd suggest you empty your pretty little head and shut your sexy mouth or I'll make sure your cock suffers a worse fate than neglect." She raised her head in challenge.

"Nah, I'm good. Do your worst." Probably not the best thing to say to a control freak. I trusted her—mostly.

"Grab the headboard, Alex. Do not let go. Fight the urge to touch me, and I'll make this so good for you." She purred, placing kisses haphazardly over my chest, down to my concave abdomen, and the last at my belly button. My eyes fought my desire to watch the tip of her tongue connecting to my burning skin each time she placed another kiss lower, inch by inch. My eyes rolled back, lost in sensations until . . . nothing.

My eyes opened groggily, confused. She sat staring at my body, diverting her gaze from my face to my shoulders. My hands gripped the bedrails like my life depended on it, warning myself of the consequences. I focused on her face moving closer to mine, then moving upward bringing her luscious body with her. I was out of my mind when her dripping wet pussy hovered over my throbbing erection. I could feel her chest beating erratically above me, mirroring my lusty need. Seneca slipped her forefinger into her mouth, wetting it thoroughly, then dragging it from my happy trail to the base of my cock. "Aww, fuck, Sen," I growled.

A wicked grin crept up her high cheekbones, promising more. She wet her finger again and reached for my seeping cock, swirling my pre-cum with a featherlight touch over my crown. I never knew she had so much restraint. Most of our fucking had been like a cockfight; antagonistic, feral, and fast. Today, though, there wasn't fucking. She showed me a completely different side of her personality. Not the feistiness I knew, but how she could contain her emotions when she chose. That her impulsive nature was manageable when given time and attention. If this kind of treatment was the prize for letting her have those things, I'd turn over the keys to the farm and let her have her way. Damn the consequences!

Pushing herself lower down my thighs, she nestled herself between my knees so her lips were perfectly lined up to lick my cock. She breathed small puffs of hot air over my crown, short circuiting my brain. My chest froze, not knowing whether I would live or die, waiting longer each time until another hot breath passed over again. She teased the tip of her tongue through my slit, watching my body convulse like a vulture waiting for its prey. She was playing with her food, and loving every fucking minute of it.

"Jesus, Sen. You're killing me." Her lips quirked and made another pass through my slit, then sat up, pleased with herself.

Sshh. She hummed. By the way her eyes shifted, I could see the wheels in her brain considering her next move. Her eyes widened, having made a decision. Before I knew it, she reached her right hand to cup my balls, squeezing a little too firmly. "Fuucck!" I bleated. She'd been so focused on the tip I didn't see that coming.

Pleased with herself, she massaged each sack, studying every gap and formation in and outside it. I felt a finger slide down the seam between them, my heart leaping out of my chest as she inserted her finger into my anus, pressing firmly.

"Fucking hell!" I screamed—a lot—not sure if I loved or hated it. "Do that again," I pleaded. Instantly, she rubbed the walnut-sized prostate until I bucked her off. *I liked it more than a lot.*

She bit her lip, "I'm learning so much about you, Mr. Valize." She pressed a different finger to her lips, reminding me to shut my mouth. Seneca repositioned herself between my thighs, pushing my knees up toward my shoulders. I'd done this to her several times to get a better angle to reach her G-spot but hadn't considered it a plus for a man. Her lips captured my head, sucking deeply, then popping off. Tiny solar flares burst behind my eyes, sending glorious chills up my spine.

One small hand coiled up and down my dick as her mouth took in the rest. She was driven and committed to her task, so, when the other hand returned to my prostate, I almost passed out. The sensations were nothing I had ever experienced before. No wonder Seneca needed me to let her have her way in bed. I was an idiot to have ever denied her.

"You're almost there, Alex. You've been very patient. Remember this moment and how it felt. More importantly, remember what it takes to bring you back here." She dove down again, doubling her efforts, her head bobbing furiously. I panted as my balls tightened and tingles streaked up my spine.

"I'm almost there," I cried. Taking advantage of my position, Seneca inserted two fingers into my ass, tearing the biggest orgasm I'd ever had. My body quaked as sweat poured out of me. The heavenly gates had opened, receiving my soul as my body succumbed to her magnificent ministrations.

"Uhhh! Fuck, Sen. That's it. That's my girl. Jesus Christ, woman. That's some Triple X porn right there. Whew!"

She continued milking my dick as she slowly removed her fingers from my ass. She knelt back, smiling profusely, her rosy cheeks beamed with pride. Fuck. I was proud of her, too. She'd been patiently waiting for the perfect time to reveal this specific wanton side of her to me. I wouldn't take it for granted. She had given me a piece of herself out of trust and respect, not whimsy or gratuity. This gift came from her soul, and I accepted it wholeheartedly.

Chapter 31

SENECA

Why I bothered calling my father at all was idiotic. I didn't need a crystal ball to know my request for him to visit would be shot down. "Honey, it's not that I don't want to see you. I do. It's that Belinda's kids are throwing her a birthday party on Friday, and her grandkids will be in town. You understand, right?"

His pathetic pleading was more of the same I expected to hear out of his spineless body. Something inside of me snapped. I was done accepting his lame excuses. He knew where to go if he wanted to spend time with me. This wasn't a relationship between a father and daughter. No, it was a symbiotic relationship with his second wife. He was a parasite trapped in her orbit that didn't need to affect me the way I'd let it in the past. Without apology, I released my inner Kraken.

"No, Dad. I don't understand. You have one daughter. One. While I don't require you to do anything for me, including respecting my feelings or situation, I require you to remember you have a child. Adult or not, I've been your daughter longer than Belinda's been your wife. I understand you have a new family now, but you could at least try to visit me any time other than the holidays. Are you aware I have a graduation ceremony coming up in May? You probably already have an excuse six months in advance as to why you won't be coming. Don't worry, I'm not sending you an invitation. Forget about me. You've made your priorities crystal clear. Take good care of yourself and have a great life. Bye."

I can't believe I finally said those words. My therapist and I have been cultivating a similar statement for two years. I kept calm, said exactly what I needed to say, and exited the situation. He didn't even so much as try to stop me from hanging up. His resignation hurt the most. Would this be the last conversation I ever had with him? The ball is in his court now.

Forcibly, I put the call in my rearview mirror. I had work to do. I moved up delivery times for all the barn material to this week. It had to be counted, categorized, and protected before the end of the day Wednesday. It may be Monday today, but I could feel the minutes closing in on my deadline two days away.

I wandered to Elias's workspace to confer on our final plans. Our Herculean project took a village. I was the mayor, Abigail was the ambassador, and Elias was, well, the rest of the village.

Knocking on the sliding barn door before entering, I slid it open slightly, stepped onto the concrete pad and walked soundlessly to his workbench. "Hi, Elias. Do you have time for a final walkthrough for the next few days?" I pulled out my customary stool, dusted off a small area, and carefully set down my folio and computer.

He made a series of guttural noises, then made me wait ten minutes. "If now isn't a good time, I can come—" he cut me off.

"Let's get this over with." He shook his head like he'd been in another world. "Sorry. I get so engrossed in my work that I forget others have a life to live. Let me grab my manifests and see what I'm expecting."

I opened my computer to review the project management flowchart I put together a few weeks ago. "I need to meet the lumber liquidator today at two and the steel guy at four over at the building site. When are the hardware people dropping off the fasteners, nails, and the like?"

He waded through a stack of papers, stopping to peruse an order. "Some time today between your other deliveries. If you need me to swing by the property to check them in, it's not a problem.

"Great," I pressed on, not looking up. "Tomorrow, we have windows, HVAC, and the City Planner to walk the property one last time. Did you make the blueprint changes he requested and file for a permit?"

"Yep. Burrams, ditches, and drainage are all fixed. I appreciated him thinking ahead about how the crops needed to drain away from the barn even though they'd be hundreds of yards away. "You know how water is," we said in unison, "It flows to the lowest possible point."

"Terrific. Tiny, Annalise, and Stephen are confirmed for Thanksgiving dinner. Derrick and half a dozen carpenter friends will be onsite by nine Friday morning. By sundown Sunday, Alex's going to have a barn."

Elias's eyes beamed brightly for his friend. They'd been through a lot of stuff over the years. Mostly good, if not tainted by his archaic parents and their lack of interest in their only son. This weekend would change the course of his friend's life and I could see the pride on his face at being able to resurrect his past into a Technicolor future.

I pressed my hand to my chest, "Oh my god, that's amazing. I hoped everyone could make it. This is going to be so much fun. Lindsey said she contacted the local news station and newspapers to cover the event and get some early exposure. She even has a few friends who asked to help. Abigail has a task team from the community gardens who will man a food tent the whole weekend. Did we forget anything?" I was jittery with nerves. Everything needed to run perfectly to reach our goal on Sunday.

He smacked his head, "Duh! Heavy equipment. Hi-lo, pneumatic tools, all the good stuff to get this sucker standing quickly. My buddies at the equipment rental place donated it all for the weekend. They'll be back early Monday morning, so we need to finish as soon as possible. I want all those pasture gates and rails dropped between the posts before the hi-lo leaves."

Shutting my laptop lid, I exclaimed, "Sounds like we have a plan, buddy."

"What plan are you talking about," a smooth, sexy voice inquired. *Oh, shit.*

"Seneca's Zen Garden pathway. It will take at least a month to receive the stone and gravel she needs for her spring project. Our timeline is in place. No need to worry," he said seamlessly. *Damn, he was good.*

Alex pulled on his stubbled chin with a finger and thumb. "Wow. I'm impressed at how quickly you've pulled this together. It's like you've been planning this for years," he laughed broadly, cracking himself up.

"Four to be precise," I said, drolly. He sidled up behind me, casually running a hand down my ass as I gathered my things. "I can't wait to see you working on it. You know. Your behind in the air and shirt dipping low so I can see your buxom boobs."

He was shameless. No amount of schooling was going to work that out of his system. I snorted, "Only for you, Alex. Too bad you'll be too busy chasing cows in a pasture to bother me. However, if you behave yourself, I will give you the honor of escorting me down the path for the first time. *I had a flash of us walking arm and arm with my mother hovering overhead.*

I shivered, my eyes fluttering at the feelings emitted by that vision. When my mother entered my consciousness, good things happened. If she could help me complete these internships, I might enjoy that walk with the man who made me want a future with him.

Three days of deliveries coupled with three days of distracting Alex from visiting his pastures. Abigail had him running into town several times a day to pick up things she "forgot" from the wine and cheese specialty store to the world renowned French bakery. Then, two towns over, he needed to pick up the best shrimp in Connecticut. When she sent him to the grocery store for ten pounds each of sliced roast beef, salami, and turkey, and everything else needed to make dozens of sandwiches for three days, he began to ask questions.

"Abigail, far be it from me to question your catering excellence, but who are you feeding with all this food? My family and Tiny will be gone Friday morning and we can't possibly eat this much lunch meat in one weekend." He stood parked in her kitchen doorway, his forearms on either side of the frame.

Abigail looked at me, but I kept my head down, hiding behind my computer. "Tell him, Seneca," she demanded, turning her back on Alex, fighting the tremors in her shoulders.

I rolled my eyes at the sheer drama of this charade. "Your sister called me this morning asking if they could stay for the weekend since the kids wanted to see Olde Mystic Village and the vernacular bridge. I couldn't deny her, so we have a few extra mouths to feed. Prepare yourself for a loud, full house. Besides, your brother might still come. Have you heard from him?"

"Huh," he muttered. "Seems like Annalise is talking to you more than me. *Women*. "As for Dane, it's a yes for Thanksgiving dinner, but he won't get here until after four. He said to start without him if we were hungry." Alex turned to leave when Elias waltzed into the kitchen.

"Where are you going? I need your help with the new office building. I know you can drywall, so join me out there when you're done in the hen house." He snapped open the fridge grabbing a bottle of water, knocking it shut with his fine ass, and air kissing his wife before exiting the side door.

"Hen house?" Alex questioned. "Did he just call me a hen?"

"Cluck cluck, baby. Pretty soon Amy the Great is gonna hunt you down and make you her new beau." Abigail clucked her tongue, getting a rise out of him.

"No fucking way. That chicken gives me the creeps. It's like she knows what I'm thinking," he said, hooking his ball cap from the hook to his head, grabbing his coat, and disappearing out the door.

I laughed, "That man is a handful. Now that he's gone, I need to meet my delivery guys. I'll be back by five and help you get the dining room table set. Do you need anything before I go?"

Abigail waved me off. "All set. Pizza tonight. Too much cooking to do before tomorrow." She worried her bottom lip looking at three to-do lists in front of her. She always had a plan. Usually a good one, too. Though most had enough holes to make Swiss cheese. She was an idea girl, and great at executing them. It was the messy stuff in the middle that tripped her up.

ALEX

Thursday morning came in with a flurry, and I wasn't talking about snow. Double ovens blasted, three adults and two kids dumped a foyer full of luggage at my feet, and, by noon, two grown-ass men were wrestling in the living room over the remote. *Yeah, one of them was me.*

"Come on! You always hog the remote on game day. I called it last year, and I'm not taking no for an answer," I bellowed, hunkering over a very relaxed, unmovable Elias, legs spread, chomping potato chips on the couch.

"No," he deadpanned. "Go to your fucking room and watch on your own fucking TV. This one is mine. Like it or lump it." *Very mature, indeed.*

"Language!" Annalise yelled.

Elias blanched. "Sorry."

Every year it was the same thing, and every year my sorry ass landed in the wingback chair drinking a beer like a petulant child. This year, though, Tiny took up the other side of the couch asking for the remote. When Elias handed it over without so much as a blink, I fumed.

"Why does Tiny get the remote?" I muttered shifting in my seat.

Elias smiled at Tiny, who smiled back, "Because Tiny is my guest, and you're my pain in the ass. Simple." Tiny ho, ho, hoed a laugh waiting for the next jab.

I scrubbed my face watching the television screen blindly. "You have to be the worst friend in the world," I crowed. "The worst!"

"Aw. Come on, you big baby. I'm not the worst. I got Tiny to stay this weekend to help us get your pasture rails set up. That's gotta be worth something." Elias waggled his brows my way followed by Tiny doing the same.

I shook my head, not hearing clearly, "You did what now?"

Elias put a chip in his mouth chomping loudly, keeping his gaze on the game. "You heard me. We're getting your precious pasture set up this weekend. You're welcome."

I jumped up from my seat with a whoop, "I—geez—fuck, yeah! Thank you so much! Now I can drive my girls to stretch their haunches. Oh, guys, thank you so much!" I ran across the room tackling Elias with a noogie on top of his chestnut locks, then over to Tiny who put his hands up like he'd kill me if I touched him. "Cool, high five then." I couldn't stop smiling all damn day and night. Sleeping would be impossible, but who needs sleep when your future started tomorrow?

"What's all the noise out here?" Abigail said, stopping in front of Elias for a chip. He wasted no time lifting her onto his lap and planting a sultry kiss to her eager lips. *Lucky fucker.* Seneca had made herself scarce so far, peeling potatoes with my sister while

Stephen took the kids out in the golf cart for a tour of the property. It would be the only quiet hour of the weekend.

As promised, Dane arrived at four with a backpack and a bouquet of flowers. *Kiss up.*

"Whoa! I don't remember Thanksgiving's like this here at the inn. It's so loud." He dropped his pack in the mudroom, and walked through to the living room with flowers stretched toward Abigail. Maybe he thought it would protect him from the kids, but it didn't protect him from Abigail who dropped from Elias's lap and wrapped herself like an alien around his maturing body. Dane wasn't a kid anymore at six feet tall. He'd filled out this past year, especially since he found a girl he wanted to impress. Software development majors weren't known for their physiques but, when Dane suggested to his Dungeons and Dragons group that they skip the game twice a week and lift some weights, he formed a following.

Abigail stopped wrapping her tiny hands around his bulging shoulders and down half his chest before I interrupted her. "Abs," I said in warning, "One more inch and I narc on you to Elias. Feeling up a minor is poor form," I said, winking at my brother.

"Minor? *Pfft.* I've been legal for three years, if you recall. I can't help it I'm irresistible."

Seneca had a talent for sliding into a room at the most inopportune times. "He sounds just like you," she pointed at me. "Congrats. You've created a clone without consummation." She clapped her hands together, cracking herself up. Once she pulled herself together, she extended her hand sincerely, "Hi. I'm Seneca. Alex's other pain in the ass. Good to meet you."

Dane looked at me with wide eyes. "Hello, Seneca," he said, skipping the handshake and leaning in for a full-body hug. "You're definitely the prettier ass by far. I'm Dane. The smarter of the two Valize brothers. It should be obvious, but I didn't want you to pity my brother because he is a bigger—."

A knowing smile was shared at my expense. I'm a big boy. I can take it. "Sorry. Our little meet and greet time is over. Dane, go to the basement and bring up six folding chairs, set them up, and get ready to mash potatoes. Thirty pounds this year. Think those big muscles of yours can handle it?" I said running my calloused hands up his arms like I wanted to feel him up. His grunt said it all.

Dinner began early at five followed by board games and drinking. My sister's kids were still on a tight schedule, so I knew when the real party could begin sooner than later. Snuggling up by the six-foot-tall fireplace with Baileys and hot chocolate was a Thanksgiving tradition. For me, this year started a new tradition of Seneca's long legs strewn over mine, and the two of us tucked under a blanket on the chaise.

Soft holiday music hummed through the living room as her warm body snuggled deeper into mine. Imagining the Farnsworth family sharing stories and promises of a bright future permeated the walls, whispering through the centuries. It occurred, touring through Mystic for the first time, the Farnsworth family didn't just live here; they thrived here, building the library, post office, orphanage, and city buildings. I loved how Abigail and now Elias were working together with their community to continue that legacy adding another whole dimension to this town with their gardens. Once Lindsey was done with our new website, Abigail could start offering gardening, cooking and pottery classes with the wheel Elias gave her years ago. Dreams came true here at the Farnsworth Inn and Eloheh Farms. I prayed mine would come true as well.

Still snuggled in with Seneca, I cleared my throat to get everyone's attention, kissing that sweet spot that drove her crazy before I began.

"Growing up, Annalise, Dane, and myself looked to our parents as protectors, guides, and, I'll say it, taskmasters. When they passed, it left a gaping hole in our family that couldn't be filled until now. You've all protected me these past few months, guided me in ways I didn't think I needed and moved me forward when I could have dug a hole and stayed buried for years." My voice caught, forcing me to pause. "I'd like to make a toast. From blood to bonds of friendship, you are my family. You are what truly matters to me, and my gratitude runs deep for each of you. Cheers!"

Several hear-hears sang out, but nothing rang brighter than Seneca shifting herself to look up at me with her big, brown soulful eyes. Moments passed as we stared into each other's eyes. Time stopped but for our hearts thumping wildly against each other. "Same," she uttered as if a sudden reality washed over her, then laid her head back down into my shoulder, sighing deeply.

Chapter 32

ALEX

There wasn't a snowflake or drop of rain that would keep me from getting those rails up today. I felt bad, okay, not so bad that our friends and family got roped into helping me. First, an early wake-up call. Then, a cold breakfast. I said, "Suck it up cupcakes, daddy needs her girls out to pasture."

Seneca had grabbed the children to gather the morning's eggs, and I shoved Dane and Tiny out to milk the cows. Abigail was a drill sergeant in the kitchen—directing traffic—and me and Elias were out loading up his truck with tools, blankets, and cases of water.

"You ready for today?" Elias inquired.

I looked at him funny. Elias didn't do small talk. "Ah, yeah. Why wouldn't I be?" I threw an air-compressor into the back of the pickup bed wondering what the hell was with him.

"Just checking. We probably won't get all the work done today and I wanted to set the right expectations. You sometimes get ahead of yourself," he said paternally.

"Thanks, Dad. I'm good. But now that you mention it, I can't thank you enough for taking time out of your busy schedule and ruining your holiday weekend to help me out. I promise I'll make it up to you one day." I slapped him on the shoulder as I crossed the drive toward the house.

"Damn straight you will!" he hollered back.

I walked into the house stopping in the bathroom for a last pit stop before announcing to everyone else to use it, too. "We are leaving in ten minutes. Five of you in Elias's pickup. Everyone else in the minivan. Someone, help Abigail get those baskets of food into the back of my truck. Now!"

As promised, we were backing out of the driveway to drive the mile and half to the service drive leading off the main road. A strange feeling came over me. The bridge between the past and the present began today. We were a long way off from resolving my land and water issues. Government involvement in my land would take time to resolve. Magnates of industry weren't going to hand over money for reparations without a fight. I needed to shut down what I couldn't control and enjoy what I could. Having friends and family at my side was the best way I could see that happening.

Elias made the turn-off driving over the small swail in the field to a small army of people standing next to mountains of lumber, steel, and equipment. *What is going on?* Elias looked at me with a stupid grin. I spun in my seat to Seneca who was grinning the same way. "What did you do?"

Tears ran down her cheeks, her chest heaving with emotion, "Bringing you back to life."

Oh my god. Oh my god. This woman.

I turned toward the front windshield, looking at an army of people in front of me. The enormity of what she accomplished, left me mute.

As she often did, Abigail squealed from the backseat, "Get me out of here! We have a barn to raise."

A what?

I scrubbed my face, "Come again?"

Elias patted my shoulder. "Let's go build your barn, buddy." He maneuvered his massive body from the front seat leaving me to digest what just happened. Seneca stayed with me, waiting quietly for—what? A complete and total meltdown? Babysit a sobbing, unworthy slob? A witness to my humility?

Her small hand pressed onto my shoulder. "You can do this, Alex. You deserve a new start. Everyone here believes in you and your future. Be the Phoenix and rise from the ashes. Prove to yourself you're more than the sum of your pieces."

How does this woman always know what I'm thinking? It's frightening. I'd often thought it was connected to her Native ancestry, but, more often, she had to be an angel on earth sent to watch over me. I crossed my hand over my chest to clutch hers, tipping my head to kiss her hand. "One day, I'll have the right words to tell you everything in my heart. Until then, please accept my undying devotion and gratitude for staying by my side and seeing me through. You're unbelievable, Seneca."

SENECA

I felt like a fairy godmother, granting wishes and making all the children happy.

Abigail was in her glory, tending to everyone's needs with food, water, and high spirits. Annalise, Stephen, and the kids organized ten tool belts with nails, hammers, measuring tapes, and the like for all our carpenters. Alex was spinning in circles, still in a dream state, and Elias and I were huddled around our blueprints with Tiny, Derrick, and all his buddies.

Elias took the helm, calling everyone to come closer, shoving a box of hard hats into the middle of the circle, and pulling me next to his side.

"Take one and wear it. I don't have insurance for stupid behavior. When in doubt, ask for help. Our goal today is to frame this bad boy. For those of you who can come back tomorrow, we'll hang a steel roof and get the exterior walls set. We'll pour concrete in the spring, but it's a dirt floor for now. Try to keep your blood off it." He winked at Derrick, reminding him of a previous incident. "With any luck, the slider doors will go in on both the long and short sides of the barn by Sunday. Work lights will run by generator once we have a place to hang them. Any questions?"

Dane shouted, "When's lunch?" He got shoved around pretty badly after that crack and kept his head down for the rest of the afternoon.

Once everyone was up to speed, he hooked up a speaker to his truck radio, blaring the best from the 80s to classic country favorites. Everyone was revved up, making a difference in Alex's life, sending my heart to the moon and back. I wanted this for him. I wanted—needed—him to feel good about himself again. Our relationship required him to find his center and stay there. Alex wasn't a depressive person. Life oppressed him into a funk that was unquestionably difficult to pull out of. I justified my involvement as his intern. Helping Mr. Valize at Eloheh Farms was my duty first. As his girlfriend, though, I wanted him to feel good about himself so he could do anything his heart desired.

Elias and I will share a timeline for each phase of this project with Alex next week. Tiny and his sister's family will leave on Sunday, along with everyone in town who needs to return to work. Dane will leave for finals on Sunday, returning in two weeks to help through his Christmas break. We hoped Alex and his brother could finally put those pasture rails in place so he could sleep again. My head was spinning with everything happening at once. I needed a moment to breathe.

Two arms slid around my freezing torso, nuzzling a cold nose to the nape of my neck. "You sure know how to make a guy happy."

Hmm. "Just this one. Do you like the layout? We can change any of the interior setup before the build-out. I hope you didn't mind that I copied the same style as your last barn with a few upgrades."

He turned me around, placing a soft kiss on my mouth. "If you mean an automated milking station, stainless steel troughs, and more windows? Then, yeah, I'm over the moon."

I smiled into his mouth, "Those and a second-story loft. I wanted you to have a calm, relaxing space instead of returning home to rest. You know all that stuff you approved at the hardware place?" His eyes went wide. "Yep, those are for your office. Not Lindsey's." It was fun to surprise Alex. The faces he made were hilarious.

"Including the giant canvas of a daisy-adorned dairy cow?" His lips pressed together, hoping that it was a joke.

I paused for effect, "No, Alex. That's for Lindsey. You're getting a giant close-up of Amy the Great sitting in Elias's shoe. It's inspiring." I burst into tears. The look on his face when I deadpanned my reply was priceless. I loved screwing with this guy.

He closed his eyes, bemused, "One day, Seneca, when I can see straight, you're going to get it bad."

I jogged in place, "Oooo. Promises. Promises. Do your worst, Alex. In the meantime, it looks like it's time to stand up the walls of your new barn."

With a quick kiss, he bolted back to the fray to discuss logistics. Elias, our mechanical genius, researched wind, sunrise and sunset, and other meteorological factoids that would optimize the barn's positioning, and decided that squaring it up fifty feet from the property line would work well. Vehicles could move around it, and no land would be wasted.

It seemed like we'd only begun when a cowbell rang. A buffet lunch was served in the covered tent, and the kids cleaned up all the garbage. Abigail and I tore everything down except the tables, then drove back to the house to assemble a snack break. An hour later, we returned to see two of the four walls shored up with huge two-by-fours and a third craned into position for the men to lock them with temporary beams. I didn't know anything about barn raising until a few weeks ago, but Derrick assured us a steel roof would save us huge amounts of money in maintenance for years to come. That one piece of information alone made the decision simple. Elias did the contracting and final measurements as Phase I came together by six that evening.

One barn raised. *Check*

One happy camper. *Check*

One happy intern. *Please hold.*

Chapter 33
SENECA

Saturday arrived with several pained expressions and moans. I sipped my morning joe with my knees tucked under me in my torn DelVal sweatshirt and plain pink and grey plaid sleep pants. "Are we there yet?" I whined into my mug.

Abigail stepped around the counter with a brown grocery bag stacked to the rim with sandwiches, chips, water, and the rest of her molasses cookies Tiny went ga-ga for at Thanksgiving dinner. When he emerged into the kitchen, it struck me if you sprinkled some white hair onto that man's beard, added some spectacles, and a red suit, Tiny would be the epitome of Santa Claus.

"You're too good to me, Abigail. Can I come back if I'm not invited to my new friend's house for Christmas? I'll build you a few of those planter boxes you liked," he said encouragingly. The man was a giant puppy dog. *Speaking of which* . . .

"Where is Benny? He'll want to say goodbye, too." On cue, you could hear the thump of his tail against the wall as he padded through the house. "There he is!"

Like in a scene from *Lassie*, Tiny bent over, scratching below his muzzle and behind his ears. "Keep a close eye on your master. He has a habit of getting into scrapes, as you know. Fetch help if he falls, and don't forget to make them brush your teeth. Whew! Your breath is rank."

I stuffed my hands on my hips, taking that personally. "He gets dental sticks every day. If he didn't eat the damn chicken poop, he'd be fine. Go on, Tiny. The open road is calling."

With many hugs and thanks, he was back in his pickup, headed back to Pennsylvania. Annalise's family trekked down the stairs exhausted. Alex came in, promising he'd load up their van before heading to the barn, but, first, he wanted to wrestle with Benny, his niece and, his nephew. I could tell how much he missed having his dog around, and, hopefully, once he was settled into his own place, he could bring him back for good. In a last-ditch effort to be the good uncle, he chased the kids around the dining room table, then the piano, and finally up the grand staircase and back down the servant stairs into the kitchen; Benny trailed and jumped behind them.

"Give your uncle a big hug and wish him well. We have to go." Stephen was a good balance of stern versus half-joking. I liked him a lot, and I was happy Annalise had a partner who kept her grounded. I suppose I'd need to be that person for Alex if we took a real stab at a relationship.

Abigail pulled four travel containers of French toast sticks and syrup from the warming tray for their ride home. I also caught another brown grocery bag of snacks and brownies to keep the little critters happy. One day, that woman would make the most perfect babies. I'm surprised it hasn't happened yet. From what I heard, they were super freaks in the sack. I wouldn't be surprised if they pushed out their own Little League team.

By eight-forty-five, Benny was the last to jump in the van after getting tons of hugs and kisses from the rest of us. He'd be back for another visit at Christmas. It was too much to care for him with everything else going on. Moments later, all our guests, sans Dane, were gone, and an eerie quiet loomed throughout the house. Looking around the kitchen, I noticed Abigail and I were the only two sitting around the island, only the ticking clock keeping us company.

"We did it," I whispered, hoping I hadn't spoken too soon. "More importantly, we survived our first Friendsgiving." I sipped my coffee in peace. "This will sound stupid, but did you already make notes for next year?"

Abigail threw her head back in jest, "Are you kidding me? I already ordered the turkey. Just kidding—Monday." We giggled, knowing she wasn't joking.

"You really outdid yourself, Abs. This weekend was by far your best-planned event. You're the hostess with the mostest and getting quite a reputation for it. I envision your planner filled with destination weddings, showers, and anniversaries; the list is endless. You'll need more staff and a staging area to handle it all. Better give Elias a heads up," I half-jested.

She bubbled her lips, sounding exhausted. "Elias doesn't need any more projects. Maybe in a few years. We've just started one that will take eighteen years to complete." She smacked her hand over her mouth, bug-eyed.

I carefully put my mug down, raced around the island, and screamed as I threw my hands around my tiny friend. "Do I get to be Aunt Sen?"

She held me tightly, weeping. "Absolutely," she said confidently, then turning a shade of green, "I'm afraid, Sen. My mom died too young for me to learn anything from her, and, well, you knew my aunt. She was as rotten as they came. What if I suck at being a mom?"

I backed my friend into a chair, handing her a box of tissues for her snotty nose. "Should I take some classes or something?" Her snarfing sounds were gross but, like Abigail, real and raw. In all this chaos, my best friend debated whether she could be a good mom. How did I miss this?

I hopped onto the counter, crossing my legs, beaming at her. "Back up a minute. Have you told Elias?"

If she could turn paler, she did. Her worried bottom lip quivered, followed by a river of tears. "I haven't told him yet!" She buried her head in her hands, ashamed. I let her self-soothe for a few minutes. It was part of her ADHD therapy, and this would be the perfect time to use it.

It was time to begin the process of *pulling* details out of her. "You found out..."

"Three weeks ago." *And she didn't tell her best friend. Argh!*

"And you're not telling him because..."

She dug her palms into her eye sockets making them squeak. "Because he's been under so much stress!" Grabbing the whisk off the stove, she marched back and forth like she wielded a magic wand. "Two people permanently moved in with us. Not that we minded. Then there was planning for the barn and everyone visiting. Thank God the harvest event ended before the madness began. Something had to give, Sen. Now there's your project, and his car business, and planning for upcoming guests, not to mention the holiday. Sen, the list goes on and on. When would I tell him? During a quiet evening bubble bath? We haven't had one of those since the day before you arrived. Life is complicated now. I don't even know if it's the right time to have a child. I finally just became an adult." *End scene.*

Dramatic monologues were Abigail's specialty. You couldn't interrupt or she'd have to start over, which came with a meltdown. They were filled with questions you didn't have time to answer. My favorite is when they are perfectly choreographed acts with props and costumes. I had a very specific role in making this play come full circle—my level head. It was my superpower used best in times of crisis so long as there weren't any other problem solvers in the bunch. Then, it was mayhem. Good news for her: everyone left, and the rest are at the barn.

"Breathe, baby," I said, pulling her in for more hugs. "This is why God gives you nine months to get your shit together. For the record, you made a great choice withholding this wonderful news until after Thanksgiving. The focus needs to be on you and Elias no—and the little peanut you made."

"Can it be a bean instead of a peanut?" she said seriously. I held her tear-streaked face in my hands.

"Call it anything you want, sweetheart. This is your bean, and you can do anything you want. You're the momma, and you'll be the best momma ever. I promise."

She stood up, gripping me hard on the shoulders. "You will be by my side every minute, right? So help me, God, you'd better not think of leaving during my time of need. I'll revoke all your aunt privileges, including spoiling my bean."

Okay. That sounded so wrong.

I crossed my heart and raised my fake scout fingers in promise. "I've got you, Abs. Promise."

"Whew!" she hollered and danced around the kitchen, collecting dirty cups, plates, and napkins. "I'm so happy someone knows. I can breathe again. Let's start making more sandwiches for the guys. Oh, and a giant thermos of hot cocoa with peppermint. Elias loves that stuff."

Another whirlwind of a day whizzed by to everyone's satisfaction. The roof was installed and secured, and several windows were placed to bring as much light as possible into the space. Alex had made a big stink about insufficient lighting in the old barn. As he put it, "I need to see my girls' tits clearly." *Such a perv.*

Elias captured Abigail around the stomach, lifted her off the ground, and whispered something that made her moan too loudly for all of us to hear.

"Stop it, you two! There are children present," Alex said, pointing his sandwich at Dane, who deadpanned back.

Dane swiped at his brother, "I have forgotten who the adult is in this family. I find the girls and keep them. You beg the girls, and they run away." *Ouch!*

By the purse of Alex's lips and tuck of his head, we were setting up for another round of World Federation Wrestling. *Yep.* Alex handed off his sandwich to me, motioning to step back.

"I'm not proud of what I'm about to do to my little brother. He knows not what he says, and, therefore, as his elder, the lessons of life fall to me to impart on his sorry ass. This shouldn't take long." A wicked snarl etched into Alex's face, and Dane panicked, slipping on the wet soil, almost taking him out before the tussle even began.

"You're a dead man!" Alex bolted after him through the barn.

"You gotta catch me, old man," Dane taunted. Sure, there was a thirteen-year difference, but I had my money on Alex. He was athletic, cunning, and knew a thing or two about combat tactics. Dane didn't stand a chance, especially since he made a logistical error climbing the loft ladder. Alex grabbed hold of his leg and hauled him down, holding him tightly by his belt loops.

The crowd went wild as the first Valize Games were completed, the elder Valize winning the prize.

"Tell me again, who can't get a woman, Dane?" This was why, as much as I wanted a sibling, taunting and torture weren't my thing. "Come on. We all know the answer."

Dane twisted his hips and freed himself from his smart-mouthed brother, feeling embarrassed. "You won this round, Alex, but next time, you're mine. You're the best womanizer. Congratulations."

Alex nodded and smiled until Dane's words finally registered. The dirt kicked up again as Dane escaped the barn unscathed. "Kids," he said, flipping his wrist into the air. Watching this display of brotherly love was heartwarming, but it was time to concede the floor to Elias, who commandeered this small army to action.

"Intermission is over. We are back to our regularly scheduled program. I need two groups to head out to pasture number one and hang those rails. We need one pasture completed this weekend." Four middle-aged men who owned neighboring farms offered their services. With a golf cart and hi-lo, making the task more efficient, I directed the next group to follow Elias to build out the loft. "We're done by daybreak today. Everything else can wait. Ladies, if you could lay out the lights, one of us will hang them before we leave."

Watching a strong man the size of an ox with a mechanical tattoo was hot. Watching another strong man, a lean, mean, fighting machine, was also hot, especially when I got to see him uninhibited and playful with his brother. Seeing Dane in action didn't hurt the eyes either. Personally, I felt strong men seemed stronger when they could share their insecurities. It was courageous and sexy.

With Alex's project under control, my sole focus shifted to my spring project. I had to travel back to campus for my semester-end synopsis paper and mentoring session with Dr. Abel. I also needed to follow up with the Lieutenant Governor to include his findings in my report. If I was lucky, I could enjoy the holidays without the stress of two internships. I needed a break—and a hot tub. *I should ask for one for Christmas.*

As Abigail drove back to the house, I broached the subject of how Abigail would tell her husband she was preggers. Nibbling on a double chocolate chip cookie, I saw her biting her lip red. She was as transparent as they came.

"You know I'm going to DelVal on Thursday, right?"

Her eyes widened, "Now that you mention it, yes. Would you like me to pack some food for the trip? Bribe Dr. Abel perhaps with an apple strudel?" We giggled, remembering his penchant for baked goods.

I nibbled again. "Not for him, though one of your Italian sub sandwiches sounds great."

"Anything for you, sweetheart," she soothed.

"Not to drive you crazy, but when will you tell Elias about the baby?" She winced at the thought. "I was thinking we could get a super sexy dress from our favorite store and you could do one of your porn star dances to reel him in like you did before." I slapped my thigh at the thought of a three-month-gone Abigail in a sequin slip dress cut up to her crotch in silver strappy sandals grinding for a shocked Elias. "You could wait until you're showing and dance for him in a tube dress. Think he'll get the picture?"

Pfft. "Seriously? Never gonna happen. That man knows when I have a pimple on my butt. He's going to know any day now." She whimpered, turning the pickup truck onto her street.

"Are you feeling sick? Anything that might give it away?" I prodded anxiously.

"Only getting up to pee every thirty minutes. These hormones are a real bitch," she cried, pulling at her ponytail.

"Well, that's good. I would hate for you to be doubled over for three months. You need a plan, Abs. Have you talked with ATG? She's always had great advice for you," I said trying to keep a straight face.

Abigail pulled into her drive, parked the car, and hopped out of the cab. We collected all our bags and coolers from the truck and dropped them on the kitchen floor. Abigail slapped her keys on the counter, announcing, "Get changed. We're going to town. The guys won't be back for hours and there has to be an outfit in my favorite store designed to drive my man wild."

"Here's what's going to happen. You distract Alex and Dane, and I'll set the mood for Elias upstairs. We'll get those decadent pastries from the French bakery around the corner from the dress shop, and I'll order an Italian feast from Mariano's to lay at his feet when he comes home. What do you think?"

It was a good start on short notice. I was impressed. "Could you have a picnic in front of the fire instead of upstairs? It would be so much easier."

"Oh my god, Seneca. Can you imagine the memories we'll make?"

Her eyes glazed over, peering into the future and looking back at what hadn't happened yet. *Welcome to Abigail's mind.* I loved it when she saw the whole night unfolding like a steamy romance novel: *I tell him I'm pregnant, and he jumps for joy.*

She grabbed my arm, "Take Dane out for beer, babes, and dancing. He'll love it and he'll be gone tomorrow. Everyone's happy!" Abigail did her happy dance grabbing her keys off the counter and dancing out the door." *I didn't even get to shower!*

We were back at the inn several hours later; Abigail bolting up the stairs to prepare for her big reveal. The deep, plunging, emerald green dress she bought at the retro thrift store screamed, "Take me!" Elias should enjoy this version of her body as much as possible because I promise it will never look like that again. My mother lamented after her baby-body never recovered. Instead, her mantra became, "My body is my badge of motherhood." Despite the truth of her statement, losing a youthful body deserved a moment of grief.

The side door slammed shut with the clumping of boots and brotherly barbs.

"You know you're a pain in my ass," Alex accused his brother playfully.

Dane tried to appeal to his brother. "But I'm your favorite pain in your ass. Face it, you're going to miss this handsome face when I leave tomorrow,"

I slid into the butler's nook, eyeing them in the kitchen, Dane waggling his eyebrows at his brother as his hands slid down his sleek planes.

Alex sighed, resigned, hanging his head. "You're absolutely right, Dane. I am going to miss you. Having you here this weekend supporting me, creating a new future for us, meant more to me than you can imagine. Our parents would be proud of us."

When he looked up, Dane rubbed his neck as a blush crept up his face, saying, "Yeah, they would." Alex stepped in front of him, solidly holding his shoulders. The scene of a surrogate father and his son took my breath away. It was Norman Rockwell-esque in composition and style. This was how fathers turned their sons into men: steadfast, levelheaded, and kind. One day, Alex would have kids of his own, and they would have an incredible man to learn from.

Dane cuffed his brother's neck, pulling him in tightly, "There is nothing I wouldn't do for you, Alex. You're more than my brother. You're my friend and mentor. I can't wait to see what you do with your new start."

"Go kick some ass on your finals. You've got this," he said, pushing him back gently. "I'll meet you at Eloheh after finals, and we'll pack up the rest of the house, okay?"

Dane nodded ruefully, stopping short when he saw me enter the kitchen.

"Hey, guys. I was thinking we'd go out to dinner tonight. Maybe grab a few beers at Lefty's sports bar? What do you think?" I reached into the fridge, grabbed a soda and cracked it open, and leaned my hip against the counter.

The guys looked at each other, exhausted. "I know you're tired, but I don't feel like cooking, and Abigail has plans with Elias that don't include an audience, if you know what I mean."

Alex shook his hands in front of his face, "Please! No details. Give us an hour to rest and shower."

Both men began unbuttoning their flannel shirts, rehashing the day as I pulled up a chair to watch them strip down to their bare chests. Alex lifted his muscled biceps over his head, summoning me like a siren to run my hands over them. I would be lying if I didn't notice the similarities between brothers; each man's loose-fitting jeans hung low on their trim hips. It was a window to Alex's youth I happily filed away. Alex may be all over the board emotionally, but there was no denying he was all man from head to toe.

Lost in my musings, Alex walked right in front of me, the top button of his jeans popped open, treating me to his happy trail and cut lower abs. I stared forward, licking my lips, oblivious to his words or brother. He caught me under the chin, raising my head to see his mouth dipping low. "Like what you see, baby?" he whispered. *Oh, fuck, yeah.*

"Uh-huh," I hummed, desperate to taste him.

He called over his shoulder, "Dane, you can have the shower first. I'll be up soon."

Dane chortled, skating past us, nudging him from behind. "I'll take my time."

"Yeah. You do that," he muttered, redirecting his attention to my face.

Barely a second went by when Alex gave his first panty-melting directive. "Take me out, Sen."

Geezus, God. Yes!

I had him unzipped freeing his bulging cock instantly. "Look at me," he commended next. "Open that porn star mouth of yours and suck me hard." I moaned deeply, anticipating his thickness in my mouth, the taste of him on my tongue. "Keep your eyes on mine, and don't take them off me. I want to see every feeling and desire that crosses your face. Understand?" he demanded, swiping his thumb over my bottom lip, making another gush of wetness soak my panties.

I stuck out my tongue, ready to receive the pool of pre-cum dripping precariously from his tip. He tapped his crown, flicking his wetness onto my waiting tongue, forcing my eyes to roll back in my head from the intensity of his stare. "Eyes on me," he growled.

Reaching for his eager cock, I grabbed him firmly at the root, guiding his length back into my hot, wet mouth. His hiss of pleasure inspired me to take more of him until his shaft bumped into the back of my throat. The sounds he made and the squelching of my gags were so erotic that I almost came myself. I tried my best to keep my eyes on him. But the allure of his taut abs bucking forward was very compelling. The motion of his hips was hypnotic as he slipped in and out of my mouth; still, I was desperate to have him inside me. Pleasing him, in all its forms, had become an addiction for me. I wanted and needed to make him happy. Contrary to everything I'd ever felt about a man, Alex niggled his way into my heart, irreversibly turning my world inside out.

It wasn't much longer until I felt his silky shaft quickening. His thrusts became erratic; his back arched. He was almost there, and I knew exactly how he wanted it.

"Fuck, Sen, I'm coming!" he shouted, pulling me back. *Not a chance.* I doubled my efforts, grabbing his ass firmly and locking his pelvis to my face. I would take every drop of his cum down my throat like a beer bong. *Shit! I am a fucking porn star.* I suppose some women would see this as wanton and shameful, but not me. I was an overachiever.

Alex gently pulled out of my mouth, giving me a minute to catch my breath before sliding his hands under my arms and lifting me to his chest. He leaned his forehead into mine, breathing erratically and straining to regain his composure. When he did, he cupped my face so reverently I thought I'd faint. "You fucking take my breath away." I smiled demurely like the proper, sweet porn star I was.

His warm breath on my face felt like a balm on my heart. Soft kisses feathered over my swollen lips whispering praises and devotion. They came out so easily I almost missed the imperceptible *love you* on his lips.

Chapter 34

ALEX

What the hell came out of my mouth?

I mean, it wasn't that I hadn't been considering how I felt about Seneca. I loved so much about her. Her long, silky hair that swished like a horse's tail. Her big brown eyes that opened up a universe of possibilities. Or her mouth. *Fuck. So talented.* Seneca was a force of nature I could trust. I relied on her to my detriment. She'd repeatedly proven herself to be a valued employee, caring friend, and confidante. So why was I hesitating to share my love for her openly?

Considering my past relationships, some tragic and others disappointing, nothing soul-crushing stood out. Being with Seneca was completely different. Something about her gave me pause unless perhaps I was the issue. Was I a commitment-phobe? Why would I be? I wanted my last relationship. I like having someone to share my day with. What wasn't I getting?

Seneca emerged from her bedroom dressed in distressed jeans that looked painted on, tucked into elaborately stitched cowboy boots. Her tight, white, long-sleeved T-shirt covering her barely perceptible nude lace bra held her luscious overflowing tits sitting high above the sterling silver and turquoise medallioned belt.

Her short-waisted jean jacket hung over her shoulders like a hug, making her a vision of simplicity. I gulped, afraid of what might come out of my mouth, though Dane had no problem cat-calling her as she walked down the grand staircase.

"Yeah, girl. Lookin' good," he jutted her chin, appraising her openly.

I cut him off, extending my hand to support her last few steps. "Are you sure we need to leave the house?" I was worse than my coveting brother.

"If any man so much as looks at you tonight, they'll be blind in an instant," I growled in her ear, kissing that sweet spot that drove her mad.

She turned her head into my mouth seductively. "I'll break one of your nuts for every man you blind. Control yourself. Half this town just helped you raise a barn. Show your gratitude by being pleasant."

I pushed her out the door, muttering, "Not a chance."

It took some prodding during dinner to figure out why it was so important to leave Abigail and Elias alone. "I can't tell you exactly. It's not my story to tell, but let's just say there will be another chick in the hen house," she giggled sweetly.

I leaned forward, nibbling on her lips, "Really? They're having a baby? Will you get to be an aunt?"

She looked offended. "Duh, yeah! This kid will need a village. Have you met the mother?" I was almost insulted on Abigail's behalf until she smacked the table. "Any idea who the uncle will be?" She eyeballed me, cocking her head to the side.

"Uh..."

"You! Ding-dong. You're going to be the uncle." *Me? With Seneca as the aunt?*

"Together?" I said stupidly.

Like blackout shutters dropping, the music faded and the air evaporated out of the room. Together, like us married, together? I was so confused. That was a pretty big leap in my book. Thinking about being in love as a fantasy was easy. But everyday life, cooking, and cleaning, and finances, and helping our friends raise their kids, well, that was quite a different story. Reality struck head on. My face must have contorted because Seneca tapped my forehead when I regained consciousness.

"Earth to Alex. Hello? You're freaking me out." She continued to smooth out my fretting bow until I breathed normally again. "Maybe we should go?" she asked, concerned.

I pushed her hands away, rubbing my eyes as if that would erase the pictures in my head. "I'm sorry. I thought you said we, as in you and me, together. Like married, together?"

Then she went silent.

Realization hit her square in the face, and she chuckled. "Huh. I see your point. Getting ahead of ourselves, aren't we?" she said dejectedly, peering into her beer. "I guess that remains to be seen. We can still be an aunt and uncle to this little person without being married, right?"

I nodded, not wanting to create more awkwardness, "Sure, we can." I snagged my full beer off the table and chugged the whole thing back. This night went from promising to perishable, and, for a change, I wasn't the one who did it.

Like zombies, we stared at people dancing to viewing mainstream and bizarre sports on the giant TVs. After ten minutes of this horrible agony, I offered to take her home. She collected her purse and I waved at Dane on the dance floor, who was getting handsy with a cute blonde. "Heading back to the house. Lock up when you get back."

The ride home was the longest, painful ride of my life. I knew the realization of us becoming an aunt and uncle didn't include us getting married. It would, however, bind us for a lifetime in other ways. I know I'm not abandoning our friends because of Seneca's issues. She'd have to figure her shit out fast, or something terrible would happen.

SENECA

I arrived at Dr. Abel's office, armed with supporting documentation for my first internship report. Olivia welcomed me with a warm hug, and I couldn't help but follow up on my email regarding Dr. Abel's state of mind.

"Olivia, is Dr. Abel, uh, feeling, okay?" I shifted my head side-to-side, feeling her out.

She looked up from her computer screen, perplexed. "As far as I know. Why?"

I fidgeted with my hands. My concerns didn't warrant me being nosey except I was. "His emails have indicated a playfulness I'm not used to. I wasn't sure if something notable had changed." I raised my eyebrows hoping it was something good.

Acknowledgment lit up her face. "Ah. That. He started dating Ms. Pearson in the oncology lab. It seems he has a whole new outlook on life." She tittered adorably like a bird.

"That would explain a few things," I said sarcastically. "Then I'm happy for him. Thanks for the intel," I smiled genuinely, walking through to the Dean's office.

An hour later, I was back in my car traveling to The Farnsworth Estate, with Dr. Abel's approval of both projects in hand. However, they did come with a warning to keep my relationships professional since I was living with friends. He was a smart man with a keen sense of how relationships can sour; his divorce barely settled looming over his head.

Because I'm me, I scrutinized every piece of our conversation over the ninety-minute drive home.

"From what I can tell, this report looks very thorough, Seneca. Although the final resolutions from Eloheh Farms can't be reached by graduation, I need you to submit a status report from the state outlining their plans, if any, for remediation. Attention to the Zen Garden and its marketing plan is your new priority. I'll send our notes and directives to Mr. Valize and ask for his sign-off and letter of recommendation for your portfolio. Mrs. McGinnis still needs to submit her expectations and deadlines before January fifth, when the new semester begins."

What a relief! I was coming into the home stretch for graduation, and I could feel a weight lifting from my shoulders. I would finally be doing something I loved for the next five months. No more cows or chickens—
except I couldn't help but love *them*. Only plants, pavers, and aesthetics that would inspire and heal. Marketing wasn't my specialty, though I knew which takeaways I wanted my visitors to experience. From there, the sky was the limit.

Working with Alex was illuminating, touching on various aspects of farming I never would have experienced at Longwood Gardens. Would I use any of these new skills in the future? Who knows? Just more skills for my life's toolbox. I'll miss spending time with Eunice, Bernice, Emma, Belinda and the other girls. Soon, Alex will have a milking system, saving him tons of time and increasing his revenue exponentially. As for my egg collecting, I think I'll keep that task. While Benny visited, he liked seeing his bird friends again and pawing at Amy the Great, the only loose chicken. They've established a quite funny relationship I should capitalized on.

The weeks before Christmas were filled with a flurry of preparations for another estate event, a Wassailing Donor dinner. Abigail could decorate this place to the hilt at five hundred dollars a ticket, serve hors d'oeuvres, champagne, and a sumptuous dinner to support the school district's performing arts programs, like the high school senior competition choir and string quartets entertaining them tonight. The evening was another way the Farnsworth family supported the community.

"Are you sure you don't want to wear a low-cut frock sans underwear and join the party?" Alex stuck out his tongue mimicking Benny begging for a treat.

"Not unless you're prepared to wear a powdered wig and wooden teeth after I knock yours out," I snarked with a sinister smile. Shudders rippled through his body at the thought, bringing me to tears.

"Looks like we're sitting upstairs on the back deck drinking hot spiked cider and eating popcorn balls," I took a large chomp out of a caramel-flavored ball already primed in my hand.

One of the things Alex and I had gotten very good at was sitting in silence—not an uncomfortable one, usually. Sometimes, we'd snuggle without talking, enjoying each other's body heat and closeness, and other times on opposite sides of the room, me reading and him watching a hockey game.

"Alex?" I nudged him, sitting on the loveseat on the slim deck under the roofline upstairs. "Are we weird?"

He bristled. "Weird? Like how? We are in so many ways, but what were you thinking?"

I pulled my knees to my chest, setting my popcorn ball to the side. "I know you're a lot older than me, but, when we hang out like this or on opposite sides of the living room, are we weird that we aren't wrapped around each other all the time?"

Over the past weeks, our conversations have become less passive-aggressive and more genuine. We worked together so much better when we just said what was on our minds instead of assuming what the other one was thinking. It was refreshing.

Turning in his seat, he studied my face. He cupped my jaw, grazing his thumb over my cheek, smiling. "Yeah, we're weird. I'm unsure if I'm speaking for both of us, but we have found a comfortable groove. A sense of trust and compatibility it took years to find. If you think I'm an old, boring man now, brace yourself for the future," he mocked me playfully.

I considered his perspective, measuring it against my childhood. My mom enjoyed her quiet time, and my dad liked to read his newspaper uninterrupted. However, they often became animated when we were all together. I was young when she died. I couldn't have known what a "normal" relationship looked like. It certainly wasn't what I was experiencing now with my dad and Belinda.

I bit my lip, "Well, you are old and slowing down and—" Like a tiger pouncing on its prey, he scooped me into his lap, growling as he nipped my skin down to my clavicle until I squealed. "Okay! Okay! You're not old!" I said, pleading for mercy.

His nips turned to kisses that melted me to my core. I loved how he made me feel even when I didn't know what I wanted to feel.

"Sen. Seriously. I'm happy to have you on my lap every night. I know your mind is always busy analyzing this and that, and I don't want to get in your way. Is that a wrong assumption?"

I think I confused myself. I responded tentatively, "Yes and no. I'm just concerned that sitting on opposite sides of the room might make us drift apart. I know we're still figuring out our relationship. I think you'd agree we are beyond friends with benefits or even employer-employee. We don't have those constraints anymore, right?"

He spun me around to straddle his lap, scanning my face carefully, "Are you saying you'd like to change the terms of our relationship to something more permanent?"

My pregnant pause made him wince. "Look, Sen. You don't have to answer now. You still have your internship to complete, and then who knows where your next project will lead you. This year might turn out to be good times in the rearview mirror." His nervous chuckle didn't do much to settle my head or my heart.

I planted a sweet kiss on his tempting lips. "Let's see how things go."

So much for a carefree evening. What did seating arrangements have to do with anything? We weren't married. We were fucking around, having a good time, and poorly testing the waters of a future that was not guaranteed. I wanted more with him, but the timing was off. How could I travel the world learning and experiencing all that horticulture offers if I'm tied down to one place? Asking him to wait for me was asinine. He *was* getting older. Fuck! He was forty. I knew he wanted kids, and a wife, and a simple life. Wasn't that why his old girlfriend left him? I respected him too much to lead him on. My point crystallized right then and there. I didn't want to make promises I couldn't keep. Nor did I want to shortchange my future at the cost of his broken heart.

Circular problems drove my obsessive behavior out of control. I jumped up from his lap, thanking him for a great night, skirting another chair as I exited the deck quickly. My heart raced as I tore through Abigail's bedroom, ignoring Elias taking a break from the party, reading on his bed. It took all my control not to slam his bedroom door as I took the side stairs, snagging my coat and stuffing my feet in my boots as I left the house. I felt claustrophobic. I jumped in the golf cart and took off over the first hill to the maple tree that provided me shelter and safety while my mind went haywire. I needed air. I needed a way out.

Chapter 35
SENECA

Problem solving was my specialty. Overanalyzing was my superpower and my kryptonite. Sitting under a half moon shining brightly on a clear winter night, days away from the winter solstice, was my perfect solitary confinement. The air was still, my nose tinged with a comforting coldness that reminded me that space and time were the true healers of my circumstance. I needed to take a step back to gain perspective I couldn't seem to grasp when snug in Alex's arms.

I was twenty-eight years young. My future was limitless with adventures untold. The captivating allure of seeing Japanese gardens in person sent fireworks off in my head. Visiting botanical gardens in Thailand, Singapore, Hawaii and the Arctic Circle, all spurred my creativity and desire to learn and roam. The juxtaposition of settling into a predictable life with a secure, sexy man doing the same thing day in and day out was suffocating. Isn't that why Meghan left? Isn't that why Alex shut off his emotional center so he wouldn't get hurt? He had been transparent with me, and I'd been a shit, hiding my plans for an exciting future in horticulture. I hated this part of being an adult. Wishing and hoping weren't strategies I could afford. I needed a real plan. Now.

ALEX

I saw her ride past the barn and over the hill, her hair whipping around her serious face. The full moon lit up the sky and, from this perspective, I could almost see her knuckles turning white on the steering wheel. We had hit an impasse. She was young, impetuous, formidable, and determined. I loved all these things about her and more, though each one came with a price tag. Seneca didn't have to spell out her dreams of traveling around the world. It had always been a part of her, like the expected wind on a spring day. Life shone down on her with a cosmic glow you had to stand back and admire in awe. I wanted her to have every experience her heart ached for. She wouldn't be happy in East Stroudsburg. It was a tiny town. Mystic wasn't much better, except tourism brought wealth to the area, bringing better opportunities for new projects. I knew this move would ultimately make me more money and offer more opportunities to grow my product line. But losing my family's land in Pennsylvania weighed heavy on my heart.

Seneca needed to find herself, without me weighing her down. We'd had fun fooling around, sharing our family stories, and establishing a new life for me. I couldn't have done it without her. She was an integral part of my life's tapestry, and I'd relish every moment we had together. I needed to take the high road here. I'd never had a woman who lit me up like she did. It wasn't only our physical connection. There was a strange kinetic energy pulling me into her inner sanctum, both mind and body. It left me breathless, sated, and safe. Seneca filled a void I didn't know I had after my parents died.

I kept a watchful eye on the horizon, making sure she returned safely. A light snow began, and my chest tightened when she'd hadn't come back yet. Two hours later the battery headlight on the golf cart peeked at the top of the hill as my breath gave way to relief. I wouldn't chase her down like I wanted to. I wouldn't pressure her for answers I knew she couldn't provide. My only source of connection was to wait on the side porch, quietly waiting with a kiss to her head and a tight hug of encouragement. It seemed paternal, but, at that moment, it was all I could offer.

Dane finished his fall semester and, as planned, met me at our old home to pack up the rest of our things. Annalise and Steven were scheduled to come over that evening and take us out to dinner, so we had a lot to accomplish before that. My biggest concern had been how to condense a century full of knickknacks, pictures, and memories into a few boxes.

I kneeled down next to a pile of framed pictures, picking up one of Dane sitting between my parents on a fishing boat excursion when he was eight. "Good times, right?" I said. handing him the photo.

He sniffed, tracing each of their faces. "It seems like a dream. We were happy, together, enjoying life then poof! It all ended. It kills me how quickly it all fell apart. It's made me stop more often to take mental snapshots of anything good in my life. If I don't, nothing becomes sacred or special."

I cuffed his neck, pulling him into an awkward-seated hug. "You're smart, Dane. Mom and Dad would have been incredibly proud of you and your accomplishments. Keep making great memories. File them away to take them out when you need them most. Just make sure you don't forget me," I joked.

Tears slipped from our eyes, sharing the most tender moment we'd had in a long while. "I will," he said smiling. "You do the same. My favorite mental picture of recent is watching how you looked at Seneca when you realized she organized your barn raising. It was magical and intimate. I think all of us blushed watching you drink her in like she stole your heart for an eternity. It was something special."

I stared at my brother and his poetic accounting of the most soul-filling moment of my life. One that Seneca gave me with an open heart without asking for anything in return. Pure, honest, and exquisite, my intern delivered everything she promised and more. How could I show her my appreciation for all her kindnesses? Her body and mind? It was an impossibility. I had to let her go and become everything she wanted to be. Now, if only I could find the words to tell her.

"I have an idea," I offered to Dane. "Why don't we just pack up everything and sort it when we find a new home. We'll toss obvious stuff like newspapers and magazines. If we know for sure we don't want it, we'll donate it. Otherwise, we don't need to aggravate ourselves with this now. Sound good?"

He scrubbed his face trying to hide his relief. "Sounds good."

I got up, leaving him to his thoughts. I carried a pile of boxes to the living room and began the same process. Since I'd already taken most of what I wanted, my room and my most precious possessions were already with me. Annalise would clean up the kitchen, the basement, and all the closets. It wasn't like she had to rush, only that I didn't want anyone to loot the house stealing our history.

Leo met me the next morning to review how the radon mitigation was being resolved. After sealing all the cracks in the foundation, adjusting the air pressure in the lower level of the house, and ensuring proper ventilation in every room, the company Leo hired installed a monitoring system. Of course, that came with a hefty bill. Leo had presented it sheepishly, but confirmed that the home was clear of radon before we arrived yesterday.

Next, he shared the latest report from the Pennsylvania Department of Environmental Protection and government cases as it related to my soil and water issues. Convoluted didn't describe what was involved.

"I wanted you to have these reports for your records. The summaries tell the whole story so far, but suffice it to say you have a multi-million dollar settlement in the making. I would secure a qualified environmental lawyer. A real shark would be best. Even though the state will work to get criminal charges against Halogen Corp., the primary company responsible for the contamination in your county, you are entitled to all kinds of personal compensation your lawyer can share with you. Be forewarned, though, this process could take years to resolve. It's a long and arduous process. However if you can keep your momentum, the financial gain for having to relocate will be substantial." Leo delivered all this in his expected nonemotional way while my insides promised to heave the moment he walked out the door.

I swallowed hard. "Thank you, Leo, for taking the lead on this. Seneca has a line on a qualified environmental lawyer. I guess I should be grateful no one was harmed, and eventually I can repay Abigail for her financial support. It just breaks my heart that this house will fall into disrepair and my land will fall to waste. Never in a million years would I have thought this could happen to me. It's tragic." I paced around the kitchen table, wondering where all our belongings would go.

Leo put his hand on my shoulder, uncharacteristically, speaking with more emotion than I'd ever heard in the twelve years I'd known him, "I'm proud of you, Alex. I can't imagine how you've kept it together during this hardship, but you've found a new beginning, and, with a little luck, this whole mess will side in your favor. What's done is done—time to move on."

Tears threatened to fall as Dane came out of his room. I introduced him to Leo as we walked him outside to his car when Dane stopped him.

"Hey, Leo. Would you do me a favor and take a few pictures of me and Alex? One on the stairs here, and one by the barn? I'd love to have one by the maple tree where we had a swing, too, if you have time. You know, for posterity."

His request split me in two. Dane was so smart and thoughtful to mark this occasion with some photos like we discussed less than an hour ago. Not all memories are good ones. Sometimes, you have to mark the bad ones, too. "Sure, son. Good idea." I quickly called Annalise to bring over Benny and join our final moments here at our family home.

For the next twenty minutes, Leo followed us around the property, catching glimpses of our past: in the hay loft, by our favorite tree, and on the family tractor that had been a fixture at Eloheh Farms for fifty years, and, finally, a few with Benny and Tiny. Yeah, we had a lot of great memories here. The bittersweet blanket of grief washed over my family. Bits and pieces of our lives flitting by yet clinging to our souls. This home would always be the haven my parents and my ancestors built to not only provide a foundation to live by, but a source of safety and love that made our lives so special. Today was a good day. Tomorrow will be better.

The U-Haul we rented came in handy moving furniture over to Annalise's home, and the rest into storage. Our final load would move with us across state lines back to Mystic. It felt like the door behind us slammed shut with only one path to go—forward. Driving alone made for deep analysis; from my time as a child to a rambunctious teenager, to a highly decorated army captain to homestead owner. Looking backward illuminated a history of challenges, great humility, and strength I couldn't have imagined mastering. Without every one of those experiences teaching me about myself, I wouldn't know how to move forward.

Pulling into the inn's driveway close to midnight, only two lights remained on: the side porch light and my bedroom light, which could only be seen from the driveway. Abigail must have kept them on. She was always so thoughtful. Exhaustion came over me, so, forgoing any unpacking, I grabbed my small duffle, peeled my brother from his pickup, and headed straight to bed.

"Dude, I can barely see straight," Dane moaned, kicking off his boots and hanging his coat.

"Ditto. Take the first room up the stairs. Abigail said she'd have it ready for . . ."

We stopped short to a kitchen full of candles, a crock-pot of beef stew, and a glittery sign saying, "Welcome Home." My eyes teared, knowing we had found a place to call home. Hugging Dane into my side, gratitude filled my heaving heart.

"Shit, Alex. They really do want us here. I just thought your friends were being nice, but look what they did," he croaked, pointing to the adorable sign and comfort-food meal at midnight. "I have no words."

I sniffed. "I do. Let's eat. I'm starving."

Chapter 36
SENECA

Christmas was two days away, and the inn's guest list tripled. Alex refused to share a bed with his brother which put me in a weird position of either imposing on Elias and Abigail or engaging in an awkward couple of days snuggling with Alex. In the past, it wouldn't have been a hardship but we were at a crossroads with limited space.

"Shut up! I'm trying to sleep here," Dane wailed, flipping away from the bed and dragging his blanket over his head.

"You shut up, asshole. I can't help that Seneca loves snuggling with me. Are her purrs of pleasure making you hard?"

Oh, he did not just say that.

"What the fuck, Alex? Don't make your brother uncomfortable. Keep your hands to yourself and I won't accidentally acknowledge them," I chastised through a devilish smile as I pushed my ass into his growing cock.

"Come on, Sen! See? My hands aren't even touching you." Alex waved his hands over my head so Dane could see. "Quit your whining, Dane. One day, you'll have a hot woman who can't resist being in your bed. Until then, take notes."

Unfucking believable. Scenes of their childhood swept through my brain. I could laugh it off, but watching these two harass each other was more entertaining than Abigail climbing up Elias for a kiss.

"Seriously, guys. It's late and our guests are expecting a quiet night's sleep. If you can't shut your mouths, I'm taking Dane's blowup, and he'll sleep with you, Alex." *This is the stuff that makes great moms.*

Harumpf. "Fine!"

Pffst. "Fine!"

Then, blessed silence. Several slow breaths later, a calloused hand slid across my stomach and up to my right breast soaking my panties. My breath hitched, leaning back into his chest giving him more access to massage me. Forcing myself to keep my breathing steady, I cupped the back of his hand and rolled forward locking it between my breasts. Wordlessly, he nudged his nose behind my ear, warm air tickling my neck.

"Mmm," I sighed enjoying the intimacy of this position.

"Mmm," he echoed, kissing me sweetly. "I missed you," he said on a sigh.

I turned my head to see his big brown eyes drinking me in. There was no denying I was falling deeper into his charms. Alex gave me a kind of stability I hadn't known was sexy. I sucked his bottom lip, tasting toothpaste on his tongue. I loved his lips. So sexy and soft. Red and full. I could kiss those lips all night long. "Humm. I don't want to, but I can't help it. You're ruining me, Alex," I said turning away yawning into a deep sleep. I couldn't tell if I was dreaming or if my subconscious was making things up, but I heard those words again, "love you," but that couldn't be right. He had to have said something else. He told me he couldn't let himself go there, and I believed him. I'm so tired. Tomorrow this will all be a dream.

Morning came quickly in darkness and always threw me into a funk. I dragged my legs off the side of the bed, sitting up confused. I turned around to an empty bed, feeling as if last night had been a dream. So why then did I feel like I missed something? I wasn't awake enough to synthesize my emotions. Frankly, I was tired of the seesawing motion of ups and downs. I didn't have the bandwidth for it. I had five months to pull together my final semester project and figure out my next move, one that might not include staying here in Mystic.

I stood and stretched, walking around the end of the bed, careful not to trip over Dane, down the hall, and into Abigail's bedroom to shower. I could hear her downstairs preparing for her guests' breakfasts while she sang Broadway tunes. *My girl loved her tunes.* After a quick rinse, I grabbed a pair of sweats and sweatshirt from her closet, dressed, and loped down the backstairs into the kitchen to help her out.

I tapped her on the shoulder as she swung her hips to the left. "Holy begeezus, you scared the crap out of me," she fanned her face with the spatula—catching her breath.

Chuckling, I grabbed the spatula out of her hands and stepped in front of the pancake griddle noticing them bubble. "How did last night go, Abs. Did Elias like the idea of becoming a real daddy?" I cracked myself up. Her playtime kink took on a whole new meaning.

Her face went somber as she rubbed her forehead with the back of her hand. "I may not have told him."

"Told him what?" Elias announced, sliding behind Abigail, hugging her tightly. She went from white to green, confusing me entirely.

She looked to me for backup but I didn't know what I was supposed to say. Last night was supposed to be transformative for both of them. Abigail was supposed to tell her husband they were pregnant. What the hell happened?

The phrase "pregnant pause" made more sense now. Elias spun her around, picked her up, and deposited her on the counter to stare her down. Abigail was a lousy liar. She didn't stand a chance against Elias who could scare the piss out of a terrorist.

She put her tiny hand on his brick wall of a chest, not letting him see her eyes.

"Abigail? Tell me what?" He tipped her chin up and held it there until she caved.

"I'm . . . pregnant," she whispered.

If ever there was a time to glimpse Elias as a young child, this was it. This massive two-hundred-and-twenty-pound goliath picked Abigail up and threw her into the air like a beachball. When he caught her, he spun her around, set her back on the counter then planted a salacious kiss not meant for public consumption to her smiling face. He was out of breath, chest heaving, and sending telepathic messages only they could understand. I didn't think her announcement could have gone better until he broke down crying into her lap.

"Princess, you're going to be a momma. My sweet girl is going to make me a father. I can't believe it. When did you find out? And, more importantly, why didn't you tell me?" He caged her in, not giving her any space to wiggle out of a straight answer.

She lifted her hands to settle on either side of his bearded face, "I was scared. I wanted to. Really. But we had a flurry of guests and parties, and now Alex and Seneca are moving in. It's been hectic. I planned on telling you right after Thanksgiving but we were raising a barn. It was crazy town around here. Please don't be mad." She pouted for effect, though real tears streaked her face. Abigail knew how to work her man. *I should probably take a note from her playbook.*

Elias shushed her, nudging her knees farther apart. "Baby, I'm the farthest thing away from mad. I don't want you to go through any of this alone. Neither of us had a great childhood, but we have each other, and my son will have the best parents of all time. And, you're done slaving around this place come January first. We're hiring you an assistant or a housekeeper, or an all-in-one person. You need your rest, and we know what happens when you don't get it, right?"

She blushed. "I become impossible and need to be disciplined," she simpered. *Jesus, these two have their roles down pat.*

I interjected obnoxiously, "Okay, you two. I'm out. Abs, the pancakes are done. I'll pour your guests drinks and then you're on your own. Congratulations to both of you. I couldn't be happier." I waved, exiting the kitchen with a glass pitcher of orange juice and served her guests. I wanted what they had. Respect for each other. Lust and playfulness that never ended. And, the transparency to admit when they were wrong without judgment.

I sighed at that. Transparency wasn't my forte and judgment seemed part of my OCD. I was more like a vault with my emotions, never wanting to inflict them on unsuspecting victims. Losing control was one of my hallmark moves not everyone got to see. But woe be unto ye who hath provoked the sleeping dragon. Let's just say it's not pretty. I gave Abigail a thrashing years ago when she left Chicago without telling me. Come to think of it, Alex got one, too, shortly after I met him. His cocky, misogynistic comments said while pizza grease dripped down my face got him into trouble with everyone else, too.

Chapter 37
SENECA

The holidays came and went with the added highlight of Lindsey and her Aunt Micha joining us for Christmas Eve. New traditions were made playing charades. I wondered if Lindsey would enjoy Dane's company as much as his attention on her suggested he did.

"I've got this," Dane insisted, dropping to all fours. "Get on my back," he demanded.

Lindsey caught onto what he was inferring and duplicated her stance on top of his. "Ready," she said giddily.

"Do it!"

She listed to one side, careful not to fall off his back.

"Building blocks," Abigail yelled.

"Sex!" Alex hollered, only to receive a roomful of glares. "Come on! She mounted him." That got a round of laughter.

Dane seemed annoyed and lifted his left hand and left knee off the floor tipping Lindsey to the point of falling.

"Leaning Tower of Pisa," I shouted triumphantly.

Everyone hooted about how they could have done it better, but I was watching how Dane stayed on the ground cradling Lindsey in the crux of his arm. As she tried to pull herself up, he rolled over on top of her, hovering. A look passed between them giving me reason to believe a new love story was starting to take shape. The rest of the holiday was layered with good food, great company and shared memories we'd all cherish.

***

It was a mild winter with some occasional whiteouts, allowing the girls to roam more often in their new pasture. Alex's chickens got a clean bill of health before the holiday, allowing him to sell his organic eggs sooner than expected. Lindsey got the green light to start advertising on the newly updated Eloheh Farm website and secure local area events for him to meet his new customers.

I was days away from ordering fifty-six hundred pavers, crushed stone, regular sand, and polymeric sand to build the winding path to a concentric circle meditation space. The project had been burning a hole in my brain for years. Now that it's weeks away from starting, I began to panic.

"Elias," I blurted out, rushing into his work garage. My chest heaved, and I bent over trying to catch my breath. "Are you sure we ordered enough materials for the path? We won't have time to place another order."

He slid himself out from underneath a 1967 Chevy El Camino. His jumpsuit fit tightly over his thick thighs and his broad chest pulled nicely. I'd never been much of a beard girl, but, when he kept it short like it was now, he was drool worthy. *And, was married to my best friend.* Staying prone with his legs wide, *distracting,* he looked me straight in the eye.

"You can't keep doing this, Seneca. We calculated your dimensions three times. We even added an extra ten feet in case some of the bricks were damaged. Everything will arrive March fifth. They will lay each palette equidistant apart. The contractor we decided on two months ago has you on their calendar to begin March tenth. In between we'll string everything off. All is good, sweetheart. Relax."

He didn't wait for my reply. He didn't even give me his signature wink. Was I freaking out for nothing?

Alex slipped into the barn and began rubbing my shoulders.

"That feels too good. Thanks," I hummed.

I could feel his breath on my neck, heating up my body. It was exactly what I needed to relax and exactly what we agreed *not* to do. When I agreed to our new arrangement, I hadn't figured out how stressed I would be. So much so that I resembled an alcoholic succumbing to a bottle of whisky.

Desperate for a fix, I broke down. I tipped my head up over my shoulder, whispering into Alex's face. "Do you have time for a private meeting in your bedroom? It's very important," I purred quietly.

He snipped my earlobe with his teeth, mirroring my whisper. "Is there something I have that you need, Sen?" He kept massaging my shoulders and kissing my neck, making it impossible for me to keep from moaning.

A loud clank hit the cement floor, and Elias rolled back out from underneath the car, annoyed. "For the love of Christ, get the hell out of here. I don't need to hear your fucking foreplay." Without another word, he returned back under the car while Alex and I giggled like teenagers.

Grabbing his elbow, I pulled him toward the sliding barn door. "You heard the man. Let's go!"

I wouldn't call the two hours we spent a fuckfest, though I will admit to walking tenderly down to dinner. I needed that release desperately. Glenda would say using sex to medicate my OCD wasn't ideal. I, however, say a girl's gotta do what a girl's gotta do. And this girl got the job done.

Later that night, after dinner, Alex invited me to check out his improvements to the barn and loft after dinner. He assured me it was safe since the City Planner and Building Department approved all the plugs, ground defaults, and switches. The lights we'd picked in November were installed and the girls had new feeding troughs and water filtration systems in place. Alex wasn't taking any chances again with tainted water purifying well beyond minimal requirements.

"Are you sure you don't have an ulterior motive for bringing me out here? It would be a good ruse for a serial killer movie. Don't tell me you've been holding back and not telling me about your darker side? This would be such an inopportune time," I said in mock insult.

He tapped out a rhythm on his steering wheel cogitating. After a moment he turned his devilish grin my way. "You got me dead to rights. Luring you out here was part of my evil plan established years ago when I first met you. Wouldn't you agree the little bit about my farm being decimated forever was clever? It took some effort, but I'm no quitter. When I kill my girlfriend, I like to do it right. Muuuuaaaahhh!"

He swerved, laughing so much that I almost peed my pants. "This is fun. Imagining you as a serial killer is laughable. You're too goofy. Sorry, my friend, you'd better find a new career."

Pulling into the newly cut dirt circle drive, he parked the truck. "Don't move," he directed with a wink, and ran around the hood. He yanked open the passenger door, offering his hand like a gentleman. As I shimmied to the running board, he flipped me over his shoulder and walked me to the main door as I smacked his tight ass. "Settle down. You can have my ass in a minute, but first . . ."

Alex set me down inside the newly lit barn. He must have come out earlier to do it. "Oh, Alex. It's incredible!" I squealed. I'd been too busy the past couple weeks to check on his progress, but holy moly, was it beautiful!

"It wasn't easy to configure. In the end we had a specialist come out to ensure we ordered enough lights in the correct configurations to get the most bang for our buck." He puffed out his chest, surveying his new kingdom. He nodded his head slowly. "Yeah, it sure is something."

I pulled him into a tight side hug taking in every detail. "You deserve every bit of it and then some. I'm so proud of you, Alex." We stared a while longer, then he grabbed my hand and dragged me around to every nook and cranny explaining all the new features of the barn and their benefits. Eunice, Bernice and the rest of his girls would be living in style. The new milking system shortened his collection time to a quarter of what it had been. This new barn was a lean, mean, producing machine.

"Alex! You brought my curtains over," I exclaimed, walking over to the wall between the main area and the milking station. "They look so cute." I fawned over my curtains, loving how he put a little bit of me in his new sanctuary.

He clucked, "And take a chance my girls won't produce because they miss their décor? Hell, no!"

I turned him toward me by his lapels, licking my lips in appreciation for his hard work and hard body. "Is there anything else you want to show me?"

He dipped his head low to mine, his eyes hooded in anticipation. "Yes, ma'am, there is, but you're going to have to crawl for it," he growled into my mouth.

"Ooh. That sounds kinky. See, you get to keep that dark side alive," I hissed, running my hands down his body.

He snorted. "If climbing a ladder is kinky, then, yeah, climb away."

The last time I was up here, it was only roughed in. No drywall, only subfloor, and one big window. The dramatic change from barren to beautiful was nothing short of spectacular. If I hadn't known I was in a barn, this incredible room could be Alex's living room in Pennsylvania. He added an entry pad before the door with a small bench for his boots, keeping the dirt out of his living space. Three daisy cow hooks hung indiscriminately on the wall above the bench for coats, and a small sign on the door said, "Alex Valize, Head Honcho, Keeper of the Cows," in an elegant scroll against a distressed tan framed background. *I'll have to ask Lindsey if she found that on Etsy or Pinterest. I'd like one made for Abigail and Elias as a thank you gift.*

A sturdy, distressed maple desk sat to the left of the window providing him good light in the day and a magnificent view of what will soon be his organic crops. He had a serene view of his cows milling around the first pasture with plans for two additional pastures later this summer. I could envision him looking out there, knowing he'd risen from the ashes. A phoenix of his own making. His rolling wood and leather boss chair swiveled on casters, allowing him to roll it over to a round, matching worktable. On the side wall was the outrageous daisy-crowned cow canvas we bought in November, along with a multi-light floor lamp directed into the room's four corners, giving it a homey glow. The opposite wall from the window sported a camel-colored futon with several denim-clothed pillows, one saying, "Whatever doesn't kill you makes you stronger." *Wasn't that the truth.* The centerpiece of this comfortable, manly room was a midnight blue jute rug. It was huge and seemed to be laid over a thick rubber mat, making it super soft to walk on.

"Alex! You have outdone yourself," I said, turning slowly in a circle, my hands on my cheeks. "The cow picture! And, aww, look. You have pictures of your family already on your desk. That's so sweet." I fawned over every detail, from the chicken coop desk organizer to a cup full of pens with silk vegetables attached to the ends. It looked like a garden was growing on his desk. "You have to tell me who helped you with this. I know it wasn't you," I taunted playfully.

His shocked look was comical. "You hurt me deep, Seneca," he cried. "You're right, though. Between Lindsey scouring Pinterest to Abigail walking over fifty rugs and laying on as many futons in her pregnant state, she decided on those two necessary pieces of décor." His smile screamed pride and accomplishment. He earned every bit of it.

I walked around the room, dragging my hand over every material and lamenting that I'd missed this part of the project. Sensing something was off, Alex asked, "Why the face, Sen?"

I turned, pressing my lips, keeping myself from blurting out my disappointment. Choosing my words carefully, I said quietly, "It looks like you are managing without me. It's bittersweet. That's all." I sat down on the futon, taking in the room from this vantage point, and saw a ceramic zen dog sitting in the corner that looked similar to Benny. *I missed that boy.*

Alex kneeled in front of me, taking my small hands in his big, calloused ones. "Our projects might be done, Sen, but I'll never manage without you. I look forward to your sass and insights. You push me to be a better man. A better partner. You may have a whole future ahead of you, but never think I'll manage better without you. I won't."

He slid his hands into my hair, his fingers pushing out the braid I'd carefully plaited earlier. He moaned as he pulled the silky strands from root to end, getting harder each time he kissed me. Our tongues chased each others like we'd chased each other's for years. It was a dance we were made to have. Angling my head to gain access to my neck, he yanked my sweater down as he placed hot, wet kisses between my breasts. He became frustrated when he couldn't get my clothes off faster.

"Fuck, Sen. I've been thinking about you laid out on this rug from the moment I rolled it open. I can't wait anymore. I want you so fucking badly." He ground his hips against mine showing me exactly what he wanted from me. I wanted him, too. I dreamt of fucking him on his new office chair, on his office floor, and, God help me, in a damn cow berth. I wanted him everywhere.

"Please tell me we can have tonight without thinking of the future. I need this, Sen. I need you." His kisses silenced the end of his thoughts probably preventing him from saying something he would regret later. I understood why, even if it caused us both pain.

"Alex, please. Make love to me." *Oh, shit! That came out all wrong.*

He paused, searching my eyes for something. Thoughts flickered across his face assessing my fear at what came out of my mouth. When he found my response lacking, he sat back on his heels, anguish furrowing his brow. I stared at him intently. I knew I'd screwed up saying those stupid words. Why did I keep word-vomiting my thoughts?

It seemed like an eternity before he spoke again. His words were soft, caring, like a prayer. "Is that what you want, Sen? You want me to make love to you? Not fuck you?" He looked so confused, so vulnerable.

Did I want that? What would it mean? It would change our relationship. I'd never made love to a man. It was always fast, hot, and animalistic at times, especially with Alex. He brought out emotions in me that I didn't know I possessed. Making love to him would be cataclysmic. I'd never be the same. Was I ready to commit myself to him?

I sat up, sliding myself out from under his legs. I took his face into mine, preparing to either ruin us or bind us together for eternity. I wasn't sure what would come out of my mouth next. I could see his heart beating wildly, though. His sapphire blue eyes faded to black. This was it. No more games or what-ifs. My heart broke at what I needed to do.

"If ever I wanted to make love to a man it would be with you, Alex. I want to tell you something, and I don't want you to respond, okay?" My mouth went dry, summoning my thoughts to come out in a coherent statement. "I love you, Alex Valize. I want you with all my heart..."

My throat closed and I gulped.

"I sense a 'but' coming," he supplied warily, waiting as I asked.

"It's true what they say about timing. It means everything. We agreed not to have expectations. I have to finish my internship and degree. I have goals and dreams I've wished to meet for a long time. I can't settle down before I've even begun to fulfill them. I don't know how long that will take. You said I could take all the time I needed, but, Alex, you are older and I know you want a family. I promised myself I wouldn't interfere with your goals and dreams either. I don't know what to do. I want you desperately, but I can't make love to you tonight. I was wrong to ask for it. I'm—I'm so sorry. Please don't hate me."

I slid my hands down his chest feeling how erratically it was beating. I was killing him, I knew it. It was killing me to say those things, too. With no other choice, I stood up, fixed my shirt and opened the loft door. "I'll see you downstairs."

Chapter 38

ALEX

What the fuck just happened?

One minute I'm ready to christen my office with my spicy vixen, and the next I'm standing there with my dick in my hand, having an existential crisis. I had whiplash from the intense heat of the moment, then felt the lick of the frigid winter air outside my window as I drove Seneca back to the house in silence. I understood what she was saying. I even appreciated her trying to protect me from herself and her decisions, but I wasn't ready to let her tell me how to feel about us or what I should be doing while she lived her life. Because, goddammit, there would be a future with her.

She attempted to jump out of the truck, when I caught her elbow. I stared deeply into her big brown eyes, making a promise I was hellbent on keeping. "We *will* figure this out, Seneca. Give it time. Believe in us, okay?"

She stared at me, uncertain of our destiny. She nodded and I released her arm, allowing her to leave. I don't know how long I sat looking out over the dark horizon, contemplating every word we'd said to one another. I tore through every precept I held about love and relationships, shearing them down to one thing: respect.

I don't know if I ever respected anyone as much as I respected Seneca. She was young chronologically, though her intellect and sensitivity were far beyond her years. She was an old soul. From what she'd told me, her mom had a keen understanding of the earth and her connection to it. She respected it, cared for it like it was her child, protecting it vigilantly. If only we would all feel the same way, we could save our planet and ourselves. It left me lacking.

There was a knock on the driver's window, waking me abruptly from my thoughts.

"Dude. Get inside. You'll freeze your ass off," Elias barked through the glass. I shook my head clear and exited the vehicle numbly. "What's going on with you? Seneca came in and ran up the stairs, barely acknowledging us."

I shoved my hands in my pockets, searching the ground for answers. "We are at an impasse in our relationship. It has nothing to do with love or wanting a future. It has more to do with timing. Elias, she's just beginning to find her way in the world, and I'm a fucking dinosaur in comparison. I need to let her explore her options, not hold her back. She wants the same thing but can't seem to let go of this invisible hold we have on each other. Hopefully, in a few months or a few years, we'll know what's to be between us. It fucking hurts like hell."

His giant hand landed on my shoulder, giving it a squeeze. "Love hurts like a motherfucker, doesn't it?"

I sighed, annoyed, "It sure as hell does."

As much as my heart said to stay and help Seneca get her project off the ground, my head said, "Get the hell out of the way." Last night, she was crystal clear about us going our separate ways. So why, then, did I still want to throw her onto the counter and fuck that stupid thought out of her beautiful brain? I've heard of men groveling for their women and judging them as weak and pussy whipped. But today, I was okay with it. I was that grown-ass man torn down by a small woman, ready to do whatever she wanted me to do if only she would agree to be mine.

Instead, I poured her morning cup of coffee, slid the mug across the island with a wry smile, and wished invisibility cloaks were real so I could watch her without showing her the lust and pain I could barely contain. *I was a miserable fool.*

Seneca deserved to be excited today. For fear of stirring the proverbial pot with our usual banter of saying, "Hey," I settled for a friendly, buddy-buddy tack allowing her to stay focused and without distractions.

"Good luck today," I forced out with as much excitement as a rejected lover could.

She cupped both hands around her coffee, adorably, like she did every morning. Blowing on the steaming liquid while still maintaining eye contact. Though today, those black eyes stared back unrequited and sorrowful. What did I think would happen overnight? A complete change of mind? *Not only was I a miserable fool but a dreamer, too.*

Seneca's materials would arrive this week and the weather report was favorable. She had several lists spread out over the back counter; more than any sane person should have, emphasizing her need for order and control. Anyone who chanced to alter her plans took their life into their own hands, especially me. I considered having a "Don't Fuck with Me" T-shirt made as a reminder, then remembered why she initially hated me in the first place.

Her big day had arrived the following day and Seneca gathered her team of minions welcoming everyone and doling out assignments.

"Our paver people have measured and tamped down the sand path we will follow. Be careful on the gravel pad. It's leveled and can't be walked on. We have to lay at least twenty feet a day to get this part of the project done by the end of March. Plant materials will arrive; by then we'll have dug holes. We'll have two weeks in April to walk my focus group through the garden, collect their reviews, and collate them into a cohesive paper." She looked upward, processing her last words. "That is to say, *I* will write the paper," she said with a self-deprecating laugh. Pivoting, she continued, "Lindsey, when will all our signs be finished?"

Lindsey looked down at her clipboard and then back to Seneca. "If all goes well, the meditation signs will be ready April fifth, and the main sign by the twentieth. The guys are trying to get it done earlier, but the details you requested might slow down the process," she said apologetically. Lindsey was a trooper. Understated, capable, and very shy. Sometimes I found it difficult to question her approach to marketing without upsetting her. She was really young, but I didn't want to discriminate against her because of it. Surprisingly clever, she exceeded all our expectations from IT to marketing without finishing college.

Seneca rolled her neck, "That will have to do. Inform me of any changes, please. Next, be conscientious of where you are using heavy equipment. I don't want any natural foliage destroyed. This is my holy ground and you will treat it with the utmost respect." *Like any of us would dare not to do so.* "Any questions?"

Derrick, our friend and carpenter chirped, "We need to talk about seating when you're finished."

Seneca slapped her forehead, dropping her clipboard to her thigh. "Yes! Right. Seating. Give me fifteen minutes and we'll knock that out." She rolled her eyes as if she was inept. I wasn't letting her feel that way.

Slipping behind her after she dismissed everyone, I spun her around, holding her hips tightly. "You will not second guess yourself. Do you understand me? You've done all the prep and you'll deal with any hiccups like a professional. Trust in your abilities, Seneca, or I swear I'll spank you." I gave her my sexiest grin and enjoyed watching her blush. She exhaled a deep, long breath and relaxed.

"Yes, sir," she whispered.

I kissed her lips softly and smacked her ass anyway. "Go kick some garden ass."

My barn was complete, shy of a few bits and pieces. My cows were happy roaming around again, and my chickens finally flew the coop into their own pen. Life was good. It was time now to get my seedlings to sprout. On the far side of the barn, the side with the best sunlight, I'd set up two-by-eights on sawhorses to hold up hundreds of seedlings. They'd stay warm until frost was no longer a concern, only needing water and a few warming lights to get them to grow. I was finally into a groove between plant care, cow care, and farmer-like things. I could feel myself becoming whole again, and it felt amazing.

Lindsey had prepared a letter we sent in late January to my old customers, suppliers, and the East Stroudsburg government officials explaining why I moved. I apologized for my quick departure and to be on the lookout for future organic products made to be shipped. Holy cow, did I get dozens of letters of support, concern, and friendship asking that I stay in touch. Even Annalise had people coming by her home offering comfort and support. A donation fund sprung up with the area Rotary Club, and, to date, has raised over fifty-two hundred dollars for my legal fees. *I was growing concerned about how many times I've teared up recently. Maybe I was in man-o-pause.*

People are surprising. Quick to condemn and just as quick to support. The community I shared in that quaint little town would never be forgotten. If the people of Mystic gave me half of what they gave me, I would be truly blessed.

Everyone here at The Farnsworth Inn and Eloheh Farms each had their pet projects to attend to. I'd put up ads for seasonal help, finding two middle-aged men and a kind, elderly woman to help till my first fields, plant, water, and tend to them until they took root. Elias was up to his eyeballs in pavers. Abigail had a full roster of guests from mid-March through October, spurring my decision to find a new place to live.

Abigail said multiple times having me stay wasn't a burden. Except, every night they couldn't rent my room equaled lost income. I knew it wasn't about the money for them. Abigail's trust was worth millions. It was my integrity that mostly suffered. She was growing a business, not a boarding house for displaced friends.

I'd seen a few lease signs nearby if I could find time to check them out. I waffled on asking Seneca to join me, though thinking she'd live with me was presumptuous. She'd put me firmly in the friend zone, cutting sex out of our relationship—for now. Even being in each other's orbit clouded both our judgment. It was undue pressure that neither of us needed. *Especially the pressure in my pants.* Seneca stayed in her bedroom until the inn became too busy, then bunked with Abigail and Elias. Awkward as it was for Elias, I think he secretly enjoyed watching his wife play sleepover with her friend. *And they thought I was the pervert. Lucky daddy!*

At dinner, I announced I had started looking for a new place to live and several forks clanked onto their plates. "This is out of the blue," Abigail cried, tears threatening to fall.

"Aw. Come on, man. I was just starting to like having you around," Elias deadpanned, murmuring under his breath, "About fucking time."

Seneca said nothing. I didn't know if that was a good or bad thing. She'd been strictly focused on her project, working every night to calculate, record, and prepare for the next day. Abigail offered sweetly, "Do you need any help finding a place? No need to hurry off, Alex. We always have room for you." She was as sweet as they came unless you pissed her off. Then, not good.

I smiled back, "I've got this. There's a place a mile from the barn that's for lease. I figured I would hole up there for the year. Besides, Dane will be back in a few months, and he'll need a place, too. It's small, but, if it works out, it will do until either my lawsuits come through or my farm takes off. I'm going over there after dinner to check it out." I bobbed my head assuring myself this was the right move. *Yep. Right move.*

By April first, I was unpacking my things, again, in my newly leased two-bedroom house. It was clean, cozy and quiet. I kept long days, and those three attributes were a dealbreaker. If all went well, I'd get Benny back from Annalise in June after she and Steven adopted their own pet. I missed having his face on my thigh and rubbing his fur while watching television. It was therapeutic. So was having Seneca in my bed. I was a desperate, lonely man.

I dropped the rest of my silverware into the drawer when I heard a soft knock. I bumped the drawer closed with my hip and went to see who'd found me. Only three people knew where I lived, so maybe...

It was Abigail with a basket bigger than her body filled with baked goods, kitchen towels, a knitted blanket, and several packages of condoms. *Bless her heart.*

"Really, Abs? I love it all, but condoms? You know I'm not fifteen, right?" I tickled her under her armpit getting a yipe and an elbow to my ribs. "Ouch!"

"Serves you right, Alex. It's always safety first. Besides, don't you plan to have company over soon?" She winked like she was having a seizure.

That would be nice. Doubtful, but nice. "One can only hope. Let me put this over here for now. What do you think? Does it look like a place I'd live in?" I watched warily as she assessed the place.

"Better than that. It looks like the new and improved Alex," she cooed. "Best of good times and great health. Elias will come by tomorrow after he lays the final pavers for Seneca." Her eyes cast down, rolling her lips in and out, preparing to say something.

"It's none of my business, Alex. You and Seneca have had a wild relationship until now. There is this weird vibe going on between you. Are you talking to each other? Is it over? I'm at a loss." She sat down at the kitchen table, making herself feel at home.

What did she want to hear? What did Seneca already tell her? It seemed like yesterday Abigail took me aside for a long walk after I'd been an ass to her best friend. She threatened me, if I didn't make it right, she'd castrate me. I felt inspired to fix the problem I caused by extending an olive branch and letting her decide if she wanted to accept it. This had been another déjà vu moment.

I sat down and took her hands in mine. "Yes, we are talking. Yes, we are mostly on the same page. No. It's not over, at least for now. Seneca needs to spread her wings and use her shiny new degree to explore the world, not be stuck in a tiny town off the east coast of nowhere. I have to let her go. It's going to kill me to do it, but I owe her that for all she's done for me. Maybe in a few years she'll decide to come back. Maybe I'll still be available. Maybe not. We need time, Abs."

Her eyes glistened with tears streaming down her face, hiccups punctuating her breathing. "I can't believe it finally happened," she mewled.

"What happened?" My brow knit in confusion.

She withdrew one hand, wiping at her smiling face, "You grew up. You're no longer the cocky, self-centered piece of shit I learned to love. I'm so happy for you and your appreciation and selflessness for my best friend. I hope you don't count her out of your life just yet. You know she's a dog with a bone when she wants something, and I have a feeling you're her bone." Her pouty lips were adorable. Another of Abigail's superpowers was her transparency. You got what you saw with her. You'd never have to wonder what was going on in her head. If she thought I still had a chance with Seneca, then I'd hold onto that hope, no matter how small it was.

I sat back in my chair, relieved. "Thank you for loving and supporting me, Abigail. You never let me down."

She blushed, then popped up from her chair beelining for the door. "Welcome home, Alex. Enjoy your goodies. Oh! Best put all those baked goods in your freezer. There's too many to eat in a week." I watched her get in her car and back out of the driveway, gaining a new appreciation for that special woman.

Chapter 39

SENECA

I feel like I'm in a tunnel with no light to guide me through. While Elias was a godsend laying pavers for me with a few of his buddies, the perfect weather the meteorologist guaranteed would come turned into two days of rain, which equaled a four-day delay. We had one more day of paving to do when I got the call from one of the nurseries shipping half my plants.

"Miss Locklear, my driver is in the hospital with gallstones. I'm afraid to tell you, my backup driver has COVID. I'd drive them myself but I'm the only other person here. I'm really sorry. I'll have them for you next Monday before noon."

My first response was *close your fucking store and drive through the night.* My second thought was to rent a step van and drive the hundred miles to get them myself. Except that's an expensive rental, and I wasn't using my own money. Instead, I put on my big girl panties and let him off the hook.

"I'm sorry your men aren't well. Of course, I can wait. Let me know immediately of any other holdups. I have a deadline to meet." This was an example of surrender Glenda said I needed to embrace. Sick drivers were out of my control. *Breathe.*

This day wasn't over. The final nail in my coffin arrived an hour later. One week before my focus group would determine my destiny, three of my signs were spelled incorrectly. The phrase, "mysteries of the universe," read "miseries of the universe." *Miseries!* The other two signs suffered the same kind of death. I knew where the disconnect happened, and it was going to break her heart when she heard about this.

Needing the problem resolved today, I walked into the little garage that was now Lindsey's office and cashier stand. She had decorated it adorably with crocheted plants, potatoes, pickles, and tomatoes, all with encouraging sayings. I loved every one of them. Lindsey didn't have a mean bone in her body, which made this visit impossibly hard.

"Hey—Lindsey. Do you have a minute?" She looked at me funny knowing something was off.

"Of course. What's up?" She stopped typing and swirled her chair around.

"Before I continue, I want you to know I am the one completely responsible for what I'm about to tell you. This is my proj—"

She cut me off, "Spill it, Seneca. I can take it."

I rubbed both sides of my jaw ready to cry, so I blurted out what I came to say. "Three of the signs are spelled wrong and need to be remade immediately."

Her jaw dropped, eyes went wide, and her shoulders rolled in as if in pain. "Oh. My. God! No!" she jerkily exhaled. My dyslexia! I swear I spell-checked everything. I'm so sorry."

I walked over to her seat and pulled her up into a hug. "That's the funny part of this problem. It wasn't that the words were spelled wrong. It's that they were the wrong words." I explained the three sayings, watching her eyes shutter closed. My heart broke for her.

"They won't be ready for the focus group!" Another realization swept over her agonized face. "We can't put them up, can we?" I shook my head, no.

I sat her back down and pulled up a chair. "I'll ask Abigail if she could design some beautifully lettered signs and we'll put them up the day of the tour so they don't get damaged. With any luck, the weather will be good and I'll still get a positive response. It was an honest mistake. I should have taken the time for a final look before sending them to the designer. I've learned a lesson, too. We'll get through this, okay?"

I waited for her nod but didn't get one. "Look at me, Lindsey. This is how we learn from our mistakes. We own it, fix it, and put best practices in place to prevent another mishap. It's over. We're moving forward."

She wiped her eyes and huffed out, "Okay. Can we fix it now and resend it before any more time lapses?" I liked her spirit and tenacity. Frankly, I'm surprised we haven't had any other mistakes. Being overworked was a surefire way to make mistakes.

"Absolutely," I said patting her back. In less than five minutes, the mistakes were fixed and forwarded, followed by a phone call I made after leaving Lindsey's office confirming the updates. The company gave me a deep discount for the re-do and promised their best to meet my deadline. I couldn't ask for anything more. *What a day!*

"Thank you for being so understanding. I feel terrible about this," Lindsey cried again, grabbing me tightly for another hug. "You're being so nice to me. I really appreciate it."

"Let's put this all behind us, okay? I have to check in with Abigail now. I'm looking forward to seeing your upcoming marketing campaigns. It's time to start building some hype. Oh! And, don't forget to reach out to every Chamber of Commerce in the tri-state area. They'll help us get the word out fast. Text if you need anything."

Before she could stop me again, I dashed out of her office and into the house to find Abigail with flour all over her face and apron.

"What the hell, Abs?" I dragged my finger along the counter lifting a quarter inch of pastry flour and showing it to her.

She looked dejected, scrunching her eyes closed. "It's a new cake recipe. It's giving me fits. It has to be sifted twice. I can't contain it!" Watching her work brought tears of joy and laughter. Abigail should have her own reality show. It would be spectacular.

I air hugged her, not wanting to be covered in it, too. "I believe in you." I pumped a fist into the air in support.

Her hand jammed into her hip, giving me a don't-fuck-with-me look, "Thanks. I'll remember that. What do you need? I'm working here."

Ah, yes. There was a reason for my visit.

"I'd like to have a small reception for my focus group after they walk the path. A small something they can munch on while filling out their survey. No one leaves without filling one out. I don't have time for emails, and reminders, and all that crap. I'm on a deadline."

She pointed across the room to be her small desk. "Grab my appointment book and flip it open. What date are you looking at?"

I flipped it open to find the workings of an eight-year-old. All manner of doodles, scratches, and stars filled the margins of every page. *Is this really how her mind worked?* "Their tour is April fifth from ten to eleven, followed by a Q&A, and filling out their survey. Let's call it eleven-fifteen. I'll make a light lunch of deli sandwiches on mini brioche buns, coleslaw and potato salad. Of course, we'll need your double fudge brownies for dessert and a variety of canned drinks. Super simple. If you could shop for it, I can make everything that morning except your dessert. They'll be done at twelve-thirty and I'll clean it all up. And good news, you don't have anything else that day," I said, smiling brightly.

Abigail blew an errant tendril out of her face, replying whimsically, "Easy-peasy. No problem. Remind me two days before. Pregnancy brain has set in, and even looking at my calendar doesn't help me remember anything."

I keep forgetting she's pregnant. She's not showing, only feeling more fatigued. Thank goodness she wasn't a barfer. That shit wipes you out. "How about I review your calendar with you at breakfast each morning and again before dinner so you can stay on top of things? It's the least I can do for all you've done for me. As soon as this project is over, I'll be your personal slave." I pressed my hands together in prayer, bowing reverently to the house princess.

She hummed aloud. "Does that mean you're sticking around until I deliver?" *That stopped me in my tracks.*

"Maybe," I said stretching out the word. "When are you due again? September?"

Her stern look took me aback, "July, Seneca. For the third time, July! Twentieth to be precise. Or as precise as a baby can be."

"Right," I muttered. "I'll definitely be here. I can't miss the little bean popping out from its momma." I twirled my hair around my finger, accepting that I wouldn't be traveling this summer. I had put in a few applications for continuing education in the Philippines, Japan, and Arizona. Having more experience in humid and arid climates would be a huge plus for my toolbelt. Additionally, those hours would count toward my master's program as soon as I figured out where that would be. I didn't have a timeline, only that I thought I would flow from one experience to the other. *Funny how life makes you flexible.*

Abigail motioned for me to sit down with her at the table. She poured two glasses of iced tea and pushed one in front of me. She looked so serious.

"You know how my brain works, right? It never shuts off. Moving at the speed of light, getting way ahead of myself." *Where was she going with this?* "Have you considered how Alex will fit into your life after graduation?"

There it was. The million-dollar question tormenting me daily for the past eight months. Before I had a chance to respond, she interjected, "Seneca. It doesn't have to be an all or nothing situation. Alex is a reasonable man. I know you love him. It's written all over your face, and, God knows, your body lights up every time he walks into a room."

I sighed as I exhaled. "I'm torn! I agree with everything you've said. Finding the balance between him and my career is killing me. I don't want to do half-measures, Abs. He deserves so much more than that." I rubbed my forehead, feeling desperate.

She took both my hands in hers over the table, squeezing them tightly. "Make him a proposal and let him decide if he's okay with it. The one thing I can tell you, from being a married woman, is negotiating is paramount to your happiness. There's always a middle ground. You just have to fight for it. Talk to him, Sen. You might be ecstatically surprised." *The mother hen in her is nesting.*

I pursed my lips contemplating her request. She wasn't wrong. Was I holding back, being stubborn about my decision to follow my heart or break his? This was agony. I needed more time. Time to finish my internship and then plan my next move. Except applications had been sent out and many more needed to be completed. Opportunities were snapped up quickly, forcing me to be reactive when I wanted to take a moment and breathe after so many months of pressure. Sadly, I didn't have that luxury. I needed to make a living and couldn't do that in a small town.

"I'll keep thinking about it. I promise." I swung our hands back and forth, sharing the heaviness of our talk. "I should check on Elias. He's supposed to finish the path today. Talk to you later."

"Come here, Seneca. I have a job for you," Elias waved me to his side affectionately. "Here," he handed me five pavers, "You get to place the final pieces to your masterpiece." I gasped looking from the heavy material to his twinkly eyes.

"Seriously? You saved these for me? I—I don't know what to say," I said through a stream of tears.

In Elias style, he proclaimed, "Say nothing. Let's get this done and check it off your list. I have a new car coming in tomorrow, so you'll be on your own from here on out."

Panic rolled over my body. This was it. I couldn't lean on anyone anymore. Elias insisted on building the path with his friends who had done this before. He didn't want me to interrupt or make changes along the way, and I honored that request. The burden of this project was mine and mine alone. I was petrified. *Enough!* Freaking out wasn't part of my itinerary. I had pavers to complete and plants arriving tomorrow.

I grabbed a kneeler and got to work placing the final pieces. I spread the polymeric sand in between the pieces, unable to see through the river of tears at having completed my dream project. "There." I sat back on my heels, admiring my handiwork, when cheers and clapping surprised me. I turned around to see all my friends standing behind me, congratulating and praising me for a job well done. If I thought I couldn't see through my tears before, I was blind now.

Alex pulled me up into his arms, letting me blubber into his chest. Four years of envisioning and planning this path were over. I could hardly contain myself. Completing this project with the people who believed in what it stood for—harmony, wholeness, abundance, and peace—Eloheh—seemed poetic. I looked to the heavens, thanking my mother for her guidance and protection as this project unfolded. Having her in my heart every step of the way brought me unlimited strength.

Alex wouldn't let go of me, no matter what direction I turned. I couldn't tell if he thought I'd leave him or if he wanted me to know he supported me the way I had supported him. *Both, I suppose.* "Look at what you achieved, Sen. It's incredible," he whispered, looking down at me lovingly.

I brushed the side of his jaw with my knuckles since my hands were filthy. "Thank you. Thank you everyone so much for being part of my village." I began crying tears of joy, again. Alex could wring his shirt out later.

Abigail pushed him out of the way, "Let the best friend through," she demanded, throwing her arms around me so fiercely I almost fell over. "I never doubted you for a moment. Congratulations, Sen. I'm so proud of you."

By the time the revelry ended and the rest of the materials were stowed away in the barn, it was near nightfall. Abigail made a delicious Italian dinner and tiramisu for dessert. Sitting at the table with my best friends, I lifted my glass.

Ahem. "I'd like to make a toast and share a revelation. Firstly, to Abigail. My benefactor, my friend, my mother at times, and my ride or die girl. None of this would have been possible without you. Secondly, to Elias for his attention to detail and engineering skills that will keep the path safe and secure for many years. And, last, but not least, Alex. For pushing me to become more than the sum of my parts. You made my project a priority in your crazy, upturned life, and I appreciate you more than words can say. Thank you all from the bottom of my heart." We clinked glasses, making cheering noises of all kinds and basking in the glow of our friendship. Everyone in my life was happy. The rest was gravy.

Chatter filled the air before I finished. "Wait! Please. My revelation. If anyone had asked me four years ago if we were as talented, resourceful, hardworking, and clever as we are today, I would have laughed them out of the room. Look at us now. Look at what we've imagined and brought to life. Our team brought them to reality. Our village overcame adversity to achieve greatness. We have done these things. Not alone, but together. Together, we are the sum of our parts—together, we make a difference. Please raise your glass again—to us. A formidable, talented, hardworking, loving, exceptional group of kinky people who have had the honor of calling each other friends. Cheers!"

Chapter 40

ALEX

Living in Mystic allowed me to plant my crops sooner than East Stroudsburg. Mid-April to late May was optimal, and I knew I was pushing the envelope on planting, but I wanted them in the ground before Seneca finished her project. I wanted to be present when she handed in her final thesis. If all went well, I wanted to whisk her off for a weekend in New York City to celebrate her graduation, her project, and us starting a new life in Mystic. Together or separately. My only concern was whether she would be leaving the estate immediately.

Since completing Seneca's pathway, she'd planted, positioned statuary, dug posts for her signage, and fine-tuned her marketing plan. I slept at the barn, maximizing every minute I had while tending to my seedlings and tweaking my automatic milking machine.

A few days later, I chanced a few minutes with what I hoped was still my girl. "Hey, Sen. Looking good." She turned to look over her shoulder, still on her hands and knees. It took great control not to objectify that tight, plump ass. We've had some incredible nights with her bottom looking like she was now.

Seneca eyeballed me, "I'm sure it does. How about you helping me up? I'm broken." She winced as I hooked my arms below her armpits, gently lifting her up. "Oh! Ow! Alex, I don't think I can stand on my own. Her eyes began to tear, and my pulse quickened. Carefully scooping her into my arms, I instructed her to wrap her arm around my neck, but she winced, trying to lift her arm. My girl was in pain. It broke my heart to see her like this. "Don't worry, baby. I've got you."

I quickly walked her down the path to the house, grabbing at the handle with only my thumb and kicking the door open.

"Hey, easy on the door!" Abigail shouted. "What's—Sen! What's wrong with her?" Her shouts turned to shrieks.

"She overdid it. I'm taking her upstairs for a bath. Would you get a cold glass of water and a bottle of ibuprofen? I'm spending the night with her on the floor. I hope she doesn't have any bulging disks. They take forever to heal."

Abigail did my bidding as I carried her up the grand staircase to what had been my bedroom. I carefully laid her on the bed then ran into the bathroom to start a steaming hot bath in the clawfoot tub. I dumped a pound of Epsom salts in to help her muscles relax, returning to her side to undress her.

"Let's get you into a hot tub, okay?"

"Okay. I'm sure I pulled a muscle. Nothing a hot bath and muscle relaxers can't fix," she mused.

I wasn't sure if she was talking herself into feeling better or believed what was coming out of her mouth. Either way, she was staying on her back tomorrow if I had to sit on her. *A burden I'd gladly take on.*

"We'll see."

I gently pulled her arms out of her fleece jacket, carefully lifting her long sleeve T-shirt over her head. She winced each time I pulled off a sleeve. Looking at her limp body made me near hysterical. It was when I was able to slip her pants off her hips without undoing the button that I noticed how much weight she had lost. She was working herself to death.

Abigail ran into the room. Hands outstretched with the water and pills. "Holy shit, Sen. You're a stick figure. Why didn't I notice you hadn't been eating?" She looked at me, frightened. "Alex? What do we do?"

I scrubbed my face, wondering the same thing. "Make her a sandwich, and I'm going to force-feed it to her while she soaks in the tub." I approached Abigail, whispering, "Every meal needs to be monitored. She'll sit at that kitchen table until her plate is empty, or I'll puree it and pour it down her throat." I was serious, but the imagery made me chuckle. Abigail saw it, too.

"I'd like to see that. Then again, I'd rather she eats it on her own. Give me a few minutes," she said wistfully and sped out the door.

I pulled off her socks and then released her perfect breasts from their harness as carefully as I could, carrying her from the bed to the hot bath and testing the water before lifting her in. *Perfect.* She tried lifting her arms to lower herself in but whimpered at the effort. It seemed every bit of her was strained beyond function.

"Sit still, woman. I won't leave your side. I'm saving my lecture for later because you're in big trouble. Big trouble," I enunciated every syllable. "Here. Open your mouth and swallow." I placed four pills on her tongue, holding the water glass close for her to drink them back. "You'll start feeling those soon."

I sat at the top of the tub, keeping a hand on her at all times, either running my fingers through her hair or massaging her biceps and neck as she struggled to exhale easily. I willed her muscles to relax, needing her pain to subside. Her body spasmed as the muscles fought to stay tight. *Why wasn't the medication working yet?*

"Alex. I'm afraid. I hurt so much," she cried out in pain.

"I know, baby. I know. Focus your mind somewhere special. Guide your muscles to relax through your thoughts. Be patient. Soon you'll feel better."

I didn't know what else to say. We could call the doctor, but they'd only give her stronger drugs. If we could get her through the night, she might not need them. I'd do everything I knew of for a strained back until she was well. It wasn't that long ago she laid on the floor with me for three days when my back went out. Her resilience was exceptional.

Abigail buzzed back into the room with a tray of food. "I brought something for you, too. It's past dinnertime. I'll check on you both later. Text me if you need anything." She kissed me on the head and patted my shoulder.

Leaning over me, she kissed her friend's face, promising everything she could promise to get her better. Abigail left the room weeping, shutting the door behind her.

I continued massaging her head, temples and neck until her breathing smoothed. When her shoulders dropped two inches, I knew the medicine was working. *Thank God.*

"Baby, let me help you eat something. You've lost a lot of weight. You need your strength to finish your project. Here, take a bite," I coaxed, willing her to eat. Thankfully, I was able to get her to eat half a sandwich before she dozed off.

The water became tepid, alerting me she needed to get warm again. I quickly grabbed several towels from the linen closet and spread them on my bed. Cautiously, I lifted her from the water carrying her dripping body back to where I could cocoon her in safety. I patted every inch of her body like she was a precious child, keeping her close, protected, and loved. Once she was dry, I pulled back the down comforter and rolled her naked body into the sheets, tucking her in. I grabbed another dry towel and slowly towel dried hair, enjoying the silky strands through my fingers.

Once I knew she was settled, I returned to the scene of the crime to put her tools away, sweeping off any remnants of dirt from the pathway. I looked up and down both sides of the pavers, noticing she'd plotted out where each plant would be planted. I'd get up early and finish the job for her so she wouldn't worry about getting behind. Her focus group would be here in a few days, and it would take that long before Seneca would be able to move easily.

Entering the house, Abigail pulled me aside, concerned, and rightfully so. "Did she eat? How is she doing? Will she be able to work again soon?" She moved from foot to foot hyped up on adrenaline.

A large hand came down on her shoulder, and a deep voice dipped close to soothe her. "She'll be fine, princess. Your bestie is a strong woman. She'll bounce back soon. Why don't you go up and keep her company?" Abigail's eyes rounded, taking his cue. She bolted up the back stairs to reach her quickly like her tail was on fire.

I looked at my best friend. It was my turn to freak out. "Elias. Seneca has to have lost ten to fifteen pounds, and I didn't fucking notice. What kind of boyfriend am I that I didn't notice?" I shoved my fingers through my long, dirty-blond hair as I paced. "Fuck!" I said, slamming the kitchen countertop.

That same hand soothing Abigail dropped onto my shoulder paternally, "The woman wears sweatshirts and baggy pants most of the time. And, if I'm not mistaken, the two of you haven't been in each other's bed in a bit." He wasn't wrong. But still…

"She looked like a little bird fallen from a tree. Broken, limp, and helpless. I don't know what else to do." I pulled my hair unforgivingly. I was the worst! I needed to know she'd be okay.

Elias brought me in for a hug. "Come here, dumbass. Give her a few days to recuperate, and you can chastise her for hours. You'd like that, right?" He guffawed. *Yeah, that would make me feel better.*

"Sure," I complied. "Thanks, buddy. I'm going upstairs for the night. I'm staying with her until she's better."

"You do that." He winked at me, walking around the kitchen cleaning up.

Abigail left for the night after I cleaned up the bathroom. I stripped out of my clothes, keeping my boxer briefs on. I slid under the covers, positioning myself as close as I could without jarring her sleeping body. I watched her for hours. Her eyes fluttered like hummingbirds. *She must be dreaming.* Tiny smirks quirked up the corners of her mouth, periodically, making me smile, too. She was so beautiful and smart. I began counting the tiny freckles across the bridge of her nose until I began to drift asleep.

Her hand reached out for me, eyes still shut. "Alex? You know I love you, right?"

My eyes blew wide open. Now, wide awake, I whispered in her ear, "I know, and I love you, too." She hummed sweetly.

"We'll figure us out. I want that. I need more time." I was speechless. Was it the drugs or her subconscious at play here? I desperately wanted the same thing. We made sense together. She only needed to find her way.

"I know you will. I'll always be yours," I whispered emphatically. She hummed again and fell back to sleep. Carefully, I tucked her to my chest, spooning her for the rest of the night.

I sent Abigail a message at five in the morning that I'd be outside working and asked if she could give Seneca more medicine at six and then feed her. She agreed, and I went out to finish planting. By seven thirty, I entered the house, kicked off my boots and coat, and collapsed onto a barstool.

Without a word, Elias slid a hot cup of coffee and an apple fritter down the countertop in silence. He walked to the servants stairs, gave me a small jut of his chin, and walked up. Our manly way of communicating was so easy. Why did words have to get in the way?

I quickly showered after Abigail left, sliding back in bed under the warm covers. Using copious amounts of argan oil, complements of Abigail, I followed the length of each of Seneca's muscled legs to its corresponding tendons. Sometimes, with my thumbs and others with the palms of my hands, I coaxed her body to let go of its tension. Beautifully sexy, sometimes painful moans emanated from her delicate throat. If I weren't trying to relax her,

I'd be mounting her lithe body and fucking her wildly. Even in sleep the magnetism between us was dynamic.

"Thank you. I'm not sure if it feels good or my muscle will explode," she whimpered in pain.

"Tell me if I'm pushing too much. Is this better?" I removed some pressure and she relaxed more into the mattress.

"Ha! You're always pushing too hard. I do like when you're hard, though." I held back a laugh. It sounded like her meds were at full force again.

An hour later, I kissed her plump, sexy lips and got dressed. Abigail generously left a tray of orange juice, fruit and hardboiled eggs on the floor for me to feed her. I brought the tray into the room and roused my delicate flower from her pseudo sleep, propping her up against several pillows.

"How are you feeling, baby?" I said pushing her hair back behind her ears. Her wild mane falling off her shoulders and sexy as fuck.

"Hmm," she cooed. "Ouch! Gaww." Her repertoire of pain was expansive. "Is this what it feels like to be run over by a car? Because it really sucks." She winced several more times as she repositioned herself to sit upright.

"I can't speak for the car part, but I feel your pain with the strain part." I leaned in and kissed her gently. "If you want, I can make the pain go away for a while," I said waggling my eyebrows.

"Go away. Thinking of sex makes my uterus spasm and that hurts, too." *Interesting.*

"I have, it on doctor's orders, I can't leave until you eat everything on this tray. You know I'm a rule follower, so eat up." I may have been too exuberant for a morning wake-up call, but I'd been up since before the sun came up and was a little punchy.

She grimaced. "All of it? I'm not that hungry," she said pushing the egg around the bowl.

"Too bad. I'm not above torturing you with my incredible humor until those plates are empty," I taunted.

"Ugh! Fine. Back up. I'll eat." Even in pain, my woman was a force of nature. A beautiful one at that.

I made myself busy straightening the covers and picking up her clothes. Since moving out, nothing in this room was technically mine, though sometimes it still felt that way. So far, she hadn't realized she was naked under those sheets. Without something to wear she wasn't going anywhere. *We'll call it house arrest.* Continuing with my mundane tasks, I alphabetized the bookshelf, dusted the room, and did an assortment of stretches.

"Are you about done? You're exhausting me," she ranted.

"Have you finished everything on that tray?" I shot back.

She wailed, "It's too much food! Can't I finish it later? I have to pee."

Seneca's brain may have wanted to pee, but her body rejected the idea of sitting up and walking across the room to pee. Giving her my support, she hobbled across the room nearly falling as she sat down on the commode. Staying close in case her legs buckled when she stood, I crossed my arms and waited for her to finish her business.

"What? Are you going to watch me pee, too?" She shot me an annoyed look.

"I'm not that kinky," I said, disgusted.

She shooed me away, "Then turn around or something." I did as she said, listening to the long stream of her release followed by a throaty sigh. "That felt good."

I think she forgot I was standing there because she froze when I turned around. "Did I say something out loud?"

I gave her a devilish smile, "Yep!" I said, popping the P.

"Sometimes I hate you, Mr. Valize." I wasn't listening, lifting her off the seat after she painfully tried to wipe herself. Back in bed, I covered her up, kissing her deeply.

She had a look in her eye like she had something to say but held back. "No you don't. Say it, Seneca. Say you love me."

Would she remember her medication-induced truth? I was petrified she wouldn't. Then what would I do? I didn't have to wait long for her answer when she said very clearly, "I love you, Alex, and I need a toothbrush." *Holy shit! She said it. She loves me.*

Do I play it cool? Or jump on her? *She's broken, man. Settle down.*

In the end, I wrapped my tongue around hers thrusting so deeply we were both heaving. I pulled back and responded, "About fucking time you said it." I kissed her nose. "I love you, too."

She smiled, tracing her index finger over my now swollen lips. "I'm staying, Alex. I'll travel sometimes. You'll come with me sometimes, too. We'll make this work. Are you okay with that?"

Am I okay with that? Fuck yeah, I'm okay with that!

"Every word of it. I love you so much. I'd do anything for you." I entrusted my heart and soul to this woman now and forever. So long as we were together, we could figure anything out.

Her eyebrow raised. "Anything?" she probed coyly.

"Anything." I kissed her deeply again.

"Including finish planting my plants?" She thought she was so clever.

"Done. Next," I huffed on my knuckles then rubbed my pec.

"Done?"

"Done. You're going to have to go bigger, Sen. I'm way ahead of you."

"Did my signs arrive? Did you confirm my focus group people? Is my website up and running? Can you write my thesis for Dr. Abel? Would you mind making a bunch of sandwiches and cleaning up the mess? How abou—"

"Enough. You can do all those things from this bed. You'll get your cell phone and computer, after you finish what's on that tray, and take a nap. You're about due for more pain meds. A heating pad will arrive today and you'll sit that pretty ass on it until I say so. Understand?"

She had the decency to look admonished. "Understood."

I handed her the tray and rubbed her feet while she ate every morsel. "I like this arrangement," she said through bites. "How about we do this every night? You can be my slave?"

Pfft. "Slave, huh. How about we take turns? You know, like a partnership. I go down on you, you go down on me. It's a win-win." I mocked her, liking how she molded into the pillows even more. Moments later, she was asleep again. I watched her for a long time, imprinting every nuance of her lovely body. She loved me enough to stay. She was strong enough to find a middle ground that didn't cut her dreams off before attempting them. She was mine.

It took four long years to put our pieces together. I had to believe there was a God, and They had a bigger plan for us than we could ever have imagined. I'll never be religious, but, if Seneca could love me, there had to be something in the heavens rooting for us to be together.

THE END

Epilogue

SENECA

It's amazing what you can achieve sitting on your ass. Three phone calls and five emails later and I had confirmed all the final pieces of my senior project. The day before my focus group arrived, I was back on my feet, albeit slowly. Our friend, Derrick, sent over his new girlfriend to massage me each day this week so I could be ready for focus group day. Lindsey, the best marketing and web person in the history of the world, called the sign company every day since her screw-up, offering them her kidney if they could not only finish the signs but install them the morning of the tour.

"You shouldn't have offered them a kidney," I admonished her for even thinking my signs were more important than her organs. "No lives would have been lost if they didn't go up on time, so, unless the apocalypse is imminent, simple begging and pleading are enough."

Her sheepish expression was enough to prove she'd learned her lesson.

My first guests were in awe of the beautiful introduction to the Zen Garden. Huge amounts of purple heather, yellow buttercup daisies, and orange day lilies would soon bloom, dotting the beds surrounding a magnificent six-foot sign at the entrance to the garden area. Everything about this project was natural. From annuals, to mulch, to meditative concepts on round wood signs and benches. Derrick was a superstar creating six wood and black steel-based benches on which guests could relax and contemplate the inspirational sayings perched just off the pathway. The crown jewel of my garden was three concentric circles winding around themselves with short, inspirational words and phrases etched into several pavers. Some phrases came from my Native background, like *ninetta* or *gaagigi*, meaning "just me" and "forever." Others were from modern poets to prominent philosophers like Confucius. One of my favorites was from my Jewish mentor, Dr. Abel, and came from the Torah—*Hineni*–Here I am. Anyone who chooses to contemplate a moment or two would understand we are all part of one. None is more important than the other, but, together, they make a whole. That was my mother's vision for me. Bringing people together to see the worldview perspective of life was the key to happiness. *I did it, Mom . . . with you by my side.*

The Q&A went really well. Only one question was asked which I wasn't able to answer. I promised to find an answer and contact them soon. I did manage to make the sandwiches, though Abigail shooed me out of the kitchen to make the salads and again to carry the trays of food outside.

"Hail to the no!" She pointed a finger at my face and sent me running outside to wait on the porch. "Girl just got her feet and she's already getting herself in trouble. Open the door!"

"Yes, ma'am!" I said, doing her bidding and saluting as she maneuvered through the opening. "You're the best, Abs, as always. Don't forget to sign me up for my indenture starting in May."

"Don't worry. I've got you down for everything," she muttered with a sardonic smile.

Several people from local garden nurseries, the Rotary Club, the Chamber of Commerce, and children from schools of all ages were oohing and aahing down the winding path. Lindsey was brilliant, anticipating that they would do the heavy lifting if they liked what they saw, getting our name in their newsletters and websites and promoting our space for events. After reviewing all the responses, I only found one concerning remark. One person disagreed when asked if they felt this project was comprehensive enough to complete a college internship. "There was no way one person did all this work. Impossible. As for being the pinnacle of a horticulture degree, I would have expected many more indigenous plant materials and more phrases incorporated from all cultures, not the few she chose. Other than that, it was fine."

I couldn't help being a little hurt. Everything he said was taken personally. I suppose I could have researched more inspirational phrases from the hundreds of religions around the world or brought in several hybrid flowers that wouldn't bloom until August. It was obvious this person didn't understand that not all flowers bloomed at the same time. More importantly, internships focus on building leadership skills, problem-solving, troubleshooting, and managing resources. This project would have taken me six months or longer to do on my own. He could stick his stupid comment up his ass.

"Will there ever be a complete consensus on a subjective topic?" Alex said to encourage me.

Elias shook his head disapprovingly, "Ignore that dumb fuck. I bet everything he does and says is negative. Let it go, Seneca." *He had a point.*

Abigail wrapped her arms around my neck and I reciprocated like we did when we were sharing secrets in high school. She staunchly reassured me, "I'm your boss, bitch. If I say it's incredible, then it is. Dr. Abel will love it, too."

We took over twenty pictures cataloging the project's intricacies, along with every sign, and several with my focus group milling around and resting on the benches with their eyes closed. It was heartwarming. *That guy can kiss my ass.* By the end of the week, two days before the end of the official semester, I hand-delivered my thesis and supporting documents to Dr. Abel, along with a bouquet of Abigail's finest spring tulips for Olivia.

"Seneca! These are beautiful. Are they from your garden?"

"Some of them. I wanted to thank you so much for everything as I trekked through my degree. You were indispensable." I hugged her before taking one last walk into Dr. Abel's office.

He stood, motioning me to sit down in the chair I'd called "mine." This could have been any meeting, any day of my college career, except it wasn't. Another chapter of my life was ending, and I felt giddy. I hoped there would be other offers to grab onto, though I highly doubted my internships, either one, warranted exclusive opportunities for more study abroad. I'd resigned myself to that and was prepared for whatever the future held for me.

"So here we are. Another year completed. Thanks for sending over your preliminary thesis so I could review it in time for you to make changes. You'll be happy to know, you don't have any changes to make," he said proudly like a doting father. "I have to say, Seneca, I wasn't sure you'd make it through all these cataclysmic dips and turns. Every plan you made burst into flames. Several decisions went out the window with new ones right behind them. I'm so impressed with how you pivoted, making accommodations for each one. You fought your OCD, asked for help, reorganized when required, and didn't lose your cool or your mind in the process. *If he only knew.* Your internships were flying successes, and I'm looking forward to seeing you back here next week for graduation."

I jumped up, dancing with my hands in the air. I knew I gave everything to these projects. I knew I'd done them well, pleasing my bosses and building new skill sets along the way. I was only concerned that I had done enough the first time, completing everything in time to graduate.

I shoved my hand forward to shake Dr. Abel's, but, instead, he pulled me into a hug. I didn't know if that was politically correct, but I didn't care. Dr. Abel wasn't only my professor and mentor. He had become a friend and father figure. One I would stay in touch with for the rest of our lives.

I returned to the inn ready to faceplant and sleep for a week, and if it weren't for Alex and Abigail talking to me through my hundred-mile trek back to the inn, I don't think I'd have made it.

"Tell me everything. Don't leave anything out," he begged me. I gave him the whole nine yards and then some.

"I'm so fucking proud of you, Sen. Words can't express how I'm feeling now. I guess I'll have to show you when you get home." His seductive tone went right to my core, pushing my pedal to the metal to get home ten minutes early. "I see you driving up. Bye!"

Car parked and backpack over my shoulder, I stopped outside the side door, enjoying the cool, spring air. In all the chaos of completing my project, I wasn't able to enjoy my creation. Tomorrow, Alex and I would walk down the path holding hands, and find the peace we'd worked so hard for these past nine months.

I opened the creaky door, dropped my things, and walked into the kitchen to a loud, "Congratulations, Seneca!" Abigail, Elias, Lindsey and Derrick all stood there beaming at me, clapping.

"Oh my god! Annalise! Steven! Tiny! And Benny!! You're here, too! I'm so happy to see you again." I crouched down and got all my doggy kisses, seeing him wiggle his butt as I loved him up.

Annalise bent down for Benny's kisses, too. "Honestly, Seneca, if it weren't for the kids distracting him, he'd have been depressed for six months. Besides, we found a rescue dog, and they said they'd to keep her until the kids finished school in two weeks. They'd do anything to find a forever home for one of their dogs." I think Benny was happy to be reunited for good. I lifted his paws and danced with him until Alex put a glass of champagne in my hand.

He quieted the room. "Thank you, everyone, for being here today. As you know, Seneca went from one internship to two. I'll skip all the details and instead tell you she completed both with flying colors. Dr. Abel sent both me and Abigail letters of appreciation and congratulations. He also sent this." He unfolded a letter he pulled from his back pocket and read:

Dear Mr. Valize and Mrs. McGinnis,

Your gracious offers to accept Seneca Locklear into your homes and businesses to complete her internships were not only gracious, but life changing.

With your letters of recommendation, I have been able to secure three opportunities for Miss Locklear's Master's program and the ability to travel abroad in exchange programs, giving her skills she may not have been able to acquire here in the United States.

Please discuss these programs with her and have her contact me at her earliest opportunity with her intentions. Brochures and itineraries are enclosed in the packet.

Thank you again for being an integral part of the Delaware Valley University Horticulture Department. People like you are making a difference in young lives.

Sincerely,

Dr. Gregory Abel
Dean of Horticulture Studies
Delaware Valley University

Holy shit!

I'd only come home and now had the chance to study abroad. I wanted to. So badly. But when I looked around the room at the people who had given me their time, friendship, expertise, love, and, let's not forget, vast amounts of money, I couldn't leave them. I'm sure I can defer these opportunities for a year with a bit of help from Dr. Abel. I need some time to decompress and reset. I wasn't giving up, only honoring my body and friends. What I couldn't, wouldn't, give up was the chance to help my best friend deliver her baby and the opportunity to build a relationship with the man I was destined to be with. On my trip home, another spirit guide showed me how to create a horticulture program right here at the Farnsworth Inn and Eloheh Farms. It was a brilliant idea and one I would fulfill, just not now. I wanted time with Alex to solidify our relationship.

Yanked from my musings, a I loud voice called from across the room. "You're getting the hell out of my house, aren't you?" Elias blustered. *Yes. I would be leaving his house.* Alex gave me the key to his rental on bent knee and asked me to move in with him. I would have been stupid to refuse.

"As soon as you carry my shit down the stairs, Big Guy," I swatted at his ginormous chest, then pulled him into a hug.

"Hey! What about me? You said you'd be my slave. You're mine from seven-thirty in the morning to six at night, Monday through Friday and half-days Saturday. This is nonnegotiable," Abigail demanded like a Smurfette. *I couldn't take her seriously with her hair all mussed up and round with a baby.*

"Yes, Your Highness. I serve at the pleasure of My Queen," I overenunciated, bowing deeply at the waist.

Alex wrapped his strong arms around my stomach, nuzzling at my ear, demanding my attention. "You're mine the rest of the time. Uninterrupted," he said, pointing at Abigail.

"Yes, sir," I purred. "Will forever be enough?" My toes curled at the possibility.

"That will do, baby. That will do."

Bonus Chapter

The Wedding

"Babe! Where did you put the can opener?" Alex yelled, walking into our room in his boxer briefs holding a can of dog food.

His new pet name for me was 'babe;' it was better than honey bear. *Yuck!*

"Top drawer to the left of the sink where it always is." We were starting to sound like an old married couple. It had only been a month since I moved in, but we fell into a rhythm that ebbed and flowed causing me to open my heart to the thought of a real home again.

Like every time in the past four years, my father let me down and bailed on my graduation. Again, he chose his new family over me. He married Belinda, and I was but a figment of his imagination. *Whatever.* I was done with the past. Alex was my future, and I'd never treat my future children the way he treated me.

"Did you find it?!" I yelled back. Annoyed at being woken up for a can opener.

Moments later he slinked back into the bedroom with his hand behind his back sporting a woody.

"I did," he said, devilishly, his eyebrows waggling as he crawled onto the bed. "That's not all I found." I was afraid. Very afraid. Especially, when he whipped out from behind his back a large pancake flipper. *Oh, no!* "I'm feeling like pancakes this morning. How about it, Sen? Want me to make you my flapjack?"

I couldn't contain my laughter at the hilarity of my hot and completely ripped boyfriend holding a kitchen utensil like Bobby Flay. "Yeah, baby. I'll give it up to my sexy chef. But this time, you have to promise to use a towel. I'm tired of washing these sheets!"

He grabbed the covers, tugging them off my warm body and flipping me to my stomach. In one smack to my ass, he'd made my panties soaked. "I could fuck you on the floor. Or against the wall. Or your favorite, in the shower. Wait. I'll save that one for when we're done making a mess in this bed." I eyed him carefully. We'd had sex in all those places and more. It's a good thing we invested in some high-end cleaning products because this place looked like a sexual crime scene. He looked me squarely in the face sizing up how serious I was about the sheets when he caved. "Fine! I'll change and wash the sheets. You drive a hard bargain. Now get on your hands and knees, woman, while I whip up the batter."

Uncovering Alex's silly side had been one of the most fulfilling parts of our new relationship. We'd both relaxed and found we were more alike than we hoped. I enjoyed goofing around at the barn, or the market, but, when he shifted into retired captain mode, it was like a transformer blowing up—explosive.

"Alex, what are you going to do to me?" I played along with this sex-themed scenario, but, seriously, I wanted to know what I was in for.

He set the flipper off to the side, then palmed each of my ass cheeks, squeezing and kneading them like they were dough. "Fuck, Sen. I never get tired of seeing you like this. I can see everything."

Uhhh. That man's dirty talk turned me into butter.

He used his knee to separate my legs even wider. His fingers plunged into my wet pussy, scooping out my essence and rubbing it slowly over my anus, arousing my senses in the best way possible. "Alex," I moaned, loving his touch and anticipating his next move.

Folding himself over my back, he captured my lips, taking them possessively between his own and sucking on my tongue. "Do you like that, baby?" He pulled back, his stare intense.

My heart fluttered, and I gulped. "Yes, Alex. Keep doing that."

Where he had plunged one finger before, he plunged two, this time assaulting my sex, causing me to gasp. Pushing my limits, he rubbed both fingers over my hole, making promises I couldn't understand. "You want me in your ass, don't you? You like when I challenge you." He didn't wait for an answer and slowly, carefully pressed his thumb past the tight-muscled ring of my ass.

Caught between a moan of pleasure and burning pain, I whined, "Oh my god, it hurts so much. I'm not sure I can do this, Alex."

He kept his thumb firmly in place, using his other hand to massage my taut ass cheeks. "Relax, Sen. You can do this. You can do anything you set your mind to, even this. There. That's right, baby. Breathe. Let me in."

I panted, trying to keep myself together. The initial stretch of his thumb began to subside and where there once was pain, now began to feel pleasure. Finally, relaxing, I closed my eyes and focused on each sensation Alex evoked.

He whispered against my ear, "You're doing great, baby. Breathe and give yourself over to me. Trust that I won't hurt you, but will fill you with a pleasure you've never dreamt of." He turned his thumb, causing me to groan. Not in pain, but in how good it started to feel. The stretch he was able to pull from my body was masterful. While his right thumb was working my ass, his left slipped underneath me finding my clit and rubbing gently.

"God, Alex. That feels so good. Yes. Keep doing that." I didn't know which intoxicating move I wanted him to keep doing, only that I wanted more of what he was doing.

He smirked. His big-mouthed, independent woman just handed over control to her smart-mouthed, sexy as fuck man. This was his nirvana. When he took control, he allowed me to eradicate every thought in my head. I never thought I could give one hundred percent of myself to anyone. I'd learned not to trust anyone but myself—until Alex.

"I want you to come for me, Sen. Give yourself over to me and come on my hand." His words encouraged me to move with his hands. How he synchronized his feather-light touch and pumping fingers brought me over the edge in epic style. Flashes of light, and a series of tremors I'd never felt before had me screaming uncontrollably.

"Fuck! Yes, yes, yes. Damn, Alex. What you do to me leaves me speechless." I rode the wave of my orgasm, shuddering as I came down, but Alex wasn't finished with me. He never was. Saying I'd stay, choosing him over any other option, unleashed a monster. He was insatiable and I loved every minute of it.

He extracted his thumb and flipped me over. Once his boxer briefs were off, he reinserted his thumb as he pushed my knees higher to my ears. He slid himself between my knees and kissed each thigh tenderly, teasing his lip closer and closer to my sopping wet pussy. A wave of tremors traveled down up my body as he drove himself once into my depth, then pulled out and drove his cock deeper to the hilt.

"God, Sen. You're so tight. I can't get enough of you. Tell me you want me," he demanded.

"I want you, Alex. So badly," I wailed. I wanted more. More than our bodies could give, more than our minds would allow. I wanted him on a cellular level that connected us through eternity. Before I could say those things, he stopped pumping into me.

Out of breath and shaking, he lowered his mouth to mine in the most reverent kiss he'd ever given me; it shook me to my core. "I love you, Seneca. I've loved you since the day I met you and more every day since then. You're mine. You'll always be mine."

Our mouths hovered over each other in awe. I pushed my hands into his dampened, dirty-blond hair, pulling him down to kiss him back. "I love you, too, Alex. I wanted to believe we weren't right for each other, but deep down, I knew it would be you who'd steal my heart."

He abandoned his thumb in my anus, focusing solely on my pussy. I could feel Alex's cock pulsing inside, begging for its release, when he hissed, "You're mine, Seneca. Feel me inside you." He shifted my hips higher, giving him a better angle to reach the exact right spot for my pleasure. "I'm going to fill you with my cum every night and day until we make a baby. Do you understand?" His hips slammed into my ass, driving deeper, his balls sounding a steady rhythm until he grunted out his release. "And, every night thereafter."

"Sen! Ahhh! Baby, you make me feel so good."

I closed my eyes, allowing my senses to coalesce inside my body and mind. Just as I hit my peak of emotional pleasure, I heard a loud smack. Realizing too late it was my ass that took the beating, I swore.

"What the fuck, Alex? Why did you do that? I was feeling so good," I whined, really pissed off at him.

He didn't even have the good sense to feel shame when he announced, "I'm hungry. I want pancakes. Let's go!"

Yanking my legs to the end of the bed, he stood and pulled me into his strong arms. "I love you so much." He knew what he was doing, buttering me up like one of his pancakes.

"You'd better because you're not getting chocolate chips in yours if you don't." And, with that, I walked naked into the kitchen and tied an apron around my body.

It took minutes to make the batter, and, in that time, Alex had stripped the bed and dumped the sheets in the laundry room. Returning to the kitchen, he wrapped his arms around me tightly and whispered sensually in my ear.

"Baby, put the whisk down."

I followed his instructions and tried to turn around.

"Stay still." Again, I obeyed.

He kissed behind my ear and down to the curve of my neck. "I want to travel the world with you. I want to watch you study plants with the same awestruck face you have when you find a new species of plants to research. I want to watch your belly swell with our child inside it. Most importantly, I want to wake up to your face every day for the rest of my life."

My mind was whirring. Every new statement made it go faster until I felt heady. What was he saying?

His right arm released my waist, then curled back around me, holding a black velvet box. "Open it," he instructed, and I did. A sparkling princess-cut diamond sat between two trillion-cut diamonds on a flat platinum band. I didn't know anything about diamonds, but, as the sun caught the stones, it blinded me. "Seneca Locklear. Will you continue to help me grow to be the husband of your dreams?"

I felt dizzy and my knees buckled. He asked me to marry him. *He asked me to marry him!* His hold on me tightened. "Hold on, babe. You're not passing out at my proposal." He scooped me up and carried me to the kitchen table. Satisfied I wouldn't fall off the chair, he removed the box from my hands and removed the ring. Sinking to one knee, naked as the day he was born, Alex Valize slid his ring onto my finger.

"Seneca, will you marry me?"

I can't say I'd been waiting for four years to be asked that question, but, in my heart I always knew he was the one for me. I tackled him to the ground, throwing my arms around his strong chest, squeezing with all my might.

"Yes!"

Two weeks later, Abigail called me in the middle of the night.

"Slave! Come now! I'm ready to drop a bowling ball on the living room floor if you don't get here now!"

"Give me the phone, woman. Sen? Yeah, get the fuck over here now! The baby is coming!" Elias growled.

After getting dressed and letting Benny out, we were at their house in ten minutes, ushering the midwife in front of us through the front door. Elias managed to get Abigail back in her bed after having stripped it of regular sheets, exposing the latex barrier sheet the midwife suggested she have ready during her final weeks of pregnancy.

"Time to breathe, Abigail. Remember what we practiced? That's right. Pant like a dog until I tell you to push. Elias, get behind her and give her something to hold onto." Alice, the midwife they'd been doing Lamaze with, was exceptional. Not only did she calm the parents, she also calmed me and Alex. *Though he did look a little pale.*

"Hey guys," Alex choked out, "I think I'm going to sit this one out." He left the room quickly, and I pulled up an antique Queen Anne's chair to the bed.

"I'm here if you need me, Abs. Keep doing everything you've learned, and in no . . ."

"Fucking hell! Get this alien out of me! Elias!" She cried into his massive, tattooed arm. He cooed in her ear terms of endearment and encouragement for over an hour. Sensing the final act of her birth, I pushed my chair over to the wall and let the rest unfold.

"Time to push, dear. Give me one big push, and the baby will be out. Come on. One big push!" Alice's orders did not fall on deaf ears. Abigail pushed like her life depended on it, and Elias had her nail marks to prove it.

I watched in amazement a life entering this world through a tiny portal between Abigail's legs. Why I ever thought Alex's cock would tear me open was ludicrous. This baby's head was more than three times that size in circumference and Abigail barely bled. *Fascinating.*

Leaving my chair, I chanced a look at my best friend and her adoring husband. These two were going to make incredible parents, and Alex and I would be the doting aunt and uncle who hid secrets from them. "You did great, you two. I'm going to scoot out and take Alex home. I'm sure Alice will take amazing care of you and the baby." I kissed their cheeks and waved at my new nephew. A miracle happened before my eyes, and I felt that same tremor I got when I felt my spirit guides move through me. This little fellow would change the world—or, at least, ours.

～

Two months later, before our final harvest, Alex and I stood at the head of my Zen meditation pathway at sunset. Tiny luminaries dotted the way on both sides up to a canopy filled with the end of season flowers grown at The Farnsworth Inn. Every piece of our ceremony came from the earth. The food, the decorations, the people . . . and our vows.

Alex extended his elbow and I looped my arm through his to hold an aromatic bundle of lavender, lemongrass, and mixed-colored zinnias wrapped in natural raffia ribbon. I wore a crown of more zinnias I'd made myself yesterday, sitting in the far field I'd sat in almost a year ago, wondering what was going to happen with my internship and Alex. Today, though, my worries were gone.

"Are you ready, Sen?" Alex rubbed the low curve of my back, left bare by the deep cut of my sustainable Tencel and Cupro dress I ordered online. It represented everything about me and my dedication to the earth.

"Absolutely. Let's do this."

Derrick played the guitar as we walked arm and arm down the two hundred feet of path, stealing glances and cracking jokes. The rest of our friends lined the path holding candles as the sun began to set igniting every shade of blistering orange to the brilliance seen in the pink and purple zinnias that circled my head. It was magical.

The music stopped, and Dane, ordained by the power of the internet, began our ceremony.

If love were a straight line, the two of you would never have met. Your paths to love are as intricate as the path you just walked down. Each one was placed with care and secured with the right intentions. We have seen firsthand what a misplaced stone can do to a relationship. It shifts out of place, causing another stone to shift with it. A relationship is the same way. You can't afford to let even one stone go unattended, for it will fester and fall, unable to come back together.

Alex. You are no stone, brother. You are an immovable boulder. But just like an ant can carry fifty times its weight, you carried me and our family home on your back for over a decade. Your strength will be your greatest asset to this marriage, but you won't have to carry it alone this time.

Seneca. As the song says, you are the wind beneath Alex's wings. You are the Earth, Wind, and Fire that will propel your family to succeed while standing in one place. You are a force that I'm happy to call my family.

Because the mosquitoes are chewing the skin off my neck, I'm skipping the rest of this ceremony until the toasts inside the barn. So, without further ado, do you, Alex, take Seneca as your lawful life partner? To have and to hold, when I'm not in the room, and cherish her to death do you part?

"I do."

Cool. Do you, Seneca, take Alex to be your lawful life partner? To have and to hold, quietly without touching my brother when I'm in the room, and cherish him to death do you part?

"I do."

Fantastic! I pronounce you husband and wife. We're all going inside while you devour your wife with an insanely long kiss. Congratulations!

Our small entourage adjourned to Elias, Abigail, and now Jacob's barn, as Alex descended upon me.

Dipping me backward, admiring my cleavage, Alex growled, "You are so fucking beautiful. Do you think our friends will notice if I tear that dress off you at the reception?" He kissed me hard once, then pulled me upright.

"Touch this dress and your dick will be swinging alongside my tits," I winked and bit his lip softly.

"God, I love you, baby. I can't wait to see the world with you."

Looking at him in his Army dress blues, I swooned. He was magnificent to look at, incredible to banter with, and ridiculous to play with when he was silly. This man is my husband. If I ever thought I'd never get ahead in life, I was sadly mistaken. For us, the winding road made us the happiest in the end, and I wouldn't have traded it for anything.

I cocked my head to the side, giving him a coy smile, "I love you, too, baby. If I were you, I'd have your bags packed by tomorrow because we're headed to Hawaii for my first workshop and our honeymoon."

ABOUT THE AUTHOR

The sassy and sensational Beth Gelman is a #1 Amazon Best-Selling Author who loves to pull your heartstrings and get you riled up with her books. She has earned honorable mentions at The Bookfest Awards and Readerviews.com for *Always Falling Behind*. In addition, *Eight Crazy One Night Stands* made her an #1 Amazon Best Selling Author. Beth brings the steam in her contemporary romances about women who speak up, take what's theirs, and embrace their wild side. Authentic, resilient, loyal, and spiritual, she's not afraid to learn, fail, speak her mind, or try new things. More importantly, she loves her husband, twins, and all the dogs in the world!

Follow me on Facebook (Beth Gelman's Author Page), Instagram, Substack, Goodreads, Bookbub, and TikTok or at www.BethGelman.com. Don't forget to join my newsletter for early access specials, pre-orders, excerpts, birthday goodies, and other nonsense.

ACKNOWLEDGEMENTS

This book began with a simple concept, a young woman who had started college long after most kids. My female main character (FMC) would have OCD, a lot of sass, and a brilliant mind—and that's where my concept ended. *Sort of.* What I didn't expect was how in-depth I would take these characters or how concerned my subconscious was about global environmental issues. My mind and spirituality's inner workings had always been connected to the indigenous North American Indian tribes. I found their ideals and ways deeply entrenched in gratitude and appreciation for Mother Earth and everything that supported it, uplifting and hopeful. They focused on simplicity and equal give and take, which are concepts our current world has sadly forgotten.

Like every book I write, there are moral questions, personal growth, and a deep desire for my characters and readers to grow. Sure, the steamy stuff is excellent escapism, but the cathartic nature of reflection and new intentions keeps spurring my desire to write—for us both!

A great many people made this book possible. Please join me in extending my heartfelt thanks to the following wonderful people and organizations.

The Sault Tribe of Chippewa Indians—Thank you Natalie Shattuck and Isabelle Osawamick for taking time to educate me on Ojibwe linguistics and Native culture. My desire to represent your people properly is paramount to my writing. The words and phrase translations are so poetic, they are transcendental.

Dalia Samansky—Where did you come from?! We are definitely *besheret*. Thank you so much for being a BETA reader, and now, friend. I loved your input, feedback, and heartfelt compliments. My respect for you and what you bring to the table is exceptional. I can't wait to do it again!

Alison Schooley—Thank you for being a BETA reader! While I value your feedback, I truly appreciate how you pointed out the depth of my characters and storylines as unique compared to many other authors you've read. *(Gushing.) Hugs.*

Renee Miller—Thank you for being a BETA reader! Your feedback and encouragement meant so much to me. I hope we can do it again!

Jane Litherland—My BETA bestie. Thank you for your continued support of my writing. I'm indebted to you for pushing through your personal trials to meet my deadline and honor your commitment to me. You're the best! One day I'm coming to meet you across the pond.

Sydney Reuben—Your sincere love and support unconditionally through the years has brought me so much joy. There is a lot of Seneca in you. You're the best Auntie I have! Love you!!

Paul Scheidler—Again, with the history lessons! Thank you so much for all your wisdom regarding the Trail of Tears and your service in Afghanistan. You have illuminated just how utterly unforgivable the way our Native Americans were treated then and now.

Amy Scheidler—Long live ATG. Without you, there'd be no confident chicken in my stories. Thank you, girl!

Leo Tucker—Leo! You may not be a chemist, but you are the world's sweetest, smartest little dog-man. Thanks for lending me your name. However, Leo, the chemist, is the antithesis of your personality. No offense.

Dr. Seymour Ziegelman—Every book needs a good doctor and a loving father who never abandons their kids. I wish Seneca had you for hers. Thanks for lending me your name for the past 28ish years.

Fran Lambert—You're Fran-tastic! Fran-omenal! Thanks for lending your maiden name and your support.

Daryl Ziegelman—Me: I'll be done in ten minutes. (7:00 pm) Daryl: I'm going to bed (9:30 pm). You're the most understanding man a wife could ever want. I love you so much!

Samantha Ziegelman—Thanks, Sweetie, for letting me run my lines with you. Your sense of humor is wicked smart, and your opinion of my work means the world to me. You complete me!

Evan Ziegelman—Me: So when you have a minute (10 pm). Evan: So, here's what you need to do (10:01 pm). God, how I love you, kid! Thanks for having my back at all hours of the night.

The Google—Having answers at my fingertips is life-altering. I'm deeply grateful for the information that is so readily accessible.

YouTube – Oh, the things I have learned! And, listened to! When you're my age, you remember digging through volumes of books, encyclopedias, and records to find the information you needed. Or search for an expert whose contact information wasn't in the phone book. YouTube is an incredible gift for me and something our youth will never truly appreciate. Here's to technology, even when it's a P.I.A!

Shout outs!

#Jones Farm – All Natural Symbiotic Farming

https://www.barrettcommunity.com/farms/jones-farm-all-natural-symbiotic-farming

#Neel Daphtary – President of Chemtech International, PA

https://chemtech-us.com/the-complete-guide-to-co2-check-valves-2/

Songlist:

Loathing—"Wicked – The Musical" reference

I Am Not Okay—Jelly Roll

Wind Beneath My Wings—Jeff Silbar and Larry Henley

DISCOVER BETH'S CATALOG AND CONTACT INFORMATION

TITLE	ISBN
The Perfect Series	
The Perfect Voice (#1)	9798989946730
The Perfect Lessons (#2)	9798990587311
Making Perfect Sense (#3)	9798990587342

Dazed and Confused Steamy Romances – **Neurodivergent Brains: ADHD, ODC & Dyslexia**

Always Falling Behind (#1)	9798989946778
Never Getting Ahead (#2)	9798992034028
Found in the Middle (#3)	9798992034035 (Spring 2026)

Standalone Novels

Socially Satisfied ~ More Than Just a Swipe	9798989946792
Eight Crazy One Night Stands	9798990587380

STAY IN TOUCH!
Email: BethGelmanWrites@gmail.com

Website:
Facebook: Beth Gelman's Author Page
Instagram: @bethgelmanwrites
TikTok: @beth.gelman.author
Amazon.com: Beth Gelman's Complete Catalog
https://www.amazon.com/dp/B0DSGP2P4W

Bookbub.com:
https://www.bookbub.com/books/never-getting-ahead-dazed-and-confused-book-2-by-beth-gelman
Goodreads.com:
https://www.goodreads.com/search?q=beth+gelman&qid=45BtBuzkM5
Barnes and Noble:
https://www.barnesandnoble.com/w/never-getting-ahead-beth-gelman/1146797637?ean=9798992034035

THANK YOU SO MUCH FOR READING MY BOOKS!
Until next time . . .

READ MORE: The Perfect Lessons

Chapter 1 Trudie

When I clicked *accept* on my registration in January and committed myself to another psychology conference, I never dreamed it would start this way. Kissing strange, beautiful men years younger than me didn't exactly fit my school's approved teacher behavior profile. But, boy, was it fun.

This was the fifth conference I'd attended since I became a middle school teacher five years ago. The niggle I had to get to the heart of my issues kept me returning each year. I hadn't been physically abused or neglected (nothing like that, thank God). Yet, some of the emotional trauma I sustained as a child lingered in my psyche, and I was determined to do whatever it took to eradicate it from my life.

My trauma was due to proximity, or lack thereof, as it related to my father. He was a CAT adjuster. Yeah, no one knew what that was. I didn't until I was twelve. He was the guy insurance companies hired to assess the damage from hurricanes, tornadoes, forest fires, and the like. One ring of the phone and he was gone—sometimes a week, sometimes longer. The longer he was gone, the greater the disaster at home when he returned. Thus, therapy and psychology conferences. Lots and lots and lots of them.

This year, the conference was in San Francisco, and I was hyped to spend a few extra days afterward seeing the sights. I booked a day trip to Yosemite, leaving at the buttcrack of dawn to see the giant sequoias, and I considered a sunset cruise on San Francisco Bay but thought it might be awkward to go alone. I hated looking desperate. Most of the time, I found like-minded people at the conferences who would hang around after the workshops were finished to check out the sights. However, being back in the dating world. I was out of practice, and honestly, I wasn't even sure what I was looking for.

Had men changed much in the six years I was dating Sam? Social media was rife with ways to attract people. But did I really want to "be" with someone or hook up? It was just too confusing. Ruby, my friend from college, always said, "Have no expectations, have no broken heart." How does one date or hook up without expectations? I wasn't opening my vajayjay to some pervert or rando to get off. I had standards! I wanted to know their name first and maybe see their current STD test results.

The fact remained, I wanted to walk away from a tryst and feel good about it, not dirty—unless, of course, I discovered I liked being a dirty girl. But seriously, that guy would have to be a god. In the meantime, I took Ruby's suggestion and kept my expectations low, hoping to be pleasantly surprised when that guy found my G-spot in the first ten minutes—not six years.

Registration for conferences always happened six months before the event, so when it was time to leave for San Francisco, I had almost forgotten about it and scrambled to find everything I needed for the trip.

My apartment was tiny—like tiny house tiny. Four hundred square feet didn't even feel big when nothing was in the place. It was a temporary situation, but it was much better than living at home like I had after college, and it was mine. I hung the flowy canary yellow drapes well below the windows to make the room look taller. That's what the home shows said to do. There wasn't much in the way of furniture—did I mention I was a poor middle school teacher—but my decor was on point. I had managed to fit in a couch that faced the window overlooking a pond stocked with lily pads, a side table sporting a green glass vintage lamp with a floral shade, and a nearly matching oversized ottoman for my aching feet. I had passed on a dining set since I landed in front of the TV most evenings when I wasn't with Sam. My sweet, kind, generally dull in the bedroom, and now ex-boyfriend, Sam. Sadly, I didn't miss spending time with him.

Sam and I had dated for six years. We started in college, and like most first loves, he swept me off my feet, feeding me slices of pizza while we snuggled on the couch watching scary movies. We did a lot of hiking in the Upper Peninsula of Michigan and had a blast on a Spanish club spring break trip to Cancun. I probably partied on the beach more than immersing myself in the culture. (And yes, it was my own culture since my family was Mexican, but we were very "Americanized.") The class was an easy A, and I knew more than enough Spanish to find a bathroom, ask for dessert, or swear at someone.

From what I knew of kissing, Sam was a good kisser and an attentive lover. He was new and fun, and we had many things in common. Still, it turned into the most predictable, boring, and vanilla love life I could imagine over the years. Thinking he was "the one" was laughable, yet I kept dating him long after college. The dealbreaker had come two months earlier when he announced he was taking a new position in Colorado and wanted me to join him. Honestly, it was an easy decision—the saddest part was throwing away a six-year investment. Romance novels would have to pick up the slack in the bedroom department, along with my trusty vibrator, Big Ben. I could always count on him—unless his batteries died.

I needed to keep the past in the past. I focused all my energy on packing, grabbing my toiletries, shoving them into my big purple suitcase, and then picking out a few practical outfits to wear during the professional workshops. I also chose a long black and red fitted dress that showcased a sexy kick-pleat along the back hem and a low-cut back that bordered on risqué to wow the crowd at the evening gala and a few flirtier casual outfits for tootling around the city at night, and I was good to go.

My rental car was waiting outside my chic apartment building. This place was a massive upgrade from the one I had out of college and was only a few miles from the busy expressway I traveled daily to get to work. The apartment itself was a standard two-bedroom arrangement. The second bedroom was too small for a bed but a great place to set up a yoga mat, a desk for writing lesson plans, and a comfy overstuffed chair for reading that I had found at a secondhand store in a quaint city a few miles away. But the best part of this place was the courtyard with a meditation fountain and a cherry blossom tree that took your breath away each springtime. A couple of wood-slatted benches and plastic Adirondack chairs sat in a circle around a firepit on the opposite side of the space. I took every opportunity to go there to clear my head, grounding myself as I maneuvered through life's obstacle course.

The ride to the airport was uneventful. However, when I arrived, gorgeous men kept appearing before my eyes while I checked my bags. My imagination jumped into high gear looking at these ripped young men with bulging arms, high cheekbones, full lips, and tight asses. I thought I was hallucinating when one of the hotties locked eyes with me and gave me a sexy smile, making me blush. I was about to say something when I heard a loud "Next," so I gave a little one-finger wave and walked up to the ticket counter.

When I finally reached my seat on the plane, I let out a deep sigh. I thought back to those guys at the ticket counter and chastised myself for even thinking about hooking up with one of them. I mean, I could have—I was young enough, and I had some nice assets, but let's face it, I was almost ten years older than most of them, and it just seemed like a male-bait situation. Regardless, I was headed out to find some answers about myself at this conference, and I needed to stay focused.

The overhead speaker called passengers to attention and to buckle up. As I snapped my belt into place, a large body plopped down next to me.

"Hello, again." A deep voice melted over me. *Mmm.*

I looked up to see the source of that yummy greeting and was paralyzed when I recognized the hottie from the ticket counter. His sexy smile gleamed as he drove his large hands through his tousled, dirty-blond hair.

Oh, shit!

"Uh, hi," I said, squishing my face into an awkward smile. A very attractive look, I'm sure.

He chuckled. "I guess we're traveling to the same place. This four-hour trip is looking better and better every minute." He used his foot to push his backpack under the seat before him and tucked a neck roll behind his head. It looked comfortable—why did I always forget to buy one of those?

My head nodded like one of those drinking bird toys, only not controlled by gravity but by the awkwardness I felt.

"Yeah, it's a long one." Silence. Awkward silence. *Come on, Trudie, you need to practice your game before you meet someone who really interests you.*

I brushed my auburn hair behind my ear and started again.

"So, what do you have planned in San Francisco?" Better.

He pivoted in his chair to get a better look at me. The flight attendant sashayed down the aisle behind him, asking him to sit facing forward for takeoff. He shifted back with a slight huff.

"Soccer training camp. I play for my university, and they send us to one of these international training camps for a week each year to prepare us for higher-level play. We used to play in the fall, but the NCCA voted to move our season to spring, so now we have an extended training schedule. No rest for the weary," he added.

I would be pissed if I didn't have three months off during the summer, but he seemed easygoing about it. As a teacher, summers were sacred. We worked our asses off during the school year, and when the bell rang in June, it was a race to our cars.

Years ago, during a takeoff, I had created a ritual of praying to the Almighty in case she was listening. Just a few prayers—to send wisdom for the pilot to land the plane safely and to send a mental blanket of white light all over me and the other passengers to bring us peace and safety while in the air. I know it sounded a little bonkers, but it has worked every time so far, so it has stayed a part of my travel routine.

I may have said some of it out loud instead of in my head since my flight buddy was eyeing me suspiciously. Thinking out loud had maybe gotten me in trouble once before. Maybe.

"You doing okay?"

"Uh, yeah. Did I say something out loud?" I asked, paranoid.

"Yeah. You did. Not a fan of flying, huh?" He helped me out.

"Did the white knuckles tip you off? Takeoffs are the worst. I'll be fine in a few minutes." I closed my eyes and tried to calm myself down. I added "mortified" to my list of issues this trip.

I was going through my prayers again, inside my head, and engaging in a breathing technique to settle myself when I felt a large, warm hand wrap around my white-knuckled one, choking the seat rest. I'm not going to lie. It felt good. Safe. Protected. All those elusive things I wanted in my life. I opened my eyes slowly, tilting my head, then back up toward our entwined hands and then back to his face.

He smiled nervously. "Is this okay?"

If I hadn't been such a head case then, I'd have considered this a violation of my personal space, but his strong reassurance left me taking my first full breath since I had walked onto this bird, so I nodded my head appreciatively.

He continued. "Good. What's your name? I'm Jared." He squeezed my hand gently.

Why was I coming up with reasons not to engage with this guy? He could know my name. I doubt he was a stalker who would hunt me down after this flight. *Just give him your fucking name!*

"Trudie," I blurted out. "It's Trudie," I whispered a second time.

I stared at his lips a little too long, I think, because he leaned his head forward, almost touching our foreheads together, and whispered, "Don't worry, I've got you. Whatever you need, I'll take care of it for you." His tone insinuated a lot more than he was saying. As his breath warmed my face, his eyes twinkled, presumably hoping to alleviate *any* discomfort I might have on this flight. I blushed at his innuendo and then looked out the window for a moment of relief.

What do you say to a guy who was that forward? I mean, it wasn't that I wouldn't want him to kiss me, touch me, or ask me to visit him in the restroom, but I didn't know who this guy was or what diseases he was walking around with. And maybe it was ridiculous to think that was what he intended to do, even if my deranged mind wanted him to.

Click here to read the rest of The Perfect Lessons!
https://www.amazon.com/dp/B0BSFX6JX7
It's a super steamy cliffhanger, so grab Making Perfect Sense, too!
https://www.amazon.com/dp/B0BRWP5857

Made in the USA
Columbia, SC
27 April 2025